LOSS AND GAIN

Visit WWW.CLUNYMEDIA.COM *for other titles from the Catholic literary tradition, including:*

ROBERT HUGH BENSON
Come Rack, Come Rope
Lord of the World

GEORGES BERNANOS
The Fearless Heart
Joy
Under the Sun of Satan

WILLA CATHER
Death Comes for the Archbishop
My Ántonia

G. K. CHESTERTON
Wanderings over the World

MYLES CONNOLLY
Dan England and the Noonday Devil
Mr. Blue

F. MARION CRAWFORD
The Saracinesca Tetralogy

A. J. CRONIN
The Keys of the Kingdom

ALICE CURTAYNE
House of Cards

GERTRUD VON LE FORT
The Veil of Veronica

MARIELLA GABLE, O.S.B. (EDITOR)
Many-Colored Fleece (*Short Stories*)
Our Father's House (*Short Stories*)

JOSÉ MARÍA GIRONELLA
The Cypresses Believe in God (TWO VOLUMES)

RUMER GODDEN
Five for Sorrow, Ten for Joy
In This House of Brede

CAROLINE GORDON & ALLEN TATE (EDITORS)
The House of Fiction (*Short Stories*)

CAROLINE GORDON
The Malefactors
The Strange Children

PAUL HORGAN
A Distant Trumpet
Humble Powers
Things As They Are

CARYLL HOUSELANDER
The Dry Wood

BRUCE MARSHALL
Father Malachy's Miracle
A Thread of Scarlet

FRANÇOIS MAURIAC
A Kiss for the Leper
The Desert of Love
Vipers' Tangle

EDWIN O'CONNOR
All in the Family

BEN J. REINHARD (TRANSLATOR)
Beowulf

IGNAZIO SILONE
Fontamara
Bread and Wine
The Seed Beneath the Snow

SIGRID UNDSET
The Burning Bush
The Wild Orchid
The Faithful Wife

LEO L. WARD
Men in the Field: Eighteen Short Stories

HELEN C. WHITE
Bird of Fire
Dust on the King's Highway
Not Built with Hands
A Watch in the Night

LOSS AND GAIN

The Story of a Convert

John Henry Newman

CLUNY
Providence, Rhode Island

CLUNY EDITION, 2024

This Cluny edition is a republication of *Loss and Gain*, first published in 1848, from the 1881 edition published by Burns and Oates.

For information regarding this title
or any other Cluny Media publication,
please write to info@clunymedia.com, or to
Cluny Media, P.O. Box 1664, Providence, RI 02901

ONLINE AT WWW.CLUNYMEDIA.COM

ISBN: 978-1685953577

Cover design by Clarke & Clarke
Cover image: John Sell Cottman, *A Castle Tower*
(*Caernarvon Castle*), undated,
watercolor on white pape
Courtesy of Wikimedia Commons

It is scarcely necessary to say that the Author submits all that he has written to the judgment of the Church, whose gift and prerogative it is to determine what is true and what is false in religious teaching.

Adhuc modicum aliquantulum,
qui venturus est, veniet, et non tardabit.
justus autem meus ex fide vivit.

DEDICATION

To the VERY REV. CHARLES W. RUSSELL, D.D.,
President OF ST. PATRICK'S COLLEGE, MAYNOOTH, &C. &C.

MY DEAR DR. RUSSELL—

Now that at length I take the step of printing my name in the Title-Page of this Volume, I trust I shall not be encroaching on the kindness you have so long shown to me, if I venture to follow it up by placing yours in the page which comes next, thus associating myself with you, and recommending myself to my readers by the association.

Not that I am dreaming of bringing down upon you, in whole or part, the criticisms, just or unjust, which lie against a literary attempt which has in some quarters been thought out of keeping with my antecedents and my position; but the warm and sympathetic interest which you took in Oxford matters thirty years ago, and the benefits which I derived personally from that interest, are reasons why I am desirous of prefixing your name to a Tale, which, whatever its faults, at least is a more intelligible and exact representation of the thoughts, sentiments, and aspirations, then and there prevailing, than was to be found in the anti-Catholic pamphlets, charges, sermons, reviews, and story-books of the day.

These reasons, too, must be my apology, should I seem to be asking your acceptance of a Volume, which, over and above its intrinsic defects, is, in its very subject and style, hardly commensurate with the theological reputation and the ecclesiastical station of the person to whom it is presented.

I am, my dear Dr. Russell,
Your affectionate friend,
John H. Newman
THE ORATORY
FEBRUARY 21, 1874

ADVERTISEMENT

THE following tale is not intended as a work of controversy in behalf of the Catholic Religion; but as a description of what is understood by few, viz. the course of thought and state of mind—or rather one such course and state—which issues in conviction of its Divine origin.

Nor is it founded on fact, to use the common phrase. It is not the history of any individual mind among the recent converts to the Catholic Church. The principal characters are imaginary; and the writer wishes to disclaim personal allusion in any. It is with this view that he has feigned ecclesiastical bodies and places, to avoid the chance, which might otherwise occur, of unintentionally suggesting to the reader real individuals, who were far from his thoughts.

At the same time, free use has been made of sayings and doings which were characteristic of the time and place in which the scene is laid. And, moreover, when, as in a tale, a general truth or fact is exhibited in individual specimens of it, it is impossible that the ideal representation should not more or less coincide, in spite of the author's endeavour, or even without his recognition, with its existing instances or champions.

It must also be added, to prevent a farther misconception, that no proper representative is intended in this tale, of the religious opinions which had lately so much influence in the University of Oxford.

FEBRURAY 21, 1848

ADVERTISEMENT TO THE SIXTH EDITION

A TALE, directed against the Oxford converts to the Catholic Faith, was sent from England to the author of this Volume in the summer of 1847, when he was resident at Santa Croce in Rome. Its contents were as wantonly and preposterously fanciful, as they were injurious to those whose motives and actions it professed to represent; but a formal criticism or grave notice of it seemed to him out of place.

The suitable answer lay rather in the publication of a second tale; drawn up with a stricter regard to truth and probability, and with at least some personal knowledge of Oxford, and some perception of the various aspects of the religious phenomenon, which the work in question handled so rudely and so unskilfully.

Especially was he desirous of dissipating the fog of pomposity and solemn pretence, which its writer had thrown around the personages introduced into it, by showing, as in a specimen, that those who were smitten with love of the Catholic Church, were nevertheless as able to write common-sense prose as other men.

Under these circumstances *Loss and Gain* was given to the public.

FEBRUARY 21, 1874

LOSS AND GAIN

The Story of a Convert

PART I

CHAPTER I

CHARLES REDING was the only son of a clergyman, who was in possession of a valuable benefice in a midland county. His father intended him for orders, and sent him at a proper age to a public school. He had long revolved in his mind the respective advantages and disadvantages of public and private education, and had decided in favour of the former. "Seclusion," he said, "is no security for virtue. There is no telling what is in a boy's heart: he may look as open and happy as usual, and be as kind and attentive, when there is a great deal wrong going on within. The heart is a secret with its Maker; no one on earth can hope to get at it or to touch it. I have a cure of souls; what do I really know of my parishioners? Nothing; their hearts are sealed books to me. And this dear boy, he comes close to me; he throws his arms round me, but his soul is as much out of my sight as if he were at the antipodes. I am not accusing him of reserve, dear fellow: his very love and reverence for me keep him in a sort of charmed solitude. I cannot expect to get at the bottom of him.

> "'Each in his hidden sphere of bliss or woe,
> Our hermit spirits dwell.'

"It is our lot here below. No one on earth can know Charles's secret thoughts. Did I guard him here at home ever so well, yet, in due time, it would be found that a serpent had crept into the heart of his innocence. Boys do not fully know what is good and what is evil; they do wrong things at first almost innocently. Novelty hides vice from them; there is no one to warn them or give them rules; and they become slaves of sin, while they are learning what sin is.

They go to the University, and suddenly plunge into excesses, the greater in proportion to their inexperience. And, besides all this, I am not equal to the task of forming so active and inquisitive a mind as his. He already asks questions which I know not how to answer. So he shall go to a public school. There he will get discipline at least, even if he has more of trial: at least he will gain habits of self-command, manliness, and circumspection; he will learn to use his eyes, and will find materials to use them upon; and thus will be gradually trained for the liberty which, any how, he must have when he goes to college."

This was the more necessary, because, with many high excellences, Charles was naturally timid and retiring, over-sensitive, and, though lively and cheerful, yet not without a tinge of melancholy in his character, which sometimes degenerated into mawkishness.

To Eton, then, he went; and there had the good fortune to fall into the hands of an excellent tutor, who, while he instructed him in the old Church-of-England principles of Mant and Doyley, gave his mind a religious impression, which secured him against the allurements of bad company, whether at the school itself, or afterwards at Oxford. To that celebrated seat of learning he was in due time transferred, being entered at St. Saviour's College; and he is in his sixth term from matriculation, and his fourth of residence, at the time our story opens.

At Oxford, it is needless to say, he had found a great number of his schoolfellows, but, it so happened, had found very few friends among them. Some were too gay for him, and he had avoided them; others, with whom he had been intimate at Eton, having high connections, had fairly cut him on coming into residence, or, being entered at other colleges, had lost sight of him. Almost everything depends at Oxford, in the matter of acquaintance, on proximity of rooms. You choose your friend, not so much by your tastes, as by your staircase. There is a story of a London tradesman who lost custom after beautifying his premises, because his entrance went up a step; and we all know how great is the difference between open and shut doors when we walk along a street of shops. In a university a youth's hours are portioned out to him. A regular man gets up and goes to chapel, breakfasts, gets up his lectures, goes to lecture, walks, dines; there is little to induce him to mount any staircase but his own; and if he does so, ten to one he finds the friend from home whom he is seeking; not to say that freshmen, who naturally have common feelings and interests, as naturally are allotted a staircase in common. And thus it was that Charles Reding was brought across William Sheffield, who had come into residence the same term as himself.

The minds of young people are pliable and elastic, and easily accommodate themselves to any one they fall in with. They find grounds of attraction both where they agree with one another and where they differ; what is congenial to themselves creates sympathy; what is correlative, or supplemental, creates admiration and esteem. And what is thus begun is often continued in after-life by the force of habit and the claims of memory. Thus, in the choice of friends, chance often does for us as much as the most careful selection could have effected. What was the character and degree of that friendship which sprang up between the freshmen Reding and Sheffield, we need not here minutely explain: it will be enough to say, that what they had in common was freshmanship, good talents, and the back staircase; and that they differed in this—that Sheffield had lived a good deal with people older than himself, had read much in a desultory way, and easily picked up opinions and facts, especially on controversies of the day, without laying anything very much to heart; that he was ready, clear-sighted, unembarrassed, and somewhat forward: Charles, on the other hand, had little knowledge as yet of principles or their bearings, but understood more deeply than Sheffield, and held more practically, what he had once received; he was gentle and affectionate, and easily led by others, except when duty clearly interfered. It should be added, that he had fallen in with various religious denominations in his father's parish, and had a general, though not a systematic, knowledge of their tenets. What they were besides, will be seen as our narrative advances.

CHAPTER II

It was a little past one P.M. when Sheffield, passing Charles's door, saw it open. The college servant had just entered with the usual half-commons for luncheon, and was employed in making up the fire. Sheffield followed him in, and found Charles in his cap and gown, lounging on the arm of his easy-chair, and eating his bread and cheese. Sheffield asked him if he slept, as well as ate and drank, "accoutred as he was."

"I am just going for a turn into the meadow," said Charles; "this is to me the best time of the year: *nunc formosissimus annus*; everything is beautiful; the laburnums are out, and the may. There is a greater variety of trees there than in any other place I know hereabouts; and the planes are so touching just now, with their small multitudinous green hands half-opened; and there are two or three such fine dark willows stretching over the Cherwell; I think some dryad inhabits them: and, as you wind along, just over your right shoulder is the Long Walk, with the Oxford buildings seen between the elms. They say there are dons here who recollect when the foliage was unbroken, nay, when you might walk under it in hard rain, and get no wet. I know I got drenched there the other day."

Sheffield laughed, and said that Charles must put on his beaver and walk with him a different way. He wanted a good walk; his head was stupid from his lectures; that old Jennings prosed so awfully upon Paley, it made him quite ill. He had talked of the Apostles as neither "deceivers nor deceived," of their "sensible miracles," and of their "dying for their testimony," till he did not know whether he himself was an *ens physiologicum* or a *totum metaphysicum*, when

Jennings had cruelly asked him to repeat Paley's argument; and because he had not given it in Jennings' words, friend Jennings had pursed up his lips, and gone through the whole again; so intent, in his wooden enthusiasm, on his own analysis of it, that he did not hear the clock strike the hour; and, in spite of the men's shuffling their feet, blowing their noses, and looking at their watches, on he had gone for a good twenty minutes past the time; and would have been going on even then, he verily believed, but for an interposition only equalled by that of the geese at the Capitol. For that, when he had got about half through his recapitulation, and was stopping at the end of a sentence to see the impression he was making, that uncouth fellow, Lively, moved by what happy inspiration he did not know, suddenly broke in, apropos of nothing, nodding his head, and speaking in a clear cackle, with, "Pray, sir, what is your opinion of the infallibility of the Pope?" Upon which every one but Jennings did laugh out: but he, *au contraire*, began to look very black; and no one can tell what would have happened, had he not cast his eyes by accident on his watch, on which he coloured, closed his book, and *instanter* sent the whole lecture out of the room.

Charles laughed in his turn, but added, "Yet, I assure you, Sheffield, that Jennings, stiff and cold as he seems, is, I do believe, a very good fellow at bottom. He has before now spoken to me with a good deal of feeling, and has gone out of his way to do me favours. I see poor bodies coming to him for charity continually; and they say that his sermons at Holy Cross are excellent."

Sheffield said he liked people to be natural, and hated that donnish manner. What good could it do? And what did it mean?

"That is what I call bigotry," answered Charles; "I am for taking every one for what he is, and not for what he is not: one has this excellence, another that; no one is everything. Why should we not drop what we don't like, and admire what we like? This is the only way of getting through life, the only true wisdom, and surely our duty into the bargain."

Sheffield thought this regular prose, and unreal. "We must," he said, "have a standard of things, else one good thing is as good as another. But I can't stand here all day," he continued, "when we ought to be walking." And he took off Charles's cap, and, placing his hat on him instead, said, "Come, let us be going."

"Then must I give up my meadow?" said Charles.

"Of course you must," answered Sheffield; "you must take a beaver walk. I want you to go as far as Oxley, a village some little way out, all the vicars of which, sooner or later, are made bishops. Perhaps even walking there may do us some good."

The friends set out, from hat to boot in the most approved Oxford bandbox-cut of trimness and prettiness. Sheffield was turning into the High Street, when Reding stopped him: "It always annoys me," he said, "to go down High Street in a beaver; one is sure to meet a proctor."

"All those University dresses are great fudge," answered Sheffield; "how are we the better for them? They are mere outside, and nothing else. Besides, our gown is so hideously ugly."

"Well, I don't go along with your sweeping condemnation," answered Charles; "this is a great place, and should have a dress. I declare, when I first saw the procession of Heads at St. Mary's, it was quite moving. First—"

"Of course the pokers," interrupted Sheffield.

"First the organ, and every one rising; then the Vice-Chancellor in red, and his bow to the preacher, who turns to the pulpit; then all the Heads in order; and lastly the Proctors. Meanwhile, you see the head of the preacher slowly mounting up the steps; when he gets in, he shuts-to the door, looks at the organ-loft to catch the psalm, and the voices strike up."

Sheffield laughed, and then said, "Well, I confess I agree with you in your instance. The preacher is, or is supposed to be, a person of talent; he is about to hold forth; the divines, the students of a great University, are all there to listen. The pageant does but fitly represent the great moral fact which is before us; I understand *this*. I don't call *this* fudge; what I mean by fudge is, outside without inside. Now I must say, the sermon itself, and not the least of all the prayer before it—what do they call it?"

"The bidding prayer," said Reding.

"Well, both sermon and prayer are often arrant fudge. I don't often go to University sermons, but I have gone often enough not to go again without compulsion. The last preacher I heard was from the country. Oh, it was wonderful! He began at the pitch of his voice, 'Ye shall pray.' What stuff! 'Ye shall *pray*'; because old Latimer or Jewell said, 'Ye shall praie,' therefore we must not say, 'Let us pray.' Presently he brought out," continued Sheffield, assuming a pompous and up-and-down tone, "'especially for that pure and apostolic branch of it *established*'—here the man rose on his toes, '*established* in these dominions.' Next came, 'for our Sovereign Lady Victoria, Queen, Defender of the Faith, in all causes and over all persons, ecclesiastical as well as civil, within these her dominions, *supreme*'—an awful pause, with an audible fall of the sermon-case on the cushion; as though nature did not contain, as if the human mind could not sustain, a bigger thought. Then followed, 'the pious and munificent founder,' in the same twang, 'of All Saints' and 'Leicester Colleges.' But his *chef-d'oeuvre* was his emphatic recognition of '*all* the doctors, *both* the proctors,' as if the numerical antithesis had a graphic power, and threw those excellent personages into a charming *tableau vivant*."

Charles was amused at all this; but he said in answer, that he never heard a sermon but it was his own fault if he did not gain good from it; and he quoted the words of his father, who, when he one day asked him if so-and-so had not preached a very good sermon, "My dear Charles," his father had said, "all sermons are good." The words, simple as they were, had retained a hold on his memory.

Meanwhile, they had proceeded down the forbidden High Street, and were crossing the bridge, when, on the opposite side, they saw before them a tall, upright man, whom Sheffield had no difficulty in recognizing as a bachelor of Nun's Hall, and a bore at least of the second magnitude. He was in cap and gown, but went on his way, as if intending, in that extraordinary guise, to take a country walk. He took the path which they were going themselves, and they tried to keep behind him; but they walked too briskly, and he too leisurely, to allow of that. It is very difficult duly to delineate a bore in a narrative, for the very reason that he *is* a bore. A tale must aim at condensation, but a bore acts in solution. It is only on the long-run that he is ascertained. Then, indeed, he is *felt*; he is oppressive; like the sirocco, which the native detects at once, while a foreigner is often at fault. *Tenet occiditque.* Did you hear him make but one speech, perhaps you would say he was a pleasant, well-informed man; but when he never comes to an end, or has one and the same prose every time you meet him, or keeps you standing till you are fit to sink, or holds you fast when you wish to keep an engagement, or hinders you listening to important conversation—then there is no mistake, the truth bursts on you, *apparent dirae facies*, you are in the clutches of a bore. You may yield, or you may flee; you cannot conquer. Hence it is clear that a bore cannot be represented in a story, or the story would be the bore as much as he. The reader, then, must believe this upright Mr. Bateman to be what otherwise he might not discover, and thank us for our consideration in not proving as well as asserting it.

Sheffield bowed to him courteously, and would have proceeded on his way; but Bateman, as became his nature, would not suffer it; he seized him. "Are you disposed," he said, "to look into the pretty chapel we are restoring on the common? It is quite a gem—in the purest style of the fourteenth century. It was in a most filthy condition, a mere cow-house; but we have made a subscription, and set it to rights."

"We are bound for Oxley," Sheffield answered; "you would be taking us out of our way."

"Not a bit of it," said Bateman; "it's not a stone's throw from the road; you must not refuse me. I'm sure you'll like it."

He proceeded to give the history of the chapel—all it had been, all it might have been, all it was not, all it was to be.

"It is to be a real specimen of a Catholic chapel," he said; "we mean to make the attempt of getting the Bishop to dedicate it to the Royal Martyr—why should not we have our St. Charles as well as the Romanists?—and it will be quite sweet to hear the vesper-bell tolling over the sullen moor every evening, in all weathers, and amid all the changes and chances of this mortal life."

Sheffield asked what congregation they expected to collect at that hour.

"That's a low view," answered Bateman; "it does not signify at all. In real Catholic churches the number of the congregation is nothing to the purpose; service is for those who come, not for those who stay away."

"Well," said Sheffield, "I understand what that means when a Roman Catholic says it; for a priest is supposed to offer sacrifice, which he can do without a congregation as well as with one. And, again, Catholic chapels often stand over the bodies of martyrs, or on some place of miracle, as a record; but our service is 'Common Prayer,' and how can you have that without a congregation?"

Bateman replied that, even if members of the University did not drop in, which he expected, at least the bell would be a memento far and near.

"Ah, I see," retorted Sheffield, "the use will be the reverse of what you said just now; it is not for those that come, but for those who stay away. The congregation is outside, not inside; it's an outside concern. I once saw a tall church-tower—so it appeared from the road; but on the sides you saw it was but a thin wall, made to look like a tower, in order to give the church an imposing effect. Do run up such a bit of a wall, and put the bell in it."

"There's another reason," answered Bateman, "for restoring the chapel, quite independent of the service. It has been a chapel from time immemorial, and was consecrated by our Catholic forefathers."

Sheffield argued that this would be as good a reason for keeping up the Mass as for keeping up the chapel.

"We do keep up the Mass," said Bateman; "we offer our Mass every Sunday, according to the rite of the English Cyprian, as honest Peter Heylin calls him; what would you have more?"

Whether Sheffield understood this or no, at least it was beyond Charles. Was the Common Prayer the English Mass, or the Communion-service, or the Litany, or the sermon, or any part of these? Or were Bateman's words really a confession that there were clergymen who actually said the Popish Mass once a week? Bateman's precise meaning, however, is lost to posterity; for they had by this time arrived at the door of the chapel. It had once been the chapel of an almshouse; a small farmhouse stood near; but, for population, it was plain no "church accommodation" was wanted. Before entering, Charles hung back, and whispered to his friend that he did not know Bateman. An introduction, in consequence, took place. "Reding of St. Saviour's—Bateman of Nun's Hall"; after which ceremony, in place of holy water, they managed to enter the chapel in company.

It was as pretty a building as Bateman had led them to expect, and very prettily done up. There was a stone altar in the best style, a credence table, a piscina, what looked like a tabernacle, and a couple of handsome brass candlesticks. Charles asked the use of the piscina—he did not know its name—and was told that there was always a piscina in the old churches in England, and that there could be no proper restoration without it. Next he asked the meaning of the beautifully wrought closet or recess above the altar; and received for answer, that "our sister churches of the Roman obedience always had a tabernacle for reserving the consecrated bread." Here Charles was brought to a stand: on which Sheffield asked the use of the niches; and was told by Bateman that images of saints were forbidden by the canon, but that his friends, in all these matters, did what they could. Lastly, he asked the meaning of the candlesticks; and was told that, Catholicly-minded as their Bishop was, they had some fear lest he would object to altar lights in service—at least at first: but it was plain that the *use* of the candlesticks was to hold candles. Having had their fill of gazing and admiring, they turned to proceed on their walk, but could not get off an invitation to breakfast, in a few days, at Bateman's lodgings in the Turl.

CHAPTER III

NEITHER of the friends had what are called *views* in religion; by which expression we do not here signify that neither had taken up a certain line of opinion, though this was the case also; but that neither of them—how could they at their age?—had placed his religion on an intellectual basis. It may be as well to state more distinctly what a "view" is, what it is to be "viewy," and what is the state of those who have no "views." When, then, men for the first time look upon the world of politics or religion, all that they find there meets their mind's eye as a landscape addresses itself for the first time to a person who has just gained his bodily sight. One thing is as far off as another; there is no perspective. The connection of fact with fact, truth with truth, the bearing of fact upon truth, and truth upon fact, what leads to what, what are points primary and what secondary—all this they have yet to learn. It is all a new science to them, and they do not even know their ignorance of it. Moreover, the world of today has no connection in their minds with the world of yesterday; time is not a stream, but stands before them round and full, like the moon. They do not know what happened ten years ago, much less the annals of a century; the past does not live to them in the present; they do not understand the worth of contested points; names have no associations for them, and persons kindle no recollections. They hear of men, and things, and projects, and struggles, and principles; but everything comes and goes like the wind, nothing makes an impression, nothing penetrates, nothing has its place in their minds. They locate nothing; they have no system. They hear and they forget; or they just recollect what they have once heard, they can't tell where. Thus they have no consistency in their arguments; that is, they argue one way today, and not exactly the other way tomorrow, but indirectly the other way, at random. Their lines of argument diverge; nothing comes to a point; there is no one centre in which their mind sits, on which their judgment of men and things proceeds. This is the state of many men all through life; and miserable politicians or Churchmen they make, unless by good luck they are in safe hands, and ruled by others, or are pledged to a course. Else they are at the mercy of the winds and waves; and, without being Radical, Whig, Tory, or Conservative, High Church or Low Church, they do Whig acts, Tory acts, Catholic acts, and heretical acts, as the fit takes them, or as events or parties drive them. And sometimes, when their self-importance is hurt, they take refuge in the idea that all this is a proof that they are unfettered, moderate, dispassionate, that they observe the mean, that they are "no party men"; when they are, in fact, the most helpless of slaves; for our strength in this world is, to be the subjects of the reason, and our liberty, to be captives of the truth.

Now Charles Reding, a youth of twenty, could not be supposed to have much of a view in religion or politics; but no clever man allows himself to judge of things simply at hap-hazard; he is obliged, from a sort of self-respect, to have some rule or other, true or false; and Charles was very fond of the maxim, which he has already enunciated, that we must measure people by what they are, and not by what they are not. He had a great notion of loving every one—of looking kindly on every one; he was pierced with the sentiment which he had seen in a popular volume of poetry, that—

"Christian souls...
Though worn and soil'd with sinful clay,
Are yet, to eyes that see them true,
All glistening with baptismal dew."

He liked, as he walked along the road, and met labourer or horseman, gentleman or beggar, to say to himself, "He is a Christian." And when he came to Oxford, he came there with an enthusiasm so simple and warm as to be almost childish. He reverenced even the velvet of the Pro.; nay, the cocked hat which preceded the Preacher had its claim on his deferential regard. Without being himself a poet, he was in the season of poetry, in the sweet springtime, when the year is most beautiful, because it is new. Novelty was beauty to a heart so open and cheerful as his; not only because it was novelty, and had its proper charm as such, but because when we first see things, we see them in a "gay confusion," which is a principal element of the poetical. As time goes on, and we number and sort and measure things—as we gain views—we advance towards philosophy and truth, but we recede from poetry.

When we ourselves were young, we once on a time walked on a hot summer-day from Oxford to Newington—a dull road, as any one who has gone it knows; yet it was new to us; and we protest to you, reader, believe it or not, laugh or not, as you will, to us it seemed on that occasion quite touchingly beautiful; and a soft melancholy came over us, of which the shadows fall even now, when we look back on that dusty, weary journey. And why? Because every object which met us was unknown and full of mystery. A tree or two in the distance seemed the beginning of a great wood, or park, stretching endlessly; a hill implied a vale beyond, with that vale's history; the bye-lanes, with their green hedges, wound and vanished, yet were not lost to the imagination. Such was our first journey; but when we had gone it several times, the mind refused to act, the scene ceased to enchant, stern reality alone remained; and we thought it one of the most tiresome, odious roads we ever had occasion to traverse.

But to return to our story. Such was Reding. But Sheffield, on the other hand, without possessing any real view of things more than Charles, was, at this time, fonder of hunting for views, and more in danger of taking up false ones. That is, he was "viewy," in a bad sense of the word. He was not satisfied intellectually with things as they are; he was critical, impatient to reduce things to system, pushed principles too far, was fond of argument, partly from pleasure in the exercise, partly because he was perplexed, though he did not lay anything very much to heart.

They neither of them felt any special interest in the controversy going on in the University and country about High and Low Church. Sheffield had a sort of contempt for it; and Reding felt it to be bad taste to be unusual or prominent in anything. An Eton acquaintance had asked him to go and hear one of the principal preachers of the Catholic party, and offered to introduce him; but he had declined it. He did not like, he said, mixing himself up with party; he had come to Oxford to get his degree, and not to take up opinions; he thought his father would not relish it; and, moreover, he felt some little repugnance to such opinions and such people, under the notion that the authorities of the University were opposed to the whole movement. He could not help looking at its leaders as demagogues; and towards demagogues he felt an unmeasured aversion and contempt. He did not see why clergymen, however respectable, should be collecting undergraduates about them; and he heard stories of their way of going on which did not please him. Moreover, he did not like the specimens of their followers whom he fell in with; they were forward, or they "talked strong," as it was called; did ridiculous, extravagant acts; and sometimes neglected their college duties for things which did not concern them. He was unfortunate, certainly: for this is a very unfair account of the most exemplary men of that day, who doubtless are still, as clergymen or laymen, the strength of the Anglican Church; but in all collections of men, the straw and rubbish (as Lord Bacon says) float on the top, while gold and jewels sink and are hidden. Or, what is more apposite still, many men, or most men, are a compound of precious and worthless together, and their worthless swims, and their precious lies at the bottom.

CHAPTER IV

Bateman was one of these composite characters: he had much good and much cleverness in him; but he was absurd, and he afforded a subject of conversation to the two friends as they proceeded on their walk. "I wish there was less of fudge and humbug everywhere," said Sheffield; "one might shovel off cartloads from this place, and not miss it."

"If you had your way," answered Charles, "you would scrape off the roads till there was nothing to walk on. We are forced to walk on what you call humbug; we put it under our feet, but we use it."

"I cannot think that; it's like doing evil that good may come. I see shams everywhere. I go into St. Mary's, and I hear men spouting out commonplaces in a deep or a shrill voice, or with slow, clear, quiet emphasis and significant eyes—as that Bampton preacher not long ago, who assured us, apropos of the resurrection of the body, that 'all attempts to resuscitate the inanimate corpse by natural methods had hitherto been experimentally abortive.' I go into the place where degrees are given—the Convocation, I think—and there one hears a deal of unmeaning Latin for hours, graces, dispensations, and proctors walking up and down for nothing; all in order to keep up a sort of ghost of things passed away for centuries, while the real work might be done in a quarter of an hour. I fall in with this Bateman, and he talks to me of rood-lofts without roods, and piscinae without water, and niches without images, and candlesticks without lights, and masses without Popery; till I feel, with Shakespeare, that 'all the world's a stage.' Well, I go to Shaw, Turner, and Brown, very different men, pupils of Dr. Gloucester—you know whom I mean—and they tell us that we ought to put up crucifixes by the wayside, in order to excite religious feeling."

"Well, I really think you are hard on all these people," said Charles; "it is all very much like declamation; you would destroy externals of every kind. You are like the man in one of Miss Edgeworth's novels, who shut his ears to the music that he might laugh at the dancers."

"What is the music to which I close my ears?" asked Sheffield.

"To the meaning of those various acts," answered Charles; "the pious feeling which accompanies the sight of the image is the music."

"To those who have the pious feeling, certainly," said Sheffield; "but to put up images in England in order to create the feeling is like dancing to create music."

"I think you are hard upon England," replied Charles; "we are a religious people."

"Well, I will put it differently: do *you* like music?"

"You ought to know," said Charles, "whom I have frightened so often with my fiddle."

"Do you like dancing?"

"To tell the truth," said Charles, "I don't."

"Nor do I," said Sheffield; "it makes me laugh to think what I have done, when a boy, to escape dancing; there is something so absurd in it; and one had to be civil and to duck to young girls who were either prim or pert. I have behaved quite rudely to them sometimes, and then have been annoyed at my ungentlemanlikeness, and not known how to get out of the scrape."

"Well, I didn't know we were so like each other in anything," said Charles; "oh, the misery I have endured, in having to stand up to dance, and to walk about with a partner!—everybody looking at me, and I so awkward. It has been a torture to me days before and after."

They had by this time come up to the foot of the rough rising ground which leads to the sort of table-land on the edge of which Oxley is placed. They stood still awhile to see some equestrians take the hurdles, then mounted the hill, and looked back upon Oxford.

"Perhaps you call those beautiful spires and towers a sham," said Charles, "because you see their tops and not their bottoms?"

"Whereabouts were we in our argument?" said the other, reminded that they had been wandering from it for the last ten minutes. "Oh, I recollect; I know what I was at. I was saying that you liked music, but didn't like dancing; music leads another person to dance, but not you; and dancing does not increase but diminishes the intensity of the pleasure you find in music. In like manner, it is a mere piece of pedantry to make a religious nation, like the English, more religious by placing images in the streets; this is not the English way, and only offends us. If it were our way, it would come naturally without any one telling us. As music incites to dancing, so religion would lead to images; but as dancing does not improve music to those who do not like dancing, so ceremonies do not improve religion to those who do not like ceremonies."

"Then do you mean," said Charles, "that the English Romanists are shams, because they use crucifixes?"

"Stop there," said Sheffield; "now you are getting upon a different subject. They believe that there is *virtue* in images; that indeed is absurd in them, but it makes them quite consistent in honouring them. They do not put up images as outward shows, merely to create feelings in the minds of beholders, as Gloucester would do, but they in good, downright earnest worship images, as being more than they seem, as being not a mere outside show. They pay them a religious worship, as having been handled by great saints years ago, as having been used in pestilences, as having wrought miracles, as having moved their eyes or bowed their heads; or, at least, as having been blessed by the priest, and been brought into connection with invisible grace. This is superstitious, but it is real."

Charles was not satisfied. "An image is a mode of teaching," he said; "do you mean to say that a person is a sham merely because he mistakes the particular mode of teaching best suited to his own country?"

"I did not say that Dr. Gloucester was a sham," answered Sheffield; "but that mode of teaching of his was among Protestants a sham and a humbug."

"But this principle will carry you too far, and destroy itself," said Charles. "Don't you recollect what Thompson quoted the other day out of Aristotle, which he had lately begun in lecture with Vincent, and which we thought so acute—that habits are created by those very acts in which they manifest themselves when created? We learn to swim well by trying to swim. Now Bateman, doubtless, wishes to *introduce* piscinae and tabernacles; and to wait, before beginning, *till* they are received, is like not going into the water till you can swim."

"Well, but what is Bateman the better when his piscinae are universal?" asked Sheffield; "what does it *mean*? In the Romish Church it has a use, I know—I don't know what—but it comes into the Mass. But if Bateman makes piscinae universal among us, what has he achieved but the reign of a universal humbug?"

"But, my dear Sheffield," answered Reding, "consider how many things there are which, in the course of time, have altered their original meaning, and yet have a meaning, though a changed one, still. The judge's wig is no sham, yet it has a history. The Queen, at her coronation, is said to wear a Roman Catholic vestment, is that a sham? Does it not still typify and impress upon us the 'divinity that doth hedge a king,' though it has lost the very meaning which the Church of Rome gave it? Or are you of the number of those, who, according to the witticism, think majesty, when deprived of its externals, a jest?"

"Then you defend the introduction of unmeaning piscinae and candlesticks?"

"I think," answered Charles, "that there's a great difference between reviving and retaining; it may be natural to retain, even while the use fails, unnatural to revive when it has failed; but this is a question of discretion and judgment."

"Then you give it against Bateman?" said Sheffield.

A slight pause ensued; then Charles added, "But perhaps these men actually do wish to introduce the realities as well as the externals: perhaps they wish to use the piscina as well as to have it... Sheffield," he continued abruptly, "why are not canonicals a sham, if piscinae are shams?"

"Canonicals," said Sheffield, as if thinking about them; "no, canonicals are no sham; for preaching, I suppose, is the highest ordinance in our Church, and has the richest dress. The robes of a great preacher cost, I know, many pounds; for there was one near us who, on leaving, had a present from the ladies of an entire set, and a dozen pair of worked slippers into the bargain. But it's all fitting, if preaching is the great office of the clergy. Next comes the Sacrament, and has the surplice and hood. And hood," he repeated, musing; "what's that for? No, it's the scarf. The hood is worn in the University pulpit; what is the scarf?—it belongs to chaplains, I believe, that is, to *persons*; I can't make a view out of it."

"My dear Sheffield," said Charles, "you have cut your own throat. Here you have been trying to give a sense to the clerical dress, and cannot; are you then prepared to call it a sham? Answer me this single question—Why does a clergyman wear a surplice when he reads prayers? Nay, I will put it more simply—Why can only a clergyman read prayers in church?—Why cannot I?"

Sheffield hesitated, and looked serious. "Do you know," he said, "you have just pitched on Jeremy Bentham's objection. In his 'Church of Englandism' he proposes, if I recollect rightly, that a parish-boy should be taught to read the Liturgy; and he asks, Why send a person to the University for three or four years at an enormous expense, why teach him Latin and Greek, on purpose to read what any boy could be taught to read at a dame's school? What is the *virtue* of a clergyman's reading? Something of this kind, Bentham says; and," he added, slowly, "to tell the truth, *I* don't know how to answer him."

Reding was surprised, and shocked, and puzzled too; he did not know what to say; when the conversation was, perhaps fortunately, interrupted.

CHAPTER V

EVERY year brings changes and reforms. We do not know what is the state of Oxley Church now; it may have rood-loft, piscina, sedilia, all new; or it may be reformed backwards, the seats on principle turning from the Communion-table, and the pulpit planted in the middle of the aisle; but at the time when these two young men walked through the churchyard, there was nothing very good or very bad to attract them within the building; and they were passing on, when they observed, coming out of the church, what Sheffield called an elderly don, a fellow of a college, whom Charles knew. He was a man of family, and had some little property of his own, had been a contemporary of his father's at the University, and had from time to time been a guest at the parsonage. Charles had, in consequence, known him from a boy; and now, since he came into residence, he had, as was natural, received many small attentions from him. Once, when he was late for his own hall, he had given him his dinner in his rooms; he had taken him out on a fishing expedition towards Faringdon; and had promised him tickets for some ladies, lionesses of his, who were coming up to the Commemoration. He was a shrewd, easy-tempered, free-spoken man, of small desires and no ambition; of no very keen sensibilities or romantic delicacies, and very little religious pretension; that is, though unexceptionable in his deportment, he hated the show of religion, and was impatient at those who affected it. He had known the University for thirty years, and formed a right estimate of most things in it. He had come out to Oxley to take a funeral for a friend, and was now returning home. He hallooed to Charles, who, though feeling at first awkward on finding himself with two such different friends and in two such different relations, was, after a time, partially restored to himself by the unconcern of Mr. Malcolm; and the three walked home together. Yet, even to the last, he did not quite know how and where to walk, and how to carry himself, particularly when they got near Oxford, and he fell in with various parties who greeted him in passing.

Charles, by way of remark, said they had been looking in at a pretty little chapel on the common, which was now in the course of repair. Mr. Malcolm laughed. "So, Charles," he said, "*you're* bit with the new fashion."

Charles coloured, and asked, "What fashion?" adding, that a friend, by accident, had taken them in.

"You ask what fashion," said Mr. Malcolm; "why, the newest, latest fashion. This is a place of fashions; there have been many fashions in my time. The greater part of the residents, that is, the boys, change once in three years; the fellows and tutors, perhaps, in half a dozen; and every generation has its own fashion. There is no principle of stability in Oxford, except the Heads, and they are always the same, and always will be the same to the end of the chapter. What is in now," he asked, "among you youngsters—drinking or cigars?"

Charles laughed modestly, and said he hoped drinking had gone out everywhere.

"Worse things may come in," said Mr. Malcolm; "but there are fashions everywhere. There was once a spouting club, perhaps it is in favour still; before it was the music-room. Once geology was all the rage; now it is theology; soon it will be architecture, or medieval antiquities, or editions and codices. Each wears out in its turn; all depends on one or two active men; but the secretary takes a wife, or the professor gets a stall; and then the meetings are called irregularly, and nothing is done in them, and so gradually the affair dwindles and dies."

Sheffield asked whether the present movement had not spread too widely through the country for such a termination; he did not know much about it himself, but the papers were full of it, and it was the talk of every neighbourhood; it was not confined to Oxford.

"I don't know about the country," said Mr. Malcolm, "that is a large question; but it has not the elements of stability here. These gentlemen will take livings and marry, and that will be the end of the business. I am not speaking against them; they are, I believe, very respectable men; but they are riding on the spring-tide of a fashion."

Charles said it was a nuisance to see the party-spirit it introduced. Oxford ought to be a place of quiet and study; peace and the Muses always went together; whereas there was talk, talk, in every quarter. A man could not go about his duties in a natural way, and take every one as he came, but was obliged to take part in questions, and to consider points which he might wish to put from him, and must sport an opinion when he really had none to give.

Mr. Malcolm assented in a half-absent way, looking at the view before him, and seemingly enjoying it. "People call this county ugly," said he, "and perhaps it is; but whether I am used to it or no, I always am pleased with it. The lights are always new; and thus the landscape, if it deserves the name, is always presented in a new dress. I have known Shotover there take the most opposite hues, sometimes purple, sometimes a bright saffron or tawny orange." Here he stopped: "Yes, you speak of party-spirit; very true, there's a good deal of it.... No, I don't think there's much," he continued, rousing; "certainly there is more division just at this minute in Oxford, but there always is division, always rivalry. The separate societies have their own interests and honour to maintain, and quarrel, as the orders do in the Church of Rome. No, that's too grand a comparison; rather, Oxford is like an almshouse for clergymen's widows.

Self-importance, jealousy, tittle-tattle are the order of the day. It has always been so in my time. Two great ladies, Mrs. Vice-Chancellor and Mrs. Divinity-Professor, can't agree, and have followings respectively: or Vice-Chancellor himself, being a new broom, sweeps all the young Masters clean out of Convocation House, to their great indignation: or Mr. Slaney, Dean of St. Peter's, does not scruple to say in a stage-coach that Mr. Wood is no scholar; on which the said Wood calls him in return 'slanderous Slaney'; or the elderly Mr. Barge, late Senior Fellow of St. Michael's, thinks that his pretty bride has not been received with due honours; or Dr. Crotchet is for years kept out of his destined bishopric by a sinister influence; or Mr. Professor Carraway has been infamously shown up, in the *Edinburgh*, by an idle fellow whom he plucked in the schools; or (*majora movemus*) three colleges interchange a mortal vow of opposition to a fourth; or the young working Masters conspire against the Heads. Now, however, we are improving; if we must quarrel, let it be the rivalry of intellect and conscience, rather than of interest or temper; let us contend for things, not for shadows."

Sheffield was pleased at this, and ventured to say that the present state of things was more real, and therefore more healthy. Mr. Malcolm did not seem to hear him, for he did not reply; and, as they were now approaching the bridge again, the conversation stopped. Sheffield looked slily at Charles, as Mr. Malcolm proceeded with them up High Street; and both of them had the triumph and the amusement of being convoyed safely past a proctor, who was patrolling it, under the protection of a Master.

CHAPTER VI

THE walk to Oxley had not been the first or the second occasion on which Charles had, in one shape or other, encountered Sheffield's views about realities and shams; and his preachments had begun to make an impression on him; that is, he felt that there was truth in them at bottom, and a truth new to him. He was not a person to let a truth sleep in his mind; though it did not vegetate very quickly, it was sure ultimately to be pursued into its consequences, and to affect his existing opinions. In the instance before us, he saw Sheffield's principle was more or less antagonistic to his own favourite maxim, that it was a duty to be pleased with every one. Contradictions could not both be real: when an affirmative was true, a negative was false. All doctrines could not be equally sound: there was a right and a wrong. The theory of dogmatic truth, as opposed to latitudinarianism (he did not know their names or their history, or suspect what was going on within him), had in the course of these his first terms, gradually begun to energise in his mind. Let him but see the absurdities of the latitudinarian principle, when carried out, and he is likely to be still more opposed to it.

Bateman, among his peculiarities, had a notion that bringing persons of contrary sentiments together was the likeliest way of making a party agreeable, or at least useful. He had done his best to give his breakfast, to which our friends were invited, this element of perfection; not, however, to his own satisfaction; for with all his efforts, he had but picked up Mr. Freeborn, a young Evangelical Master, with whom Sheffield was acquainted; a sharp, but not very wise freshman, who, having been spoiled at home, and having plenty of money, professed to be *aesthetic*, and kept his college authorities in a perpetual fidget lest he should some morning wake up a Papist; and a friend of his, a nice, modest-looking youth, who, like a mouse, had keen darting eyes, and ate his bread and butter in absolute silence.

They had hardly seated themselves, and Sheffield was pouring out coffee, and a plate of muffins was going round, and Bateman was engaged, saucepan in hand, in the operation of landing his eggs, now boiled, upon the table, when our flighty youth, whose name was White, observed how beautiful the Catholic custom was of making eggs the emblem of the Easter-festival. "It is truly Catholic," said he; "for it is retained in parts of England, you have it in Russia, and in Rome itself, where an egg is served up on every plate through the Easter-week, after being, I believe, blessed; and it is as expressive and significant as it is Catholic."

"Beautiful indeed!" said their host; "so pretty, so sweet; I wonder whether our Reformers thought of it, or the profound Hooker—he was full of types—or Jewell. You recollect the staff Jewell gave Hooker: that was a type. It was like the sending of Elisha's staff by his servant to the dead child."

"Oh, my dear, dear Bateman," cried Sheffield, "you are making Hooker Gehazi!"

"That's just the upshot of such trifling," said Mr. Freeborn; "you never know where to find it; it proves anything, and disproves anything."

"That is only till it's sanctioned," said White; "When the Catholic Church sanctions it, we're safe."

"Yes, we're safe," said Bateman; "it's safe when it's Catholic."

"Yes," continued White, "things change their nature altogether when they are taken up by the Catholic Church: that's how we are allowed to do evil that good may come."

"What's that?" said Bateman.

"Why," said White, "the Church makes evil good."

"My dear White," said Bateman gravely, "that's going too far; it is indeed."

Mr. Freeborn suspended his breakfast operations, and sat back in his chair.

"Why," continued White, "is not idolatry wrong—yet image-worship is right?"

Mr. Freeborn was in a state of collapse.

"That's a bad instance, White," said Sheffield; "there *are* people in the world who are uncatholic enough to think image-worship is wrong, as well as idolatry."

"A mere Jesuitical distinction," said Freeborn with emotion.

"Well," said White, who did not seem in great awe of the young M.A., though some years, of course, his senior, "I will take a better instance: who does not know that baptism gives grace? Yet there were heathen baptismal rites, which, of course, were devilish."

"I should not be disposed, Mr. White, to grant you so much as you would wish," said Freeborn, "about the virtue of baptism."

"Not about Christian baptism?" asked White.

"It is easy," answered Freeborn, "to mistake the sign for the thing signified."

"Not about Catholic baptism?" repeated White.

"Catholic baptism is a mere deceit and delusion," retorted Mr. Freeborn.

"Oh, my dear Freeborn," interposed Bateman, "now *you* are going too far; you are indeed."

"Catholic, Catholic—I don't know what you mean," said Freeborn.

"I mean," said White, "the baptism of the one Catholic Church of which the Creed speaks: it's quite intelligible."

"But what do you mean by the Catholic Church?" asked Freeborn.

"The Anglican," answered Bateman.

"The Roman," answered White; both in the same breath.

There was a general laugh.

"There is nothing to laugh at," said Bateman; "Anglican and Roman are one."

"One! impossible," cried Sheffield.

"Much worse than impossible," observed Mr. Freeborn.

"I should make a distinction," said Bateman: "I should say, they are one, except the corruptions of the Romish Church."

"That is, they are one, except where they differ," said Sheffield.

"Precisely so," said Bateman.

"Rather, *I* should say," objected Mr. Freeborn, "two, except where they agree."

"That's just the issue," said Sheffield; "Bateman says that the Churches are one except when they are two; and Freeborn says that they are two except when they are one."

It was a relief at this moment that the cook's boy came in with a dish of hot sausages; but though a relief, it was not a diversion; the conversation proceeded. Two persons did not like it; Freeborn, who was simply disgusted at the doctrine, and Reding, who thought it a bore; yet it was the bad luck of Freeborn forthwith to set Charles against him, as well as the rest, and to remove the repugnance which he had to engage in the dispute. Freeborn, in fact, thought theology itself a mistake, as substituting, as he considered, worthless intellectual notions for the vital truths of religion; so he now went on to observe, putting down his knife and fork, that it really was to him inconceivable, that real religion should depend on metaphysical distinctions, or outward observances; that it was quite a different thing in Scripture; that Scripture said much of faith and holiness, but hardly a word about Churches and forms. He proceeded to say that it was the great and evil tendency of the human mind to interpose between itself and its Creator some self-invented mediator, and it did not matter at all whether that human device was a rite, or a creed, or a form of prayer, or good works, or communion with particular Churches—all were but "flattering unctions to the soul," if they were considered necessary; the only safe way of using them was to use them with the feeling that you might dispense with them; that none of them went to the root of the matter, for that faith, that is, firm belief that God had forgiven you, was the one thing needful; that where that one thing was present, everything else was superfluous; that where it was wanting, nothing else availed. So strongly did he hold this, that (he confessed he put it pointedly, but still not untruly), where true faith was present, a person might be anything in profession; an Arminian, a Calvinist, an Episcopalian, a Presbyterian, a Swedenborgian—nay, a Unitarian—he would go further, looking at White, a Papist, yet be in a state of salvation.

Freeborn came out rather more strongly than in his sober moments he would have approved; but he was a little irritated, and wished to have his turn of speaking. It was altogether a great testification.

"Thank you for your liberality to the poor Papists," said White; "it seems they are safe if they are hypocrites, professing to be Catholics, while they are Protestants in heart."

"Unitarians, too," said Sheffield, "are debtors to your liberality; it seems a man need not fear to believe too little, so that he feels a good deal."

"Rather," said White, "if he believes himself forgiven, he need not believe anything else."

Reding put in his word; he said that in the Prayer Book, belief in the Holy Trinity was represented, not as an accident, but as "before all things" necessary to salvation.

"That's not a fair answer, Reding," said Sheffield; "what Mr. Freeborn observed was, that there's no creed in the Bible; and you answer that there is a creed in the Prayer Book."

"Then the Bible says one thing, and the Prayer Book another," said Bateman.

"No," answered Freeborn; "The Prayer Book only *deduces* from Scripture; the Athanasian Creed is a human invention; true, but human, and to be received, as one of the Articles expressly says, because 'founded on Scripture.' Creeds are useful in their place, so is the Church; but neither Creed nor Church is religion."

"Then why do you make so much of your doctrine of 'faith only'?" said Bateman; "for that is not in Scripture, and is but a human deduction."

"*My* doctrine!" cried Freeborn; "why it's in the Articles; the Articles expressly say that we are justified by faith only."

"The Articles are not Scripture any more than the Prayer Book," said Sheffield.

"Nor do the Articles say that the doctrine they propound is

necessary for salvation," added Bateman.

All this was very unfair on Freeborn, though he had provoked it. Here were four persons on him at once, and the silent fifth apparently a sympathiser. Sheffield talked through malice; White from habit; Reding came in because he could not help it; and Bateman spoke on principle; he had a notion that he was improving Freeborn's views by this process of badgering. At least he did not improve his temper, which was suffering. Most of the party were undergraduates; he (Freeborn) was a Master; it was too bad of Bateman. He finished in silence his sausage, which had got quite cold. The conversation flagged; there was a rise in toast and muffins; coffee-cups were put aside, and tea flowed freely.

CHAPTER VII

FREEBORN did not like to be beaten; he began again. Religion, he said, was a matter of the heart; no one could interpret Scripture rightly whose heart was not right. Till our eyes were enlightened, to dispute about the sense of Scripture, to attempt to deduce from Scripture, was beating about the bush: it was like the blind disputing about colours.

"If this is true," said Bateman, "no one ought to argue about religion at all; but you were the first to do so, Freeborn."

"Of course," answered Freeborn, "those who have *found* the truth are the very persons to argue, for they have the gift."

"And the very last persons to persuade," said Sheffield; "for they have the gift all to themselves."

"Therefore true Christians should argue with each other, and with no one else," said Bateman.

"But those are the very persons who don't want it," said Sheffield; "reasoning must be for the unconverted, not for the converted. It is the means of seeking."

Freeborn persisted that the reason of the unconverted was carnal, and that such could not understand Scripture.

"I have always thought," said Reding, "that reason was a general gift, though faith is a special and personal one. If faith is really rational, all ought to see that it is rational; else, from the nature of the case, it is not rational."

"But St. Paul says," answered Freeborn, "that 'to the natural man the things of the Spirit are foolishness.'"

"But how are we to arrive at truth at all," said Reding, "except by reason? It is the appointed method for our guidance. Brutes go by instinct, men by reason."

They had fallen on a difficult subject; all were somewhat puzzled except White, who had not been attending, and was simply wearied; he now interposed. "It would be a dull world," he said, "if men went by reason: they may think they do, but they don't. Really, they are led by their feelings, their affections, by the sense of the beautiful, and the good, and the holy. Religion is the beautiful; the clouds, sun, and sky, the fields and the woods, are religion."

"This would make all religions true," said Freeborn, "good and bad."

"No," answered White, "heathen rites are bloody and impure, not beautiful; and Mahometanism is as cold and as dry as any Calvinistic meeting. The Mahometans have no altars or priests, nothing but a pulpit and a preacher."

"Like St. Mary's," said Sheffield.

"Very like," said White; "we have no life or poetry in the Church of England; the Catholic Church alone is beautiful. You would see what I mean if you went into a foreign cathedral, or even into one of the Catholic churches in our large towns. The celebrant, deacon, and subdeacon, acolytes with lights, the incense, and the chanting—all combine to one end, one act of worship. You feel it *is* really a worshipping; every sense, eyes, ears, smell, are made to know that worship is going on. The laity on the floor saying their beads, or making their acts; the choir singing out the *Kyrie*; and the priest and his assistants bowing low, and saying the *Confiteor* to each other. This is worship, and it is far above reason."

This was spoken with all his heart; but it was quite out of keeping with the conversation which had preceded it, and White's poetry was almost as disagreeable to the party as Freeborn's prose.

"White, you should turn Catholic out and out," said Sheffield.

"My dear good fellow," said Bateman, "think what you are saying. You can't really have gone to a schismatical chapel. Oh, for shame!"

Freeborn observed, gravely, that if the two Churches *were* one, as had been maintained, he could not see, do what he would, why it was wrong to go to and fro from one to the other.

"You forget," said Bateman to White, "you have, or might have, all this in your own Church, without the Romish corruptions."

"As to the Romish corruptions," answered White, "I know very little about them."

Freeborn groaned audibly.

"I know very little about them," repeated White eagerly, "very little; but what is that to the purpose? We must take things as we find them. I don't like what is bad in the Catholic Church, if there is bad, but what is good. I do not go to it for what is bad, but for what is good. You can't deny that what I admire is very good and beautiful. Only you try to introduce it into your own Church. You would give your ears, you know you would, to hear the *Dies irae*."

Here a general burst of laughter took place. White was an Irishman. It was a happy interruption; the party rose up from table, and a tap at that minute, which sounded at the door, succeeded in severing the thread of the conversation.

It was a printseller's man with a large book of plates.

"Well timed," said Bateman—"put them down, Baker: or rather give them to me—I can take the opinion of you men on a point I have much at heart. You know I wanted you, Freeborn, to go with me to see my chapel; Sheffield and Reding have looked into it. Well now, just see here."

He opened the portfolio; it contained views of the Campo Santo at Pisa. The leaves were slowly turned over in silence, the spectators partly admiring, partly not knowing what to think, partly wondering at what was coming.

"What do you think my plan is?" he continued. "You twitted me, Sheffield, because my chapel would be useless. Now I mean to get a cemetery attached to it; there is plenty of land; and then the chapel will become a chantry. But now, what will you say if we have a copy of these splendid medieval monuments round the burial-place, both sculpture and painting? Now, Sheffield, Mr. Critic, what do you say to that?"

"A most admirable plan," said Sheffield, "and quite removes my objections.... A chantry! what is that? Don't they say Mass in it for the dead?"

"Oh, no, no, no," said Bateman, in fear of Freeborn; "we'll have none of your Popery. It will be a simple, guileless chapel, in which the Church Service will be read."

Meanwhile Sheffield was slowly turning over the plates. He stopped at one. "What will you do with that figure?" he said, pointing to a Madonna.

"Oh, it will be best, most prudent, to leave it out; certainly, certainly."

Sheffield soon began again: "But look here, my good fellow, what do you do with these saints and angels? Do see, why here's a complete legend; do you mean to have this? Here's a set of miracles, and a woman invoking a saint in heaven."

Bateman looked cautiously at them, and did not answer. He would have shut the book, but Sheffield wished to see some more. Meanwhile he said, "Oh yes, true, there *are* some things; but I have an expedient for all this; I mean to make it all allegorical. The Blessed Virgin shall be the Church, and the saints shall be cardinal and other virtues; and as to that saint's life, St. Ranieri's, it shall be a Catholic 'Pilgrim's Progress.'"

"Good! then you must drop all these popes and bishops, copes and chalices," said Sheffield; "and have their names written under the rest, that people mayn't take them for saints and angels. Perhaps you had better have scrolls from their mouths, in old English. This St. Thomas is stout; make him say, 'I am Mr. Dreadnought,' or 'I am Giant Despair'; and, since this beautiful saint bears a sort of dish, make her 'Mrs. Creature Comfort.' But look here," he continued, "a whole set of devils; are *these* to be painted up?"

Bateman attempted forcibly to shut the book; Sheffield went on: "St. Anthony's temptations; what's this? Here's the fiend in the shape of a cat on a wine-barrel."

"Really, really," said Bateman, disgusted, and getting possession of it, "you are quite offensive, quite. We will look at them when you are more serious."

Sheffield indeed was very provoking, and Bateman more good-humoured than many persons would have been in his place. Meanwhile Freeborn, who had had his gown in his hand the last two minutes, nodded to his host, and took his departure by himself; and White and Willis soon followed in company.

"Really," said Bateman to Sheffield, when they were gone, "you and White, each in his own way, are so very rash in your mode of speaking, and before other people, too. I wished to teach Freeborn a little good Catholicism, and you have spoilt all. I hoped something would have come out of this breakfast. But only think of White! it will all out. Freeborn will tell it to his set. It is very bad, very bad indeed. And you, my friend, are not much better; never serious. What *could* you mean by saying that our Church is not one with the Romish? It was giving Freeborn such an advantage."

Sheffield looked provokingly easy; and, leaning with his back against the mantelpiece, and his coat-tail almost playing with the spout of the kettle, replied, "You had a most awkward team to drive."

Then he added, looking sideways at him, with his head back, "And why had you, O most correct of men, the audacity to say that the English Church and the Romish Church *were* one?"

"It must be so," answered Bateman; "there is but one Church—the Creed says so; would you make two?"

"I don't speak of doctrine," said Sheffield, "but of fact. I didn't mean to say that there *were* two *Churches*; nor to deny that there was one *Church*. I but denied the fact, that what are evidently two bodies were one body."

Bateman thought awhile; and Charles employed himself in scraping down the soot from the back of the chimney with the poker. He did not wish to speak, but he was not sorry to listen to such an argument.

"My good fellow," said Bateman, in a tone of instruction, "you are making a distinction between a Church and a body which I don't quite comprehend. You say that there are two bodies, and yet but one Church. If so, the Church is not a body, but something abstract, a mere name, a general idea; is *that* your meaning? If so, you are an honest Calvinist."

"You are another," answered Sheffield; "for if you make two visible Churches, English and Romish, to be one Church, that one Church must be invisible, not visible. Thus, if I hold an abstract Church, you hold an invisible one."

"I do not see that," said Bateman.

"Prove the two Churches to be one," said Sheffield, "and then I'll prove something else."

"Some paradox?" said Bateman.

"Of course," answered Sheffield, "a huge one; but yours, not mine. Prove the English and Romish Churches to be in any sense one, and I will prove by parallel arguments that in the same sense we and the Wesleyans are one."

This was a fair challenge. Bateman, however, suddenly put on a demure look, and was silent. "We are on sacred subjects," he said at length in a subdued tone, "we are on very sacred subjects; we must be reverent," and he drew a very long face.

Sheffield laughed out, nor could Reding stand it. "What is it?" cried Sheffield; "don't be hard on me? What have I done? Where did the sacredness begin? I eat my words."

"Oh, he meant nothing," said Charles, "indeed he did not; he's more serious than he seems; do answer him; I am interested."

"Really, I do wish to treat the subject gravely," said Sheffield; "I will begin again. I am very sorry, indeed I am. Let me put the objection more reverently."

Bateman relaxed: "My good Sheffield," he said, "the thing is irreverent, not the manner. It is irreverent to liken your holy mother to the Wesleyan schismatics."

"I repent, I do indeed," said Sheffield; "it was a wavering of faith; it was very unseemly, I confess it. What can I say more? Look at me; won't this do? But now tell me, do tell me, *how* are we one body with the Romanists, yet the Wesleyans not one body with us?"

Bateman looked at him, and was satisfied with the expression of his face. "It's a strange question for you to ask," he said; "I fancied you were a sharper fellow. Don't you see that we have the apostolical succession as well as the Romanists?"

"But Romanists say," answered Sheffield, "that that is not enough for unity; that we ought to be in communion with the Pope."

"That's their mistake," answered Bateman.

"That's just what the Wesleyans say of us," retorted Sheffield, "when we won't acknowledge *their* succession; they say it's our mistake."

"Their succession!" cried Bateman; "they have no succession."

"Yes, they have," said Sheffield; "they have a ministerial succession."

"It isn't apostolical," answered Bateman.

"Yes, but it is evangelical, a succession of doctrine," said Sheffield.

"Doctrine! Evangelical!" cried Bateman; "whoever heard! that's not enough; doctrine is not enough without bishops."

"And succession is not enough without the Pope," answered Sheffield.

"They act against the bishops," said Bateman, not quite seeing whither he was going.

"And we act against the Pope," said Sheffield.

"We say that the Pope isn't necessary," said Bateman.

"And they say that bishops are not necessary," returned Sheffield.

They were out of breath, and paused to see where they stood. Presently Bateman said, "My good sir, this is a question of *fact*, not of argumentative cleverness. The question is, whether it is not *true* that bishops are necessary to the notion of a Church, and whether it is not *false* that Popes are necessary."

"No, no," cried Sheffield, "the question is this, whether obedience to our bishops is not necessary to make Wesleyans one body with us, and obedience to their Pope necessary to make us one body with the Romanists. You maintain the one, and deny the other; I maintain both. Maintain both, or deny both: I am consistent; you are inconsistent."

Bateman was puzzled.

"In a word," Sheffield added, "succession is not unity, any more than doctrine."

"Not unity? What then is unity?" asked Bateman.

"Oneness of polity," answered Sheffield.

Bateman thought awhile. "The idea is preposterous," he said: "here we have *possession*; here we are established since King Lucius's time, or since St. Paul preached here; filling the island; one continuous Church; with the same territory, the same succession, the same hierarchy, the same civil and political position, the same churches. Yes," he proceeded, "we have the very same fabrics, the memorials of a thousand years, doctrine stamped and perpetuated in stone; all the mystical teaching of the old saints. What have the Methodists to do with Catholic rites? With altars, with sacrifice, with rood-lofts, with fonts, with niches?—they call it all superstition."

"Don't be angry with me, Bateman," said Sheffield, "and, before going, I will put forth a parable. Here's the Church of England, as like a Protestant Establishment as it can stare; bishops and people, all but a few like yourselves, call it Protestant; the living body calls itself Protestant; the living body abjures Catholicism, flings off the name and the thing, hates the Church of Rome, laughs at sacramental power, despises the Fathers, is jealous of priestcraft, is a Protestant reality, is a Catholic sham. This existing reality, which is alive and no mistake, you wish to top with a filagree-work of screens, dorsals, pastoral staffs, croziers, mitres, and the like. Now most excellent Bateman, will you hear my parable? Will you be offended at it?"

Silence gave consent, and Sheffield proceeded.

"Why, once on a time a negro boy, when his master was away, stole into his wardrobe, and determined to make himself fine at his master's expense. So he was presently seen in the streets, naked as usual, but strutting up and down with a cocked hat on his head, and a pair of white kid gloves on his hands."

"Away with you! get out, you graceless, hopeless fellow!" said Bateman, discharging the sofa-bolster at his head. Meanwhile Sheffield ran to the door, and quickly found himself with Charles in the street below.

CHAPTER VIII

Sheffield and Charles may go their way; but we must follow White and Willis out of Bateman's lodgings. It was a Saint's day, and they had no lectures; they walked arm-in-arm along Broad Street, evidently very intimate, and Willis found his voice: "I can't bear that Freeborn," said he, "he's such a prig; and I like him the less because I am obliged to know him."

"You knew him in the country, I think?" said White.

"In consequence, he has several times had me to his spiritual tea-parties, and has introduced me to old Mr. Grimes, a good, kind-hearted old *fogie*, but an awful evangelical, and his wife worse. Grimes is the old original religious tea-man, and Freeborn imitates him. They get together as many men as they can, perhaps twenty freshmen, bachelors, and masters, who sit in a circle, with cups and saucers in their hands and hassocks at their knees. Some insufferable person of Capel Hall or St. Mark's, who hardly speaks English, under pretence of asking Mr. Grimes some divinity question, holds forth on original sin, or justification, or assurance, monopolizing the conversation. Then tea-things go, and a portion of Scripture comes instead; and old Grimes expounds; very good it is, doubtless, though he is a layman. He's a good old soul; but no one in the room can stand it; even Mrs. Grimes nods over her knitting, and some of the dear brothers breathe very audibly. Mr. Grimes, however, hears nothing but himself. At length he stops; his hearers wake up, and the hassocks begin. Then we go; and Mr. Grimes and the St. Mark's man call it a profitable evening. I can't make out why any one goes twice; yet some men never miss."

"They all go on faith," said White: "faith in Mr. Grimes."

"Faith in old Grimes," said Willis; "an old half-pay lieutenant!"

"Here's a church open," said White; "that's odd; let's go in."

They entered; an old woman was dusting the pews as if for service. "That will be all set right," said Willis; "we must have no women, but sacristans and servers."

"Then, you know, all these pews will go to the right about. Did you ever see a finer church for a function?"

"Where would you put the sacristy?" said Willis; "that closet is meant for the vestry, but would never be large enough."

"That depends on the number of altars the church admits," answered White; "each altar must have its own dresser and wardrobe in the sacristy."

"One," said Willis, counting, "where the pulpit stands, that'll be the high altar; one quite behind, that may be Our Lady's; two, one on each side of the chancel—four already; to whom do you dedicate them?"

"The church is not wide enough for those side ones," said White.

"Oh, but it is," said Willis; "I have seen, abroad, altars with only one step to them, and they need not be very broad. I think, too, this wall admits of an arch—look at the depth of the window; *that* would be a gain of room."

"No," persisted White; "the chancel is too narrow"; and he began to measure the floor with his pocket-handkerchief. "What would you say is the depth of an altar from the wall?" he asked.

On looking up he saw some ladies in the church whom he and Willis knew—the pretty Miss Boltons—very Catholic girls, and really kind, charitable persons into the bargain. We cannot add, that they were much wiser at that time than the two young gentlemen whom they now encountered; and if any fair reader thinks our account of them a reflection on Catholic-minded ladies generally, we beg distinctly to say, that we by no means put them forth as a type of a class; that among such persons were to be found, as we know well, the gentlest spirits and the tenderest hearts; and that nothing short of severe fidelity to historical truth keeps us from adorning these two young persons in particular with that prudence and good sense with which so many such ladies were endowed. These two sisters had open hands, if they had not wise heads; and their object in entering the church (which was not the church of their own parish) was to see the old woman, who was at once a subject and instrument of their bounty, and to say a word about her little grandchildren, in whom they were interested. As may be supposed, they did not know much of matters ecclesiastical, and they knew less of themselves; and the latter defect White could not supply, though he was doing, and had done, his best to remedy the former deficiency; and every meeting did a little.

The two parties left the church together, and the gentlemen saw the ladies home. "We were imagining, Miss Bolton," White said, walking at a respectful distance from her, "we were imagining St. James's a Catholic church, and trying to arrange things as they ought to be."

"What was your first reform?" asked Miss Bolton.

"I fear," answered White, "it would fare hard with your *protégée*, the old lady who dusts out the pews."

"Why, certainly," said Miss Bolton, "because there would be no pews to dust."

"But not only in office, but in person, or rather in character, she must make her exit from the church," said White.

"Impossible," said Miss Bolton; "are women, then, to remain Protestants?"

"Oh, no," answered White, "the good lady will reappear, only in another character; she will be a widow."

"And who will take her present place?"

"A sacristan," answered White; "a sacristan in a cotta. Do you like the short cotta or the long?" he continued, turning to the younger lady.

"I?" answered Miss Charlotte; "I always forget, but I think you told us the Roman was the short one; I'm for the short cotta."

"You know, Charlotte," said Miss Bolton, "that there's a great reform going on in England in ecclesiastical vestments."

"I hate all reforms," answered Charlotte, "from the Reformation downwards. Besides, we have got some way in our cope; you have seen it, Mr. White? It's such a sweet pattern."

"Have you determined what to do with it?" asked Willis.

"Time enough to think of that," said Charlotte; "it'll take four years to finish."

"Four years!" cried White; "we shall be all real Catholics by then; England will be converted."

"It will be done just in time for the Bishop," said Charlotte.

"Oh, it's not good enough for him!" said Miss Bolton; "but it may do in church for the *Asperges*. How different all things will be!" continued she; "I don't quite like, though, the idea of a cardinal in Oxford. Must we be so very Roman? I don't see why we might not be quite Catholic without the Pope."

"Oh, you need not be afraid," said White sagely; "things don't go so apace. Cardinals are not so cheap."

"Cardinals have so much state and stiffness," said Miss Bolton: "I hear they never walk without two servants behind them; and they always leave the room directly dancing begins."

"Well, I think Oxford must be just cut out for cardinals," said Miss Charlotte; "can anything be duller than the President's parties? I can fancy Dr. Bone a cardinal, as he walks round the parks."

"Oh, it's the genius of the Catholic Church," said White; "you will understand it better in time. No one is his own master; even the Pope cannot do as he will; he dines by himself, and speaks by precedent."

"Of course he does," said Charlotte, "for he is infallible."

"Nay, if he makes mistakes in the functions," continued White, "he is obliged to write them down and confess them, lest they should be drawn into precedents."

"And he is obliged, during a function, to obey the master of ceremonies, against his own judgment," said Willis.

"Didn't you say the Pope confessed, Mr. White?" asked Miss Bolton; "it has always puzzled me whether the Pope was obliged to confess like another man."

"Oh, certainly," answered White, "every one confesses."

"Well," said Charlotte, "I can't fancy Mr. Hurst of St. Peter's, who comes here to sing glees, confessing, or some of the grave heads of houses, who bow so stiffly."

"They will all have to confess," said White.

"All?" asked Miss Bolton; "you don't mean converts confess? I thought it was only old Catholics."

There was a little pause.

"And what will the heads of houses be?" asked Miss Charlotte.

"Abbots or superiors," answered White; "they will bear crosses; and when they say Mass, there will be a lighted candle in addition."

"What a good portly abbot the Vice-Chancellor will make!" said Miss Bolton.

"Oh, no; he's too short for an abbot," said her sister; "but you have left out the Chancellor himself: you seem to have provided for every one else; what will become of him?"

"The Chancellor is my difficulty," said White gravely.

"Make him a Knight-Templar," said Willis.

"The Duke's a queer hand," said White, still thoughtfully: "there's no knowing what he'll come to. A Knight-Templar—yes; Malta is now English property; he might revive the order."

The ladies both laughed.

"But you have not completed your plan, Mr. White," said Miss Bolton: "the heads of houses have got wives; how can they become monks?"

"Oh, the wives will go into convents," said White: "Willis and I have been making inquiries in the High Street, and they are most satisfactory. Some of the houses there were once university-halls and inns, and will easily turn back into convents: all that will be wanted is grating to the windows."

"Have you any notion what order they ought to join?" said Miss Charlotte.

"That depends on themselves," said White: "no compulsion whatever must be put on them. *They* are the judges. But it would be useful to have two convents, one of an active order, and one contemplative: Ursuline for instance, and Carmelite of St. Theresa's reform."

Hitherto their conversation had been on the verge of jest and earnest; now it took a more pensive tone.

"The nuns of St. Theresa are very strict, I believe, Mr. White," said Miss Bolton.

"Yes," he made reply; "I have fears for the Mrs. Wardens and Mrs. Principals who at their age undertake it."

They had got home, and White politely rang the bell.

"Younger persons," said he tenderly, "are too delicate for such a sacrifice."

Louisa was silent; presently she said, "And what will you be, Mr. White?"

"I know not," he answered; "I have thought of the Cistercians; they never speak."

"Oh, the dear Cistercians!" she said; "St. Bernard wasn't it? Sweet, heavenly man, and so young! I have seen his picture: such eyes!"

White was a good-looking man. The nun and the monk looked at each other very respectfully, and bowed; the other pair went through a similar ceremony; then it was performed diagonally. The two ladies entered their home; the two gentlemen retired.

We must follow the former upstairs. When they entered the drawing-room they found their mother sitting at the window in her bonnet and shawl, dipping into a chance volume in that unsettled state which implies that a person is occupied, if it may be so called, in waiting, more than in anything else.

"My dear children," she said as they entered, "where *have* you been? The bells have stopped a good quarter of an hour: I fear we must give up going to church this morning."

"Impossible, dear mamma," answered Miss Bolton; "we went out punctually at half-past nine; we did not stop two minutes at your worsted-shop; and here we are back again."

"The only thing we did besides," said Charlotte, "was to look in at St. James's, as the door was open, to say a word or two to poor old Wiggins. Mr. White was there, and his friend Mr. Willis; and they saw us home."

"Oh, I understand," answered Mrs. Bolton; "that is the way when young gentlemen and ladies get together: but at any rate we are late for church."

"Oh, no," said Charlotte, "let us set out directly, we shall get in by the first lesson."

"My dear child, how can you propose such a thing?" said her mother: "I would not do so for any consideration; it is so very disgraceful. Better not go at all."

"Oh, dearest mamma," said the elder sister, "this certainly *is* a prejudice. Why always come in at one time? There is something so formal in people coming in all at once, and waiting for each other. It is surely more reasonable to come in when you can: so many things may hinder persons."

"Well, my dear Louisa," said her mother, "I like the old way. It used always to be said to us, Be in your seats before 'When the wicked man,' and at latest before the 'Dearly Beloved.' That's the good old-fashioned way. And Mr. Jones and Mr. Pearson used always to sit at least five minutes in the desk to give us some law, and used to look round before beginning; and Mr. Jones used frequently to preach against late comers. I can't argue, but it seems to me reasonable that good Christians should hear the whole service. They might as well go out before it's over."

"Well, but, mamma," said Charlotte, "so it *is* abroad: they come in and go out when they please. It's so devotional."

"My dear girl," said Mrs. Bolton, "I am too old to understand all this; it's beyond me. I suppose Mr. White has been saying all this to you. He's a good young man, very amiable and attentive. I have nothing to say against him, except that he *is* young, and he'll change his view of things when he gets older."

"While we talk, time's going," said Louisa; "is it quite impossible we should still go to church?"

"My dear Louisa, I would not walk up the aisle for the world; positively I should sink into the earth: such a bad example! How can you dream of such a thing?"

"Then I suppose nothing's to be done," said Louisa, taking off her bonnet; "but really it is very sad to make worship so cold and formal a thing. Twice as many people would go to church if they might be late."

"Well, my dear, all things are changed now: in my younger days Catholics were the formal people, and we were the devotional; now it's just the reverse."

"But isn't it so, dear mamma?" said Charlotte, "isn't it something much more beautiful, this continued concourse, flowing and ebbing, changing yet full, than a way of praying which is as wooden as the reading-desk?—it's so free and natural."

"Free and easy, *I* think," said her mother; "for shame, Charlotte! how can you speak against the beautiful Church Service; you pain me."

"I don't," answered Charlotte; "it's a mere puritanical custom, which is no more part of our Church than the pews are."

"Common Prayer is offered to all who can come," said Louisa; "Church should be a privilege, not a mere duty."

"Well, my dear love, this is more than I can follow. There was young George Ashton—he always left before the sermon; and when taxed with it, he said he could not bear an heretical preacher; a boy of eighteen!"

"But, dearest mamma," said Charlotte, "what *is* to be done when a preacher is heretical? What else can be done?—it's so distressing to a Catholic mind."

"Catholic, Catholic!" cried Mrs. Bolton, rather vexed; "give me good old George the Third and the Protestant religion. Those were the times! Everything went on quietly then. We had no disputes or divisions; no differences in families. But now it is all otherwise. My head is turned, I declare; I hear so many strange, out-of-the-way things."

The young ladies did not answer; one looked out of the window, the other prepared to leave the room.

"Well it's a disappointment to us all," said their mother; "you first hindered me going, then I have hindered you. But I suspect, dear Louisa, mine is the greater disappointment of the two."

Louisa turned round from the window.

"I value the Prayer Book as you cannot do, my love," she continued; "for I have known what it is to one in deep affliction. May it be long, dearest girls, before you know it in a similar way; but if affliction comes on you, depend on it, all these new fancies and fashions will vanish from you like the wind, and the good old Prayer Book alone will stand you in any stead."

They were both touched.

"Come, my dears; I have spoken too seriously," she added. "Go and take your things off, and come and let us have some quiet work before luncheon-time."

CHAPTER IX

Some persons fidget at intellectual difficulties, and, successfully or not, are ever trying to solve them. Charles was of a different cast of temper; a new idea was not lost on him, but it did not distress him, if it was obscure, or conflicted with his habitual view of things. He let it work its way and find its place, and shape itself within him, by the slow spontaneous action of the mind. Yet perplexity is not in itself a pleasant state; and he would have hastened its removal, had he been able.

By means of conversations such as those which we have related (to which many others might be added, which we spare the reader's patience), and from the diversities of view which he met with in the University, he had now come, in the course of a year, to one or two conclusions, not very novel, but very important: first, that there are a great many opinions in the world on the most momentous subjects; secondly, that all are not equally true; thirdly, that it is a duty to hold true opinions; and, fourthly, that it is uncommonly difficult to get hold of them. He had been accustomed, as we have seen, to fix his mind on persons, not on opinions, and to determine to like what was good in every one; but he had now come to perceive that, to say the least, it was not respectable in any great question to hold false opinions. It did not matter that such false opinions were sincerely held—he could not feel that respect for a person who held what Sheffield called a sham, with which he regarded him who held a reality. White and Bateman were cases in point; they were very good fellows, but he could not endure their unreal way of talking, though they did not feel it to be unreal themselves. In like manner, if the Roman Catholic system was untrue, so far was plain (putting aside higher considerations), that a person who believed in the power of saints, and prayed to them, was an actor in a great sham, let him be as sincere as he would. He mistook words for things, and so far forth, he could not respect him more than he respected White or Bateman. And so of a Unitarian; if he believed the power of unaided human nature to be what it was not; if by birth man is fallen, and he thought him upright, he was holding an absurdity. He might redeem and cover this blot by a thousand excellences, but a blot it would remain; just as we should feel a handsome man disfigured by the loss of an eye or a hand. And so, again, if a professing Christian made the Almighty a being of simple benevolence, and He was, on the contrary, what the Church of England teaches, a God who punishes for the sake of justice, such a person was making an idol or unreality the object of his religion, and (apart from more serious thoughts about him) so far he could not respect him. Thus the principle of dogmatism gradually became an essential element in Charles's religious views.

Gradually, and imperceptibly to himself; for the thoughts which we have been tracing only came on him at spare times, and were taken up at intervals from the point at which they were laid down. His lectures and other duties of the place, his friends and recreations, were the staple of the day; but there was this undercurrent ever in motion, and sounding in his mental ear as soon as other sounds were hushed. As he dressed in the morning, as he sat under the beeches of his college-garden, when he strolled into the meadow, when he went into the town to pay a bill or make a call, when he threw himself on his sofa after shutting his oak at night, thoughts cognate with those which have been described were busy within him.

Discussions, however, and inquiries, as far as Oxford could afford matter for them, were for a while drawing to an end; for Trinity Sunday was now past, and the Commemoration was close at hand. On the Sunday before it, the University sermon happened to be preached by a distinguished person, whom that solemnity brought up to Oxford; no less a man than the Very Rev. Dr. Brownside, the new Dean of Nottingham, some time Huntingdonian Professor of Divinity, and one of the acutest, if not soundest academical thinkers of the day. He was a little, prim, smirking, be-spectacled man, bald in front, with curly black hair behind, somewhat pompous in his manner, with a clear musical utterance, which enabled one to listen to him without effort. As a divine, he seemed never to have had any difficulty on any subject; he was so clear or so shallow, that he saw to the bottom of all his thoughts: or, since Dr. Johnson tells us that "all shallows are clear," we may perhaps distinguish him by both epithets. Revelation to him, instead of being the abyss of God's counsels, with its dim outlines and broad shadows, was a flat, sunny plain, laid out with straight macadamised roads. Not, of course, that he denied the Divine incomprehensibility itself, with certain heretics of old; but he maintained that in Revelation all that was mysterious had been left out, and nothing given us but what was practical, and directly concerned us. It was, moreover, to him a marvel, that every one did not agree with him in taking this simple, natural view, which he thought almost self-evident; and he attributed the phenomenon, which was by no means uncommon, to some want of clearness of head, or twist of mind, as the case might be. He was a popular preacher; that is, though he had few followers, he had numerous hearers; and on this occasion the church was overflowing with the young men of the place.

He began his sermon by observing, that it was not a little remarkable that there were so few good reasoners in the world, considering that the discursive faculty was one of the characteristics of man's nature, as contrasted with brute animals. It had indeed been said that brutes reasoned; but this was an analogical sense of the word "reason," and an instance of that very ambiguity of language, or confusion of thought, on which he was animadverting. In like manner, we say that the *reason* why the wind blows is, that there is a change of temperature in the atmosphere; and the *reason* why the bells ring is, because the ringers pull them; but who would say that the wind *reasons* or that bells *reason*? There was, he believed, no well-ascertained fact (an emphasis on the word *fact*) of brutes reasoning. It had been said, indeed, that that sagacious animal, the dog, if, in tracking his master, he met three ways, after smelling the two, boldly pursued the third without any such previous investigation; which, if true, would be an instance of a disjunctive hypothetical syllogism. Also Dugald Stewart spoke of the case of a monkey cracking nuts behind a door, which, not being a strict imitation of anything which he could have actually seen, implied an operation of abstraction, by which the clever brute had first ascended to the general notion of nut-crackers, which perhaps he had seen in a particular instance, in silver or in steel, at his master's table, and then descending, had embodied it, thus obtained, in the shape of an expedient of his own devising. This was what had been said: however, he might assume on the present occasion, that the faculty of reasoning was characteristic of the human species; and, this being the case, it certainly was remarkable that so few persons reasoned well.

After this introduction, he proceeded to attribute to this defect the number of religious differences in the world. He said that the most celebrated questions in religion were but verbal ones; that the disputants did not know their own meaning, or that of their opponents; and that a spice of good logic would have put an end to dissensions, which had troubled the world for centuries—would have prevented many a bloody war, many a fierce anathema, many a savage execution, and many a ponderous folio. He went on to imply that in fact there was no truth or falsehood in the received dogmas in theology; that they were modes, neither good nor bad in themselves, but personal, national, or periodic, in which the intellect reasoned upon the great truths of religion; that the fault lay, not in holding them, but in insisting on them, which was like insisting on a Hindoo dressing like a Fin, or a regiment of dragoons using the boomarang.

He proceeded to observe, that from what he had said, it was plain in what point of view the Anglican formularies were to be regarded; viz. they were *our* mode of expressing everlasting truths, which might be as well expressed in other ways, as any correct thinker would be able to see. Nothing, then, was to be altered in them; they were to be retained in their integrity; but it was ever to be borne in mind that they were Anglican theology, not theology in the abstract; and that, though the Athanasian Creed was good for us, it did not follow that it was good for our neighbours; rather, that what seemed the very reverse might suit others better, might be *their* mode of expressing the same truths.

He concluded with one word in favour of Nestorius, two for Abelard, three for Luther, "that great mind," as he worded it, "who saw that churches, creeds, rites, persons, were nought in religion, and that the inward spirit, *faith*," as he himself expressed it, "was all in all"; and with a hint that nothing would go well in the University till this great principle was so far admitted, as to lead its members—not, indeed, to give up their own distinctive formularies, no—but to consider the direct contradictories of them equally pleasing to the divine Author of Christianity.

Charles did not understand the full drift of the sermon; but he understood enough to make him feel that it was different from any sermon he had heard in his life. He more than doubted, whether, if his good father had heard it, he would not have made it an exception to his favourite dictum. He came away marvelling with himself what the preacher could mean, and whether he had misunderstood him. Did he mean that Unitarians were only bad reasoners, and might be as good Christians as orthodox believers? He could mean nothing else. But what if, after all, he was right? He indulged the thought awhile. "Then every one is what Sheffield calls a sham, more or less; and there was no reason for being annoyed at any one. Then I was right originally in wishing to take every one for what he was. Let me think; every one a sham...shams are respectable, or rather no one is respectable. We can't do without some outward form of belief; one is not truer than another; that is, all are equally true.... *All* are true.... That is the better way of taking it; none are shams, all are true.... All are *true*! impossible! one as true as another! why then it is as true that our Lord is a mere man, as that He is God. He could not possibly mean this; what *did* he mean?"

So Charles went on, painfully perplexed, yet out of this perplexity two convictions came upon him, the first of them painful too; that he could not take for gospel everything that was said, even by authorities of the place and divines of name; and next, that his former amiable feeling of taking every one for what he was, was a dangerous one, leading with little difficulty to a sufferance of every sort of belief, and legitimately terminating in the sentiment expressed in Pope's Universal Prayer, which his father had always held up to him as a pattern specimen of shallow philosophism:

"Father of all, in every age,
In every clime adored,
By saint, by savage, and by sage,
Jehovah, Jove, or Lord."

CHAPTER X

Charles went up this term for his first examination, and this caused him to remain in Oxford some days after the undergraduate part of his college had left for the Long Vacation. Thus he came across Mr. Vincent, one of the junior tutors, who was kind enough to ask him to dine in Common-room on Sunday, and on several mornings made him take some turns with him up and down the Fellows' walk in the college garden.

A few years make a great difference in the standing of men at Oxford, and this made Mr. Vincent what is called a don in the eyes of persons who were very little younger than himself. Besides, Vincent looked much older than he really was; he was of a full habit, with a florid complexion and large blue eyes, and showed a deal of linen at his bosom, and full wristbands at his cuffs. Though a clever man, and a hard reader and worker, and a capital tutor, he was a good feeder as well; he ate and drank, he walked and rode, with as much heart as he lectured in Aristotle, or crammed in Greek plays. What is stranger still, with all this he was something of a valetudinarian. He had come off from school on a foundation fellowship, and had the reputation both at school and in the University of being a first-rate scholar. He was a strict disciplinarian in his way, had the undergraduates under his thumb, and having some *bonhomie* in his composition, was regarded by them with mingled feelings of fear and good will. They laughed at him, but carefully obeyed him. Besides this he preached a good sermon, read prayers with unction, and in his conversation sometimes had even a touch of evangelical spirituality. The young men even declared they could tell how much port he had taken in Common-room by the devoutness of his responses in evening-chapel; and it was on record that once, during the Confession, he had, in the heat of his contrition, shoved over the huge velvet cushion in which his elbows were imbedded upon the heads of the gentlemen commoners who sat under him.

He had just so much originality of mind as gave him an excuse for being "his own party" in religion, or what he himself called being "no party man"; and just so little that he was ever mistaking shams for truths, and converting pompous nothings into oracles. He was oracular in his manner, denounced parties and party-spirit, and thought to avoid the one and the other by eschewing all persons, and holding all opinions. He had a great idea of the *via media* being the truth; and to obtain it, thought it enough to flee from extremes, without having any very definite mean to flee to. He had not clearness of intellect enough to pursue a truth to its limits, nor boldness enough to hold it in its simplicity; but he was always saying things and unsaying them, balancing his thoughts in impossible attitudes, and guarding his words by unintelligible limitations. As to the men and opinions of the day and place, he would in the main have agreed with them, had he let himself alone; but he was determined to have an intellect of his own, and this put him to great shifts when he would distinguish himself from them. Had he been older than they, he would have talked of "young heads," "hot heads," and the like; but since they were grave and cool men, and outran him by fourteen or fifteen years, he found nothing better than to shake his head, mutter against party-spirit, refuse to read their books, lest he should be obliged to agree with them, and make a boast of avoiding their society. At the present moment he was on the point of starting for a continental tour to recruit himself after the labours of an Oxford year; meanwhile he was keeping hall and chapel open for such men as were waiting either for Responsions, or for their battel money; and he took notice of Reding as a clever, modest youth of whom something might be made. Under this view of him, he had, among other civilities, asked him to breakfast a day or two before he went down.

A tutor's breakfast is always a difficult affair both for host and guests; and Vincent piqued himself on the tact with which he managed it. The material part was easy enough; there were rolls, toast, muffins, eggs, cold lamb, strawberries, on the table; and in due season the college-servant brought in mutton-cutlets and broiled ham; and every one ate to his heart's, or rather his appetite's, content. It was a more arduous undertaking to provide the running accompaniment of thought, or at least of words, without which the breakfast would have been little better than a pig-trough. The conversation or rather mono-polylogue, as some great performer calls it, ran in somewhat of the following strain:

"Mr. Bruton," said Vincent, "what news from Staffordshire? Are the potteries pretty quiet now? Our potteries grow in importance. You need not look at the cup and saucer before you, Mr. Catley; those came from Derbyshire. But you find English crockery everywhere on the Continent. I myself found half a willow-pattern saucer in the crater of Vesuvius. Mr. Sikes, I think *you* have *been* in Italy?"

"No, sir," said Sikes; "I was near going; my family set off a fortnight ago, but I was kept here by these confounded smalls."

"Your *Responsiones*," answered the tutor in a tone of rebuke; "an unfortunate delay for you, for it is to be an unusually fine season, if the meteorologists of the sister University are right in their predictions. Who is in the Responsion schools, Mr. Sikes?"

"Butson of Leicester is the strict one, sir; he plucks one man in three. He plucked last week Patch of St. George's, and Patch has taken his oath he'll shoot him; and Butson has walked about ever since with a bulldog."

"These are reports, Mr. Sikes, which often flit about, but must not be trusted. Mr. Patch could not have given a better proof that his rejection was deserved."

A pause—during which poor Vincent hastily gobbled up two or three mouthfuls of bread and butter, the knives and forks meanwhile clinking upon his guests' plates.

"Sir, is it true," began one of his guests at length, "that the old Principal is going to be married?"

"These are matters, Mr. Atkins," answered Vincent, "which we should always inquire about at the fountain-head; *antiquam exquirite matrem*, or rather *patrem*; ha, ha! Take some more tea, Mr. Reding; it won't hurt your nerves. I am rather choice in my tea; this comes overland through Russia; the sea-air destroys the flavour of our common tea. Talking of air, Mr. Tenby, I think you are a chemist. Have you paid attention to the recent experiments on the composition and resolution of air? Not? I am surprised at it; they are well worth your most serious consideration. It is now pretty well ascertained that inhaling gases is the cure for all kinds of diseases. People are beginning to talk of the gas-cure, as they did of the water-cure. The great foreign chemist, Professor Scaramouch, has the credit of the discovery. The effects are astounding, quite astounding; and there are several remarkable coincidences. You know medicines are always unpleasant, and so these gases are always fetid. The Professor cures by stenches, and has brought his science to such perfection that he actually can classify them. There are six elementary stenches, and these spread into a variety of subdivisions? What do you say, Mr. Reding? Distinctive? Yes, there is something very distinctive in smells. But what is most gratifying of all, and is the great coincidence I spoke of, his ultimate resolution of fetid gases assigns to them the very same precise number as is given to existing complaints in the latest treatises on pathology. Each complaint has its gas. And, what is still more singular, an exhausted receiver is a specific for certain desperate disorders. For instance, it has effected several cures of hydrophobia. Mr. Seaton," he continued to a freshman, who, his breakfast finished, was sitting uncomfortably on his chair, looking down and playing with his knife—"Mr. Seaton, you are looking at that picture"—it was almost behind Seaton's back—"I don't wonder at it; it was given me by my good old mother, who died many years ago. It represents some beautiful Italian scenery."

Vincent stood up, and his party after him, and all crowded round the picture.

"I prefer the green of England," said Reding.

"England has not that brilliant variety of colour," said Tenby.

"But there is something so soothing in green."

"You know, of course, Mr. Reding," said the tutor, "that there is plenty of green in Italy, and in winter even more than in England; only there are other colours too."

"But I can't help fancying," said Charles, "that that mixture of colours takes off from it the repose of English scenery."

"The repose, for instance," said Tenby, "of Binsey Common, or Port Meadow in winter."

"Say in summer," said Reding; "if you choose place, I will choose time. I think the University goes down just when Oxford begins to be most beautiful. The walks and meadows are so fragrant and bright now, the hay half carried, and the short new grass appearing."

"Reding ought to live here all through the Long," said Tenby: "does any one live through the Vacation, sir, in Oxford?"

"Do you mean they die before the end of it, Mr. Tenby?" asked Vincent. "It can't be denied," he continued, "that many, like Mr. Reding, think it a most pleasant time. *I* am fond of Oxford; but it is not my *habitat* out of term-time."

"Well, I think I should like to make it so," said Charles, "but, I suppose, undergraduates are not allowed."

Mr. Vincent answered with more than necessary gravity, "No"; it rested with the Principal; but he conceived that he would not consent to it. Vincent added that certainly there *were* parties who remained in Oxford through the Long Vacation. It was said mysteriously.

Charles answered that, if it was against college rules, there was no help for it; else, were he reading for his degree, he should like nothing better than to pass the Long Vacation in Oxford, if he might judge by the pleasantness of the last ten days.

"That is a compliment, Mr. Reding, to your company," said Vincent.

At this moment the door opened, and in came the manciple with the dinner paper, which Mr. Vincent had formally to run his eye over. "Watkins," he said, giving it back to him, "I almost think today is one of the Fasts of the Church. Go and look, Watkins, and bring me word."

The astonished manciple, who had never been sent on such a commission in his whole career before, hastened out of the room, to task his wits how best to fulfil it. The question seemed to strike the company as forcibly, for there was a sudden silence, which was succeeded by a shuffling of feet and a leave-taking; as if, though they had secured their ham and mutton at breakfast, they did not like to risk their dinner. Watkins returned sooner than could have been expected. He said that Mr. Vincent was right; today he had found was "the feast of the Apostles."

"The Vigil of St. Peter, you mean, Watkins," said Mr. Vincent; "I thought so. Then let us have a plain beefsteak and a saddle of mutton; no Portugal onions, Watkins, or currant-jelly; and some simple pudding, Charlotte pudding, Watkins—that will do."

Watkins vanished. By this time, Charles found himself alone with the college authority; who began to speak to him in a more confidential tone.

"Mr. Reding," said he, "I did not like to question you before the others, but I conceive you had no particular *meaning* in your praise of Oxford in the Long Vacation? In the mouths of some it would have been suspicious."

Charles was all surprise.

"To tell the truth, Mr. Reding, as things stand," he proceeded, "it is often a mark of *party*, this residence in the Vacation; though, of course, there is nothing in the *thing* itself but what is perfectly natural and right."

Charles was all attention.

"My good sir," the tutor proceeded, "avoid parties; be sure to avoid party. You are young in your career among us. I always feel anxious about young men of talent; there is the greatest danger of the talent of the University being absorbed in party."

Reding expressed a hope that nothing he had done had given cause to his tutor's remark.

"No," replied Mr. Vincent, "no"; yet with some slight hesitation; "no, I don't know that it has. But I have thought some of your remarks and questions at lecture were like a person pushing things *too far*, and wishing to form a *system*."

Charles was so much taken aback by the charge, that the unexplained mystery of the Long Vacation went out of his head. He said he was "very sorry," and "obliged"; and tried to recollect what he could have said to give ground to Mr. Vincent's remark. Not being able at the moment to recollect, he went on. "I assure you, sir, I know so little of parties in the place, that I hardly know their leaders. I have heard persons mentioned, but, if I tried, I think I should, in some cases, mismatch names and opinions."

"I believe it," said Vincent; "but you are young; I am cautioning you against *tendencies*. You may suddenly find yourself absorbed before you know where you are."

Charles thought this a good opportunity of asking some questions in detail, about points which puzzled him. He asked whether Dr. Brownside was considered a safe divine to follow.

"I hold, d'ye see," answered Vincent, "that all errors are counterfeits of truth. Clever men say true things, Mr. Reding, true in their substance, but," sinking his voice to a whisper, "they go *too far*. It might even be shown that all sects are in one sense but parts of the Catholic Church. I don't say true parts, that is a further question; but they *embody* great *principles*. The Quakers represent the principle of simplicity and evangelical poverty; they even have a dress of their own, like monks. The Independents represent the rights of the laity; the Wesleyans cherish the devotional principle; the Irvingites, the symbolical and mystical; the High Church party, the principle of obedience; the Liberals are the guardians of reason. No party, then, I conceive, is entirely right or entirely wrong. As to Dr. Brownside, there certainly have been various opinions entertained about his divinity; still, he is an able man, and I think you will gain *good*, gain *good* from his teaching. But mind, I don't *recommend* him; yet I respect him, and I consider that he says many things very well worth your attention. I would advise you, then, to accept the *good* which his sermons offer, without committing yourself to the *bad*. That, depend upon it, Mr. Reding, is the golden though the obvious rule in these matters."

Charles said, in answer, that Mr. Vincent was overrating his powers; that he had to learn before he could judge; and that he wished very much to know whether Vincent could recommend him any book, in which he might see at once *what* the true Church-of-England doctrine was on a number of points which perplexed him.

Mr. Vincent replied, he must be on his guard against dissipating his mind with such reading, at a time when his University duties had a definite claim upon him. He ought to avoid all controversies of the day, all authors of the day. He would advise him to read *no* living authors. "Read dead authors alone," he continued; "dead authors are safe. Our great divines," and he stood upright, "were models; 'there were giants on the earth in those days,' as King George the Third had once said of them to Dr. Johnson. They had that depth, and power, and gravity, and fulness, and erudition; and they were so racy, always racy, and what might be called English. They had that richness, too, such a mine of thought, such a world of opinion, such activity of mind, such inexhaustible resource, such diversity, too. Then they were so eloquent; the majestic Hooker, the imaginative Taylor, the brilliant Hall, the learning of Barrow, the strong sense of South, the keen logic of Chillingworth, good, honest old Burnet," etc., etc.

There did not seem much reason why he should stop at one moment more than another; at length, however, he did stop. It was prose, but it was pleasant prose to Charles; he knew just enough about these writers to feel interested in hearing them talked about, and to him Vincent seemed to be saying a good deal, when in fact he was saying very little. When he stopped, Charles said he believed that there were persons in the University who were promoting the study of these authors.

Mr. Vincent looked grave. "It is true," he said; "but, my young friend, I have already hinted to you that indifferent things are perverted to the purposes of *party*. At this moment the names of some of our greatest divines are little better than a watchword by which the opinions of living individuals are signified."

"Which opinions, I suppose," Charles answered, "are not to be found in those authors."

"I'll not say that," said Mr. Vincent. "I have the greatest respect for the individuals in question, and I am not denying that they have done good to our Church by drawing attention in this lax day to the old Church-of-England divinity. But it is one thing to agree with these gentlemen; another," laying his hand on Charles's shoulder, "another to belong to their party. Do not make man your master; get good from all; think well of all persons, and you will be a wise man."

Reding inquired, with some timidity, if this was not something like what Dr. Brownside had said in the University pulpit; but perhaps the latter advocated a toleration of opinions in a different sense? Mr. Vincent answered rather shortly, that he had not heard Dr. Brownside's sermon; but, for himself, he had been speaking only of persons in our own communion.

"Our Church," he said, "admitted of great liberty of thought within her pale. Even our greatest divines differed from each other in many respects; nay, Bishop Taylor differed from himself. It was a great principle in the English Church. Her true children agree to differ. In truth," he continued, "there is that robust, masculine, noble independence in the English mind, which refuses to be tied down to artificial shapes, but is like, I will say, some great and beautiful production of nature—a tree, which is rich in foliage and fantastic in limb, no sickly denizen of the hothouse, or helpless dependent of the garden wall, but in careless magnificence sheds its fruits upon the free earth, for the bird of the air and the beast of the field, and all sorts of cattle, to eat thereof and rejoice."

When Charles came away, he tried to think what he had gained by his conversation with Mr. Vincent; not exactly what he had wanted, some practical rules to guide his mind and keep him steady; but still some useful hints. He had already been averse to parties, and offended at what he saw of individuals attached to them. Vincent had confirmed him in his resolution to keep aloof from them, and to attend to his duties in the place. He felt pleased to have had this talk with him; but what could he mean by suspecting a tendency in himself to push things too far, and thereby to implicate himself in party? He was obliged to resign himself to ignorance on the subject, and to be content with keeping a watch over himself in future.

CHAPTER XI

No opportunity has occurred of informing the reader that, during the last week or two, Charles had accidentally been a good deal thrown across Willis, the *umbra* of White at Bateman's breakfast-party. He had liked his looks on that occasion, when he was dumb; he did not like him so much when he heard him talk; still he could not help being interested in him, and not the least for this reason, that Willis seemed to have taken a great fancy to himself. He certainly did court Charles, and seemed anxious to stand well with him. Charles, however, did not like his mode of talking better than he did White's; and when he first saw his rooms, there was much in them which shocked both his good sense and his religious principles. A large ivory crucifix, in a glass case, was a conspicuous ornament between the windows; an engraving, representing the

Blessed Trinity, as is usual in Catholic countries, hung over the fire-place, and a picture of the Madonna and St. Dominic was opposite to it. On the mantelpiece were a rosary, a thuribulum, and other tokens of Catholicism, of which Charles did not know the uses; a missal, ritual, and some Catholic tracts, lay on the table; and, as he happened to come on Willis unexpectedly, he found him sitting in a vestment more like a cassock than a reading-gown, and engaged upon some portion of the Breviary. Virgil and Sophocles, Herodotus and Cicero seemed, as impure pagans, to have hid themselves in corners, or flitted away, before the awful presence of the Ancient Church. Charles had taken upon himself to protest against some of these singularities, but without success.

On the evening before his departure for the country he had occasion to go towards Folly Bridge to pay a bill, when he was startled, as he passed what he had ever taken for a dissenting chapel, to see Willis come out of it. He hardly could believe he saw correctly; he knew, indeed, that Willis had been detained in Oxford, as he had been himself; but what had compelled him to a visit so extraordinary as that which he had just made, Charles had no means of determining.

"Willis!" he cried, as he stopped.

Willis coloured, and tried to look easy.

"Do come a few paces with me," said Charles. "What in the world has taken you there? Is it not a dissenting meeting?"

"Dissenting meeting!" cried Willis, surprised and offended in his turn: "what on earth could make you think I would go to a dissenting meeting?"

"Well, I beg your pardon," said Charles; "I recollect now: it's the exhibition room. However, *once* it *was* a chapel: that's my mistake. Isn't it what is called 'the Old Methodist Chapel?' I never was there; they showed there the *Dio-astro-doxon*, so I think they called it." Charles talked on, to cover his own mistake, for he was ashamed of the charge he had made.

Willis did not know whether he was in jest or earnest. "Reding," he said, "don't go on; you offend me."

"Well, what is it?" said Charles.

"You know well enough," answered Willis, "though you wish to annoy me."

"I don't indeed."

"It's the Catholic church," said Willis.

Reding was silent a moment; then he said, "Well, I don't think you have mended the matter; it *is* a dissenting meeting, call it what you will, though not the kind of one I meant."

"What can you mean?" asked Willis.

"Rather, what mean *you* by going to such places?" retorted Charles; "why, it is against your oath."

"My oath! what oath?"

"There's not an oath now; but there was an oath till lately," said Reding; "and we still make a very solemn engagement. Don't you recollect your matriculation at the Vice-Chancellor's, and what oaths and declarations you made?"

"I don't know what I made: my tutor told me nothing about it. I signed a book or two."

"You did more," said Reding. "I was told most carefully. You solemnly engaged to keep the statutes; and one statute is, not to go into any dissenting chapel or meeting whatever."

"Catholics are not Dissenters," said Willis.

"Oh, don't speak so," said Charles; "you know it's meant to include them. The statute wishes us to keep from all places of worship whatever but our own."

"But it is an illegal declaration or vow," said Willis, "and so not binding."

"Where did you find that get-off?" said Charles; "the priest put that into your head."

"I don't know the priest; I never spoke a word to him," answered Willis.

"Well, any how, it's not your own answer," said Reding; "and does not help you. I am no casuist; but if it is an illegal engagement you should not continue to enjoy the benefit of it."

"What benefit?"

"Your cap and gown; a university education; the chance of a scholarship or fellowship. Give up these, and then plead, if you will, and lawfully, that you are quit of your engagement; but don't sail under false colours: don't take the benefit and break the stipulation."

"You take it too seriously; there are half a hundred statutes *you* don't keep, any more than I. You are most inconsistent."

"Well, if we don't keep them," said Charles, "I suppose it is in points where the authorities don't enforce them; for instance, they don't mean us to dress in brown, though the statutes order it."

"But they *do* mean to keep you from walking down High Street in beaver," answered Willis; "for the Proctors march up and down, and send you back, if they catch you."

"But *this* is a different matter," said Reding, changing his ground; "this is a matter of religion. It can't be right to go to strange places of worship or meetings."

"Why," said Willis, "if we are one Church with the Roman Catholics, I can't make out for the life of me how it's wrong for us to go to them or them to us."

"I'm no divine, I don't understand what is meant by one Church," said Charles; "but I know well that there's not a bishop, not a clergyman, not a sober churchman in the land but would give it against you. It's a sheer absurdity."

"Don't talk in that way," answered Willis, "please don't. I feel all my heart drawn to the Catholic worship; our own service is so cold."

"That's just what every stiff Dissenter says," answered Charles; "every poor cottager, too, who knows no better, and goes after the Methodists—after her dear Mr. Spoutaway or the preaching cobbler. *She* says (I have heard them), 'Oh, sir, I suppose we ought to go where we get most good. Mr. So-and-so goes to my heart—he goes through me.'"

Willis laughed; "Well, not a bad reason, as times go, *I* think," said he: "poor souls, what better means of judging have they? How can you hope they will like 'the Scripture moveth us'? Really you are making too much of it. This is only the second time I have been there, and, I tell you in earnest, I find my mind filled with awe and devotion there; as I think you would too. I really am better for it; I cannot pray in church; there's a bad smell there, and the pews hide everything; I can't see through a deal board. But here, when I went in, I found all still, and calm, the space open, and, in the twilight, the Tabernacle just visible, pointed out by the lamp."

Charles looked very uncomfortable. "Really, Willis," he said, "I don't know what to say to you. Heaven forbid that I should speak against the Roman Catholics; I know nothing about them. But *this* I know, that you are not a Roman Catholic, and have no business there. If they have such sacred things among them as those you allude to, still these are not yours; you are an intruder. I know nothing about it; I don't like to give a judgment, I am sure. But it's a tampering with sacred things; running here and there, touching and tasting, taking up, putting down. I don't like it," he added, with vehemence; "it's taking liberties with God."

"Oh, my dear Reding, please don't speak so very severely," said poor Willis; "now what have I done more than you would do yourself, were you in France or Italy? Do you mean to say you wouldn't enter the churches abroad?"

"I will only decide about what is before me," answered Reding; "when I go abroad, then will be the time to think about your question. It is quite enough to know what we ought to do at the moment, and I am clear you have been doing wrong. How did you find your way there?"

"White took me."

"Then there is one man in the world more thoughtless than

you: do many of the gownsmen go there?"

"Not that I know of; one or two have gone from curiosity; there is no practice of going, at least this is what I am told."

"Well," said Charles, "you must promise me you will not go again. Come, we won't part till you do."

"That is too much," said Willis, gently; then, disengaging his arm from Reding's, he suddenly darted away from him, saying, "Good-bye, good-bye; to our next merry meeting—*au revoir*."

There was no help for it. Charles walked slowly home, saying to himself: "What if, after all, the Roman Catholic Church is the true Church? I wish I knew what to believe; no one will tell me what to believe; I am so left to myself." Then he thought: "I suppose I know quite enough for practice—more than I *do* practise; and I ought surely to be contented and thankful."

CHAPTER XII

Charles was an affectionate son, and the Long Vacation passed very happily at home. He was up early, and read steadily till luncheon, and then he was at the service of his father, mother, and sisters for the rest of the day. He loved the calm, quiet country; he loved the monotonous flow of time, when each day is like the other; and, after the excitement of Oxford, the secluded parsonage was like a haven beyond the tossing of the waves. The whirl of opinions and perplexities which had encircled him at Oxford now were like the distant sound of the ocean—they reminded him of his present security. The undulating meadows, the green lanes, the open heath, the common with its wide-spreading dusky elms, the high timber which fringed the level path from village to village, ever and anon broken and thrown into groups, or losing itself in copses—even the gate, and the stile, and the turnpike-road had the charm, not of novelty, but of long familiar use; they had the poetry of many recollections. Nor was the dilapidated, deformed church, with its outside staircases, its unsightly galleries, its wide intruded windows, its uncouth pews, its low table, its forlorn vestry, and its damp earthy smell, without its pleasant associations to the inner man; for there it was that for many a year, Sunday after Sunday, he had heard his dear father read and preach; there were the old monuments, with Latin inscriptions and strange devices, the black boards with white letters, the Resurgams and grinning skulls, the fire-buckets, the faded militia-colours, and, almost as much a fixture, the old clerk, with a Welsh wig over his ears, shouting the responses out of place—which had arrested his imagination, and awed him when a child. And then there was his home itself; its well-known rooms, its pleasant routine, its order, and its comfort—an old and true friend, the dearer to him because he had made new ones. "Where I shall be in time to come I know not," he said to himself; "I am but a boy; many things which I have not a dream of, which my imagination cannot compass, may come on me before I die—if I live; but here at least, and now, I am happy, and I will enjoy my happiness. Some say that school is the pleasantest time of one's life; this does not exclude college. I suppose care is what makes life so wearing. At present I have no care, no responsibility; I suppose I shall feel a little when I go up for my degree. Care is a terrible thing; I have had a little of it at times at school. What a strange thing to fancy, I shall be one day twenty-five or thirty! How the weeks are flying by! the Vacation will soon be over. Oh, I am so happy, it quite makes me afraid. Yet I shall have strength for my day."

Sometimes, however, his thoughts took a sadder turn, and he anticipated the future more vividly than he enjoyed the present. Mr. Malcolm had come to see them, after an absence from the parsonage for several years: his visit was a great pleasure to Mr. Reding, and not much less to himself, to whom a green home and a family circle were agreeable sights, after his bachelor-life at college. He had been a great favourite with Charles and his sisters as children, though now his popularity with them for the most part rested on the memory of the past. When he told them amusing stories, or allowed them to climb his knee and take off his spectacles, he did all that was necessary to gain their childish hearts; more is necessary to conciliate the affection of young men and women; and thus it is not surprising that he lived in their minds principally by prescription. He neither knew this, nor would have thought much about it if he had; for, like many persons of advancing years, he made himself very much his own centre, did not care to enter into the minds of others, did not consult for them, or find his happiness in them. He was kind and friendly to the young people, as he would be kind to a canary-bird or a lap-dog; it was a sort of external love; and, though they got on capitally with him, they did not miss him when gone, nor would have been much troubled to know that he was never to come again. Charles drove him about the country, stamped his letters, secured him his newspapers from the neighbouring town, and listened to his stories about Oxford and Oxford men. He really liked him, and wished to please him; but, as to consulting him in any serious matter, or going to him for comfort in affliction, he would as soon have thought of betaking him to Dan the pedlar, or old Isaac who played the Sunday bassoon.

"How have your peaches been this year, Malcolm?" said Mr. Reding one day after dinner to his guest.

"You ought to know that we have no peaches in Oxford," answered Mr. Malcolm.

"My memory plays me false, then: I had a vision of, at least, October peaches on one occasion, and fine ones too."

"Ah, you mean at old Tom Spindle's, the jockey's," answered Mr. Malcolm; "it's true, he had a bit of a brick wall, and was proud of it. But peaches come when there is no one in Oxford to eat them; so either the tree, or at least the fruit, is a great rarity there. Oxford wasn't so empty once; you have old mulberry-trees there in record of better days."

"At that time, too," said Charles, "I suppose, the more expensive fruits were not cultivated. Mulberries are the witness, not only of a full college, but of simple tastes."

"Charles is secretly cutting at our hothouse here," said Mr. Reding; "as if our first father did not prefer fruits and flowers to beef and mutton."

"No, indeed," said Charles, "I think peaches capital things; and as to flowers, I am even too fond of scents."

"Charles has some theory, then, about scents, I'll be bound," said his father; "I never knew a boy who so placed his likings and dislikings on fancies. He began to eat olives directly he read the Œdipus of Sophocles; and, I verily believe, will soon give up oranges from his dislike to King William."

"Every one does so," said Charles: "who would not be in the fashion? There's Aunt Kitty, she calls a bonnet, 'a sweet' one year, which makes her 'a perfect fright' the next."

"You're right, papa, in this instance," said his mother; "I know he has some good reason, though I never can recollect it, why he smells a rose, or distils lavender. What is it, my dear Mary?"

"'Relics ye are of Eden's bowers,'" said she.

"Why, sir, that was precisely your own reason just now," said Charles to his father.

"There's more than that," said Mrs. Reding, "if I knew what it was."

"He thinks the scent more intellectual than the other senses," said Mary, smiling.

"Such a boy for paradoxes!" said his mother.

"Well, so it is in a certain way," said Charles, "but I can't explain. Sounds and scents are more ethereal, less material; they have no shape—like the angels."

Mr. Malcolm laughed. "Well, I grant it, Charles," he said; "they are length without breadth!"

"Did you ever hear the like?" said Mrs. Reding, laughing too;

"don't encourage him, Mr. Malcolm; you are worse than he. Angels length without breadth!"

"They pass from place to place, they come, they go," continued Mr. Malcolm.

"They conjure up the past so vividly," said Charles.

"But sounds surely more than scents," said Mr. Malcolm.

"Pardon me; the reverse as *I* think," answered Charles.

"That *is* a paradox, Charles," said Mr. Malcolm; "the smell of roast-beef never went further than to remind a man of dinner; but sounds are pathetic and inspiring."

"Well, sir, but think of this," said Charles, "scents are complete in themselves, yet do not consist of parts. Think how very distinct the smell of a rose is from a pink, a pink from a sweet-pea, a sweet-pea from a stock, a stock from lilac, lilac from lavender, lavender from jasmine, jasmine from honeysuckle, honeysuckle from hawthorn, hawthorn from hyacinth, hyacinth"—

"Spare us," interrupted Mr. Malcolm; "you are going through the index of Loudon!"

"And these are only the scents of flowers; how different flowers smell from fruits, fruits from spices, spices from roast-beef or pork-cutlets, and so on. Now, what I was coming to is this—these scents are perfectly distinct from each other, and *sui generis*; they never can be confused; yet each is communicated to the apprehension in an instant. Sights take up a great space, a tune is a succession of sounds; but scents are at once specific and complete, yet indivisible. Who can halve a scent? They need neither time nor space; thus they are immaterial or spiritual."

"Charles hasn't been to Oxford for nothing," said his mother, laughing and looking at Mary; "this is what I call chopping logic!"

"Well done, Charles," cried Mr. Malcolm; "and now, since you have such clear notions of the power of smells, you ought, like the man in the story, to be satisfied with smelling at your dinner, and grow fat upon it. It's a shame you sit down to table."

"Well, sir," answered Charles, "some people *do* seem to thrive on snuff at least."

"For shame, Charles!" said Mr. Malcolm; "you have seen me use the common-room snuff-box to keep myself awake after dinner; but nothing more. I keep a box in my pocket merely as a bauble—it was a present. You should have lived when I was young. There was old Dr. Troughton of Nun's Hall, he carried his snuff loose in his pocket; and old Mrs. Vice-Principal Daffy used to lay a train along her arm, and fire it with her nose. Doctors of medicine took it as a preservative against infection, and doctors of divinity against drowsiness in church."

"They take wine against infection now," said Mr. Reding; "it's a much surer protective."

"Wine?" cried Mr. Malcolm; "oh, they didn't take less wine then, as you and I know. On certain solemn occasions they made a point of getting drunk, the whole college, from the Vice-Principal or Sub-Warden down to the scouts. Heads of houses were kept in order by their wives; but I assure you the jolly god came *very* near Mr. Vice-Chancellor himself. There was old Dr. Sturdy of St. Michael's, a great martinet in his time. One day the King passed through Oxford; Sturdy, a tall, upright, iron-faced man, had to meet him in procession at Magdalen Bridge, and walked down with his pokers before him, gold and silver, vergers, cocked hats, and the rest. There wasn't one of them that wasn't in liquor. Think of the good old man's horror, Majesty in the distance, and his own people swaying to and fro under his very nose, and promising to leave him for the gutter before the march was ended."

"No one can get tipsy with snuff, I grant," said Mr. Reding; "but if wine has done some men harm it has done others a deal of good."

"Hair-powder is as bad as snuff," said Mary, preferring the former subject; "there's old Mr. Butler of Cooling, his wig is so large and full of powder that when he nods his head I am sure to sneeze."

"Ah, but all these are accidents, young lady," said Mr. Malcolm, put out by this block to the conversation, and running off somewhat testily in another direction; "accidents after all. Old people are always the same; so are young. Each age has its own fashion: if Mr. Butler wore no wig, still there would be something about him odd and strange to young eyes. Charles, don't you be an old bachelor. No one cares for old people. Marry, my dear boy; look out betimes for a virtuous young woman, who will make you an attentive wife."

Charles slightly coloured, and his sister laughed as if there was some understanding between them.

Mr. Malcolm continued: "Don't wait till you want some one to buy flannel for your rheumatism or gout; marry betimes."

"You will let me take my degree first, sir?" said Charles.

"Certainly, take your M.A.'s if you will; but don't become an old Fellow. Don't wait till forty; people make the strangest mistakes."

"Dear Charles will make a kind and affectionate husband, I am sure," said his mother, "when the time comes; and come it will, though not just yet. Yes, my dear boy," she added, nodding at him, "you will not be able to escape your destiny, when it comes."

"Charles, you must know," said Mr. Reding to his guest, "is romantic in his notions just now. I believe it is that he thinks no one good enough for him. Oh, my dear Charlie, don't let me pain you, I meant nothing serious; but somehow he has not hit it off very well with some young ladies here, who expected more attention than he cared to give."

"I am sure," said Mary, "Charles is most attentive whenever there is occasion, and always has his eyes about him to do a service; only he's a bad hand at small-talk."

"All will come in time, my dear," said his mother; "a good son makes a good husband."

"And a very loving papa," said Mr. Malcolm.

"Oh, spare me, sir," said poor Charles; "how have I deserved this?"

"Well," proceeded Mr. Malcolm, "and young ladies ought to

marry betimes too."

"Come, Mary, *your* turn is coming," cried Charles; and taking his sister's hand, he threw up the sash, and escaped with her into the garden.

They crossed the lawn, and took refuge in a shrubbery. "How strange it is!" said Mary, as they strolled along the winding walk; "we used to like Mr. Malcolm so, as children; but now—I like him *still*, but he is not the same."

"We are older," said her brother; "different things take us now."

"He used to be so kind," continued she; "when he was coming, the day was looked out for; and mamma said, 'Take care you be good when Mr. Malcolm comes.' And he was sure to bring a twelfth-cake, or a Noah's ark, or something of the sort. And then he romped with us, and let us make fun of him."

"Indeed it isn't he that is changed," said Charles, "but we; we are in the time of life to change; we have changed already, and shall change still."

"What a mercy it is," said his sister, "that we are so happy among ourselves as a family! If we change, we shall change together, as apples of one stock; if one fails, the other does. Thus we are always the same to each other."

"It is a mercy, indeed," said Charles; "we are so blest that I am sometimes quite frightened."

His sister looked earnestly at him. He laughed a little to turn off the edge of his seriousness. "You would know what I mean, dear Mary, if you had read Herodotus. A Greek tyrant feared his own excessive prosperity, and therefore made a sacrifice to fortune. I mean, he gave up something which he held most precious; he took a ring from his finger and cast it into the sea, lest the Deity should afflict him, if he did not afflict himself."

"My dear Charles," she answered, "if we do but enjoy God's gifts thankfully, and take care not to set our hearts on them or to abuse them, we need not fear for their continuance."

"Well," said Charles, "there's one text which has ever dwelt on my mind, 'Rejoice with trembling.' I can't take full, unrestrained pleasure in anything."

"Why not, if you look at it as God's gift?" asked Mary.

"I don't defend it," he replied; "it's my way; it may be a selfish prudence, for what I know; but I am sure that, did I give my heart to any creature, I should be withdrawing it from God. How easily could I idolize these sweet walks, which we have known for so many years!"

They walked on in silence. "Well," said Mary, "whatever we lose, no change can affect us as a family. While we are we, we are to each other what nothing external can be to us, whether as given or as taken away."

Charles made no answer.

"What has come to you, dear Charles?" she said, stopping and looking at him; then, gently removing his hair and smoothing his forehead, she said, "you are so sad today."

"Dearest Mary," he made answer, "nothing's the matter, indeed. I think it is Mr. Malcolm who has put me out. It's so stupid to talk of the prospects of a boy like me. Don't look so, I mean nothing; only it annoys me."

Mary smiled.

"What I mean is," continued Charles, "that we can rely on nothing here, and are fools if we build on the future."

"We can rely on each other," she repeated.

"Ah, dear Mary, don't say so; it frightens me."

She looked round at him surprised, and almost frightened herself.

"Dearest," he continued, "I mean nothing; only everything is so uncertain here below."

"We are sure of each other, Charles."

"Yes, Mary," and he kissed her affectionately, "it is true, most true"; then he added, "all I meant was that it seems presumptuous to say so. David and Jonathan were parted; St. Paul and St. Barnabas."

Tears stood in Mary's eyes.

"Oh, what an ass I am," he said, "for thus teasing you about nothing; no, I only mean that there is One *only* who cannot die, who never changes, only One. It can't be wrong to remember this. Do you recollect Cowper's beautiful lines? I know them without having learned them—they struck me so much the first time I read them"; and he repeated them:

Thou art the source and centre of all minds,
Their only point of rest, Eternal Word.
From Thee departing, they are lost, and rove
At random, without honour, hope, or peace.
From Thee is all that soothes the life of man,
His high endeavour and his glad success,
His strength to suffer and his will to serve.
But oh, Thou Sovereign Giver of all good,
Thou art of all Thy gifts Thyself the crown;
Give what Thou canst, without Thee we are poor,
And with Thee rich, take what Thou wilt away.

CHAPTER XIII

October came at length, and with it Charles's thoughts were turned again to Oxford. One or two weeks passed by; then a few days; and it was time to be packing. His father parted with him with even greater emotion than when he first went to school. He would himself drive him in the phaeton to the neighbouring town, from which the omnibus ran to the railroad, though he had the gout flying about him; and when the moment for parting came he could not get himself to give up his hand, as if he had something to say which he could not recollect or master.

"Well, Christmas will soon come," he said; "we must part, it's no use delaying it. Write to us soon, dear boy; and tell us all about yourself and your matters. Tell us about your friends; they are nice young men apparently: but I have great confidence in your prudence; you have more prudence than some of them. Your tutor seems a valuable man, from what you tell me," he went on repeating what had passed between him and Charles many times before; "a sound, well-judging man, that Mr. Vincent. Sheffield is too clever; he is young; you have an older head. It's no good my going on; I have said all this before; and you may be late for the train. Well, God bless you, my dearest Charlie, and make you a blessing. May you be happier and better than your father! I have ever been blest all my life long—wonderfully blest. Blessings have been poured on me from my youth, far above my deserts; may they be doubled upon you! Good-bye, my beloved Charles, good-bye!"

Charles had to pass a day or two at the house of a relative who lived a little way out of London. While he was there a letter arrived for him, forwarded from home; it was from Willis, dated from London, and announced that he had come to a very important decision, and should not return to Oxford. Charles was fairly in the world again, plunged into the whirl of opinions: how sad a contrast to his tranquil home! There was no mistaking what the letter meant; and he set out at once with the chance of finding the writer at the house from which he dated it. It was a lodging at the west-end of town; and he reached it about noon.

He found Willis in company with a person apparently two or three years older. Willis started on seeing him.

"Who would have thought! what brings you here?" he said; "I thought you were in the country." Then to his companion, "This is the friend I was speaking to you about, Morley. A happy meeting; sit down, dear Reding; I have much to tell you."

Charles sat down all suspense, looking at Willis with such keen anxiety that the latter was forced to cut the matter short. "Reding,

I am a Catholic."

Charles threw himself back in his chair, and turned pale.

"My dear Reding, what is the matter with you? Why don't you speak to me?"

Charles was still silent; at last, stooping forward, with his elbows on his knees, and his head on his hands, he said, in a low voice, "O Willis, what have you done!"

"Done?" said Willis; "what *you* should do, and half Oxford besides. O Reding, I'm so happy!"

"Alas, alas!" said Charles; "but what is the good of my staying?—all good attend you, Willis; good-bye!"

"No, my good Reding, you don't leave me so soon, having found me so unexpectedly; and you have had a long walk, I dare say; sit down, there's a good fellow; we shall have luncheon soon, and you must not go without taking your part in it." He took Charles's hat from him, as he spoke; and Charles, in a mixture of feelings, let him have his way.

"O Willis, so you have separated yourself from us for ever!" he said; "you have taken your course, we keep ours: our paths are different."

"Not so," said Willis; "you must follow me, and we shall be one still."

Charles was half offended; "Really I must go," he said, and he rose; "you must not talk in that manner."

"Pray, forgive me," answered Willis; "I won't do so again; but I could not help it; I am not in a common state, I'm so happy!"

A thought struck Reding. "Tell me, Willis," he said, "your exact position; in what sense are you a Catholic? What is to prevent your returning with me to Oxford?"

His companion interposed: "I am taking a liberty perhaps," he said; "but Mr. Willis has been regularly received into the Catholic Church."

"I have not introduced you," said Willis. "Reding, let me

introduce Mr. Morley; Morley, Mr. Reding. Yes, Reding, I owe it to him that I am a Catholic. I have been on a tour with him abroad. We met with a good priest in France, who consented to receive my abjuration."

"Well, I think he might profitably have examined into your state of mind a little before he did so," said Reding; "*you* are not the person to become a Catholic, Willis."

"What do you mean?"

"Because," answered Reding, "you are more of a Dissenter than a Catholic. I beg your pardon," he added, seeing Willis look up sharply, "let me be frank with you, pray do. You were attached to the Church of Rome, not as a child to a mother, but in a wayward roving way, as a matter of fancy or liking, or (excuse me) as a greedy boy to something nice; and you pursued your object by disobeying the authorities set over you."

It was as much as Willis could bear; he said, he thought he recollected a text about "obeying God *rather* than men."

"I *see* you have disobeyed men," retorted Charles; "I *trust* you have been obeying God."

Willis thought him rude, and would not speak.

Mr. Morley began: "If you knew the circumstances better," he said, "you would doubtless judge differently. I consider Mr. Willis to be just the very person on whom it was incumbent to join the Church, and who will make an excellent Catholic. You must blame, not the venerable priest who received him, but me. The good man saw his devotion, his tears, his humility, his earnest desire; but the state of his mind he learned through me, who speak French better than Mr. Willis. However, he had quite enough conversation with him in French and Latin. He could not reject a postulant for salvation; it was impossible. Had you been he, you would have done the same."

"Well, sir, perhaps I have been unjust to him and you," said Charles; "however, I cannot augur well of this."

"You are judging, sir," answered Mr. Morley, "let me say it, of things you do not know. You do not know what the Catholic religion is, you do not know what its grace is, or the gift of faith."

The speaker was a layman; he spoke with earnestness the more intense, because quiet. Charles felt himself reproved by his manner; his good taste suggested to him that he had been too vehement in the presence of a stranger; yet he did not feel the less confidence in his cause. He paused before he answered; then he said briefly, that he was aware that he did not know the Roman Catholic religion, but he knew Mr. Willis. He could not help giving his opinion that good would not come of it.

"*I* have ever been a Catholic," said Mr. Morley; "so far I cannot judge of members of the Church of England; but this I know, that the Catholic Church is the only true Church. I may be wrong in many things; I cannot be wrong in this. This too I know, that the Catholic faith is one, and that no other Church has faith. The Church of England has no faith. You, my dear sir, have not faith."

This was a home-thrust; the controversies of Oxford passed before Reding's mind; but he instantly recovered himself. "You cannot expect," said he, smiling, "that I, almost a boy, should be able to argue with yourself, or to defend my Church or to explain her faith. I am content to hold that faith, to hold what she holds, without professing to be a divine. This is the doctrine which I have been taught at Oxford. I am under teaching there, I am not yet taught. Excuse me, then, if I decline an argument with you. With Mr. Willis, it is natural that I should argue; we are equals, and understand each other; but I am no theologian."

Here Willis cried out, "O my dear Reding, what I say is, 'Come and see.' Don't stand at the door arguing; but enter the great home of the soul, enter and adore."

"But," said Reding, "surely God wills us to be guided by reason; I don't mean that reason is everything, but it is at least something. Surely we ought not to act without it, against it."

"But is not doubt a dreadful state?" said Willis; "a most perilous state? No state is safe but that of faith. Can it be safe to be without faith? Now *have* you faith in your Church? I know you well enough to know you have not; where, then, are you?"

"Willis, you have misunderstood me most extraordinarily," said Charles: "ten thousand thoughts pass through the mind, and if it is safe to note down and bring against a man his stray words, I suppose there's nothing he mayn't be accused of holding. You must be alluding to some half-sentence or other of mine, which I have forgotten, and which was no real sample of my sentiments. Do you mean I have no worship? And does not worship presuppose faith? I have much to learn, I am conscious; but I wish to learn it from the Church under whose shadow my lot is cast, and with whom I am content."

"He confesses," said Willis, "that he has no faith; he confesses that he is in doubt. My dear Reding, can you sincerely plead that you are in invincible ignorance after what has passed between us? Now, suppose for an instant that Catholicism is true, is it not certain that you now have an opportunity of embracing it? And if you do not, are you in a state to die in?"

Reding was perplexed how to answer; that is, he could not with the necessary quickness analyze and put into words the answer which his reason suggested to Willis's rapid interrogatories. Mr. Morley had kept silence, lest Charles should have two upon him at once; but when Willis paused, and Charles did not reply, he interposed. He said that all the calls in Scripture were obeyed with promptitude by those who were called; and that our Lord would not suffer one man even to go and bury his father. Reding answered, that in those cases the voice of Christ was actually heard; He was on earth, in bodily presence; now, however, the very question was, *which* was the voice of Christ; and whether the Church of Rome did or did not speak with the voice of Christ—that surely we ought to act prudently; that Christ could not wish us to act otherwise; that, for himself, he had no doubt that he was in the place where Providence wished him to be; but, even if he had any doubts whether Christ was calling him elsewhere (which he had not), but if he had, he should certainly think that Christ called him in the way and method of careful examination—that prudence was the divinely appointed means of coming at the truth.

"Prudence!" cried Willis, "such prudence as St. Thomas's, I suppose, when he determined to see before believing."

Charles hesitated to answer.

"I see it," continued Willis; and, starting up, he seized his arm; "come, my dear fellow, come with me directly; let us go to the good priest who lives two streets off. You shall be received this very day. On with your hat." And, before Charles could show any resistance, he was half out of the room.

He could not help laughing, in spite of his vexation; he disengaged his arm, and deliberately sat down. "Not so fast," he said; "we are not quite this sort of person."

Willis looked awkward for a moment; then he said, "Well, at least you must go into a retreat; you must go forthwith. Morley, do you know when Mr. de Mowbray or Father Agostino gives his next retreat? Reding, it is just what you want, just what all Oxford men want; I think you will not refuse me."

Charles looked up in his face, and smiled. "It is not my line," he said at length. "I am on my way to Oxford. I must go. I came here to be of use to you; I can be of none, so I must go. Would I *could* be of service; but it is hopeless. Oh, it makes my heart ache!" And he went on brushing his hat with his glove, as if on the point of rising, yet loth to rise.

Morley now struck in: he spoke all along like a gentleman, and a man of real piety, but with a great ignorance of Protestants, or how they were to be treated.

"Excuse me, Mr. Reding," he said, "if before you go, I say one word. I feel very much for the struggle which is going on in your mind; and I am sure it is not for such as me to speak harshly or unkindly to you. The struggle between conviction and motives of this world is often long; may it have a happy termination in your case! Do not be offended if I suggest to you that the dearest and closest ties, such as your connection with the Protestant Church involves, may be on the side of the world in certain cases. It is a sort of martyrdom to have to break such; but they who do so have a martyr's reward. And, then, at a University you have so many inducements to fall in with the prevailing tone of thought; prospects, success in life, good opinion of friends—all these things are against you. They are likely to choke the good seed. Well, I could have wished that you had been able to follow the dictates of conscience at once; but the conflict must continue its appointed time; we will hope that all will end well."

"I can't persuade these good people," thought Charles, as he closed the street-door after him, "that I am not in a state of conviction, and struggling against it; how absurd! Here I come to reclaim a deserter, and I am seized even bodily, and against my will all but hurried into a profession of faith. Do these things happen to people every day? Or is there some particular fate with me thus to be brought across religious controversies which I am not up to? I a Roman Catholic! what a contrast all this with quiet Hartley!" naming his home. As he continued to think on what had passed he was still less satisfied with it or with himself. He had gone to lecture, and he had been lectured; and he had let out his secret state of mind: no, not let out, he had nothing to let out. He had indeed implied that he was inquiring after religious truth, but every Protestant inquires; he would not be a Protestant if he did not. Of course he was seeking the truth; it was his duty to do so; he recollected distinctly his tutor laying down, on one occasion, the duty of private judgment. This was the very difference between Protestants and Catholics; Catholics begin with faith, Protestants with inquiry; and he ought to have said this to Willis. He was provoked he had not said it; it would have simplified the question, and shown how far he was from being unsettled. Unsettled! it was most extravagant. He wished this had but struck him during the conversation, but it was a relief that it struck him now; it reconciled him to his position.

CHAPTER XIV

THE first day of Michaelmas term is, to an undergraduate's furniture, the brightest day of the year. Much as Charles regretted home, he rejoiced to see old Oxford again. The porter had acknowledged him at the gate, and the scout had smiled and bowed, as he ran up the worn staircase and found a blazing fire to welcome him. The coals crackled and split, and threw up a white flame in strong contrast with the newly-blackened bars and hobs of the grate. A shining copper kettle hissed and groaned under the internal torment of water at boiling point. The chimney-glass had been cleaned, the carpet beaten, the curtains fresh glazed. A tea-tray and tea commons were placed on the table; besides a battel paper, two or three cards from tradesmen who desired his patronage, and a note from a friend whose term had already commenced. The porter came in with his luggage, and had just received his too ample remuneration, when, through the closing door, in rushed Sheffield in his travelling dress.

"Well, old fellow, how are you?" he said, shaking both of Charles's hands, or rather arms, with all his might; "here we are all again; I am just come like you. Where have you been all this time? Come, tell us all about yourself. Give me some tea, and let's have a good jolly chat." Charles liked Sheffield, he liked Oxford, he was pleased to get back; yet he had some remains of home-sickness on him, and was not quite in cue for Sheffield's good-natured boisterousness. Willis's matter, too, was still on his mind. "Have you heard the news?" said Sheffield; "I have been long enough in college to pick it up. The kitchen-man was full of it as I passed along. Jack's a particular friend of mine, a good honest fellow, and has all the gossip of the place. I don't know what it means, but Oxford has just now a very bad inside. The report is, that some of the men have turned Romans; and they say that there are strangers going about Oxford whom no one knows anything of. Jack, who is a bit of a divine himself, says he heard the Principal say that, for certain, there were Jesuits at the bottom of it; and I don't know what he means, but he declares he saw with his own eyes the Pope walking down High Street with the priest. I asked him how he knew it; he said he knew the Pope by his slouching hat and his long beard; and the porter told him it was the Pope. The Dons have met several times; and several tutors are to be discommoned, and their names stuck up against the buttery-door. Meanwhile the Marshal, with two bull-dogs, is keeping guard before the Catholic chapel; and, to complete it, that old drunken fellow Topham is reported, out of malice, when called in to cut the Warden of St. Mary's hair, to have made a clean white tonsure atop of him."

"My dear Sheffield, how you run on!" said Reding. "Well, do you know, I can tell you a piece of real news bearing on these reports, and not of the pleasantest. Did you know Willis of St. George's?"

"I think I once saw him at wine in your rooms; a modest, nice-looking fellow, who never spoke a word."

"Ah, I assure you, he has a tongue in his head when it suits him," answered Charles: "yet I do think," he added, musingly, "he's very much changed, and not for the better."

"Well, what's the upshot?" asked Sheffield.

"He has turned Catholic," said Charles.

"What a fool!" cried Sheffield.

There was a pause. Charles felt awkward: then he said, "I can't say I was surprised; yet I should have been less surprised at White."

"Oh, White won't turn Catholic," said Sheffield; "he hasn't it in him. He's a coward."

"Fools and cowards!" answered Charles: "thus you divide the world, Sheffield? Poor Willis!" he added; "one must respect a man who acts according to his conscience."

"What can he know of conscience?" said Sheffield; "the idea of his swallowing, of his own free-will, the heap of rubbish which every Catholic has to believe! in cold blood tying a collar round his neck, and politely putting the chain into the hands of a priest! … And then the Confessional! 'Tis marvellous!" and he began to break the coals with the poker. "It's very well," he continued, "if a man is born a Catholic; I don't suppose they really believe what they are obliged to profess; but how an Englishman, a gentleman, a man here at Oxford, with all his advantages, can so eat dirt, scraping and picking up all the dead lies of the dark ages—it's a miracle!"

"Well, if there is anything that recommends Romanism to me," said Charles, "it is what you so much dislike: I'd give twopence, if some one, whom I could trust, would say to me, 'This is true; this is not true.' We should be saved this eternal wrangling. Wouldn't you be glad if St. Paul could come to life? I've often said to myself, 'Oh, that I could ask St. Paul this or that!'"

"But the Catholic Church isn't St. Paul quite, I guess," said Sheffield.

"Certainly not; but supposing you *did* think it had the inspiration of an Apostle, as the Roman Catholics do, what a comfort it would be to know, beyond all doubt, what to believe about God, and how to worship and please Him! I mean, *you* said, 'I can't believe this or that'; now you ought to have said, 'I can't believe the Pope has *power* to *decide* this or that.' If he had, you ought to believe it, whatever it is, and not to say, 'I can't believe.'"

Sheffield looked hard at him: "We shall have you a papist some of these fine days," said he.

"Nonsense," answered Charles; "you shouldn't say such things, even in jest."

"I don't jest; I am in earnest: you are plainly on the road."

"Well, if I am, you have put me on it," said Reding, wishing to get away from the subject as quick as he could; "for you are ever talking against shams, and laughing at King Charles and Laud, Bateman, White, rood-lofts, and piscinas."

"Now you are a Puseyite," said Sheffield in surprise.

"You give me the name of a very good man, whom I hardly know by sight," said Reding; "but I mean, that nobody knows what to believe, no one has a definite faith, but the Catholics and the Puseyites; no one says, 'This is true, that is false; this comes from the Apostles, that does not.'"

"Then would you believe a Turk," asked Sheffield, "who came to you with his 'One Allah, and Mahomet his Prophet'?"

"I did not say a creed was everything," answered Reding, "or that a religion could not be false which had a creed; but a religion can't be true which has none."

"Well, somehow that doesn't strike me," said Sheffield.

"Now there was Vincent at the end of term, after you had gone down," continued Charles; "you know I stayed up for Littlego; and he was very civil, very civil indeed. I had a talk with him about Oxford parties, and he pleased me very much at the time; but afterwards, the more I thought of what he said, the less was I satisfied; that is, I had got nothing definite from him. He did not say, 'This is true, that is false'; but 'Be true, be true, be good, be good, don't go too far, keep in the mean, have your eyes about you, eschew parties, follow our divines, all of them';—all which was but putting salt on the bird's tail. I want some practical direction, not abstract truths."

"Vincent is a humbug," said Sheffield.

"Dr. Pusey, on the other hand," continued Charles, "is said always to be decisive. He says, 'This is Apostolic, that's in the Fathers; St. Cyprian says this, St. Augustine denies that; this is safe, that's wrong; I bid you, I forbid you.' I understand all this; but I don't understand having duties put on me which are too much for me. I don't understand, I dislike, having a will of my own, when I have not the means to use it justly. In such a case, to tell me to act of myself, is like Pharaoh setting the Israelites to make bricks without straw. Setting me to inquire, to judge, to decide, forsooth! it's absurd; who has taught me?"

"But the Puseyites are not always so distinct," said Sheffield; "there's Smith, he never speaks decidedly in difficult questions. I know a man who was going to remain in Italy for some years, at a distance from any English chapel—he could not help it—and who came to ask him if he might communicate in the Catholic churches; he could not get an answer from him; he would not say yes or no."

"Then he won't have many followers, that's all," said Charles.

"But he has more than Dr. Pusey," answered Sheffield.

"Well, I can't understand it," said Charles; "he ought not; perhaps they won't stay."

"The truth is," said Sheffield, "I suspect he is more of a sceptic at bottom."

"Well, I honour the man who builds up," said Reding, "and I despise the man who breaks down."

"I am inclined to think you have a wrong notion of building up and pulling down," answered Sheffield; "Coventry, in his 'Dissertations,' makes it quite clear that Christianity is not a religion of doctrines."

"Who is Coventry?"

"Not know Coventry? He is one of the most original writers of the day; he's an American, and, I believe, a congregationalist. Oh, I assure you, you should read Coventry, although he is wrong on the question of Church-government: you are not well *au courant* with the literature of the day unless you do. He is no party man; he is a correspondent of the first men of the day; he stopped with the Dean of Oxford when he was in England, who has published an English edition of his 'Dissertations,' with a Preface; and he and Lord Newlights were said to be the two most witty men at the meeting of the British Association, two years ago."

"I don't like Lord Newlights," said Charles, "he seems to me to have no principle; that is, no fixed, definite religious principle. You don't know where to find him. This is what my father thinks; I have often heard him speak of him."

"It's curious you should use the word *principle*," said Sheffield; "for it is that which Coventry lays such stress on. He says that Christianity has no creed; that this is the very point in which it is distinguished from other religions; that you will search the New Testament in vain for a creed; but that Scripture is full of *principles*. The view is very ingenious, and seemed to me true, when I read the book. According to him, then, Christianity is not a religion of doctrines or mysteries; and if you are looking for dogmatism in Scripture, it's a mistake."

Charles was puzzled. "Certainly," he said, "at first sight there *is* no creed in Scripture.—No creed in Scripture," he said slowly, as if thinking aloud; "no creed in Scripture, *therefore* there is no creed. But the Athanasian Creed," he added quickly, "is *that* in Scripture? It either *is* in Scripture, or it is *not*. Let me see, it either is there, or it is not.... What was it that Freeborn said last term?... Tell me, Sheffield, would the Dean of Oxford say that the Creed was in Scripture or not? Perhaps you do not fairly explain Coventry's view; what is your impression?"

"Why, I will tell you frankly, my impression is, judging from his Preface, that he would not scruple to say that it is not in Scripture, but a scholastic addition."

"My dear fellow," said Charles, "do you mean that he, a dignitary of the Church, would say that the Athanasian Creed was a mistake, because it represented Christianity as a revelation of doctrines or mysteries to be received on faith?"

"Well, I may be wrong," said Sheffield, "but so I understood him."

"After all," said Charles sadly, "it's not so much more than that other Dean, I forget his name, said at St. Mary's before the Vacation;

it's part of the same system. Oh, it was after you went down, or just at the end of term: you don't go to sermons; I'm inclined not to go either. I can't enter upon the Dean's argument; it's not worth while. Well," he added, standing up and stretching himself, "I am tired with the day, yet it has not been a fatiguing one either; but London is so bustling a place."

"You wish me to say good-night," said Sheffield. Charles did not deny the charge; and the friends parted.

CHAPTER XV

There could not have been a lecture more unfavourable for Charles's peace of mind than that in which he found himself this term placed; yet, so blind are we to the future, he hailed it with great satisfaction, as if it was to bring him an answer to the perplexities into which Sheffield, Bateman, Freeborn, White, Willis, Mr. Morley, Dr. Brownside, Mr. Vincent, and the general state of Oxford, had all, in one way or other, conspired to throw him. He had shown such abilities in the former part of the year, and was reading so diligently, that his tutors put him prematurely into the lecture upon the Articles. It was a capital lecture so far as this, that the tutor who gave it had got up his subject completely. He knew the whole history of the Articles, how they grew into their present shape, with what fortunes, what had been added, and when, and what omitted. With this, of course, was joined an explanation of the text, as deduced, as far as could be, from the historical account thus given. Not only the British, but the foreign Reformers were introduced; and nothing was wanting, at least in the intention of the lecturer, for fortifying the young inquirer in the doctrine and discipline of the Church of England.

It did not produce this effect on Reding. Whether he had expected too much, or whatever was the cause, so it was that he did but feel more vividly the sentiment of the old father in the comedy, after consulting the lawyers, "*Incertior sum multo quam ante.*" He saw that the profession of faith contained in the Articles was but a patchwork of bits of orthodoxy, Lutheranism, Calvinism, and Zuinglism; and this too on no principle; that it was but the work of accident, if there be such a thing as accident; that it had come down in the particular shape in which the English Church now receives it, when it might have come down in any other shape; that it was but a toss-up that Anglicans at this day were not Calvinists, or Presbyterians, or Lutherans, equally well as Episcopalians. This historical fact did but clench the difficulty, or rather impossibility, of saying what the faith of the English Church was. On almost every point of dispute the authoritative standard of doctrine was vague or inconsistent, and there was an imposing weight of external testimony in favour of opposite interpretations. He stopped after lecture once or twice, and asked information of Mr. Upton, the tutor, who was quite ready to give it; but nothing came of these applications as regards the object which led him to make them.

One difficulty which Charles experienced was to know whether, according to the Articles, Divine truth was directly *given* us, or whether we had to *seek* it for ourselves from Scripture. Several Articles led to this question; and Mr. Upton, who was a High Churchman, answered him that the saving doctrine neither was *given* nor was to be *sought*, but that it was *proposed* by the Church, and *proved* by the individual. Charles did not see this distinction between *seeking* and *proving*; for how can we *prove* except by *seeking* (in Scripture) for *reasons*? He put the question in another form, and asked if the Christian Religion allowed of private judgment? This was no abstruse question, and a very practical one. Had he asked a Wesleyan or Independent, he would have had an unconditional answer in the affirmative; had he asked a Catholic, he would have been told that we used our private judgment to find the Church, and then in all matters of faith the Church superseded it; but from this Oxford divine he could not get a distinct answer. First he was told that doubtless we *must* use our judgment in the determination of religious doctrine; but next he was told that it was sin (as it undoubtedly is) to doubt the dogma of the Blessed Trinity. Yet, while he was told that to doubt of that doctrine was a sin, he was told in another conversation that our highest state here is one of doubt. What did this mean? Surely certainty was simply necessary on *some* points, as on the Object of worship; how could we worship what we doubted of? The two acts were contrasted by the Evangelist; when the disciples saw our Lord after the resurrection, "they worshipped Him, *but* some doubted"; yet, in spite of this, he was told that there was "impatience" in the very idea of desiring certainty.

At another time he asked whether the anathemas of the Athanasian Creed applied to all its clauses; for instance, whether it is necessary to salvation to hold that there is "*unus aeternus*" as the Latin has it; or "such as the Father,...such the Holy Ghost"; or that the Holy Ghost is "by Himself God and Lord"; or that Christ is one "by the taking of the manhood into God?" He could get no answer. Mr. Upton said that he did not like extreme questions; that he could not and did not wish to answer them; that the Creed was written against heresies, which no longer existed, as a sort of *protest*. Reding asked whether this meant that the Creed did not contain a distinctive view of its own, which alone was safe, but was merely a negation of error. The clauses, he observed, were positive, not negative. He could get no answer farther than that the Creed taught that the doctrines of "the Trinity" and "the Incarnation" were "necessary to salvation," it being apparently left uncertain *what* those doctrines consisted in. One day he asked how grievous sins were to be forgiven which were committed after baptism, whether by faith, or not at all in this life. He was answered that the Articles said nothing on the subject; that the Romish doctrine of pardon and purgatory was false; and that it was well to avoid both curious questions and subtle answers.

Another question turned up at another lecture, viz. whether the Real Presence meant a Presence of Christ in the elements, or in the soul, i.e. in the faith of the recipient; in other words, whether the Presence was really such, or a mere name. Mr. Upton pronounced it an open question. Another day Charles asked whether Christ was present in fact, or only in effect. Mr. Upton answered decidedly "in effect," which seemed to Reding to mean no real presence at all.

He had had some difficulty in receiving the doctrine of eternal punishment; it had seemed to him the hardest doctrine of Revelation. Then he said to himself, "But what is faith in its very notion but an acceptance of the word of God when reason seems to oppose it? How is it faith at all if there is nothing to try it?" This thought fully satisfied him. The only question was, *Is* it part of the revealed word? "I can believe it," he said, "if I know for certain that I *ought* to believe it; but if I am not bound to believe it, I can't believe it." Accordingly he put the question to Mr. Upton whether it was a doctrine of the Church of England; that is, whether it came under the subscription to the Articles. He could obtain no answer. Yet if he did *not* believe this doctrine, he felt the whole fabric of his faith shake under him. Close upon it came the doctrine of the Atonement.

It is difficult to give instances of this kind, without producing the impression on the reader's mind that Charles was forward and captious in his inquiries. Certainly Mr. Upton had his own thoughts about him, but he never thought his manner inconsistent with modesty and respect towards himself.

Charles naturally was full of the subject, and would have disclosed his perplexities to Sheffield, had he not had a strong anticipation that this would have been making matters worse. He thought Bateman, however, might be of some service, and he disburdened himself to him in the course of a country walk. What was he to do? For on his entrance he had been told that when he took his degree he should have to sign the Articles, not on faith as then, but on reason; yet they were unintelligible; and how could he prove what he could not construe?

Bateman seemed unwilling to talk on the subject; at last he said, "Oh, my dear Reding, you really are in an excited state of mind; I don't like to talk to you just now, for you will not see things in a straightforward way and take them naturally. What a bug-bear you are conjuring up! You are in an Article lecture in your second year; and hardly have you commenced, but you begin to fancy what you will, or will not think at the end of your time. Don't ask about the Articles now; wait at least till you have seen the lecture through."

"It really is not my way to be fussed or to fidget," said Charles, "though I own I am not so quiet as I ought to be. I hear so many different opinions in conversation; then I go to church, and one preacher deals his blows at another; lastly, I betake myself to the Articles, and really I cannot make out what they would teach me. For instance, I cannot make out their doctrine about faith, about the sacraments, about predestination, about the Church, about the inspiration of Scripture. And their tone is so unlike the Prayer Book. Upton has brought this out in his lectures most clearly."

"Now, my most respectable friend," said Bateman, "do think for a moment what men have signed the Articles. Perhaps King Charles himself; certainly Laud, and all the great Bishops of his day, and of the next generation. Think of the most orthodox Bull, the singularly learned Pearson, the eloquent Taylor, Montague, Barrow, Thorndike, good dear Bishop Horne, and Jones of Nayland. Can't you do what they did?"

"The argument is a very strong one," said Charles; "I have felt it: you mean, then, I must sign on faith."

"Yes, certainly, if necessary," said Bateman.

"And how am I to sign as a Master, and when I am ordained?" asked Charles.

"That's what I mean by fidgeting," answered Bateman. "You are not content with your day; you are reaching forward to live years hence."

Charles laughed. "It isn't quite that," he said, "I was but testing your advice; however, there's some truth in it." And he changed the subject.

They talked awhile on indifferent matters; but on a pause Charles's thoughts fell back again to the Articles. "Tell me, Bateman," he said, "as a mere matter of curiosity, how *you* subscribed when you took your degree."

"Oh, I had no difficulty at all," said Bateman; "the examples of Bull and Pearson were enough for me."

"Then you signed on faith."

"Not exactly, but it was that thought which smoothed all difficulties."

"Could you have signed without it?"

"How can you ask me the question? Of course."

"Well, do tell me, then, what was your *ground*?"

"Oh, I had many grounds. I can't recollect in a moment what happened some time ago."

"Oh, then it was a matter of difficulty; indeed, you said so just now."

"Not at all: my only difficulty was, not about myself, but how to state the matter to other people."

"What! some one suspected you?"

"No, no; you are quite mistaken. I mean, for instance, the Article says that we are justified by faith only; now the Protestant sense of this statement is point blank opposite to our standard divines: the question was, what I was to say when asked *my* sense of it."

"I understand," said Charles; "now tell me how you solved the problem."

"Well, I don't deny that the Protestant sense is heretical," answered Bateman; "and so is the Protestant sense of many other things in the Articles; but then we need not take them in the

Protestant sense."

"Then in what sense?"

"Why, first," said Bateman, "we need not take them in any sense at all. Don't smile; listen. Great authorities, such as Laud or Bramhall, seem to have considered that we only sign the Articles as articles of peace; not as really holding them, but as not opposing them. Therefore, when we sign the Articles, we only engage not to preach against them."

Reding thought; then he said: "Tell me, Bateman, would not this view of subscription to the Articles let the Unitarians into the Church?"

Bateman allowed it would, but the Liturgy would still keep them out. Charles then went on to suggest that *they* would take the Liturgy as a Liturgy of peace too. Bateman began again.

"If you want some tangible principle," he said, "for interpreting Articles and Liturgy, I can give you one. You know," he continued, after a short pause, "what it is *we* hold? Why, we give the Articles a Catholic interpretation."

Charles looked inquisitive.

"It is plain," continued Bateman, "that no document can be a dead letter; it must be the expression of some mind; and the question here is, *whose* is what may be called the voice which speaks the Articles. Now, if the Bishops, Heads of houses, and other dignitaries and authorities were unanimous in their religious views, and one and all said that the Articles meant this and not that, they, as the imponents, would have a right to interpret them; and the Articles would mean what those great men said they meant. But they do not agree together; some of them are diametrically opposed to others. One clergyman denies Apostolical Succession, another affirms it; one denies the Lutheran justification, another maintains it; one denies the inspiration of Scripture, a second holds Calvin to be a saint, a third considers the doctrine of sacramental grace a superstition, a fourth takes part with Nestorius against the Church, a fifth is a Sabellian. It is plain, then, that the Articles have no sense at all, if the collective voice of Bishops, Deans, Professors, and the like is to be taken. They cannot supply what schoolmen call the *form* of the Articles. But perhaps the writers themselves of the Articles will supply it? No; for, first, we don't know for certain who the writers were; and next, the Articles have gone through so many hands, and so many mendings, that some at least of the original authors would not like to be responsible for them. Well, let us go to the Convocations which ratified them: but they, too, were of different sentiments; the seventeenth century did not hold the doctrine of the sixteenth. Such is the state of the case. On the other hand, *we* say that if the Anglican Church be a part of the one Church Catholic, it must, from the necessity of the case, hold Catholic doctrine. Therefore, the whole Catholic Creed, the acknowledged doctrine of the Fathers, of St. Ignatius, St. Cyprian, St. Augustin, St. Ambrose, is the *form*, is the one true sense and interpretation of the Articles. They may be ambiguous in themselves; they may have been worded with various intentions by the individuals concerned in their composition; but these are accidents; the Church knows nothing of individuals; she interprets herself."

Reding took some time to think over this. "All this," he said, "proceeds on the fundamental principle that the Church of England is an integral part of that visible body of which St. Ignatius, St. Cyprian, and the rest were Bishops; according to the words of Scripture, 'one body, one faith.'"

Bateman assented; Charles proceeded: "Then the Articles must not be considered primarily as teaching; they have no one sense in themselves; they are confessedly ambiguous: they are compiled from heterogeneous sources; but all this does not matter, for all must be interpreted by the teaching of the Catholic Church."

Bateman agreed in the main, except that Reding had stated the case rather too strongly.

"But what if their letter *contradicts* a doctrine of the Fathers?

Am I to force the letter?"

"If such a case actually happened, the theory would not hold," answered Bateman; "it would only be a gross quibble. You can in no case sign an Article in a sense which its words will not bear. But, fortunately, or rather providentially, this is not the case; we have merely to explain ambiguities, and harmonize discrepancies. The Catholic interpretation does no greater violence to the text than *any other* rule of interpretation will be found to do."

"Well, but I know nothing of the Fathers," said Charles; "others too are in the same condition; how am I to learn practically to interpret the Articles?"

"By the Prayer Book; the Prayer Book is the voice of the Fathers."

"How so?"

"Because the Prayer Book is confessedly ancient, while the Articles are modern."

Charles kept silence again. "It is very plausible," he said; he thought on. Presently he asked: "Is this a *received* view?"

"*No* view is received," said Bateman; "the Articles themselves are received, but there is no authoritative interpretation of them at all. That's what I was saying just now; Bishops and Professors don't agree together."

"Well," said Charles, "is it a *tolerated* view?"

"It has certainly been strongly opposed," answered Bateman; "but it has never been condemned."

"That is no answer," said Charles, who saw by Bateman's manner how the truth lay. "Does any one Bishop hold it? Did any one Bishop ever hold it? Has it ever been formally admitted as tenable by any one Bishop? Is it a view got up to meet existing difficulties, or has it an historical existence?"

Bateman could give but one answer to these questions, as they were successively put to him.

"I thought so," said Charles, when he had made his answer: "I know, of course, whose view you are putting before me, though I never heard it drawn out before. It is specious, certainly: I don't see but it might have done, had it been tolerably sanctioned; but you have no sanction to show me. It is, as it stands, a mere theory struck out by individuals. Our Church *might* have adopted this mode of interpreting the Articles; but from what you tell me, it certainly *has not* done so. I am where I was."

CHAPTER XVI

THE thought came across Reding whether perhaps, after all, what is called Evangelical Religion was not the true Christianity: its professors, he knew, were active and influential, and in past times had been much persecuted. Freeborn had surprised and offended him at Bateman's breakfast-party before the Vacation; yet Freeborn had a serious manner about him, and perhaps he had misunderstood him. The thought, however, passed away as suddenly as it came, and perhaps would not have occurred to him again, when an accident gave him some data for determining the question.

One afternoon he was lounging in the Parks, gazing with surprise on one of those extraordinary lights for which the neighbourhood of Oxford is at that season celebrated, and which, as the sun went down, was colouring Marston, Elsfield, and their half-denuded groves with a pale gold-and-brown hue, when he found himself overtaken and addressed by the said Freeborn *in propriâ personâ*. Freeborn liked a *tête-à-tête* talk much better than a dispute in a party; he felt himself at more advantage in long leisurely speeches, and he was soon put out of breath when he had to bolt-out or edge-in his words amid the ever-varying voices of a breakfast-table. He thought the present might be a good opportunity of doing good to a poor youth who did not know chalk from cheese, and who, by his means, might be, as he would word it, "savingly converted." So they got into conversation, talked of Willis's step, which Freeborn called awful; and, before Charles knew where he was, he found himself asking Freeborn what he meant by "faith."

"Faith," said Freeborn, "is a Divine gift, and is the instrument of our justification in God's sight. We are all by nature displeasing to Him, till He justifies us freely for Christ's sake. Faith is like a hand, appropriating personally the merits of Christ, who is our justification. Now, what can we want more, or have more, than those merits? Faith, then, is everything, and does everything for us. You see, then, how important it is to have a right view about justification by faith only. If we are sound on this capital point, everything else may take its chance; we shall at once see the folly of contending about ceremonies, about forms of Church-government, about, I will even say, sacraments or creeds. External things will, in that case, either be neglected, or will find a subordinate place."

Reding observed that of course Freeborn did not mean to say that good works were not necessary for obtaining God's favour; "but if they were, how was justification by faith only?"

Freeborn smiled, and said that he hoped Reding would have clearer views in a little time. It was a very simple matter. Faith not only justified, it regenerated also. It was the root of sanctification, as well as of Divine acceptance. The same act, which was the means of bringing us into God's favour, secured our being meet for it. Thus good works were secured, because faith would not be true faith unless it were such as to be certain of bringing forth good works in due time.

Reding thought this view simple and clear, though it unpleasantly reminded him of Dr. Brownside. Freeborn added that it was a doctrine suited to the poor, that it put all the gospel into a nutshell, that it dispensed with criticism, primitive ages, teachers—in short, with authority in whatever form. It swept theology clean away. There was no need to mention this last consequence to Charles; but he passed it by, wishing to try the system on its own merits.

"You speak of *true* faith," he said, "as producing good works: you say that no faith justifies *but* true faith, and true faith produces good works. In other words, I suppose, faith, which is *certain to be fruitful*, or *fruitful* faith, justifies. This is very like saying that faith and works are the joint means of justification."

"Oh, no, no," cried Freeborn, "that is deplorable doctrine: it is quite opposed to the gospel, it is anti-Christian. We are justified by faith only, apart from good works."

"I am in an Article lecture just now," said Charles, "and Upton told us that we must make a distinction of *this* kind; for instance, the Duke of Wellington is Chancellor of the University, but, though he is as much Chancellor as Duke, still he sits in the House of Lords as Duke, not as Chancellor. Thus, although faith is as truly fruitful as it is faith, yet it does not justify as being fruitful, but as being faith. Is this what you mean?"

"Not at all," said Freeborn; "that was Melancthon's doctrine; he explained away a cardinal truth into a mere matter of words; he made faith a mere symbol, but this is a departure from the pure gospel: faith is the *instrument*, not a *symbol* of justification. It is, in truth, a mere *apprehension*, and nothing else: the seizing and clinging which a beggar might venture on when a king passed by. Faith is as poor as Job in the ashes: it is like Job stripped of all pride and pomp and good works: it is covered with filthy rags: it is without anything good: it is, I repeat, a mere apprehension. Now you see what I mean."

"I can't believe I understand you," said Charles: "you say that to have faith is to seize Christ's merits; and that we have them, if we will but seize them. But surely not every one who seizes them, gains them; because dissolute men, who never have a dream of thorough repentance or real hatred of sin, would gladly seize and appropriate them, if they might do so. They would like to get to heaven for nothing. Faith, then, must be some particular *kind* of apprehension; *what* kind? Good works cannot be mistaken, but an 'apprehension' may. What, then, is a true apprehension? What *is* faith?"

"What need, my dear friend," answered Freeborn, "of knowing metaphysically what true faith is, if we have it and enjoy it? I do not know what bread is, but I eat it; do I wait till a chemist analyzes it? No, I eat it, and I feel the good effects afterwards. And so let us be content to know, not what faith *is*, but what it *does*, and enjoy our blessedness in possessing it."

"I really don't want to introduce metaphysics," said Charles, "but I will adopt your own image. Suppose I suspected the bread before me to have arsenic in it, or merely to be unwholesome, would it be wonderful if I tried to ascertain how the fact stood?"

"Did you do so this morning at breakfast?" asked Freeborn.

"I did not suspect my bread," answered Charles.

"Then why suspect faith?" asked Freeborn.

"Because it is, so to say, a new substance"—Freeborn sighed—"because I am not used to it, nay, because I suspect it. I must say *suspect* it; because, though I don't know much about the matter, I know perfectly well, from what has taken place in my father's parish, what excesses this doctrine may lead to, unless it is guarded. You say that it is a doctrine for the poor; now they are very likely to mistake one thing for another; so indeed is every one. If, then, we are told, that we have but to apprehend Christ's merits, and need not trouble ourselves about anything else; that justification has taken place, and works will follow; that all is done, and that salvation is complete, while we do but continue to have faith; I think we ought to be pretty sure that we *have* faith, real faith, a real apprehension, before we shut up our books and make holiday."

Freeborn was secretly annoyed that he had got into an argument, or pained, as he would express it, at the pride of Charles's natural man, or the blindness of his carnal reason; but there was no help for it, he must give him an answer.

"There are, I know, many kinds of faith," he said; "and of course you must be on your guard against mistaking false faith for true faith. Many persons, as you most truly say, make this mistake; and most important is it, all important I should say, to go right. First, it is evident that it is not mere belief in facts, in the being of a God, or in the historical event that Christ has come and gone. Nor is it the submission of the reason to mysteries; nor, again, is it that sort of trust which is required for exercising the gift of miracles. Nor is it knowledge and acceptance of the contents of the Bible. I say, it is not knowledge, it is not assent of the intellect, it is not historical faith, it is not dead faith: true justifying faith is none of these—it is seated in the heart and affections." He paused, then added: "Now, I suppose, for practical purposes, I have described pretty well what justifying faith is."

Charles hesitated: "By describing what it is *not*, you mean," said he; "justifying faith, then, is, I suppose, living faith."

"Not so fast," answered Freeborn.

"Why," said Charles, "if it's not dead faith, it's living faith."

"It's neither dead faith nor living," said Freeborn, "but faith, simple faith, which justifies. Luther was displeased with Melancthon for saying that living and operative faith justified. I have studied the question very carefully."

"Then do *you* tell me," said Charles, "what faith is, since I do not explain it correctly. For instance, if you said (what you don't say), that faith was submission of the reason to mysteries, or acceptance of Scripture as an historical document, I should know perfectly well what you meant; *that* is information: but when you say, that faith which justifies is an *apprehension* of Christ, that it is *not* living faith, or fruitful faith, or operative, but a something which in fact and actually is distinct from these, I confess I feel perplexed."

Freeborn wished to be out of the argument. "Oh," he said, "if you really once experienced the power of faith—how it changes the heart, enlightens the eyes, gives a new spiritual taste, a new sense to the soul; if you once knew what it was to be blind, and then to see, you would not ask for definitions. Strangers need verbal descriptions; the heirs of the kingdom enjoy. Oh, if you could but be persuaded to put off high imaginations; to strip yourself of your proud self, and to *experience* in yourself the wonderful change, you would live in praise and thanksgiving, instead of argument and criticism."

Charles was touched by his warmth; "But," he said, "we ought to act by reason; and I don't see that I have more, or so much, reason to listen to you, as to listen to the Roman Catholic, who tells me I cannot possibly have that certainty of faith before believing, which on believing will be divinely given me."

"Surely," said Freeborn, with a grave face, "you would not compare the spiritual Christian, such as Luther, holding his cardinal doctrine about justification, to any such formal, legal, superstitious devotee as Popery can make, with its carnal rites and quack remedies, which never really cleanse the soul or reconcile it to God?"

"I don't like you to talk so," said Reding; "I know very little about the real nature of Popery; but when I was a boy I was once, by chance, in a Roman Catholic chapel; and I really never saw such devotion in my life—the people all on their knees, and most earnestly attentive to what was going on. I did not understand what that was; but I am sure, had you been there, you never would have called their religion, be it right or wrong, an outward form or carnal ordinance."

Freeborn said it deeply pained him to hear such sentiments, and to find that Charles was so tainted with the errors of the day; and he began, not with much tact, to talk of the Papal Antichrist, and would have got off to prophecy, had Charles said a word to afford fuel for discussion. As he kept silence, Freeborn's zeal burnt out, and there was a break in the conversation.

After a time, Reding ventured to begin again.

"If I understand you," he said, "faith carries its own evidence with it. Just as I eat my bread at breakfast without hesitation about its wholesomeness, so, when I have really faith, I know it beyond mistake, and need not look out for tests of it?"

"Precisely so," said Freeborn; "you begin to see what I mean; you grow. The soul is enlightened to see that it has real faith."

"But how," asked Charles, "are we to rescue those from their dangerous mistake, who think they have faith, while they have not? Is there no way in which they can find out that they are under a delusion?"

"It is not wonderful," said Freeborn, "though there be no way. There are many self-deceivers in the world. Some men are self-righteous, trust in their works, and think they are safe when they are in a state of perdition; no formal rules *can* be given by which their reason might for certain detect their mistake. And so of false faith."

"Well, it does seem to me wonderful," said Charles, "that there is no natural and obvious warning provided against this delusion; wonderful that false faith should be so exactly like true faith that there is nothing to determine their differences from each other. Effects imply causes: if one apprehension of Christ leads to good works, and another does not, there must be something *in* the one which is not *in* the other. *What* is a false apprehension of Christ wanting in, which a true apprehension has? The word *apprehension* is so vague; it conveys no definite idea to me, yet justification depends on it. Is a false apprehension, for instance, wanting in repentance and amendment?"

"No, no," said Freeborn; "true faith is complete without conversion; conversion follows; but faith is the root."

"Is it the love of God which distinguishes true faith from false?"

"Love?" answered Freeborn; "you should read what Luther says in his celebrated comment on the Galatians. He calls such a doctrine '*pestilens figmentum*,' '*diaboli portentum*'; and cries out against the Papists, '*Pereant sophistae cum suâ maledictâ glossâ!*'"

"Then it differs from false faith in nothing."

"Not so," said Freeborn; "it differs from it in its fruits: 'By their fruits ye shall know them.'"

"This is coming round to the same point again," said Charles;

"fruits come after; but a man, it seems, is to take comfort in his justification *before* fruits come, before he knows that his faith will produce them."

"Good works are the *necessary* fruits of faith," said Freeborn; "so says the Article."

Charles made no answer, but said to himself, "My good friend here certainly has not the clearest of heads"; then aloud, "Well, I despair of getting at the bottom of the subject."

"Of course," answered Freeborn, with an air of superiority, though in a mild tone, "it is a very simple principle, '*Fides justificat ante et sine charitate*'; but it requires a Divine light to embrace it."

They walked awhile in silence; then, as the day was now closing in, they turned homewards, and parted company when they came to the Clarendon.

CHAPTER XVII

Freeborn was not the person to let go a young man like Charles without another effort to gain him; and in a few days he invited him to take tea at his lodgings. Charles went at the appointed time, through the wet and cold of a dreary November evening, and found five or six men already assembled. He had got into another world; faces, manners, speeches, all were strange, and savoured neither of Eton, which was his own school, nor of Oxford itself. He was introduced, and found the awkwardness of a new acquaintance little relieved by the conversation which went on. It was a dropping fire of serious remarks; with pauses, relieved only by occasional "ahems," the sipping of tea, the sound of spoons falling against the saucers, and the blind shifting of chairs as the flurried servant-maid of the lodgings suddenly came upon them from behind, with the kettle for the teapot, or toast for the table. There was no nature or elasticity in the party, but a great intention to be profitable.

"Have you seen the last *Spiritual Journal*?" asked No. 1 of No. 2 in a low voice.

No. 2 had just read it.

"A very remarkable article that," said No. 1, "upon the deathbed of the Pope."

"No one is beyond hope," answered No. 2.

"I have heard of it, but not seen it," said No. 3.

A pause.

"What is it about?" asked Reding.

"The late Pope Sixtus the Sixteenth," said No. 3; "he seems to have died a believer."

A sensation. Charles looked as if he wished to know more.

"The *Journal* gives it on excellent authority," said No. 2; "Mr. O'Niggins, the agent for the Roman Priest Conversion Branch Tract Society, was in Rome during his last illness. He solicited an audience with the Pope, which was granted to him. He at once began to address him on the necessity of a change of heart, belief in the one Hope of sinners, and abandonment of all creature mediators. He announced to him the glad tidings, and assured him there was pardon for all. He warned him against the figment of baptismal regeneration; and then, proceeding to apply the word, he urged him, though in the eleventh hour, to receive the Bible, the whole Bible, and nothing but the Bible. The Pope listened with marked attention, and displayed considerable emotion. When it was ended, he answered Mr. O'Niggins that it was his fervent hope that they two would not die without finding themselves in one communion, or something of the sort. He declared moreover, what was astonishing, that he put his sole trust in Christ, 'the source of all merit,' as he expressed it—a remarkable phrase."

"In what language was the conversation carried on?" asked Reding.

"It is not stated," answered No. 2; "but I am pretty sure Mr. O'Niggins is a good French scholar."

"It does not seem to me," said Charles, "that the Pope's admissions are greater than those made continually by certain members of our own Church, who are nevertheless accused of Popery."

"But they are extorted from such persons," said Freeborn, "while the Pope's were voluntary."

"The one party go back into darkness," said No. 3; "the Pope was coming forward into light."

"One ought to interpret everything for the best in a real Papist," said Freeborn, "and everything for the worst in a Puseyite. That is both charity and common sense."

"This was not all," continued No. 2; "he called together the Cardinals, protested that he earnestly desired God's glory, said that inward religion was all in all, and forms were nothing without a contrite heart, and that he trusted soon to be in Paradise—which, you know, was a denial of the doctrine of Purgatory."

"A brand from the burning, I do hope," said No. 3.

"It has frequently been observed," said No. 4, "nay it has struck me myself, that the way to convert Romanists is first to convert the Pope."

"It is a sure way, at least," said Charles timidly, afraid he was saying too much; but his irony was not discovered.

"Man cannot do it," said Freeborn; "it's the power of faith. Faith can be vouchsafed even to the greatest sinners. You see now, perhaps," he said, turning to Charles, "better than you did, what I meant by faith the other day. This poor old man could have no merit; he had passed a long life in opposing the Cross. Do your difficulties continue?"

Charles had thought over their former conversation very carefully several times, and he answered, "Why, I don't think they do to the same extent."

Freeborn looked pleased.

"I mean," he said, "that the idea hangs together better than I thought it did at first."

Freeborn looked puzzled.

Charles, slightly colouring, was obliged to proceed, amid the profound silence of the whole party. "You said, you know, that justifying faith was without love or any other grace besides itself, and that no one could at all tell what it was, except afterwards, from its fruits; that there was no test by which a person could examine himself, whether or not he was deceiving himself when he thought he had faith, so that good and bad might equally be taking to themselves the promises and the privileges peculiar to the gospel. I thought this a hard doctrine certainly at first; but, then, afterwards it struck me that faith is perhaps a result of a previous state of mind, a blessed result of a blessed state, and therefore may be considered the reward of previous obedience; whereas sham faith, or what merely looks like faith, is a judicial punishment."

In proportion as the drift of the former part of this speech was uncertain, so was the conclusion very distinct. There was no mistake, and an audible emotion.

"There is no such thing as previous merit," said No. 1; "all is of grace."

"Not merit, I know," said Charles, "but"—

"We must not bring in the doctrine of *de condigno* or *de congruo*," said No. 2.

"But surely," said Charles, "it is a cruel thing to say to the unlearned and the multitude, 'Believe, and you are at once saved; do not wait for fruits, rejoice at once,' and neither to accompany this announcement by any clear description of what faith is, nor to secure them by previous religious training against self-deception!"

"That is the very gloriousness of the doctrine," said Freeborn, "that it is preached to the worst of mankind. It says, 'Come as you are; don't attempt to make yourselves better. Believe that salvation is yours, and it is yours: good works follow after.'"

"On the contrary," said Charles, continuing his argument, "when it is said that justification follows upon baptism, we have an intelligible something pointed out, which every one can ascertain. Baptism is an external unequivocal token; whereas that a man has this secret feeling called faith, no one but himself can be a witness, and he is not an unbiassed one."

Reding had at length succeeded in throwing that dull tea-table into a state of great excitement. "My dear friend," said Freeborn, "I had hoped better things; in a little while, I hope, you will see things differently. Baptism is an outward rite; what is there, can there be, spiritual, holy, or heavenly in baptism?"

"But you tell me faith too is not spiritual," said Charles.

"*I* tell you!" cried Freeborn, "when?"

"Well," said Charles, somewhat puzzled, "at least you do not think it holy."

Freeborn was puzzled in his turn.

"If it is holy," continued Charles, "it has something good in it; it has some worth; it is not filthy rags. All the good comes afterwards, you said. You said that its fruits were holy, but that it was nothing at all itself."

There was a momentary silence, and some agitation of thought.

"Oh, faith is certainly a holy feeling," said No. 1.

"No, it is spiritual, but not holy," said No. 2; "it is a mere act, the apprehension of Christ's merits."

"It is seated in the affections," said No. 3; "faith is a feeling of the heart; it is trust, it is a belief that Christ is *my* Saviour; all this is distinct from holiness. Holiness introduces self-righteousness. Faith is peace and joy, but it is not holiness. Holiness comes after."

"Nothing can cause holiness but what is holy; this is a sort of axiom," said Charles; "if the fruits are holy, faith, which is the root, is holy."

"You might as well say that the root of a rose is red, and of a lily white," said No. 3.

"Pardon me, Reding," said Freeborn, "it is, as my friend says, an *apprehension*. An apprehension is a seizing; there is no more holiness in justifying faith, than in the hand's seizing a substance which comes in its way. This is Luther's great doctrine in his 'Commentary' on the Galatians. It is nothing in itself—it is a mere instrument; this is what he teaches, when he so vehemently resists the notion of justifying faith being accompanied by love."

"I cannot assent to that doctrine," said No. 1; "it may be true in a certain sense, but it throws stumbling-blocks in the way of seekers. Luther could not have meant what you say, I am convinced. Justifying faith is always accompanied by love."

"That is what I thought," said Charles.

"That is the Romish doctrine all over," said No. 2; "it is the doctrine of Bull and Taylor."

"Luther calls it, '*venenum infernale*,'" said Freeborn.

"It is just what the Puseyites preach at present," said No. 3.

"On the contrary," said No. 1, "it is the doctrine of Melancthon. Look here," he continued, taking his pocketbook out of his pocket, "I have got his words down as Shuffleton quoted them in the Divinity-school the other day: '*Fides significat fiduciam; in fiducidâ inest dilectio; ergo etiam dilectione sumus justi.*'"

Three of the party cried "Impossible!" The paper was handed round in solemn silence.

"Calvin said the same," said No. 1 triumphantly.

"I think," said No. 4, in a slow, smooth, sustained voice, which contrasted with the animation which had suddenly inspired the conversation, "that the con-tro-ver-sy, ahem, may be easily arranged. It is a question of words between Luther and Melancthon. Luther says, ahem, 'faith is *without* love,' meaning, 'faith without love justifies.' Melancthon, on the other hand, says, ahem, 'faith is *with* love,' meaning, 'faith justifies with love.' Now both are true: for, ahem, faith-without-love *justifies*, yet faith justifies *not-without-love*."

There was a pause, while both parties digested this explanation.

"On the contrary," he added, "it is the Romish doctrine that faith-with-love justifies."

Freeborn expressed his dissent; he thought this the doctrine of Melancthon which Luther condemned.

"You mean," said Charles, "that justification is given to faith *with* love, not to faith *and* love."

"You have expressed my meaning," said No. 4.

"And what is considered the difference between *with* and *and*?" asked Charles.

No. 4 replied without hesitation, "Faith is the *instrument*, love the *sine quâ non*."

Nos. 2 and 3 interposed with a protest; they thought it "legal" to introduce the phrase *sine quâ non*; it was introducing *conditions*. Justification was unconditional.

"But is not faith a condition?" asked Charles.

"Certainly not," said Freeborn; "'condition' is a legal word. How can salvation be free and full, if it is conditional?"

"There are no conditions," said No. 3; "all must come from the heart. We believe with the heart, we love from the heart, we obey with the heart; not because we are obliged, but because we have a new nature."

"Is there no obligation to obey?" said Charles, surprised.

"No obligation to the regenerate," answered No. 3; "they are above obligation; they are in a new state."

"But surely Christians are under a law," said Charles.

"Certainly not," said No. 2; "the law is done away in Christ."

"Take care," said No. 1; "that borders on Antinomianism."

"Not at all," said Freeborn; "an Antinomian actually holds that he may break the law: a spiritual believer only holds that he is not bound to keep it."

Now they got into a fresh discussion among themselves; and, as it seemed as interminable as it was uninteresting, Reding took an opportunity to wish his host a good night, and to slip away. He never had much leaning towards the evangelical doctrine; and Freeborn and his friends, who knew what they were holding a great deal better than the run of their party, satisfied him that he had not much to gain by inquiring into that doctrine farther. So they will vanish in consequence from our pages.

CHAPTER XVIII

When Charles got to his room he saw a letter from home lying on his table; and, to his alarm, it had a deep black edge. He tore it open. Alas, it announced the sudden death of his dear father! He had been ailing some weeks with the gout, which at length had attacked his stomach, and carried him off in a few hours.

O my poor dear Charles, I sympathize with you keenly all that long night, and in that indescribable waking in the morning, and that dreary day of travel which followed it! By the afternoon you were at home. O piercing change! it was but six or seven weeks before that you had passed the same objects the reverse way, with what different feelings, and oh, in what company, as you made for the railway omnibus! It was a grief not to be put into words; and to meet mother, sisters—and the Dead!…

The funeral is over by some days; Charles is to remain at home the remainder of the term, and does not return to Oxford till towards the end of January. The signs of grief have been put away; the house looks cheerful as before; the fire as bright, the mirrors as clear, the furniture as orderly; the pictures are the same, and the ornaments on the mantelpiece stand as they have stood, and the French clock tells the hour, as it has told it, for years past. The inmates of the parsonage wear, it is most true, the signs of a heavy bereavement; but they converse as usual, and on ordinary subjects; they pursue the same employments, they work, they read, they walk in the garden, they dine. There is no change except in the inward consciousness of an overwhelming loss. *He* is not there, not merely on this day or that, for so it well might be; he is not merely away, but, as they know well, he is gone and will not return. That he is absent now is but a token and a memorial to their minds that he will be absent always. But especially at dinner; Charles had to take a place which he had sometimes filled, but then as the deputy, and in the presence of him whom now he succeeded. His father, being not much more than a middle-aged man, had been accustomed to carve himself. And when at the meal of the day Charles looked up, he had to encounter the troubled look of one, who, from her place at table, had before her eyes a still more vivid memento of their common loss—*aliquid desideraverunt oculi.*

Mr. Reding had left his family well provided for; and this, though a real alleviation of their loss in the event, perhaps augmented the pain of it at the moment. He had ever been a kind indulgent father. He was a most respectable clergyman of the old school; pious in his sentiments, a gentleman in his feelings, exemplary in his social relations. He was no reader, and never had been in the way to gain theological knowledge; he sincerely believed all that was in the Prayer Book, but his sermons were very rarely doctrinal. They were sensible, manly discourses on the moral duties. He administered Holy Communion at the three great festivals, saw his Bishop once or twice a year, was on good terms with the country gentlemen in his neighbourhood, was charitable to the poor, hospitable in his housekeeping, and was a staunch though not a violent supporter of the Tory interest in his county. He was incapable of anything harsh, or petty, or low, or uncourteous; and died esteemed by the great houses about him, and lamented by his parishioners.

It was the first great grief poor Charles had ever had, and he felt it to be real. How did the small anxieties which had of late teased him, vanish before this tangible calamity! He then understood the difference between what was real and what was not. All the doubts, inquiries, surmises, views, which had of late haunted him on theological subjects, seemed like so many shams, which flitted before him in sun-bright hours, but had no root in his inward nature, and fell from him, like the helpless December leaves, in the hour of his affliction. He felt now *where* his heart and his life lay. His birth, his parentage, his education, his home, were great realities; to these his being was united; out of these he grew. He felt he must be what Providence had made him. What is called the pursuit of truth, seemed an idle dream. He had great tangible duties to his father's memory, to his mother and sisters, to his position; he felt sick of all theories, as if they had taken him in; and he secretly resolved never more to have anything to do with them. Let the world go on as it might, happen what would to others, his own place and his own path were clear. He would go back to Oxford, attend steadily to his books, put aside all distractions, avoid bye-paths, and do his best to acquit himself well in the schools. The Church of England as it was, its Articles, bishops, preachers, professors, had sufficed for much better persons than he was; they were good enough for him. He could not do better than imitate the life and death of his beloved father; quiet years in the country at a distance from all excitements, a round of pious, useful works among the poor, the care of a village school, and at length the death of the righteous.

At the moment, and for some time to come, he had special duties towards his mother; he wished, as far as might be, to supply to her the place of him she had lost. She had great trials before her still; if it was a grief to himself to leave Hartley, what would it be to her? Not many months would pass before she would have to quit a place ever dear, and now sacred in her thoughts; there was in store for her the anguish of dismantling the home of many years, and the toil and whirl of packing; a wearied head and an aching heart at a time when she would have most need of self-possession and energy.

Such were the thoughts which came upon him again and again in those sorrowful weeks. A leaf had been turned over in his life; he could not be what he had been. People come to man's estate at very different ages. Youngest sons in a family, like monks in a convent, may remain children till they have reached middle age; but the elder, should their father die prematurely, are suddenly ripened into manhood, when they are almost boys. Charles had left Oxford a clever unformed youth; he returned a man.

PART II

CHAPTER I

About three miles from Oxford a thickly-wooded village lies on the side of a steep, long hill or chine, looking over the Berkshire woods, and commanding a view of the many-turreted city itself. Over its broad summit once stretched a chestnut forest; and now it is covered with the roots of trees, or furze, or soft turf. The red sand which lies underneath contrasts with the green, and adds to its brilliancy; it drinks in, too, the rain greedily, so that the wide common is nearly always fit for walking; and the air, unlike the heavy atmosphere of the University beneath it, is fresh and bracing. The gorse was still in bloom, in the latter end of the month of June, when Reding and Sheffield took up their abode in a small cottage at the upper end of this village—so hid with trees and girt in with meadows that for the stranger it was hard to find—there to pass their third and last Long Vacation before going into the schools.

A year and a half had passed since Charles's great affliction, and the time had not been unprofitably spent either by himself or his friend. Both had read very regularly, and Sheffield had gained the Latin verse into the bargain. Charles had put all religious perplexities aside; that is, he knew of course many more persons of all parties than he did before, and became better acquainted with their tenets and their characters, but he did not dwell upon anything which he met with, nor attempt to determine the merits or solve the difficulties of this or that question. He took things as they came; and, while he gave his mind to his books, he thankfully availed himself of the religious privileges which the College system afforded him. Nearly a year still remained before his examination; and, as Mrs. Reding had not as yet fully arranged her plans, but was still, with her daughters, passing from friend to friend, he had listened to Sheffield's proposal to take a tutor for the Vacation, and to find a site for their studies in the neighbourhood of Oxford. There was every prospect of their both obtaining the highest honours which the schools award: they both were good scholars, and clever men; they had read regularly, and had had the advantage of able lectures.

The side of the hill forms a large, sweeping hollow or theatre just on one side of the village of Horsley. The two extreme points may be half a mile across; but the distance is increased to one who follows the path which winds through the furze and fern along the ridge. Their tutor had been unable to find lodgings in the village; and, while the two young men lived on one extremity of the sweep we have been describing, Mr. Carlton, who was not above three years older than they, had planted himself at a farmhouse upon the other. Besides, the farmhouse suited him better, as being nearer to a hamlet which he was serving during the Vacation.

"I don't think you like Carlton as well as I do," said Reding to Sheffield, as they lay on the green sward with some lighter classic in their hands, waiting for dinner, and watching their friend as he approached them from his lodgings. "He is to me so taking a man; so equable, so gentle, so considerate—he brings people together, and fills them with confidence in himself and friendly feeling towards each other, more than any person I know."

"You are wrong," said Sheffield, "if you think I don't value him extremely, and love him too; it's impossible not to love him. But he's not the person quite to get influence over me."

"He's too much of an Anglican for you," said Reding.

"Not at all," said Sheffield, "except indirectly. My quarrel with him is, that he has many original thoughts, and holds many profound truths in detail, but is quite unable to see how they lie to each other, and equally unable to draw consequences. He never sees a truth until he touches it; he is ever groping and feeling, and, as in hide-and-seek, continually burns without discovering. I know there are ten thousand persons who cannot see an inch before their nose, and who can comfortably digest contradictions; but Carlton is really a clever man; he is no common thinker; this makes it so provoking. When I write an essay for him—I know I write obscurely, and often do not bring out the sequence of my ideas in due order, but, so it is—he is sure to cut out the very thought or statement on which I especially pride myself, on which the whole argument rests, which binds every part together; and he coolly tells me that it is extravagant or far-fetched—not seeing that by leaving it out he has made nonsense of the rest. He is a man to rob an arch of its keystone, and then quietly to build his house upon it."

"Ah, your old failing again," said Reding; "a craving after views. Now, what I like in Carlton, is that repose of his—always saying enough, never too much; never boring you, never taxing you; always practical, never in the clouds. Save me from a viewy man; I could not live with him for a week, present company always excepted."

"Now, considering how hard I have read, and how little I have talked this year past, that is hard on me," said Sheffield. "Did not I go to be one of old Thruston's sixteen pupils, last Long? He gave us capital feeds, smoked with us, and coached us in Ethics and Agamemnon. He knows his books by heart, can repeat his plays backwards, and weighs out his Aristotle by grains and pennyweights; but, for generalizations, ideas, poetry, oh, it was desolation—it was a darkness which could be felt!"

"And you stayed there just six weeks out of four months, Sheffield," answered Reding.

Carlton had now joined them, and, after introductory greetings on both sides, he too threw himself upon the turf. Sheffield said: "Reding and I were disputing just now whether Nicias was a party man."

"Of course you first defined your terms," said Carlton.

"Well," said Sheffield, "I mean by a party man, one who not only belongs to a party, but who has the *animus* of party. Nicias did not make a party, he found one made. He found himself at the head of it; he was no more a party man than a prince who was born the head of his state."

"I should agree with you," said Carlton; "but still I should like to know what a party is, and what a party man."

"A party," said Sheffield, "is merely an extra-constitutional or extra-legal body."

"Party action," said Charles, "is the exertion of influence instead of law."

"But supposing, Reding, there is no law existing in the quarter where influence exerts itself?" asked Carlton.

Charles had to explain: "Certainly," he said, "the State did not legislate for all possible contingencies."

"For instance," continued Carlton, "a prime minister, I have understood, is not acknowledged in the Constitution; he exerts influence beyond the law, but not, in consequence, against any existing law; and it would be absurd to talk of him as a party man."

"Parliamentary parties, too, are recognised among us," said Sheffield, "though extra-constitutional. We call them parties; but who would call the Duke of Devonshire or Lord John Russell, in a bad sense, a party man?"

"It seems to me," said Carlton, "that the formation of a party is merely a recurrence to the original mode of forming into society. You recollect Deioces; he formed a party. He gained influence; he laid the foundation of social order."

"Law certainly begins in influence," said Reding, "for it presupposes a lawgiver; afterwards it supersedes influence; from that time the exertion of influence is a sign of party."

"Too broadly said, as you yourself just now allowed," said Carlton: "you should say that law *begins* to supersede influence, and that *in proportion* as it supersedes it, does the exertion of influence involve party action. For instance, has not the Crown an immense personal influence? We talk of the Court *party*; yet it does not interfere with law, it is intended to conciliate the people to the law."

"But it is recognized by law and constitution," said Charles, "as was the Dictatorship."

"Well, then, take the influence of the clergy," answered Carlton; "we make much of that influence as a principle supplemental to the law, and as a support to the law, yet not created or defined by the law. The law does not recognize what some one calls truly a 'resident gentleman' in every parish. Influence, then, instead of law is not necessarily the action of party."

"So again, national character is an influence distinct from the law," said Sheffield, "according to the line, '*Quid leges sine moribus*?'"

"Law," said Carlton, "is but gradually formed and extended. Well, then, so far as there is no law, there is the reign of influence; there is party without of necessity *party* action. This is the justification of Whigs and Tories at the present day; to supply, as Aristotle says on another subject, the defects of the law. Charles I exerted a regal, Walpole a ministerial influence; but influence, not law, was the operating principle in both cases. The object or the means might be wrong, but the process could not be called party action."

"You would justify, then," said Charles, "the associations or confraternities which existed, for instance, in Athens; not, that is, if they 'took the law into their own hands,' as the phrase goes, but if there was no law to take, or if there was no constituted authority to take it of right. It was a recurrence to the precedent of Deioces."

"Manzoni gives a striking instance of this in the beginning of his *Promessi Sposi*," said Sheffield, "when he describes that protection, which law ought to give to the weak, as being in the sixteenth century sought and found almost exclusively in factions or companies. I don't recollect particulars, but he describes the clergy as busy in extending their immunities, the nobility their privileges, the army their exemptions, the trades and artisans their guilds. Even the lawyers formed a union, and medical men a corporation."

"Thus constitutions are gradually moulded and perfected," said Carlton, "by extra-constitutional bodies, either coming under the protection of law, or else being superseded by the law's providing for their objects. In the middle ages the Church was a vast extra-constitutional body. The German and Anglo-Norman sovereigns sought to bring its operation *under* the law; modern parliaments have superseded its operation *by law*. Then the State wished to gain the right of investitures; now the State marries, registers, manages the poor, exercises ecclesiastical jurisdiction instead of the Church."

"This will make ostracism parallel to the Reformation or the Revolution," said Sheffield; "there is a battle of influence against influence, and one gets rid of the other; law or constitution does not come into question, but the will of the people or of the court ejects, whether the too-gifted individual, or the monarch, or the religion. What was not under the law could not be dealt with, had no claim to be dealt with, by the law."

"A thought has sometimes struck me," said Reding, "which falls in with what you have been saying. In the last half-century there has been a gradual formation of the popular party in the State, which now tends to be acknowledged as constitutional, or is already so acknowledged. My father never could endure newspapers—I mean the system of newspapers; he said it was a new power in the State. I am sure I am not defending what he was thinking of, the many bad proceedings, the wretched principles, the arrogance and tyranny of newspaper writers, but I am trying the subject by the test of your theory. The great body of the people are very imperfectly represented in parliament; the Commons are not their voice, but the voice of certain great interests. Consequently the press comes in—to do that which the constitution does not do—to form the people into a vast mutual-protection association. And this is done by the same right that Deioces had to collect people about him; it does not interfere with the existing territory of the law, but builds where the constitution has not made provision. It *tends*, then, ultimately to be recognised by the constitution."

"There is another remarkable phenomenon of a similar kind

now in process of development," said Carlton, "and that is, the influence of agitation. I really am not politician enough to talk of it as good or bad; one's natural instinct is against it; but it may be necessary. However, agitation is getting to be recognised as the legitimate instrument by which the masses make their desires known, and secure the accomplishment of them. Just as a bill passes in parliament, after certain readings, discussions, speeches, votings, and the like, so the process by which an act of the popular will becomes law is a long agitation, issuing in petitions, previous to and concurrent with the parliamentary process. The first instance of this was about fifty or sixty years ago, when... Hallo!" he cried, "who is this cantering up to us?"

"I declare it is old Vincent," said Sheffield.

"He is to come to dine," said Charles, "just in time."

"How are you, Carlton?" cried Vincent. "How d'ye do, Mr. Sheffield? Mr. Reding, how d'ye do? Acting up to your name, I suppose, for you were ever a reading man. For myself," he continued, "I am just now an eating man, and am come to dine with you, if you will let me. Have you a place for my horse?"

There was a farmer near who could lend a stable; so the horse was led off by Charles; and the rider, without any delay—for the hour did not admit it—entered the cottage to make his brief preparation for dinner.

CHAPTER II

In a few minutes all met together at table in the small parlour, which was room of all work in the cottage. They had not the whole house, limited as were its resources; for it was also the habitation of a gardener, who took his vegetables to the Oxford market, and whose wife (what is called) *did* for his lodgers.

Dinner was suited to the apartment, apartment to the dinner.

The book-table had been hastily cleared for a cloth, not over white, and, in consequence, the sole remaining table, which acted as side-board, displayed a relay of plates and knives and forks, in the midst of octavos and duodecimos, bound and unbound, piled up and thrown about in great variety of shapes. The other ornaments of this side-table were an ink-glass, some quires of large paper, a straw hat, a gold watch, a clothes-brush, some bottles of ginger-beer, a pair of gloves, a case of cigars, a neck-handkerchief, a shoe-horn, a small slate, a large clasp-knife, a hammer, and a handsome inlaid writing-desk.

"I like these rides into the country," said Vincent, as they began eating, "the country loses its effect on me when I live in it, as you do; but it is exquisite as a zest. Visit it, do not live in it, if you would enjoy it. Country air is a stimulus; stimulants, Mr. Reding, should not be taken too often. You are of the country party. I am of no party. I go here and there—like the bee—I taste of everything, I depend on nothing."

Sheffield said that this was rather belonging to all parties than to none.

"That is impossible," answered Vincent; "I hold it to be altogether impossible. You can't belong to two parties; there's no fear of it; you might as well attempt to be in two places at once. To be connected with both is to be united with neither. Depend on it, my young friend, antagonist principles correct each other. It's a piece of philosophy which one day you will thank me for, when you are older."

"I have heard of an American illustration of this," said Sheffield, "which certainly confirms what you say, sir. Professors in the United States are sometimes of two or three religions at once, according as we regard them historically, personally, or officially. In this way, perhaps, they hit the mean."

Vincent, though he so often excited a smile in others, had no humour himself, and never could make out the difference between irony and earnest. Accordingly he was brought to a stand.

Charles came to his relief. "Before dinner," he said, "we were sporting what you will consider a great paradox, I am afraid; that parties were good things, or rather necessary things."

"You don't do me justice," answered Vincent, "if this is what you think I deny. I halve your words; parties are not good, but necessary; like snails, I neither envy them their small houses, nor try to lodge in them myself."

"You mean," said Carlton, "that parties do our dirty work; they are our beasts of burden; we could not get on without them, but we need not identify ourselves with them; we may keep aloof."

"That," said Sheffield, "is something like those religious professors who say that it is sinful to engage in worldly though necessary occupations; but that the reprobate undertake them, and work for the elect."

"There will always be persons enough in the world who like to be party men, without being told to be so," said Vincent; "it's our business to turn them to account, to use them, but to keep aloof. I take it, all parties are partly right, only they go too far. I borrow from each, I co-operate with each, as far as each is right, and no further. Thus I get good from all, and I do good to all; for I countenance each, so far as it is true."

"Mr. Carlton meant more than that, sir," said Sheffield; "he meant that the existence of parties was not only necessary and useful, but even right."

"Mr. Carlton is not the man to make paradoxes," said Vincent; "I suspect he would not defend the extreme opinions, which, alas, exist among us at present, and are progressing every day."

"I was speaking of political parties," said Carlton, "but I am disposed to extend what I said to religious also."

"But, my good Carlton," said Vincent, "Scripture speaks against religious parties."

"Certainly I don't wish to oppose Scripture," said Carlton, "and

I speak under correction of Scripture; but I say this, that whenever and wherever a church does not decide religious points, so far does it leave the decision to individuals; and, since you can't expect all people to agree together, you must have different opinions; and the expression of those different opinions, by the various persons who hold them, is what is called a party."

"Mr. Carlton has been great, sir, on the general subject before dinner," said Sheffield, "and now he draws the corollary, that whenever there are parties in a church, a church may thank itself for them. They are the certain effect of private judgment; and the more private judgment you have, the more parties you will have. You are reduced, then, to this alternative, no toleration or else party; and you must recognise party, unless you refuse toleration."

"Sheffield words it more strongly than I should do," said Carlton; "but really I mean pretty much what he says. Take the case of the Roman Catholics; they have decided many points of theology, many they have not decided; and wherever there is no ecclesiastical decision, there they have at once a party, or what they call a 'school'; and when the ecclesiastical decision at length appears, then the party ceases. Thus you have the Dominicans and Franciscans contending about the Immaculate Conception; they went on contending because authority did not at once decide the question. On the other hand, when Jesuits and Jansenists disputed on the question of grace, the Pope gave it in favour of the Jesuits, and the controversy at once came to an end."

"Surely," said Vincent, "my good and worthy friend, the Rev. Charles Carlton, Fellow of Leicester, and sometime Ireland Essayist, is not preferring the Church of Rome to the Church of England?"

Carlton laughed; "You won't suspect me of that, I think," he answered; "no; all I say is, that our Church, from its constitution, admits, approves of private judgment; and that private judgment, so far forth as it is admitted, necessarily involves parties; the slender private judgment allowed in the Church of Rome admitting occasional or local parties, and the ample private judgment allowed in our Church recognizing parties as an element of the Church."

"Well, well, my good Carlton," said Vincent, frowning and looking wise, yet without finding anything particular to say.

"You mean," said Sheffield, "if I understand you, that it is a piece of mawkish hypocrisy to shake the head and throw up the eyes at Mr. this or that for being the head of a religious party, while we return thanks for our pure and reformed Church; because purity, reformation, apostolicity, toleration, all these boasts and glories of the Church of England, establish party action and party spirit as a cognate blessing, for which we should be thankful also. Party is one of our greatest ornaments, Mr. Vincent."

"A sentiment or argument does not lose in your hands," said Carlton; "but what I meant was simply that party leaders are not dishonourable in the Church, unless Lord John Russell or Sir Robert Peel hold a dishonourable post in the State."

"My young friend," said Vincent, finishing his mutton, and pushing his plate from him, "my two young friends—for Carlton is not much older than Mr. Sheffield—may you learn a little more judgment. When you have lived to my age" (viz. two or three years beyond Carlton's) "you will learn sobriety in all things. Mr. Reding, another glass of wine. See that poor child, how she totters under the gooseberry-pudding; up, Mr. Sheffield, and help her. The old woman cooks better than I had expected. How do you get your butcher's meat here, Carlton? I should have made the attempt to bring you a fine jack I saw in our kitchen, but I thought you would have no means of cooking it."

Dinner over, the party rose, and strolled out on the green. Another subject commenced.

"Was not Mr. Willis of St. George's a friend of yours, Mr. Reding?" asked Vincent.

Charles started.

"I knew him a little… I have seen him several times."

"You know he left us," continued Vincent, "and joined the Church of Rome. Well, it is credibly reported that he is returning."

"A melancholy history, anyhow," answered Charles; "most melancholy, if this is true."

"Rather," said Vincent, setting him right, as if he had simply made a verbal mistake, "a most happy termination, you mean; the only thing that was left for him to do. You know he went abroad. Any one who is inclined to Romanize should go abroad; Carlton, we shall be sending you soon. Here things are softened down; there you see the Church of Rome as it really is. I have been abroad, and should know it. Such heaps of beggars in the streets of Rome and Naples; so much squalidness and misery; no cleanliness; an utter want of comfort; and such superstition; and such an absence of all true and evangelical seriousness. They push and fight while Mass is going on; they jabber their prayers at railroad speed; they worship the Virgin as a goddess; and they see miracles at the corner of every street. Their images are awful, and their ignorance prodigious. Well, Willis saw all this; and I have it on good authority," he said mysteriously, "that he is thoroughly disgusted with the whole affair, and is coming back to us."

"Is he in England now?" asked Reding.

"He is said to be with his mother in Devonshire, who, perhaps you know, is a widow; and he has been too much for her. Poor silly fellow, who would not take the advice of older heads! A friend once sent him to me; I could make nothing of him. I couldn't understand his arguments, nor he mine. It was no good; he would make trial himself, and he has caught it."

There was a short pause in the conversation; then Vincent added, "But such perversions, Carlton, I suppose, thinks to be as necessary as parties in a pure Protestant Church."

"I can't say you satisfy me, Carlton," said Charles; "and I am happy to have the sanction of Mr. Vincent. Did political party make men rebels, then would political party be indefensible; so is religious, if it leads to apostasy."

"You know the Whigs *were* accused in the last war," said Sheffield, "of siding with Bonaparte; accidents of this kind don't affect general rules or standing customs."

"Well, independent of this," answered Charles, "I cannot think religious parties defensible on the considerations which justify political. There is, to my feelings, something despicable in heading a religious party."

"Was Loyola despicable," asked Sheffield, "or St. Dominic?"

"They had the sanction of their superiors," said Charles.

"You are hard on parties surely, Reding," said Carlton; "a man may individually write, preach, and publish what he believes to be the truth, without offence; why, then, does it begin to be wrong when he does so together with others?"

"Party tactics are a degradation of the truth," said Charles.

"We have heard, I believe, before now," said Carlton, "of Athanasius against the whole world, and the whole world against Athanasius."

"Well," answered Charles, "I will but say this, that a party man must be very much above par or below it."

"There, again, I don't agree," said Carlton; "you are supposing the leader of a party to be conscious of what he is doing; and, being conscious, he may be, as you say, either much above or below the average; but a man need not realise to himself that he is forming a party."

"That's more difficult to conceive," said Vincent, "than any statement which has been hazarded this afternoon."

"Not at all difficult," answered Carlton: "do you mean that there is only one way of gaining influence? Surely there is such a thing as unconscious influence?"

"I'd as easily believe," said Vincent, "that a beauty does not know her charms."

“That’s narrow-minded,” retorted Carlton: “a man sits in his room and writes, and does not know what people think of him.”

“I’d believe it less,” persisted Vincent: “beauty is a fact; influence is an effect. Effects imply agents, agency, will and consciousness.”

“There are different modes of influence,” interposed Sheffield; “influence is often spontaneous and almost necessary.”

“Like the light on Moses’ face,” said Carlton.

“Bonaparte is said to have had an irresistible smile,” said Sheffield.

“What is beauty itself, but a spontaneous influence?” added Carlton; “don’t you recollect ‘the lovely young Lavinia’ in Thomson?”

“Well, gentlemen,” said Vincent, “when I am Chancellor I will give a prize essay on ‘Moral Influence, its Kinds and Causes,’ and Mr. Sheffield shall get it; and as to Carlton, he shall be my Poetry Professor when I am Convocation.”

You will say, good reader, that the party took a very short stroll on the hill, when we tell you that they were now stooping their heads at the lowly door of the cottage; but the terse *littera scripta* abridges wondrously the rambling *vox emissa*; and there might be other things said in the course of the conversation which history has not condescended to record. Anyhow, we are obliged now to usher them again into the room where they had dined, and where they found tea ready laid, and the kettle speedily forthcoming. The bread and butter were excellent; and the party did justice to them, as if they had not lately dined. “I see you keep your tea in tin cases,” said Vincent; “I am for glass. Don’t spare the tea, Mr. Reding; Oxford men do not commonly fail on that head. Lord Bacon says the first and best juice of the grape, like the primary, purest, and best comment on Scripture, is not pressed and forced out, but consists of a natural exudation. This is the case in Italy at this day; and they call the juice ‘*lagrima*.’ So it is with tea, and with coffee too. Put in a large quantity, pour on the water, turn off the liquor; turn it off at once—don’t let it stand; it becomes poisonous. I am a great patron of tea; the poet truly says, 'It cheers, but not inebriates.' It has sometimes a singular effect upon my nerves; it makes me whistle—so people tell me; I am not conscious of it. Sometimes, too, it has a dyspeptic effect. I find it does not do to take it too hot; we English drink our liquors too hot. It is not a French failing; no, indeed. In France, that is, in the country, you get nothing for breakfast but acid wine and grapes; this is the other extreme, and has before now affected me awfully. Yet acids, too, have a soothing sedative effect upon one; lemonade especially. But nothing suits me so well as tea. Carlton," he continued mysteriously, "do you know the late Dr. Baillie's preventive of the flatulency which tea produces? Mr. Sheffield, do you?" Both gave up. "Camomile flowers; a little camomile, not a great deal; some people chew rhubarb, but a little camomile in the tea is not perceptible. Don't make faces, Mr. Sheffield; a little, I say; a little of everything is best—*ne quid nimis*. Avoid all extremes. So it is with sugar. Mr. Reding, you are putting too much into your tea. I lay down this rule: sugar should not be a substantive ingredient in tea, but an adjective; that is, tea has a natural roughness; sugar is only intended to remove that roughness; it has a negative office; when it is more than this, it is too much. Well, Carlton, it is time for me to be seeing after my horse. I fear he has not had so pleasant an afternoon as I. I have enjoyed myself much in your suburban villa. What a beautiful moon! but I have some very rough ground to pass over. I daren't canter over the ruts with the gravel-pits close before me. Mr. Sheffield, do me the favour to show me the way to the stable. Good-bye to you, Carlton; good night, Mr. Reding."

When they were left to themselves Charles asked Carlton if he really meant to acquit of party spirit the present party leaders in Oxford. "You must not misunderstand me," answered he; "I do not know much of them, but I know they are persons of great merit and high character, and I wish to think the best of them. They are most unfairly attacked, that is certain; however, they are accused of wishing to make a display, of aiming at influence and power, of loving agitation, and so on. I cannot deny that some things they have done have an unpleasant appearance, and give plausibility to the charge. I wish they had, at certain times, acted otherwise. Meanwhile, I do think it but fair to keep in view that the existence of parties is no fault of theirs. They are but claiming their birthright as Protestants. When the Church does not speak, others will speak instead; and learned men have the best right to speak. Again, when learned men speak, others will attend to them; and thus the formation of a party is rather the act of those who follow than of those who lead."

CHAPTER III

SHEFFIELD had some friends residing at Chalton, a neighbouring village, with a scholar of St. Michael's, who had a small cure with a house on it. One of them, indeed, was known to Reding also, being no other than our friend White, who was going into the schools, and during the last six months had been trying to make up for the time he had wasted in the first years of his residence. Charles had lost sight of him, or nearly so, since he first knew him; and at their time of life so considerable an interval could not elapse without changes in the character for good or evil, or for both. Carlton and Charles, who were a good deal thrown together by Sheffield's frequent engagements with the Chalton party, were just turning homewards in their walk one evening when they fell in with White, who had been calling at Mr. Bolton's in Oxford, and was returning. They had not proceeded very far before they were joined by Sheffield and Mr. Barry, the curate of Chalton; and thus the party was swelled to five.

"So you are going to lose Upton?" said Barry to Reding; "a capital tutor; you can ill spare him. Who comes into his place?"

"We don't know," answered Charles; "the Principal will call up one of the Junior Fellows from the country, I believe."

"Oh, but you won't get a man like Upton," said Carlton; "he knew his subject so thoroughly. His lecture in the Agricola, I've heard your men say, might have been published. It was a masterly, minute running comment on the text, quite exhausting it."

"Yes, it was his forte," said Charles; "yet he never loaded his lectures; everything he said had a meaning, and was wanted."

"He has got a capital living," said Barry; "a substantial modern house, and by the rail only an hour from London."

"And 500*l.* a year," said White; "Mr. Bolton went over the living, and told me so. It's in my future neighbourhood; a very beautiful country, and a number of good families round about."

"They say he's going to marry the Dean of Selsey's daughter," said Barry; "do you know the family? Miss Juliet, the thirteenth, a very pretty girl."

"Yes," said White, "I know them all; a most delightful family; Mrs. Bland is a charming woman, so very ladylike. It's my good luck to be under the Dean's jurisdiction; I think I shall pull with him capitally."

"He's a clever man," said Barry; "his charges are always well written; he had a high name in his day at Cambridge."

"Hasn't he been lately writing against your friends here, White?" said Sheffield.

"*My* friends!" said White; "whom can you mean? He has written against parties and party leaders; and with reason, I think. Oh, yes; he alluded to poor Willis and some others."

"It was more that that," insisted Sheffield; "he charged against certain sayings and doings at St. Mary's."

"Well, I for one cannot approve of all that is uttered from the pulpit there," said White; "I know for a fact that Willis refers with great satisfaction to what he heard there as inclining him to Romanism."

"I wish preachers and hearers would all go over together at once, and then we should have some quiet time for proper University studies," said Barry.

"Take care what you are saying, Barry," said Sheffield; "you mean present company excepted. You, White, I think, come under the denomination of hearers?"

"I!" said White; "no such thing. I have been to hear him before now, as most men have; but I think him often very injudicious, or worse. The tendency of his preaching is to make one dissatisfied with one's own Church."

"Well," said Sheffield, "one's memory plays one tricks, or I should say that a friend of mine had said ten times as strong things against our Church as any preacher in Oxford ever did."

"You mean me," said White, with earnestness; "you have misunderstood me grievously. I have ever been most faithful to the Church of England. You never heard me say anything inconsistent with the warmest attachment to it. I have never, indeed, denied the claims of the Romish Church to be a branch of the Catholic Church, nor will I—that's another thing quite; there are many things which we might borrow with great advantage from the Romanists. But I have ever loved, and hope I shall ever venerate, my own Mother, the Church of my baptism."

Sheffield made an odd face, and no one spoke. White continued, attempting to preserve an unconcerned manner: "It is remarkable," he said, "that Mr. Bolton—who, though a layman, and no divine, is a sensible, practical, shrewd man—never liked that pulpit; he always prophesied no good would come of it."

The silence continuing, White presently fell upon Sheffield. "I defy you," he said, with an attempt to be jocular, "to prove what you have been hinting; it is a great shame. It's so easy to speak against men, to call them injudicious, extravagant, and so on. You are the only person—"

"Well, well, I know it, I know it," said Sheffield; "we're only canonizing you, and I am the devil's advocate."

Charles wanted to hear something about Willis; so he turned

the current of White's thoughts by coming up and asking him whether there was any truth in the report he had heard from Vincent several weeks before; had White heard from him lately? White knew very little about him definitely, and was not able to say whether the report was true or not. So far was certain, that he had returned from abroad and was living at home. Thus he had not committed himself to the Church of Rome, whether as a theological student or as a novice; but he could not say more. Yes, he had heard one thing more; and the subject of a letter which he had received from him corroborated it—that he was very strong on the point that Romanism and Anglicanism were two religions; that you could not amalgamate them; that you must be Roman or Anglican, but could not be Anglo-Roman or Anglo-Catholic. "This is what a friend told me. In his letter to myself," White continued, "I don't know quite what he meant, but he spoke a good deal of the necessity of faith in order to be a Catholic. He said no one should go over merely because he thought he should like it better; that he had found out by experience that no one could live on sentiment; that the whole system of worship in the Romish Church was different from what it is in our own; nay, the very idea of worship, the idea of prayers; that the doctrine of intention itself, viewed in all its parts, constituted a new religion. He did not speak of himself definitely, but he said generally that all this might be a great discouragement to a convert, and throw him back. On the whole, the tone of his letter was like a person disappointed, and who might be reclaimed; at least, so I thought."

"He is a wiser, even if he is a sadder man," said Charles: "I did not know he had so much in him. There is more reflection in all this than so excitable a person, as he seemed to me, is capable of exercising. At the same time there is nothing in all this to prove that he is sorry for what he has done."

"I have granted this," said White; "still the effect of the letter was to keep people back from following him, by putting obstacles in their way; and then we must couple this with the fact of his going home."

Charles thought awhile. "Vincent's testimony," he said, "is either a confirmation or a mere exaggeration of what you have told me, according as it is independent or not." Then he said to himself, "White, too, has more in him than I thought; he really has spoken about Willis very sensibly: what has come to him?"

The paths soon divided; and while the Chalton pair took the right hand, Carlton and his pupils turned to the left. Soon Carlton parted from the two friends, and they reached their cottage just in time to see the setting sun.

CHAPTER IV

A FEW days later, Carlton, Sheffield, and Reding were talking together after dinner out of doors about White.

"How he is altered," said Charles, "since I first knew him!"

"Altered!" cried Sheffield; "he was a playful kitten once, and now he is one of the dullest old tabbies I ever came across."

"Altered for the better," said Charles; "he has now a steady sensible way of talking; but he was not a very wise person two years ago; he is reading, too, really hard."

"He has some reason," said Sheffield, "for he is sadly behindhand; but there is another cause of his steadiness which perhaps you know."

"I! no indeed," answered Charles.

"I thought of course you knew it," said Sheffield; "you don't mean to say you have not heard that he is engaged to some Oxford girl?"

"Engaged!" cried Charles, "how absurd!"

"I don't see that at all, my dear Reding," said Carlton. "It's not as if he could not afford it; he has a good living waiting for him;

and, moreover, he is thus losing no time, which is a great thing in life. Much time is often lost. White will soon find himself settled in every sense of the word, in mind, in life, in occupation."

Charles said that there was one thing which could not help surprising him, namely, that when White first came up he was so strong in his advocacy of clerical celibacy. Carlton and Sheffield laughed. "And do you think," said the former, "that a youth of eighteen can have an opinion on such a subject, or knows himself well enough to make a resolution in his own case? Do you really think it fair to hold a man committed to all the random opinions and extravagant sayings into which he was betrayed when he first left school?"

"He had read some ultra-book or other," said Sheffield; "or had seen some beautiful nun sculptured on a chancel-screen, and was carried away by romance—as others have been and are."

"Don't you suppose," said Carlton, "that those good fellows who now are so full of 'sacerdotal purity,' 'angelical blessedness,' and so on, will one and all be married by this time ten years?"

"I'll take a bet of it," said Sheffield: "one will give in early, one late, but there is a time destined for all. Pass some ten or twelve years, as Carlton says, and we shall find A.B. on a curacy, the happy father of ten children; C.D. wearing on a long courtship till a living falls; E.F. in his honeymoon; G.H. lately presented by Mrs. H. with twins; I.K. full of joy, just accepted; L.M. may remain what Gibbon calls 'a column in the midst of ruins,' and a very tottering column too."

"Do you really think," said Charles, "that people mean so little what they say?"

"You take matters too seriously, Reding," answered Carlton; "who does not change his opinions between twenty and thirty? A young man enters life with his father's or tutor's views; he changes them for his own. The more modest and diffident he is, the more faith he has, so much the longer does he speak the words of others; but the force of circumstances, or the vigour of his mind, infallibly obliges him at last to have a mind of his own; that is, if he is good for anything."

"But I suspect," said Reding, "that the last generation, whether of fathers or tutors, had no very exalted ideas of clerical celibacy."

"Accidents often clothe us with opinions which we wear for a time," said Carlton.

"Well, I honour people who wear their family suit; I don't honour those at all who begin with foreign fashions and then abandon them."

"A few years more of life," said Carlton, smiling, "will make your judgment kinder."

"I don't like talkers," continued Charles; "I don't think I ever shall; I hope not."

"I know better what's at the bottom of it," said Sheffield; "but I can't stay; I must go in and read; Reding is too fond of a gossip."

"Who talks so much as you, Sheffield?" said Charles.

"But I talk fast when I talk," answered he, "and get through a great deal of work; then I give over: but you prose, and muse, and sigh, and prose again." And so he left them.

"What does he mean?" asked Carlton.

Charles slightly coloured and laughed: "You are a man I say things to, I don't to others," he made answer; "as to Sheffield, he fancies he has found it out of himself."

Carlton looked round at him sharply and curiously.

"I am ashamed of myself," said Charles, laughing and looking confused; "I have made you think that I have something important to tell, but really I have nothing at all."

"Well, out with it," said Carlton.

"Why, to tell the truth—no, really, it is too absurd. I have made a fool of myself."

He turned away, then turned back, and resumed:

"Why, it was only this, that Sheffield fancies I have some sneaking kindness for...celibacy myself."

"Kindness for whom?" said Carlton.

"Kindness for celibacy."

There was a pause, and Carlton's face somewhat changed.

"Oh, my dear good fellow," he said kindly, "so you are one of them; but it will go off."

"Perhaps it will," said Charles: "oh, I am laying no stress upon it. It was Sheffield who made me mention it."

A real difference of mind and view had evidently been struck upon by two friends, very congenial and very fond of each other. There was a pause for a few seconds.

"You are so sensible a fellow, Reding," said Carlton, "it surprises me that you should take up this notion."

"It's no new notion taken up," answered Charles; "you will smile, but I had it when a boy at school, and I have ever since fancied that I should never marry. Not that the feeling has never intermitted, but it is the habit of my mind. My general thoughts run in that one way, that I shall never marry. If I did, I should dread Thalaba's punishment."

Carlton put his hand on Reding's shoulder, and gently shook him to and fro; "Well, it surprises me," he said; then, after a pause, "I have been accustomed to think both celibacy and marriage good in their way. In the Church of Rome great good, I see, comes of celibacy; but depend on it, my dear Reding, you are making a great blunder if you are for introducing celibacy into the Anglican Church."

"There's nothing against it in Prayer Book or Articles," said Charles.

"Perhaps not; but the whole genius, structure, working of our Church goes the other way. For instance, we have no monasteries to relieve the poor; and if we had, I suspect, as things are, a parson's wife would, in practical substantial usefulness, be infinitely superior to all the monks that were ever shaven. I declare, I think the Bishop of Ipswich is almost justified in giving out that none but married men have a chance of preferment from him; nay, the Bishop of Abingdon, who makes a rule of bestowing his best livings as marriage portions to the most virtuous young ladies in his diocese." Carlton spoke with more energy than was usual with him.

Charles answered, that he was not looking to the expediency or feasibility of the thing, but at what seemed to him best in itself, and what he could not help admiring. "I said nothing about the celibacy of clergy," he observed, "but of celibacy generally."

"Celibacy has no place in our idea or our system of religion, depend on it," said Carlton. "It is nothing to the purpose, whether there is anything in the Articles against it; it is not a question about formal enactments, but whether the genius of Anglicanism is not utterly at variance with it. The experience of three hundred years is surely abundant for our purpose; if we don't know what our religion is in that time, what time will be long enough? There are forms of religion which have not lasted so long from first to last. Now enumerate the cases of celibacy for celibacy's sake in that period, and what will be the sum total of them? Some instances there are; but even Hammond, who died unmarried, was going to marry, when his mother wished it. On the other hand, if you look out for types of our Church can you find truer than the married excellence of Hooker the profound, Taylor the devotional, and Bull the polemical? The very first reformed primate is married; in Pole and Parker, the two systems, Roman and Anglican, come into strong contrast."

"Well, it seems to me as much a yoke of bondage," said Charles, "to compel marriage as to compel celibacy, and that is what you are really driving at. You are telling me that any one is a black sheep who does not marry."

"Not a very practical difficulty to you at this moment," said Carlton; "no one is asking you to go about on Coelebs' mission just now, with Aristotle in hand and the class-list in view."

"Well, excuse me," said Charles, "if I have said anything very foolish; you don't suppose I argue on such subjects with others."

CHAPTER V

THEY had by this time strolled as far as Carlton's lodgings, where the books happened to be on which Charles was at that time more immediately employed; and they took two or three turns under some fine beeches which stood in front of the house before entering it.

"Tell me, Reding," said Carlton, "for really I don't understand, what are your reasons for admiring what, in truth, is simply an unnatural state."

"Don't let us talk more, my dear Carlton," answered Reding; "I shall go on making a fool of myself. Let well alone, or bad alone, pray do."

It was evident that there was some strong feeling irritating him inwardly; the manner and words were too serious for the occasion. Carlton, too, felt strongly upon what seemed at first sight a very secondary question, or he would have let it alone, as Charles asked him.

"No; as we are on the subject, let me get at your view," said he. "It was said in the beginning, 'Increase and multiply'; therefore celibacy is unnatural."

"Supernatural," said Charles, smiling.

"Is not that a word without an idea?" asked Carlton. "We are taught by Butler that there is an analogy between nature and grace; else you might parallel paganism to nature, and where paganism is contrary to nature, say that it is supernatural. The Wesleyan convulsions are preternatural; why not supernatural?"

"I really think that our divines, or at least some of them, are on my side here," said Charles—"Jeremy Taylor, I believe."

"You have not told me what you mean by supernatural," said Carlton; "I want to get at what *you* think, you know."

"It seems to me," said Charles, "that Christianity, being the perfection of nature, is both like it and unlike it—like it, where it is the same or as much as nature; unlike it, where it is as much and more.

I mean by supernatural the perfection of nature."

"Give me an instance," said Carlton.

"Why, consider, Carlton; our Lord says, 'Ye have heard that it has been said of old time—but *I* say unto you'; that contrast denotes the more perfect way, or the gospel... He came not to destroy, but to fulfil the law... I can't recollect of a sudden...oh, for instance, *this* is a case in point; He abolished a permission which had been given to the Jews because of the hardness of their hearts."

"Not quite in point," said Carlton, "for the Jews, in their divorces, had fallen *below* nature. 'Let no man put asunder,' was the rule in Paradise."

"Still, surely the idea of an Apostle, unmarried, pure, in fast and nakedness, and at length a martyr, is a higher idea than that of one of the old Israelites sitting under his vine and fig-tree, full of temporal goods, and surrounded by sons and grandsons. I am not derogating from Gideon or Caleb; I am adding to St. Paul."

"St. Paul's is a very particular case," said Carlton.

"But he himself lays down the general maxim, that it is 'good' for a man to continue as he was."

"There we come to a question of criticism, what 'good' means: I may think it means 'expedient,' and what he says about the 'present distress' confirms it."

"Well, I won't go to criticism," said Charles; "take the text, 'in sin hath my mother conceived me.' Do not these words show that, over and above the doctrine of original sin, there is (to say the least) great risk of marriage leading to sin in married people?"

"My dear Reding," said Carlton, astonished, "you are running into Gnosticism."

"Not knowingly or willingly," answered Charles; "but understand what I mean. It's not a subject I can talk about; but it seems to me, without of course saying that married persons must sin (which would be Gnosticism), that there is a danger of sin. But don't let me say more on this point."

"Well," said Carlton, after thinking awhile, "*I* have been accustomed to consider Christianity as the perfection of man as a whole, body, soul, and spirit. Don't misunderstand me. Pantheists say body and intellect, leaving out the moral principle; but I say spirit as well as mind. Spirit, or the principle of religious faith and obedience, should be the master principle, the *hegemonicon.* To this both intellect and body are subservient; but as this supremacy does not imply the ill-usage, the bondage of the intellect, neither does it of the body; both should be well treated."

"Well, I think, on the contrary, it does imply in one sense the bondage of intellect and body too. What is faith but the submission of the intellect? And as 'every high thought is brought into captivity,' so are we expressly told to bring the body into subjection too. They are both well treated, when they are treated so as to be made fit instruments of the sovereign principle."

"That is what I call unnatural," said Carlton.

"And it is what I mean by supernatural," answered Reding, getting a little too earnest.

"How is it supernatural, or adding to nature, to destroy a part of it?" asked Carlton.

Charles was puzzled. It was a way, he said, *towards* perfection; but he thought that perfection came after death, not here. Our nature could not be perfect with a corruptible body; the body was treated now as a body of death.

"Well, Reding," answered Carlton, "you make Christianity a very different religion from what our Church considers it, I really think"; and he paused awhile.

"Look here," he proceeded, "how can we rejoice in Christ, as having been redeemed by Him, if we are in this sort of gloomy penitential state? How much is said in St. Paul about peace, thanksgiving, assurance, comfort, and the like! Old things are passed away; the Jewish law is destroyed; pardon and peace are come; *that* is the Gospel."

"Don't you think, then," said Charles, "that we should grieve for the sins into which we are daily betrayed, and for the more serious offences which from time to time we may have committed?"

"Certainly; we do so in Morning and Evening Prayer, and in the Communion Service."

"Well, but supposing a youth, as is so often the case, has neglected religion altogether, and has a whole load of sins, and very heinous ones, all upon him—do you think that, when he turns over a new leaf, and comes to Communion, he is, on saying the Confession (saying it with that contrition with which such persons ought to say it), pardoned at once, and has nothing more to fear about his past sins?"

"I should say, 'Yes,'" answered Carlton.

"Really," said Charles thoughtfully.

"Of course," said Carlton, "I suppose him truly sorry or penitent: whether he is so or not his future life will show."

"Well, somehow, I cannot master this idea," said Charles; "I think most serious persons, even for a little sin, would go on fidgeting themselves, and would not suppose they gained pardon directly they asked for it."

"Certainly," answered Carlton; "but God pardons those who do not pardon themselves."

"That is," said Charles, "who *don't* at once feel peace, assurance, and comfort; who *don't* feel the perfect joy of the Gospel."

"Such persons grieve, but rejoice too," said Carlton.

"But tell me, Carlton," said Reding; "is, or is not, their not forgiving themselves, their sorrow and trouble, pleasing to God?"

"Surely."

"Thus a certain self-infliction for sin committed is pleasing to Him; and, if so, how does it matter whether it is inflicted on mind or body?"

"It is not properly a self-infliction," answered Carlton; "self-infliction implies intention; grief at sin is something spontaneous.

When you afflict yourself on purpose, then at once you pass from pure Christianity."

"Well," said Charles, "I certainly fancied that fasting, abstinence, labours, celibacy, might be taken as a make-up for sin. It is not a very far-fetched idea. You recollect Dr. Johnson's standing in the rain in the market-place at Lichfield when a man, as a penance for some disobedience to his father when a boy?"

"But, my dear Reding," said Carlton, "let me bring you back to what you said originally, and to my answer to you, which what you now say only makes more apposite. You began by saying that celibacy was a perfection of nature, now you make it a penance; first it is good and glorious, next it is a medicine and punishment."

"Perhaps our highest perfection here is penance," said Charles; "but I don't know; I don't profess to have clear ideas upon the subject. I have talked more than I like. Let us at length give over."

They did, in consequence, pass to other subjects connected with Charles's reading; then they entered the house, and set to upon Polybius; but it could not be denied that for the rest of the day Carlton's manner was not quite his own, as if something had annoyed him. Next morning he was as usual.

CHAPTER VI

It is impossible to stop the growth of the mind. Here was Charles with his thoughts turned away from religious controversy for two years, yet with his religious views progressing, unknown to himself, the whole time. It could not have been otherwise, if he was to live a religious life at all. If he was to worship and obey his Creator, intellectual acts, conclusions, and judgments, must accompany that worship and obedience. He might not realize his own belief till questions had been put to him; but then a single discussion with a friend, such as the above with Carlton, would bring out what he really did hold to his own apprehension—would ascertain for him the limits of each opinion as he held it, and the inter-relations of opinion with opinion. He had not yet given names to these opinions, much less had they taken a theological form; nor could they, under his circumstances, be expressed in theological language; but here he was, a young man of twenty-two, professing in an hour's conversation with a friend, what really were the Catholic doctrines and usages of penance, purgatory, councils of perfection, mortification of self, and clerical celibacy. No wonder that all this annoyed Carlton, though he no more than Charles perceived that all this Catholicism did in fact lie hid under his professions; but he felt, in what Reding put out, the presence of something, as he expressed it, "very unlike the Church of England"; something new and unpleasant to him, and withal something which had a body in it, which had a momentum, which could not be passed over as a vague, sudden sound or transitory cloud, but which had much behind it, which made itself felt, which struck heavily.

And here we see what is meant when a person says that the Catholic system comes home to his mind, fulfils his ideas of religion, satisfies his sympathies, and the like; and thereupon becomes a Catholic. Such a person is often said to go by private judgment, to be choosing his religion by his own standard of what a religion ought to be. Now it need not be denied that those who are external to the Church must begin with private judgment; they use it in order ultimately to supersede it; as a man out of doors uses a lamp in a dark night, and puts it out when he gets home. What would be thought of his bringing it into his drawing-room? What would the goodly company there assembled before a genial hearth and under glittering chandeliers, the bright ladies and the well-dressed gentlemen, say to him if he came in with a great-coat on his back, a hat on his head, an umbrella under his arm, and a large stable-lantern in his hand? Yet what would be thought, on the other hand, if he precipitated himself into the inhospitable night and the war of the elements in his ball-dress? "When the king came in to see the guests, he saw a man who had not on a wedding-garment"; he saw a man who determined to live in the Church as he had lived out of it, who would not use his privileges, who would not exchange reason for faith, who would not accommodate his thoughts and doings to the glorious scene which surrounded him, who was groping for the hidden treasure and digging for the pearl of price in the high, lustrous, all-jewelled Temple of the Lord of Hosts; who shut his eyes and speculated, when he might open them and see. There is no absurdity, then, or inconsistency in a person first using his private judgment and then denouncing its use. Circumstances change duties.

But still, after all, the person in question does not, strictly speaking, judge of the external system presented to him by his private ideas, but he brings in the dicta of that system to confirm and to justify certain private judgments and personal feelings and habits already existing. Reding, for instance, felt a difficulty in determining how and when the sins of a Christian are forgiven; he had a great notion that celibacy was better than married life. He was not the first person in the Church of England who had had such thoughts; to numbers, doubtless, before him they had occurred; but these numbers had looked abroad, and seen nothing around them to justify what they felt, and their feelings had, in consequence, either festered within them, or withered away. But when a man, thus constituted within, falls under the shadow of Catholicism without, then the mighty Creed at once produces an influence upon him. He see that it justifies his thoughts, explains his feelings; he understands that it numbers, corrects, harmonizes, completes them; and he is led to ask what is the authority of this foreign teaching; and then, when he finds it is what was once received in England from north to south, in England from the very time that Christianity was introduced here; that, as far as historical records go, Christianity and Catholicism are synonymous; that it is still the faith of the largest section of the Christian world; and that the faith of his own country is held nowhere but within her own limits and those of her own colonies; nay, further, that it is very difficult to say what faith she has, or that she has any—then he submits himself to the Catholic Church, not by a process of criticism, but as a pupil to a teacher.

In saying this, of course it is not denied, on the one hand, that there may be persons who come to the Catholic Church on imperfect motives, or in a wrong way; who choose it by criticism, and who, unsubdued by its majesty and its grace, go on criticizing when they are in it; and who, if they persist and do not learn humility, may criticize themselves out of it again. Nor is it denied, on the other hand, that some who are not Catholics may possibly choose (for instance) Methodism, in the above moral way, viz. because it confirms and justifies the inward feeling of their hearts. This is certainly possible in idea, though what there is venerable, awful, superhuman, in the Wesleyan Conference to persuade one to take it as a prophet, is a perplexing problem; yet, after all, the matter of fact we conceive to lie the other way, viz. that Wesleyans and other sectaries put themselves above their system, not below it; and though they may in bodily position "sit under" their preacher, yet in the position of their souls and spirits, minds and judgments, they are exalted high above him.

But to return to the subject of our narrative. What a mystery is the soul of man! Here was Charles, busy with Aristotle and Euripides, Thucydides and Lucretius, yet all the while growing towards the Church, "to the measure of the age of the fulness of Christ." His mother had said to him that he could not escape his destiny; it was true, though it was to be fulfilled in a way which she, affectionate heart, could not compass, did not dream of. He could not escape the destiny of being one of the elect of God; he could not escape that destiny which the grace of his Redeemer had stamped on his soul in baptism, which his good angel had seen written there, and had done his zealous part to keep inviolate and bright, which his own co-operation with the influences of Heaven had confirmed and secured. He could not escape the destiny, in due time, in God's time—though it might be long, though angels might be anxious, though the Church might plead as if defrauded of her promised increase of a stranger, yet a son; yet come it must, it was written in Heaven, and the slow wheels of time each hour brought it nearer—he could not ultimately escape his destiny of becoming a Catholic. And even before that blessed hour, as an opening flower scatters sweets, so the strange unknown odour, pleasing to some, odious to others, went abroad from him upon the winds, and made them marvel what could be near them, and make them look curiously and anxiously at him, while he was unconscious of his own condition. Let us be patient with him, as his Maker is patient, and bear that he should do a work slowly which he will do well.

Alas! while Charles had been growing in one direction, Sheffield had been growing in another; and what that growth had been will appear from a conversation which took place between the two friends, and which shall be related in the following chapter.

CHAPTER VII

Carlton had opened the small church he was serving for Saints'-day services during the Long Vacation; and not being in the way to have any congregation, and the church at Horsley being closed except on Sundays, he had asked his two pupils to help him in this matter, by walking over with him on St. Matthew's day, which, as the season was fine, and the walk far from a dull one, they were very glad to do. When church was over Carlton had to attend a sick call which lay still farther from Horsley, and the two young men walked back together.

"I did not know that Carlton was so much of a party man," said Sheffield; "did not his reading the Athanasian Creed strike you?"

"That's no mark of party, surely," answered Charles.

"To read it on days like these, I think, *is* a mark of party; it's going out of the way."

Charles did not see how obeying in so plain a matter the clear direction of the Prayer Book could be a party act.

"Direction!" said Sheffield, "as if the question were not, is that direction now binding? The sense, the understanding of the Church of this day determines its obligation."

"The *prima facie* view of the matter," said Charles, "is, that they who do but follow what the Prayer Book enjoins are of all people farthest from being a party."

"Not at all," said Sheffield; "rigid adherence to old customs surely may be the badge of a party. Now consider; ten years ago, before the study of Church-history was revived, neither Arianism nor Athanasianism were thought of at all, or, if thought of, they were considered as questions of words, at least as held by most minds—one as good as the other."

"I should say so, too, in one sense," said Charles, "that is, I should hope that numbers of persons, for instance, the unlearned, who were in Arian communities spoke Arian language, and yet did not mean it. I think I have heard that some ancient missionary of the Goths or Huns was an Arian."

"Well, I will speak more precisely," said Sheffield: "an Oxford man, some ten years since, was going to publish a history of the Nicene Council, and the bookseller proposed to him to prefix an engraving of St. Athanasius, which he had found in some old volume. He was strongly dissuaded from doing so by a brother clergyman, not from any feeling of his own, but because 'Athanasius was a very unpopular name among us.'"

"One swallow does not make a spring," said Charles.

"This clergyman," continued Sheffield, "was a friend of the most High-Church writers of the day."

"Of course," said Reding, "there has always been a heterodox school in our Church—I know that well enough—but it never has been powerful. Your lax friend was one of them."

"I believe not, indeed," answered Sheffield; "he lived out of controversy, was a literary, accomplished person, and a man of piety to boot. He did not express any feeling of his own; he did but witness to a fact, that the name of Athanasius was unpopular."

"So little was known about history," said Charles, "this is not surprising. St. Athanasius, you know, did not write the Creed called after him. It is possible to think him intemperate, without thinking the Creed wrong."

"Well, then, again; there's Beatson, Divinity Professor; no one will call him in any sense a party man; he was put in by the Tories, and never has committed himself to any liberal theories in theology. Now, a man who attended his private lectures assures me that he told the men, 'D'ye see,' said he, 'I take it, that the old Church-of-England mode of handling the Creed went out with Bull. After Locke wrote, the old orthodox phraseology came into disrepute.'"

"Well, perhaps he meant," said Charles, "that learning died away, which was the case. The old theological language is plainly a learned language; when fathers and schoolmen were not read, of course it would be in abeyance; when they were read again, it has revived."

"No, no," answered Sheffield, "he said much more on another occasion. Speaking of Creeds, and the like, 'I hold,' he said, 'that the majority of the educated laity of our Church are Sabellians.'"

Charles was silent, and hardly knew what reply to make. Sheffield went on: "I was present some years ago, when I was quite a boy, when a sort of tutor of mine was talking to one of the most learned and orthodox divines of the day, a man whose name has never been associated with party, and the near relation and connection of high dignitaries, about a plan of his own for writing a history of the Councils. This good and able man listened with politeness, applauded the project; then added, in a laughing way, 'You know you have chosen just the dullest subject in Church history. Now the Councils begin with the Nicene Creed, and embrace nearly all doctrinal subjects whatever.'"

"My dear Sheffield," said Charles, "you have fallen in with a particular set or party of men yourself; very respectable, good men, I don't doubt, but no fair specimens of the whole Church."

"I don't bring them as authorities," answered Sheffield, "but as witnesses."

"Still," said Charles, "I know perfectly well, that there was a controversy at the end of the last century between Bishop Horsley and others, in which he brought out distinctly one part at least of the Athanasian doctrine."

"His controversy was not a defence of the Athanasian Creed, I know well," said Sheffield; "for the subject came into Upton's Article-lecture; it was with Priestley; but, whatever it was, divines would only think it all very fine, just as his 'Sermons on Prophecy.' It is another question whether they would recognize the worth either of the one or of the other. They receive the scholastic terms about the Trinity just as they receive the doctrine that the Pope is Antichrist. When Horsley says the latter, or something of the kind, good old clergymen say, 'Certainly, certainly, oh yes, it's the old Church-of-England doctrine,' thinking it right, indeed, to be maintained, but not caring themselves to maintain it, or at most professing it just when mentioned, but not really thinking about it from one year's end to the other. And so with regard to the doctrine of the Trinity, they say, 'the great Horsley,' 'the powerful Horsley'; they don't indeed dispute his doctrine, but they don't care about it; they look on him as a doughty champion, armed *cap-à-pie*, who has put down dissent, who has cut off the head of some impudent non-protectionist, or insane chartist, or spouter in a vestry, who, under cover of theology, had run a tilt against tithes and church-rates."

"I can't think so badly of our present divines," said Charles; "I know that in this very place there are various orthodox writers, whom no one would call party men."

"Stop," said Sheffield, "understand me, I was not speaking *against* them. I was but saying that these anti-Athanasian views were not unfrequent. I have been in the way of hearing a good deal on the subject at my private tutor's, and have kept my eyes about me since I have been here. The Bishop of Derby was a friend of Sheen's, my private tutor, and got his promotion when I was with the latter; and Sheen told me that he wrote to him on that occasion, 'What shall I read? I don't know anything of theology.' I rather think he was recommended, or proposed to read Scott's Bible."

"It's easy to bring instances," said Charles, "when you have all your own way; what you say is evidently all an *ex-parte* statement."

"Take again Shipton, who died lately," continued Sheffield; "what a high position he held in the Church; yet it is perfectly well known that he thought it a mistake to use the word 'Person' in the doctrine of the Trinity. What makes this stranger is, that he was so very severe on clergymen (Tractarians, for instance) who evade the sense of the Articles. Now he was a singularly honest, straightforward man; he despised money; he cared nothing for public opinion; yet he was a Sabellian. Would he have eaten the bread of the Church, as it is called, for a day, unless he had felt that his opinions were not inconsistent with his profession as Dean of Bath, and Prebendary of Dorchester? Is it not plain that he considered the practice of the Church to have modified, to have re-interpreted its documents?"

"Why," said Charles, "the practice of the Church cannot make black white; or, if a sentence means yes, make it mean no. I won't deny that words are often vague and uncertain in their sense, and frequently need a comment, so that the teaching of the day has great influence in determining their sense; but the question is, whether the counter-teaching of every dean, every prebendary, every clergyman, every bishop in the whole Church, could make the Athanasian Creed Sabellian; I think not."

"Certainly not," answered Sheffield; "but the clergymen I speak of simply say that they are not bound to the details of the Creed, only to the great outline that there is *a* Trinity."

"Great outline!" said Charles, "great stuff! an Unitarian would not deny that. He, of course, believes in Father, Son, and Holy Spirit; though he thinks the Son a creature, and the Spirit an influence."

"Well, I don't deny," said Sheffield, "that if Dean Shipton was a sound member of the Church, Dr. Priestley might have been also. But my doubt is, whether, if the Tractarian school had not risen, Priestley might not have been, had he lived to this time, I will not say a positively sound member, but sound enough for preferment."

"*If* the Tractarian school had not risen! that is but saying if our Church was other than it is. What is that school but a birth, an offspring of the Church? And if the Church had not given birth to one party of men for its defence, it would have given birth to another."

"No, no," said Sheffield, "I assure you the old school of doctrine was all but run out when they began; and I declare I wish they had let things alone. There was the doctrine of the Apostolical Succession; a few good old men were its sole remaining professors in the Church; and a great ecclesiastical personage, on one occasion, quite scoffed at their persisting to hold it. He maintained the doctrine went out with the non-jurors. 'You are so few,' he said, 'that we can count you.'"

Charles was not pleased with the subject, on various accounts. He did not like what seemed to him an attack of Sheffield's upon the Church of England; and, besides, he began to feel uncomfortable misgivings and doubts whether that attack was not well founded, to which he did not like to be exposed. Accordingly he kept silence, and, after a short interval, attempted to change the subject; but Sheffield's hand was in, and he would not be balked; so he presently began again. "I have been speaking," he said, "of the liberal section of our Church. There are four parties in the Church. Of these the old Tory, or country party, which is out-and-out the largest, has no opinion at all, but merely takes up the theology or no-theology of the day, and cannot properly be said to 'hold' what the Creed calls 'the Catholic faith.' It does not deny it; it may not knowingly disbelieve it; but it gives no signs of actually holding it, beyond the fact that it treats it with respect. I will venture to say, that not a country parson of them all, from year's end to year's end, makes once a year what Catholics call 'an act of faith' in that special and very distinctive mystery contained in the clauses of the Athanasian Creed."

Then, seeing Charles looked rather hurt, he added, "I am not speaking of any particular clergyman here or there, but of the great majority of them. After the Tory party comes the Liberal; which also dislikes the Athanasian Creed, as I have said. Thirdly, as to the Evangelical; I know you have one of the Nos. of the 'Tracts for the Times' about objective faith. Now that tract seems to prove that the Evangelical party is implicitly Sabellian, and is tending to avow that belief. This too has been already the actual course of Evangelical doctrine both on the Continent and in America. The Protestants of Geneva, Holland, Ulster, and Boston have all, I believe, become Unitarians, or the like. Dr. Adam Clarke too, the celebrated Wesleyan, held the distinguishing Sabellian tenet, as Doddridge is said to have done before him. All this considered, I do think I have made out a good case for my original assertion, that at this time of day it is a party thing to go out of the way to read the Athanasian Creed."

"I don't agree with you at all," said Charles; "you say a great deal more than you have a warrant to do, and draw sweeping conclusions from slender premisses. This, at least, is what it seems to me. I wish too you would not so speak of 'making out a case.' It is as if these things were mere topics for disputation. And I don't like your taking the wrong side; you are rather fond of doing so."

"Reding," answered Sheffield, "I speak what I think, and ever will do so; I will be no party man. I don't attempt, like Vincent, to unite opposites. He is of all parties, I am of none. I think I see pretty well the hollowness of all."

"O my dear Sheffield," cried Charles, in distress, "think what you are saying; you don't mean what you say. You are speaking as if you thought that belief in the Athanasian Creed was a mere party opinion."

Sheffield first was silent; then he said, "Well, I beg your pardon, if I have said anything to annoy you, or have expressed myself intemperately. But surely one has no need to believe what so many people either disbelieve or disregard."

The subject then dropped; and presently Carlton overtook them on the farmer's pony, which he had borrowed.

CHAPTER VIII

Reding had for near two years put aside his doubts about the Articles; but it was like putting off the payment of a bill—a respite, not a deliverance. The two conversations which we have been recording, bringing him to issue on most important subjects first with one, then with another, of two intimate friends, who were bound by the Articles as well as he, uncomfortably reminded him of his debt to the University and Church; and the nearer approach of his examination and degree inflicted on him the thought that the time was coming when he must be prepared to discharge it.

One day, when he was strolling out with Carlton, toward the end of the Vacation, he had been led to speak of the number of religious opinions and parties in Oxford, which had so many bad effects, making so many talk, so many criticise, and not a few perhaps doubt about truth altogether. Then he said that, evil as it was in a place of education, yet he feared it was unavoidable, if Carlton's doctrine about parties were correct; for if there was a place where differences of religious opinions would show themselves, it would be in a university.

"I am far from denying it," said Carlton; "but all systems have their defects; no polity, no theology, no ritual is perfect. One only came directly and simply from Heaven, the Jewish; and even that was removed because of its unprofitableness. This is no derogation from the perfection of Divine Revelation, for it arises from the subject-matter on and through which it operates." There was a pause; then Carlton went on: "It is the fault of most young thinkers to be impatient, if they do not find perfection in everything; they are 'new brooms.'" Another pause; he went on again: "What form of religion is *less* objectionable than ours? You *see* the inconveniences of your own system, for you experience them; you have not felt, and cannot know, those of others."

Charles was still silent, and went on plucking and chewing leaves from the shrubs and bushes through which their path winded. At length he said, "*I* should not like to say it to any one but you, Carlton, but, do you know, I was very uncomfortable about the Articles, going on for two years since; I really could not understand them, and their history makes matters worse. I put the subject from me altogether; but now that my examination and degree are coming on, I must take it up again."

"You must have been put into the Article-lecture early," said Carlton.

"Well, perhaps I was not up to the subject," answered Charles.

"I didn't mean that," said Carlton; "but as to the thing itself, my dear fellow, it happens every day, and especially to thoughtful people like yourself. It should not annoy you."

"But my fidget is," said Charles, "lest my difficulties should return, and I should not be able to remove them."

"You should take all these things calmly," said Carlton; "all things, as I have said, have their difficulties. If you wait till everything is as it should be or might be conceivably, you will do nothing, and will lose life. The moral and social world is not an open country; it is already marked and mapped out; it has its roads. You can't go across country; if you attempt a steeple-chase, you will break your neck for your pains. Forms of religion are facts; they have each their history. They existed before you were born, and will survive you. You must choose, you cannot make."

"I know," said Reding, "I can't make a religion, nor can I perhaps find one better than my own. I don't want to do so; but this is not my difficulty. Take your own image. I am jogging along my own old road, and lo, a high turnpike, fast locked; and my poor pony can't clear it. I don't complain; but there's the fact, or at least may be."

"The pony must," answered Carlton; "or if not, there must be some way about; else what is the good of a road? In religion all roads have their obstacles; one has a strong gate across it, another goes through a bog. Is no one to go on? Is religion to be at a deadlock? Is Christianity to die out? Where else will you go? Not surely to Methodism, or Plymouth-brotherism. As to the Romish Church, I suspect it has more difficulties than we have. You *must* sacrifice your private judgment."

"All this is very good," answered Charles; "but what is very expedient still may be very impossible. The finest words about the necessity of getting home before nightfall will not enable my poor little pony to take the gate."

"Certainly not," said Carlton; "but if you had a command from a benevolent Prince, your own Sovereign and Benefactor, to go along the road steadily till evening, and he would meet you at the end of your journey, you would be quite sure that he who had appointed the end had also assigned the means. And, in the difficulty in question, you ought to look out for some mode of opening the gate, or some gap in the hedge, or some parallel cut, some way or other, which would enable you to turn the difficulty."

Charles said that somehow he did not like this mode of arguing; it seemed dangerous; he did not see whither it went, where it ended. Presently he said, abruptly, "Why do you think there are more difficulties in the Church of Rome?"

"Clearly there are," answered Carlton; "if the Articles are a crust, is not Pope Pius's Creed a bone?"

"I don't know Pope Pius's Creed," said Charles; "I know very little about the state of the case, certainly. What does it say?"

"Oh, it includes transubstantiation, purgatory, saint-worship, and the rest," said Carlton; "I suppose you could not quite subscribe these?"

"It depends," answered Charles slowly, "on this—on what authority they came to me." He stopped, and then went on: "Of course I could, if they came to me on the same authority as the doctrine of the Blessed Trinity comes. Now, the Articles come on no authority; they are the views of persons in the 16th century; and, again, it is not clear how far they are, or are not, modified by the unauthoritative views of the 19th. I am obliged, then, to exercise my own judgment; and I candidly declare to you, that my judgment is unequal to so great a task. At least, this is what troubles me, whenever the subject rises in my mind; for I have put it from me."

"Well, then," said Carlton, "take them on *faith*."

"You mean, I suppose," said Charles, "that I must consider our Church *infallible*."

Carlton felt the difficulty; he answered, "No, but you must act *as if* it were infallible, from a sense of duty."

Charles smiled; then he looked grave; he stood still, and his eyes fell. "If I *am* to make a Church infallible," he said, "if I *must* give up private judgment, if I *must* act on faith, there *is* a Church which has a greater claim on us all than the Church of England."

"My dear Reding," said Carlton, with some emotion, "where did you get these notions?"

"I don't know," answered Charles; "somebody has said that they were in the air. I have talked to no one, except one or two arguments I had with different persons in my first year. I have driven the subject from me; but when I once begin, you see it will out."

They walked on awhile in silence. "Do you really mean to say," asked Carlton at length, "that it is so difficult to understand and receive the Articles? To me they are quite clear enough, and speak the language of common sense."

"Well, they seem to me," said Reding, "sometimes inconsistent with themselves, sometimes with the Prayer Book; so that I am suspicious of them; I don't know *what* I am signing when I sign, yet I ought to sign *ex-animo*. A blind submission I could make; I cannot make a blind declaration."

"Give me some instances," said Carlton.

"For example," said Charles, "they distinctly receive the Lutheran doctrine of justification by faith only, which the Prayer Book virtually opposes in every one of its Offices. They refer to the Homilies as authority, yet the Homilies speak of the books of the Apocrypha as inspired, which the Articles implicitly deny. The Articles about Ordination are in their spirit contrary to the Ordination Service. One Article on the Sacraments speaks the doctrine of Melancthon, another that of Calvin. One Article speaks of the Church's authority in controversies of faith, yet another makes Scripture the ultimate appeal. These are what occur to me at the moment."

"Surely, many of these are but verbal difficulties, at the very first glance," said Carlton, "and all may be surmounted with a little care."

"On the other hand, it has struck me," continued Charles, "that the Church of Rome is undeniably consistent in her formularies; this is the very charge some of our writers make upon her, that she is so systematic. It may be a hard, iron system, but it is consistent."

Carlton did not wish to interrupt him, thinking it best to hear his whole difficulty; so Charles proceeded: "When a system is consistent, at least it does not condemn itself. Consistency is not truth, but truth is consistency. Now, I am not a fit judge whether or not a certain system is true, but I may be quite a judge whether it is consistent with itself. When an oracle equivocates it carries with it its own condemnation. I almost think there is something in Scripture on this subject, comparing in this respect the pagan and the inspired prophecies. And this has struck me, too, that St. Paul gives this very account of a heretic, that he is 'condemned of himself,' bearing his own condemnation on his face. Moreover, I was once in the company of Freeborn (I don't know if you are acquainted with him) and others of the Evangelical party, and they showed plainly, if they were to be trusted, that Luther and Melancthon did not agree together on the prime point of justification by faith; a circumstance which had not come into the Article-lecture. Also I have read somewhere, or heard in some sermon, that the ancient heretics always were inconsistent, never could state plainly their meaning, much less agree together; and thus, whether they would or no, could not help giving to the simple a warning of their true character, as if by their rattle."

Charles stopped; presently he continued: "This too has struck me; that either there is no prophet of the truth on earth, or the Church of Rome is that prophet. That there is a prophet still, or apostle, or messenger, or teacher, or whatever he is to be called, seems evident by our believing in a visible Church. Now common sense tells us what a messenger from God must be; first, he must not contradict himself, as I have just been saying. Again, a prophet of God can allow of no rival, but denounces all who make a separate claim, as the prophets do in Scripture. Now, it is impossible to say whether our Church acknowledges or not Lutheranism in Germany, Calvinism in Switzerland, the Nestorian and Monophysite bodies in the East. Nor does it clearly tell us what view it takes of the Church of Rome. The only place where it recognizes its existence is in the Homilies, and there it speaks of it as Antichrist. Nor has the Greek Church any intelligible position in Anglican doctrine. On the other hand, the Church of Rome has this *prima facie* mark of a prophet, that, like a prophet in Scripture, it admits no rival, and anathematizes all doctrine counter to its own. There's another thing: a prophet of God is of course at home with his message; he is not helpless and do-nothing in the midst of errors and in the war of opinions. He knows what has been given him to declare, how far it extends; he can act as an umpire; he is equal to emergencies. This again tells in favour of the Church of Rome. As age after age comes she is ever on the alert, questions every new comer, sounds the note of alarm, hews down strange doctrine, claims and locates and perfects what is new and true. The Church of Rome inspires me with confidence; I feel I can trust her. It is another thing whether she is true; I am not pretending now to decide that. But I do not feel the like trust in our own Church. I love her more than I trust her. She leaves me without faith. Now you see the state of my mind." He fetched a deep, sharp sigh, as if he had got a load off him.

"Well," said Carlton, when he had stopped, "this is all very pretty theory; whether it holds in matter of fact, is another question. We have been accustomed hitherto to think Chillingworth right, when he talks of popes against popes, councils against councils, and so on. Certainly you will not be allowed by Protestant controversialists to assume this perfect consistency in Romish doctrine. The truth is, you have read very little; and you judge of truth, not by facts, but by notions; I mean, you think it enough if a notion hangs together; though you disavow it, still, in matter of fact, consistency *is* truth to you. Whether facts answer to theories you cannot tell, and you don't inquire. Now I am not well read in the subject, but I know enough to be sure that Romanists will have more work to prove their consistency than you anticipate. For instance, they appeal to the Fathers, yet put the Pope above them; they maintain the infallibility of the Church, and prove it by Scripture, and then they prove Scripture by the Church. They think a General Council infallible, *when*, but not *before*, the Pope has ratified it; Bellarmine, I think, gives a list of General Councils which have erred. And I never have been able to make out the Romish doctrine of Indulgences."

Charles thought over this; then he said, "Perhaps the case is as you say, that I ought to know the matter of fact more exactly before attempting to form a judgment on the subject; but, my dear Carlton, I protest to you, and you may think with what distress I say it, that if the Church of Rome is as ambiguous as our own Church, I shall be in the way to become a sceptic, on the very ground that I shall have no competent authority to tell me what to believe. The Ethiopian said, 'How can I know, unless some man do teach me?' and St. Paul says, 'Faith cometh by hearing.' If no one claims my faith, how can I exercise it? At least I shall run the risk of becoming a Latitudinarian; for if I go by Scripture only, certainly there is no creed given us in Scripture."

"Our business," said Carlton, "is to make the best of things, not the worst. Do keep this in mind; be on your guard against a strained and morbid view of things. Be cheerful, be natural, and all will be easy."

"You are always kind and considerate," said Charles; "but, after all—I wish I could make you see it—you have not a word to say by way of meeting my original difficulty of subscription. How am I to leap over the wall? It's nothing to the purpose that other communions have their walls also."

They now neared home, and concluded their walk in silence, each being fully occupied with the thoughts which the conversation had suggested.

CHAPTER IX

The Vacation passed away silently and happily. Day succeeded day in quiet routine employments, bringing insensible but sure accessions to the stock of knowledge and to the intellectual proficiency of both our students. Historians and orators were read for a last time, and laid aside; sciences were digested; commentaries were run through; and analyses and abstracts completed. It was emphatically a silent toil. While others might be steaming from London to Bombay or the Havannah, and months in the retrospect might look like years, with Reding and Sheffield the week had scarcely begun when it was found to be ending; and when October came, and they saw their Oxford friends again, at first they thought they had a good deal to say to them, but when they tried, they found it did but concern minute points of their own reading and personal matters; and they were reduced to silence with the wish to speak.

The season had changed, and reminded them that Horsley was a place for summer sojourn, not a dwelling. There were heavy raw fogs hanging about the hills, and storms of wind and rain. The grass no longer afforded them a seat; and when they betook themselves indoors it was discovered that the doors and windows did not shut close, and that the chimney smoked. Then came those fruits, the funeral feast of the year, mulberries and walnuts; the tasteless, juiceless walnut; the dark mulberry, juicy but severe, and mouldy withal, as gathered not from the tree, but from the damp earth. And thus that green spot itself weaned them from the love of it. Charles looked around him, and rose to depart as a *conviva satur*. "*Edisti satis, tempus abire*" seemed written upon all. The swallows had taken leave; the leaves were paling; the light broke late, and failed soon. The hopes of spring, the peace and calm of summer, had given place to the sad realities of autumn. He was hurrying to the world, who had been up on the mount; he had lived without jars, without distractions, without disappointments; and he was now to take them as his portion. For he was but a child of Adam; Horsley had been but a respite; and he had vividly presented to his memory the sad reverse which came upon him two years before—what a happy summer—what a forlorn autumn! With these thoughts, he put up his books and papers, and turned his face towards St. Saviour's.

Oxford, too, was not quite what it had been to him; the freshness of his admiration for it was over; he now saw defects where at first all was excellent and good; the romance of places and persons had passed away. And there were changes too: of his contemporaries some had already taken their degrees and left; others were reading in the country; others had gone off to other Colleges on

Fellowships. A host of younger faces had sprung up in hall and chapel, and he hardly knew their names. Rooms which formerly had been his familiar lounge were now tenanted by strangers, who claimed to have that right in them which, to his imagination, could only attach to those who had possessed them when he himself came into residence. The College seemed to have deteriorated; there was a rowing set, which had not been there before, a number of boys, and a large proportion of snobs.

But, what was a real trouble to Charles, it got clearer and clearer to his apprehension that his intimacy with Sheffield was not quite what it had been. They had, indeed, passed the Vacation together, and saw of each other more than ever: but their sympathies in each other were not as strong, they had not the same likings and dislikings; in short, they had not such congenial minds as they fancied when they were freshmen. There was not so much heart in their conversations, and they more easily endured to miss each other's company. They were both reading for honours—reading hard; but Sheffield's whole heart was in his work, and religion was but a secondary matter to him. He had no doubts, difficulties, anxieties, sorrows, which much affected him. It was not the certainty of faith which made a sunshine to his soul, and dried up the mists of human weakness; rather, he had no perceptible need within him of that vision of the Unseen which is the Christian's life. He was unblemished in his character, exemplary in his conduct; but he was content with what the perishable world gave him. Charles's characteristic, perhaps above anything else, was an habitual sense of the Divine Presence; a sense which, of course, did not insure uninterrupted conformity of thought and deed to itself, but still there it was—the pillar of the cloud before him and guiding him. He felt himself to be God's creature, and responsible to Him—God's possession, not his own. He had a great wish to succeed in the schools; a thrill came over him when he thought of it; but ambition was not his life; he could have reconciled himself in a few minutes to failure. Thus disposed, the only subjects on which the two friends freely talked together were connected with their common studies. They read together, examined each other, used and corrected each other's papers, and solved each other's difficulties. Perhaps it scarcely came home to Sheffield, sharp as he was, that there was any flagging of their intimacy. Religious controversy had been the food of his active intellect when it was novel; now it had lost its interest, and his books took its place. But it was far different with Charles; he had felt interest in religious questions for their own sake; and when he had deprived himself of the pursuit of them it had been a self-denial. Now, then, when they seemed forced on him again, Sheffield could not help him, where he most wanted the assistance of a friend.

A still more tangible trial was coming on him. The reader has to be told that there was at that time a system of espionage prosecuted by various well-meaning men, who thought it would be doing the University a service to point out such of its junior members as were what is called "papistically inclined." They did not perceive the danger such a course involved of disposing young men towards Catholicism, by attaching to them the bad report of it, and of forcing them farther by inflicting on them the inconsistencies of their position. Ideas which would have lain dormant or dwindled away in their minds were thus fixed, defined, located within them; and the fear of the world's censure no longer served to deter, when it had been actually incurred. When Charles attended the tea-party at Freeborn's he was on his trial; he was introduced not only into a school, but into an inquisition; and since he did not promise to be a subject for spiritual impression, he was forthwith a subject for spiritual censure. He became a marked man in the circles of Capel Hall and St. Mark's. His acquaintance with Willis; the questions he had asked at the Article-lecture; stray remarks at wine-parties—were treasured up, and strengthened the case against him. One time, on coming into his rooms, he found Freeborn, who had entered to pay him a call, prying into his books. A volume of sermons, of the school of the day, borrowed of a friend for the sake of illustrating Aristotle, lay on his table; and in his bookshelves one of the more philosophical of the "Tracts for the Times" was stuck in between a Hermann *De Metris* and a Thucydides. Another day his bedroom door was open, and No. 2 of the tea-party saw one of Overbeck's sacred prints pinned up against the wall.

Facts like these were, in most cases, delated to the Head of the House to which a young man belonged; who, as a vigilant guardian of the purity of his undergraduates' Protestantism, received the information with thankfulness, and perhaps asked the informer to dinner. It cannot be denied that in some cases this course of action succeeded in frightening and sobering the parties towards whom it was directed. White was thus reclaimed to be a devoted son and useful minister of the Church of England; but it was a kill-or-cure remedy, and not likely to answer with the more noble or the more able minds. What effect it had upon Charles, or whether any, must be determined by the sequel; here it will suffice to relate interviews which took place between him and the Principal and Vice-Principal of his College in consequence of it.

CHAPTER X

When Reding presented himself to the Vice-Principal, the Rev. Joshua Jennings, to ask for leave to reside in lodgings for the two terms previous to his examination, he was met with a courteous but decided refusal. It took him altogether by surprise; he had considered the request as a mere matter of form. He sat half a minute silent, and then rose to take his departure. The colour came to his cheek; it was a repulse inflicted only on idle men who could not be trusted beyond the eye of the Dean of the College.

The Vice-Principal seemed to expect him to ask the reason of his proceeding; as Charles, in his confusion, did not seem likely to do so, he condescended to open the conversation. It was not meant as any reflection, he said, on Mr. Reding's moral conduct; he had ever been a well-conducted young man, and had quite carried out the character with which he had come from school; but there were duties to be observed towards the community, and its undergraduate portion must be protected from the contagion of principles which were too rife at the moment. Charles was, if possible, still more surprised, and suggested that there must be some misunderstanding if he had been represented to the Vice-Principal as connected with any so-called party in the place. "You don't mean to deny that there *is* a party, Mr. Reding," answered the College authority, "by that form of expression?" He was a lean, pale person, with a large hook-nose and spectacles; and seemed, though a liberal in creed, to be really a nursling of that early age when Anabaptists fed the fires of Smithfield. From his years, practised talent, and position, he was well able to browbeat an unhappy juvenile who incurred his displeasure; and, though he really was a kind-hearted man at bottom, he not unfrequently misused his power. Charles did not know how to answer his question; and on his silence it was repeated. At length he said that really he was not in a condition to speak against any one; and if he spoke of a so-called party, it was that he might not seem disrespectful to some who might be better men than himself. Mr. Vice was silent, but not from being satisfied.

"What would *you* call a party, Mr. Reding?" he said at length; "what would be your definition of it?"

Charles paused to think; at last he said: "Persons who band together on their own authority for the maintenance of views of their own."

"And will you say that these gentlemen have not views of their own?" asked Mr. Jennings.

Charles assented.

"What is your view of the Thirty-nine Articles?" said the Vice-Principal abruptly.

"*My* view!" thought Charles; "what can he mean? My *view* of the Articles! like my opinion of things in general. Does he mean my 'view' whether they are English or Latin, long or short, good or bad, expedient or not, Catholic or not, Calvinistic or Erastian?"

Meanwhile Jennings kept steadily regarding him, and Charles got more and more confused. "I think," he said, making a desperate snatch at authoritative words, "I think that the Articles 'contain a godly and wholesome doctrine, and necessary for these times.'"

"*That* is the Second Book of Homilies, Mr. Reding, not the Articles. Besides, I want your own opinion on the subject." He proceeded, after a pause: "What is justification?"

"Justification," said Charles, repeating the word, and thinking; then, in the words of the Article, he went on: "We are accounted righteous before God, but only for the merit of our Lord Jesus Christ, by faith, and not by our own works and deservings."

"Right," said Jennings; "but you have not answered my question. What *is* justification?"

This was very hard, for it was one of Charles's puzzles what justification was in itself, for the Articles do not define it any more than faith. He answered to this effect, that the Articles did not define it. The Vice-Principal looked dissatisfied.

"Can General Councils err?"

"Yes," answered Charles. This was right.

"What do Romanists say about them?"

"They think they err, too." This was all wrong.

"No," said Jennings, "they think them infallible."

Charles was silent; Jennings tried to force his decision upon him.

At length Charles said that "Only some General Councils were admitted as infallible by the Romanists, and he believed that Bellarmine gave a list of General Councils which had erred."

Another pause, and a gathering cloud on Jennings' brow.

He returned to his former subject. "In what sense do you understand the Articles, Mr. Reding?" he asked. That was more than

Charles could tell; he wished very much to know the right sense of them; so he beat about for the *received* answer.

"In the sense of Scripture," he said. This was true, but nugatory.

"Rather," said Jennings, "you understand Scripture in the sense of the Articles."

Charles assented for peace-sake. But his concession availed not; the Vice-Principal pursued his advantage.

"They must not interpret each other, Mr. Reding, else you revolve in a circle. Let me repeat my question. In what sense do you interpret the Articles?"

"I wish to take them," Reding answered, "in the general and received sense of our Church, as all our divines and present Bishops take them."

The Vice-Principal looked pleased. Charles could not help being candid, and said in a lower tone, as if words of course, "That is, on faith."

This put all wrong again. Jennings would not allow this; it was a blind, Popish reliance; it was very well, when he first came to the University, before he had read the Articles, to take them on trust; but a young man who had had the advantages of Mr. Reding, who had been three years at St. Saviour's College, and had attended the Article-lectures, ought to hold the received view, not only as being received, but as his own, with a free intellectual assent. He went on to ask him by what texts he proved the Protestant doctrine of justification. Charles gave two or three of the usual passages with such success, that the Vice-Principal was secretly beginning to relent, when, unhappily, on asking a last question as a matter of course, he received an answer which confirmed all his former surmises.

"What is our Church's doctrine concerning the intercession of Saints?"

Charles said that he did not recollect that it had expressed any opinion on the subject. Jennings bade him think again; Charles thought in vain.

"Well, what is your opinion of it, Mr. Reding?"

Charles, believing it to be an open point, thought he should be safe in imitating "our Church's" moderation. "There are different opinions on the subject," he said: "some persons think they intercede for us, others, that they do not. It is easy to go into extremes; perhaps better to avoid such questions altogether; better to go by Scripture; the book of Revelation speaks of the intercession of Saints, but does not expressly say that they intercede for us," etc.

Jennings sat upright in his easy-chair, with indignation mounting into his forehead. At length his face became like night. "*That* is your opinion, Mr. Reding."

Charles began to be frightened.

"Please to take up that Prayer Book and turn to the 22nd Article. Now begin reading it."

"The Romish doctrine," said Charles—"the Romish doctrine concerning purgatory, pardon, worshipping and adoration as well of images as of relics, and also invocation of Saints"—

"Stop there," said the Vice-Principal; "read those words again."

"And also invocation of Saints."

"Now, Mr. Reding."

Charles was puzzled, thought he had made some blunder, could not find it, and was silent.

"Well, Mr. Reding?"

Charles at length said that he thought Mr. Jennings had spoken about *intercession*.

"So I did," he made answer.

"And this," said Charles timidly, "speaks of *invocation*."

Jennings gave a little start in his arm-chair, and slightly coloured. "Eh?" he said; "give me the book." He slowly read the Article, and then cast a cautious eye over the page before and after. There was no help for it. He began again.

"And so, Mr. Reding, you actually mean to shelter yourself by that subtle distinction between invocation and intercession; as if

Papists did not invoke in order to gain the Saints' intercession, and as if the Saints were not supposed by them to intercede in answer to invocation? The terms are correlative. Intercession of Saints, instead of being an extreme only, as you consider, is a Romish abomination. I am ashamed of you, Mr. Reding; I am pained and hurt that a young man of your promise, of good ability, and excellent morals, should be guilty of so gross an evasion of the authoritative documents of our Church, such an outrage upon common sense, so indecent a violation of the terms on which alone he was allowed to place his name on the books of this society. I could not have a clearer proof that your mind has been perverted—I fear I must use a stronger term, debauched—by the sophistries and jesuistries which unhappily have found entrance among us. Good morning, Mr. Reding."

So it was a thing settled: Charles was to be sent home—an endurable banishment.

Before he went down he paid a visit of form to the old Principal—a worthy man in his generation, who before now had been a good parish priest, had instructed the ignorant and fed the poor; but now in the end of his days, falling on evil times, was permitted, for inscrutable purposes, to give evidence of that evil puritanical leaven which was a secret element of his religion. He had been kind to Charles hitherto, which made his altered manner more distressing to him.

"We had hoped," he said, "Mr. Reding, that so good a young man as you once were would have gained a place on some foundation, and been settled here, and been a useful man in his generation, sir; and a column, a buttress of the Church of England, sir. Well, sir, here are my best wishes for you, sir. When you come up for your Master's degree, sir—no, I think it is your Bachelor's—which is it, Mr. Reding, are you yet a Bachelor? Oh, I see your gown."

Charles said he had not yet been into the schools.

"Well, sir, when you come up to be examined, I should say—to be examined—we will hope that in the interval, reflection, and study, and absence perhaps from dangerous companions, will have brought you to a soberer state of mind, Mr. Reding."

Charles was shocked at the language used about him. "Really, sir," he said, "if you knew me better, you would feel that I am likely neither to receive nor do harm by remaining here between this and Easter."

"What! remain here, sir, with all the young men about?" asked Dr. Bluett, with astonishment, "with all the young men about you, sir?"

Charles really had not a word to say; he did not know himself in so novel a position. "I cannot conceive, sir," he said, at last, "why I should be unfit company for the gentlemen of the College."

Dr. Bluett's jaw dropped, and his eyes assumed a hollow aspect. "You will corrupt their minds, sir," he said—"you will corrupt their minds." Then he added, in a sepulchral tone, which came from the very depths of his inside: "You will introduce them, sir, to some subtle Jesuit—to some subtle Jesuit, Mr. Reding."

CHAPTER XI

Mrs. Reding was by this time settled in the neighbourhood of old friends in Devonshire; and there Charles spent the winter and early spring with her and his three sisters, the eldest of whom was two years older than himself.

"Come, shut your dull books, Charles," said Caroline, the youngest, a girl of fourteen; "make way for the tea; I am sure you have read enough. You sometimes don't speak a word for an hour together; at least, you might tell us what you are reading about."

"My dear Carry, you would not be much the wiser if I did," answered Charles; "it is Greek history."

"Oh," said Caroline, "I know more than you think; I have read

Goldsmith, and good part of Rollin, besides Pope's Homer."

"Capital!" said Charles; "well, I am reading about Pelopidas—who was he?"

"Pelopidas!" answered Caroline, "I ought to know. Oh, I recollect, he had an ivory shoulder."

"Well said, Carry; but I have not yet a distinct idea of him either. Was he a statue, or flesh and blood, with this shoulder of his?"

"Oh, he was alive; somebody ate him, I think."

"Well, was he a god or a man?" said Charles.

"Oh, it's a mistake of mine," said Caroline; "he was a goddess, the ivory-footed—no, that was Thetis."

"My dear Caroline," said her mother, "do not talk so at random; think before you speak; you know better than this."

"She has, ma'am," said Charles, "what Mr. Jennings would call 'a very inaccurate mind.'"

"I recollect perfectly now," said Caroline, "he was a friend of Epaminondas."

"When did he live?" asked Charles. Caroline was silent.

"Oh, Carry," said Eliza, "don't you recollect the *memoria technica*?"

"I never could learn it," said Caroline; "I hate it."

"Nor can I," said Mary; "give me good native numbers; they are sweet and kindly, like flowers in a bed; but I don't like your artificial flower-pots."

"But surely," said Charles, "a *memoria technica* makes you recollect a great many dates which you otherwise could not?"

"The crabbed names are more difficult even to pronounce than the numbers to learn," said Caroline.

"That's because you have very few dates to get up," said Charles; "but common writing is a *memoria technica*."

"That's beyond Caroline," said Mary.

"What are words but artificial signs for ideas?" said Charles; "they are more musical, but as arbitrary. There is no more reason why the sound 'hat' should mean the particular thing so called, which we put on our heads, than why 'abul-distof' should stand for 1520."

"Oh, my dear child," said Mrs. Reding, "how you run on! Don't be paradoxical."

"My dear mother," said Charles, coming round to the fire, "I don't want to be paradoxical; it's only a generalization."

"Keep it, then, for the schools, my dear; I dare say it will do you good there," continued Mrs. Reding, while she continued her hemming; "poor Caroline will be as much put to it in logic as in history."

"I am in a dilemma," said Charles, as he seated himself on a little stool at his mother's feet; "for Carry calls me stupid if I am silent, and you call me paradoxical if I speak."

"Good sense," said his mother, "is the golden mean."

"And what is common sense?" said Charles.

"The silver mean," said Eliza.

"Well done," said Charles; "it is small change for every hour."

"Rather," said Caroline, "it is the copper mean, for we want it, like alms for the poor, to give away. People are always asking *me* for it. If I can't tell who Isaac's father was, Mary says, 'O Carry, where's your common sense?' If I am going out of doors, Eliza runs up, 'Carry,' she cries, 'you haven't common sense; your shawl's all pinned awry.' And when I ask mamma the shortest way across the fields to Dalton, she says, 'Use your common sense, my dear.'"

"No wonder you have so little of it, poor dear child," said Charles; "no bank could stand such a run."

"No such thing," said Mary; "it flows into her bank ten times as fast as it comes out. She has plenty of it from us; and what she does with it no one can make out; she either hoards or she speculates."

"'Like the great ocean,'" said Charles, "'which receives the rivers, yet is not full.'"

"That's somewhere in Scripture," said Eliza.

"In the 'Preacher,'" said Charles, and he continued the quotation;

"'All things are full of labour, man cannot utter it; the eye is not satisfied with seeing, nor the ear filled with hearing.'"

His mother sighed; "Take my cup, my love," she said; "no more."

"I know why Charles is so fond of the 'Preacher,'" said Mary; "it's because he's tired of reading; 'much study is a weariness to the flesh.' I wish we could help you, dear Charles."

"My dear boy, I really think you read too much," said his mother; "only think how many hours you have been at it today. You are always up one or two hours before the sun; and I don't think you have had your walk today."

"It's so dismal walking alone, my dear mother; and as to walking with you and my sisters, it's pleasant enough, but no exercise."

"But, Charlie," said Mary, "that's absurd of you; these nice sunny days, which you could not expect at this season, are just the time for long walks. Why don't you resolve to make straight for the plantations, or to mount Hart Hill, or go right through Dun Wood and back?"

"Because all woods are dun and dingy just now, Mary, and not green. It's quite melancholy to see them."

"Just the finest time of the year," said his mother; "it's universally allowed; all painters say that the autumn is the season to see a landscape in."

"All gold and russet," said Mary.

"It makes me melancholy," said Charles.

"What! the beautiful autumn make you melancholy?" asked his mother.

"Oh, my dear mother, you mean to say that I am paradoxical again; I cannot help it. I like spring; but autumn saddens me."

"Charles always says so," said Mary; "he thinks nothing of the rich hues into which the sober green changes; he likes the dull uniform of summer."

"No, it is not that," said Charles; "I never saw anything so gorgeous as Magdalen Water-walk, for instance, in October; it is quite wonderful, the variety of colours. I admire, and am astonished; but I cannot love or like it. It is because I can't separate the look of things from what it portends; that rich variety is but the token of disease and death."

"Surely," said Mary, "colours have their own intrinsic beauty; we may like them for their own sake."

"No, no," said Charles, "we always go by association; else why not admire raw beef, or a toad, or some other reptiles, which are as beautiful and bright as tulips or cherries, yet revolting, because we consider what they are, not how they look?"

"What next?" said his mother, looking up from her work; "my dear Charles, you are not serious in comparing cherries to raw beef or to toads?"

"No, my dear mother," answered Charles, laughing, "no, I only say that they look like them, not are like them."

"A toad look like a cherry, Charles!" persisted Mrs. Reding.

"Oh, my dear mother," he answered, "I can't explain; I really have said nothing out of the way. Mary does not think I have."

"But," said Mary, "why not associate pleasant thoughts with autumn?"

"It is impossible," said Charles; "it is the sick season and the deathbed of Nature. I cannot look with pleasure on the decay of the mother of all living. The many hues upon the landscape are but the spots of dissolution."

"This is a strained, unnatural view, Charles," said Mary; "shake yourself, and you will come to a better mind. Don't you like to see a rich sunset? Yet the sun is leaving you."

Charles was for a moment posed; then he said, "Yes, but there was no autumn in Eden; suns rose and set in Paradise, but the leaves were always green, and did not wither. There was a river to feed them. Autumn is the 'fall.'"

"So, my dearest Charles," said Mrs. Reding, "you don't go out walking these fine days because there was no autumn in the garden of Eden?"

"Oh," said Charles, laughing, "it is cruel to bring me so to book. What I meant was, that my reading was a direct obstacle to walking, and that the fine weather did not tempt me to remove it."

"I am glad we have you here, my dear," said his mother, "for we can force you out now and then; at College I suspect you never walk at all."

"It's only for a time, ma'am," said Charles; "when my examination is over, I will take as long walks as I did with Edward Gandy that winter after I left school."

"Ah, how merry you were then, Charles!" said Mary; "so happy with the thoughts of Oxford before you!"

"Ah, my dear," said Mrs. Reding, "you'll then walk too much, as you now walk too little. My good boy, you are so earnest about everything."

"It's a shame to find fault with him for being diligent," said Mary: "you like him to read for honours, I know, mamma; but if he is to get them he must read a great deal."

"True, my love," answered Mrs. Reding; "Charles is a dear good fellow, I know. How glad we all shall be to have him ordained, and settled in a curacy!"

Charles sighed. "Come, Mary," he said, "give us some music, now the urn has gone away. Play me that beautiful air of Beethoven, the one I call 'The Voice of the Dead.'"

"Oh, Charles, you do give such melancholy names to things!" cried Mary.

"The other day," said Eliza, "we had a most beautiful scent wafted across the road as we were walking, and he called it 'the Ghost of the Past'; and he says that the sound of the Eolian harp is 'remorseful.'"

"Now, you'd think all that very pretty," said Charles, "if you saw it in a book of poems; but you call it melancholy when I say it."

"Oh, yes," said Caroline, "because poets never mean what they say, and would not be poetical unless they were melancholy."

"Well," said Mary, "I play to you, Charles, on this one condition, that you let me give you some morning a serious lecture on that melancholy of yours, which, I assure you is growing on you."

CHAPTER XII

Charles's perplexities rapidly took a definite form on his coming into Devonshire. The very fact of his being at home, and not at Oxford where he ought to have been, brought them before his mind; and the near prospect of his examination and degree justified the consideration of them. No addition indeed was made to their substance, as already described; but they were no longer vague and indistinct, but thoroughly apprehended by him; nor did he make up his mind that they were insurmountable, but he saw clearly what it was that had to be surmounted. The particular form of argument into which they happened to fall was determined by the circumstances in which he found himself at the time, and was this, viz. how he could subscribe the Articles *ex animo*, without faith, more or less, in his Church as the imponent; and next, how he could have faith in her, her history and present condition being what they were. The fact of these difficulties was a great source of distress to him. It was aggravated by the circumstance that he had no one to talk to, or to sympathize with him under them. And it was completed by the necessity of carrying about with him a secret which he dared not tell to others, yet which he foreboded must be told one day. All this was the secret of that depression of spirits which his sisters had observed in him.

He was one day sitting thoughtfully over the fire with a book in his hand, when Mary entered. "I wish you would teach *me* the art of reading Greek in live coals," she said.

"Sermons in stones, and good in everything," answered Charles.

"You do well to liken yourself to the melancholy Jaques," she replied.

"Not so," said he, "but to the good Duke Charles, who was banished to the green forest."

"A great grievance," answered Mary, "we being the wild things with whom you are forced to live. My dear Charles," she continued, "I hope the tittle-tattle that drove you here does not still dwell on your mind."

"Why, it is not very pleasant, Mary, after having been on the best terms with the whole College, and in particular with the Principal and Jennings, at last to be sent down, as a rowing-man might be rusticated for tandem-driving. You have no notion how strong the old Principal was, and Jennings too."

"Well, my dearest Charles, you must not brood over it," said Mary, "as I fear you are doing."

"I don't see where it is to end," said Charles; "the Principal expressly said that my prospects at the University were knocked up. I suppose they would not give me a testimonial, if I wished to stand for a fellowship anywhere."

"Oh, it is a temporary mistake," said Mary; "I dare say by this time they know better. And it's one great gain to have you with us; we, at least, ought to be obliged to them."

"I have been so very careful, Mary," said Charles; "I have never been to the evening-parties, or to the sermons which are talked about in the University. It's quite amazing to me what can have put it into their heads. At the Article-lecture I now and then asked a question, but it was really because I wished to understand and get up the different subjects. Jennings fell on me the moment I entered his room. I can call it nothing else; very civil at first in his manner, but there was something in his eye before he spoke which told me at once what was coming. It's odd a man of such self-command as he should not better hide his feelings; but I have always been able to see what Jennings was thinking about."

"Depend on it," said his sister, "you will think nothing of it whatever this time next year. It will be like a summer-cloud, come and gone."

"And then it damps me, and interrupts me in my reading. I fall back thinking of it, and cannot give my mind to my books, or exert myself. It is very hard."

Mary sighed; "I wish I could help you," she said; "but women can do so little. Come, let me take the fretting, and you the reading; that'll be a fair division."

"And then my dear mother too," he continued; "what will she think of it when it comes to her ears? And come it must."

"Nonsense," said Mary, "don't make a mountain of a mole-hill. You will go back, take your degree, and nobody will be the wiser."

"No, it can't be so," said Charles seriously.

"What do you mean?" asked Mary.

"These things don't clear off in that way," said he; "it is no summer-cloud; it may turn to rain, for what they know."

Mary looked at him with some surprise.

"I mean," he said, "that I have no confidence that they will let me take my degree, any more than let me reside there."

"That is very absurd," said she; "it's what I meant by brooding over things, and making mountains of mole-hills."

"My sweet Mary," he said, affectionately taking her hand, "my only real confidant and comfort, I would tell you something more, if you could bear it."

Mary was frightened, and her heart beat. "Charles," she said, withdrawing her hand, "any pain is less than to see you thus. I see too clearly that something is on your mind."

Charles put his feet on the fender, and looked down.

"I *can't* tell you," he said, at length, with vehemence; then, seeing by her face how much he was distressing her, he said, half-laughing, as if to turn the edge of his words, "My dear Mary, when people bear witness against one, one can't help fearing that there is, perhaps, something to bear witness against."

"Impossible, Charles! *you* corrupt other people! *you* falsify the Prayer Book and Articles! impossible!"

"Mary, which do you think would be the best judge whether my face was dirty and my coat shabby, you or I? Well, then, perhaps Jennings, or at least common report, knows more about me than I do myself."

"You must not speak in this way," said Mary, much hurt; "you really do pain me now. What can you mean?"

Charles covered his face with his hands, and at length said: "It's no good; you can't assist me here; I only pain you. I ought not to have begun the subject."

There was a silence.

"My dearest Charles," said Mary tenderly, "come, I will bear anything, and not be annoyed. Anything better than to see you go on in this way. But really you frighten me."

"Why," he answered, "when a number of people tell me that Oxford is not my place, not my position, perhaps they are right; perhaps it isn't."

"But is that really all?" she said; "who wants you to lead an Oxford life? Not we."

"No, but Oxford implies taking a degree—taking orders."

"Now, my dear Charles, speak out; don't drop hints; let me know"; and she sat down with a look of great anxiety.

"Well," he said, making an effort; "yet I don't know where to begin; but many things have happened to me, in various ways, to show me that I have not a place, a position, a home, that I am not made for, that I am a stranger in, the Church of England."

There was a dreadful pause; Mary turned very pale; then, darting at a conclusion with precipitancy, she said quickly, "You mean to say, you are going to join the Church of Rome, Charles."

"No," he said, "it is not so. I mean no such thing; I mean just what I say; I have told you the whole; I have kept nothing back. It is this, and no more—that I feel out of place."

"Well, then," she said, "you must tell me more; for, to my apprehension, you mean just what I have said, nothing short of it."

"I can't go through things in order," he said; "but wherever I go, whomever I talk with, I feel him to be another sort of person from what I am. I can't convey it to you; you won't understand me; but the words of the Psalm, 'I am a stranger upon earth,' describe what I always feel. No one thinks or feels like me. I hear sermons, I talk on religious subjects with friends, and every one seems to bear witness against me. And now the College bears its witness, and sends me down."

"Oh, Charles," said Mary, "how changed you are!" and tears came into her eyes; "you used to be so cheerful, so happy. You took such pleasure in every one, in everything. We used to laugh and say, 'All Charlie's geese are swans.' What has come over you?" She paused, and then continued: "Don't you recollect those lines in the 'Christian Year'? I can't repeat them; we used to apply them to you; something about hope or love 'making all things bright with her own magic smile.'"

Charles was touched when he was reminded of what he had been three years before; he said: "I suppose it is coming out of shadows into realities."

"There has been much to sadden you," she added, sighing; "and now these nasty books are too much for you. Why should you go up for honours? What's the good of it?"

There was a pause again.

"I wish I could bring home to you," said Charles, "the number of intimations, as it were, which have been given me of my uncongeniality, as it may be called, with things as they are. What perhaps most affected me, was a talk I had with Carlton, whom I have lately been reading with; for, if I could not agree with *him*, or rather, if *he* bore witness against me, who could be expected to say a word for me? I cannot bear the pomp and pretence which I see everywhere.

I am not speaking against individuals; they are very good persons, I know; but, really, if you saw Oxford as it is! The Heads with such large incomes; they are indeed very liberal of their money, and their wives are often simple, self-denying persons, as every one says, and do a great deal of good in the place; but I speak of the system. Here are ministers of Christ with large incomes, living in finely furnished houses, with wives and families, and stately butlers and servants in livery, giving dinners all in the best style, condescending and gracious, waving their hands and mincing their words, as if they were the cream of the earth, but without anything to make them clergymen but a black coat and a white tie. And then Bishops or Deans come, with women tucked under their arm; and they can't enter church but a fine powdered man runs first with a cushion for them to sit on, and a warm sheepskin to keep their feet from the stones."

Mary laughed: "Well, my dear Charles," she said, "I did not think you had seen so much of Bishops, Deans, Professors, and Heads of houses at St. Saviour's; you have kept good company."

"I have my eyes about me," said Charles, "and have had quite opportunities enough; I can't go into particulars."

"Well, you have been hard on them, I think," said Mary; "when a poor old man has the rheumatism," and she sighed a little, "it is hard he mayn't have his feet kept from the cold."

"Ah, Mary, I can't bring it home to you! but you must, please, throw yourself into what I say, and not criticize my instances or my terms. What I mean is, that there is a worldly air about everything, as unlike as possible the spirit of the Gospel. I don't impute to the dons ambition or avarice; but still, what Heads of houses, Fellows, and all of them evidently put before them as an end is, to enjoy the world in the first place, and to serve God in the second. Not that they don't make it their final object to get to heaven; but their immediate object is to be comfortable, to marry, to have a fair income, station, and respectability, a convenient house, a pleasant country, a sociable neighbourhood. There is nothing high about them. I declare I think the Puseyites are the only persons who have high views in the whole place; I should say, the only persons who profess them, for I don't know them to speak about them." He thought of White.

"Well, you are talking of things I don't know about," said Mary; "but I can't think all the young clever men of the place are looking out for ease and comfort; nor can I believe that in the Church of Rome money has always been put to the best of purposes."

"I said nothing about the Church of Rome," said Charles; "why do you bring in the Church of Rome? That's another thing altogether. What I mean is, that there is a worldly smell about Oxford which I can't abide. I am not using 'worldly' in its worse sense. People are religious and charitable; but—I don't like to mention names—but I know various dons, and the notion of evangelical poverty, the danger of riches, the giving up all for Christ, all those ideas which are first principles in Scripture, as I read it, don't seem to enter into their idea of religion. I declare, I think that is the reason why the Puseyites are so unpopular."

"Well, I can't see," said Mary, "why you must be disgusted with the world, and with your place and duties in it, because there are worldly people in it."

"But I was speaking of Carlton," said Charles; "do you know, good fellow as he is—and I love, admire, and respect him exceedingly—he actually laid it down almost as an axiom, that a clergyman of the English Church ought to marry? He said that celibacy might be very well in other communions, but that a man made himself a fool, and was out of joint with the age, who remained single in the Church of England."

Poor Charles was so serious, and the proposition which he related was so monstrous, that Mary, in spite of her real distress, could not help laughing out. "I really cannot help it," she said; "well, it really was a most extraordinary statement, I confess. But, my dear Charlie, you are not afraid that he will carry you off against your will, and marry you to some fair lady before you know where you are?"

"Don't talk in that way, Mary," said Charles; "I can't bear a joke just now. I mean, Carlton is so sensible a man, and takes so just a view of things, that the conviction flashed on my mind, that the Church of England really was what he implied it to be—a form of religion very unlike that of the Apostles."

This sobered Mary indeed. "Alas," she said, "we have got upon very different ground now; not what our Church thinks of you, but what you think of our Church." There was a pause. "I thought this was at the bottom," she said; "I never could believe that a parcel of people, some of whom you cared nothing for, telling you that you were not in your place, would make you think so, unless you first felt it yourself. That's the real truth; and then you interpret what others say in your own way." Another uncomfortable pause. Then she continued: "I see how it will be. When you take up a thing, Charles, I know well you don't lay it down. No, you have made up your mind already. We shall see you a Roman Catholic."

"Do *you* then bear witness against me, Mary, as well as the rest?" said he sorrowfully.

She saw her mistake. "No," she answered; "all I say is, that it rests with yourself, not with others. *If* you have made up your mind, there's no help for it. It is not others who drive you, who bear witness against you. Dear Charles, don't mistake me, and don't deceive yourself. You have a strong *will*."

At this moment Caroline entered the room. "I could not think where you were, Mary," she said; "here Perkins has been crying after you ever so long. It's something about dinner; I don't know what. We have hunted high and low, and never guessed you were helping Charles at his books." Mary gave a deep sigh, and left the room.

CHAPTER XIII

NEITHER to brother nor to sister had the conversation been a satisfaction or relief. "I can go nowhere for sympathy," thought Charles; "dear Mary does not understand me more than others. I can't bring out what I mean and feel; and when I attempt to do so, my statements and arguments seem absurd to myself. It has been a great effort to tell her; and in one sense it is a gain, for it is a trial over. Else I have taken nothing by my move, and might as well have held my tongue. I have simply pained her without relieving myself. By-the-bye, she has gone off believing about twice as much as the fact. I was going to set her right when Carry came in. My only difficulty is about taking orders; and she thinks I am going to be a Roman Catholic. How absurd! but women will run on so; give an inch, and they take an ell. I know nothing of the Roman Catholics. The simple question is, whether I should go to the Bar or the Church. I declare, I think I have made vastly too much of it myself. I ought to have begun this way with her—I ought to have said, 'D'you know, I have serious thoughts of reading law?' I've made a hash of it."

Poor Mary, on the other hand, was in a confusion of thought and feeling as painful as it was new to her; though for a time household matters and necessary duties towards her younger sisters occupied her mind in a different direction. She had been indeed taken at her word; little had she expected what would come on her when she engaged to "take the fretting, while he took the reading." She had known what grief was, not so long ago; but not till now had she known anxiety. Charles's state of mind was a matter of simple astonishment to her. At first it quite frightened and shocked her; it was as if Charles had lost his identity, and had turned out some one else. It was like a great breach of trust. She had seen there was a good deal in the newspapers about the "Oxford party" and their doings; and at different places, where she had been on visits, she had heard of churches being done up in the new fashion, and clergymen being accused, in consequence, of Popery—a charge which she had laughed at. But now it was actually brought home to her door that there was something in it. Yet it was to her incomprehensible, and she hardly knew where she was. And that, of all persons in the world, her brother, her own Charles, with whom she had been one heart and soul all their lives—one so cheerful, so religious, so good, so sensible, so cautious—that he should be the first specimen that crossed her path of the new opinions—it bewildered her.

And where *had* he got his notions?—Notions! she could not call them notions; he had nothing to say for himself. It was an infatuation; he, so clever, so sharp-sighted, could say nothing better in defence of himself than that Mrs. Bishop of Monmouth was too pretty, and that old Dr. Stock sat upon a cushion. Oh, sad, sad indeed! How was it he could be so insensible to the blessings he gained from his Church, and had enjoyed all his life? What could he need? *She* had no need at all: going to church was a pleasure to her. She liked to hear the Lessons and the Collects, coming round year after year, and marking the seasons. The historical books and prophets in summer; then the "stir-up" Collect just before Advent; the beautiful Collects in Advent itself, with the Lessons from Isaiah reaching on through Epiphany; they were quite music to the ear. Then the Psalms, varying with every Sunday; they were a perpetual solace to her, ever old yet ever new. The occasional additions, too—the Athanasian Creed, the Benedictus, Deus misereatur, and Omnia opera, which her father had been used to read at certain great feasts; and the beautiful Litany. What could he want more? Where could he find so much? Well, it was a mystery to her; and she could only feel thankful that *she* was not exposed to the temptations, whatever they were, which had acted on the powerful mind of her brother.

Then, she had anticipated how pleasant it would be when Charles was a clergyman, and she should hear him preach; when there would be one whom she would have a right to ask questions and to consult whenever she wished. This prospect was at an end; she could no longer trust him: he had given a shake to her confidence which it never could recover; it was gone for ever. They were all of them women but he; he was their only stay, now that her father had been taken away. What was now to become of them? To be abandoned by her own brother! oh, how terrible!

And how was she to break it to her mother? For broken it must be sooner or later. She could not deceive herself; she knew her brother well enough to feel sure that, when he had really got hold of a thing, he would not let it go again without convincing reasons; and what reasons there could be for letting it go she could not conceive, if there could be reasons for taking it up. The taking it up baffled all reason, all calculation. Well, but how was her mother to be told of it? Was it better to let her suspect it first, and so break it to her, or to wait till the event happened? The problem was too difficult for the present, and she must leave it.

This was her state for several days, till her fever of mind gradually subsided into a state of which a dull anxiety was a latent but habitual element, leaving her as usual at ordinary times, but every now and then betraying itself by sudden sharp sighs or wanderings of thought. Neither brother nor sister, loving each other really as much as ever, had quite the same sweetness and evenness of temper as was natural to them; self-control became a duty, and the evening circle was duller than before, without any one being able to say why. Charles was more attentive to his mother; he no more brought his books into the drawing-room, but gave himself to her company. He read to them, but he had little to talk about; and Eliza and Caroline both wished his stupid examination, past and over, that he might be restored to his natural liveliness.

As to Mrs. Reding, she did not observe more than that her son was a very hard student, and grudged himself a walk or ride, let the day be ever so fine. She was a mild, quiet person, of keen feelings and precise habits; not very quick at observation; and, having lived all her life in the country, and till her late loss having scarcely known what trouble was, she was singularly unable to comprehend how things could go on in any way but one. Charles had not told her the real cause of his spending the winter at home, thinking it would be a needless vexation to her; much less did he contemplate harassing her with the recital of his own religious difficulties, which were not appreciable by her, and issued in no definite result. To his sister he did attempt an explanation of his former conversation, with a view of softening the extreme misgivings which it had created in her mind. She received it thankfully, and professed to be relieved by it; but the blow was struck, the suspicion was lodged deep in her mind—he was still Charles, dear to her as ever, but she never could rid herself of the anticipation which on that occasion she had expressed.

CHAPTER XIV

ONE morning he was told that a gentleman had asked for him, and been shown into the dining-room. Descending, he saw the tall slender figure of Bateman, now a clergyman, and lately appointed curate of a neighbouring parish. Charles had not seen him for a year and a half, and shook hands with him very warmly, complimenting him on his white neckcloth, which somehow, he said, altered him more than he could have expected. Bateman's manner certainly was altered; it might be the accident of the day, but he did not seem quite at his ease; it might be that he was in a strange house, and was likely soon to be precipitated into the company of ladies, to which he had never been used. If so, the trial was on the point of beginning, for Charles said instantly that he must come and see his mother, and of course meant to dine with them; the sky was clear, and there was an excellent footpath between Boughton and Melford. Bateman could not do this, but he would have the greatest pleasure in being introduced to Mrs. Reding; so he stumbled after Charles into the drawing-room, and was soon conversing with her and the young ladies.

"A charming prospect you have here, ma'am," said Bateman, "when you are once inside the house. It does not promise outside so extensive a view."

"No, it is shut in with trees," said Mrs. Reding; "and the brow of the hill changes its direction so much that at first I used to think the prospect ought to be from the opposite windows."

"What is that high hill?" said Bateman.

"It is Hart Hill," said Charles; "there's a Roman camp atop of it."

"We can see eight steeples from our windows," said Mrs. Reding—"ring the bell for luncheon, my dear."

"Ah, our ancestors, Mrs. Reding," said Bateman, "thought more of building churches than we do; or rather than we have done, I should say, for now it is astonishing what efforts are made to add to our ecclesiastical structures."

"Our ancestors did a good deal too," said Mrs. Reding; "how many churches, my dear, were built in London in Queen Anne's time? St. Martin's was one of them."

"Fifty," said Eliza.

"Fifty were intended," said Charles.

"Yes, Mrs. Reding," said Bateman; "but by ancestors I meant the holy Bishops and other members of our Catholic Church previously to the Reformation. For, though the Reformation was a great blessing" (a glance at Charles), "yet we must not, in justice, forget what was done by English Churchmen before it."

"Ah, poor creatures," said Mrs. Reding, "they did one good thing in building churches; it has saved us much trouble."

"Is there much church-restoration going on in these parts?" said Bateman, taken rather aback.

"My mother has but lately come here, like yourself," said Charles; "yes, there is some; Barton Church, you know," appealing to Mary.

"Have your walks extended so far as Barton?" said Mary to Bateman.

"Not yet, Miss Reding, not yet," answered he; "of course they are destroying the pews."

"They are to put in seats," said Charles, "and of a very good pattern."

"Pews are intolerable," said Bateman; "yet the last generation of incumbents contentedly bore them; it is wonderful!"

A not unnatural silence followed this speech. Charles broke it by asking if Bateman intended to do anything in the improvement line at Melford.

Bateman looked modest.

"Nothing of any consequence," he said; "some few things were done; but he had a rector of the old school, poor man, who was an enemy to that sort of thing."

It was with some malicious feeling, in consequence of his attack on clergymen of the past age, that Charles pressed his visitor to give an account of his own reforms.

"Why," said Bateman, "much discretion is necessary in these matters, or you do as much harm as good; you get into hot water with churchwardens and vestries, as well as with old rectors, and again with the gentry of the place, and please no one. For this reason I have made no attempt to introduce the surplice into the pulpit except on the great festivals, intending to familiarize my parishioners to it by little and little. However, I wear a scarf or stole, and have taken care that it should be two inches broader than usual; and I always wear the cassock in my parish. I hope you approve of the cassock, Mrs. Reding?"

"It is a very cold dress, sir—that's my opinion—when made of silk or bombazeen; and very unbecoming too, when worn by itself."

"Particularly behind," said Charles; "it is quite unshapely."

"Oh, I have remedied that," said Bateman; "you have noticed, Miss Reding, I dare say, the Bishop's short cassock. It comes to the knees, and looks much like a continuation of a waistcoat, the straight-cut coat being worn as usual. Well, Miss Reding, I have adopted the same plan with the long cassock; I put my coat over it."

Mary had difficulty to keep from smiling; Charles laughed out. "Impossible, Bateman," he said; "you don't mean you wear your tailed French coat over your long straight cassock reaching to your ankles?"

"Certainly," said Bateman gravely; "I thus consult for warmth and appearance too; and all my parishioners are sure to know me. I think this a great point, Miss Reding: I hear the little boys as I pass say, 'That's the parson.'"

"I'll be bound they do," said Charles.

"Well," said Mrs. Reding, surprised out of her propriety, "did one ever hear the like!"

Bateman looked round at her, startled and frightened.

"You were going to speak of your improvements in your church," said Mary, wishing to divert his attention from her mother.

"Ah, true, Miss Reding, true," said Bateman, "thank you for reminding me; I have digressed to improvements in my own dress. I should have liked to have pulled down the galleries and lowered the high pews; that, however, I could not do. So I have lowered the pulpit some six feet. Now by doing so, first I give a pattern in my own person of the kind of condescension or lowliness to which I would persuade my people. But this is not all; for the consequence of lowering the pulpit is that no one in the galleries can see or hear me preach; and this is a bonus on those who are below."

"It's a broad hint, certainly," said Charles.

"But it's a hint for those below also," continued Bateman; "for no one can see or hear me in the pews either, till the sides are lowered."

"One thing only is wanting besides," said Charles, smiling and looking amiable, lest he should be saying too much; "since you are full tall, you must kneel when you preach, Bateman, else you will undo your own alterations."

Bateman looked pleased. "I have anticipated you," he said; "I preach sitting. It is more comformable to antiquity and to reason to sit than to stand."

"With these precautions," said Charles, "I really think you might have ventured on your surplice in the pulpit every Sunday. Are your parishioners contented?"

"Oh, not at all, far from it," cried Bateman; "but they can do nothing. The alteration is so simple."

"Nothing besides?" asked Charles.

"Nothing in the architectural way," answered he; "but one thing more in the way of observances. I have fortunately picked up a very fair copy of Jewell, black-letter; and I have placed it in church, securing it with a chain to the wall, for any poor person who wishes to read it. Our church is emphatically the 'poor man's church,' Mrs. Reding."

"Well," said Charles to himself, "I'll back the old parsons against the young ones any day, if this is to be their cut." Then aloud: "Come, you must see our garden; take up your hat, and let's have a turn in it. There's a very nice terrace-walk at the upper end."

Bateman accordingly, having been thus trotted out for the amusement of the ladies, was now led off again, and was soon in the aforesaid terrace-walk, pacing up and down in earnest conversation with Charles.

"Reding, my good fellow," said he, "what is the meaning of this report concerning you, which is everywhere about?"

"I have not heard it," said Charles abruptly.

"Why, it is this," said Bateman; "I wish to approach the subject with as great delicacy as possible: don't tell me if you don't like it, or tell me just as much as you like; yet you will excuse an old friend. They say you are going to leave the Church of your baptism for the Church of Rome."

"Is it widely spread?" asked Charles coolly.

"Oh, yes; I heard it in London; have had a letter mentioning it from Oxford; and a friend of mine heard it given out as positive at a visitation dinner in Wales."

"So," thought Charles, "you are bringing *your* witness against me as well as the rest."

"Well but, my good Reding," said Bateman, "why are you silent? Is it true—is it true?"

"What true? That I am a Roman Catholic? Oh, certainly; don't you understand, that's why I am reading so hard for the schools?" said Charles.

"Come, be serious for a moment, Reding," said Bateman, "do be serious. Will you empower me to contradict the report, or to negative it to a certain point, or in any respect?"

"Oh, to be sure," said Charles, "contradict it, by all means, contradict it entirely."

"May I give it a plain, unqualified, unconditional, categorical, flat denial?" asked Bateman.

"Of course, of course."

Bateman could not make him out, and had not a dream how he was teasing him. "I don't know where to find you," he said. They paced down the walk in silence.

Bateman began again. "You see," he said, "it would be such a wonderful blindness, it would be so utterly inexcusable in a person like yourself, who had known *what* the Church of England was; not a Dissenter, not an unlettered layman; but one who had been at Oxford, who had come across so many excellent men, who had seen what the Church of England could be, her grave beauty, her orderly and decent activity; who had seen churches decorated as they should be, with candlesticks, ciboriums, faldstools, lecterns, antependiums, piscinas, rood-lofts, and sedilia; who, in fact, had seen the Church Service *carried out*, and could desiderate nothing—tell me, my dear good Reding," taking hold of his button-hole, "what is it you want—what is it? Name it."

"That you would take yourself off," Charles would have said, had he spoken his mind; he merely said, however, that really he desiderated nothing but to be believed when he said that he had no intention of leaving his own Church. Bateman was incredulous, and thought him close. "Perhaps you are not aware," he said, "how much is known of the circumstances of your being sent down. The old Principal was full of the subject."

"What! I suppose he told people right and left," said Reding.

"Oh, yes," answered Bateman; "a friend of mine knows him, and happening to call on him soon after you went down, had the whole story from him. He spoke most kindly of you, and in the highest terms; said that it was deplorable how much your mind was warped by the prevalent opinions, and that he should not be surprised if it turned out you were a Romanist even while you were at St. Saviour's; anyhow, that you would be one day a Romanist for certain, for that you held that the saints reigning with Christ interceded for us in heaven. But what was stronger, when the report got about, Sheffield said that he was not surprised at it, that he always prophesied it."

"I am much obliged to him," said Charles.

"However, you warrant me," said Bateman, "to contradict it—so I understand you—to contradict it peremptorily; that's enough for me. It's a great relief; it's very satisfactory. Well, I must be going."

"I don't like to seem to drive you away," said Charles, "but really you must be going if you want to get home before nightfall. I hope you don't feel lonely or overworked where you are. If you are so at any time, don't scruple to drop in to dinner here; nay, we can take you in for a night, if you wish it."

Bateman thanked him, and they proceeded to the hall-door together; when they were nearly parting, Bateman stopped and said, "Do you know, I should like to lend you some books to read. Let me send up to you Bramhall's Works, Thorndike, Barrow on the Unity of the Church, and Leslie's Dialogues on Romanism. I could name others, but content myself with these at present. They perfectly settle the matter; you can't help being convinced. I'll not say a word more; good-bye to you, good-bye."

CHAPTER XV

Much as Charles loved and prized the company of his mother and sisters he was not sorry to have gentlemen's society, so he accepted with pleasure an invitation which Bateman sent him to dine with him at Melford. Also he wished to show Bateman, what no protestation could effect, how absurdly exaggerated were the reports which were circulated about him. And as the said Bateman, with all his want of common sense, was really a well-informed man, and well read in English divines, he thought he might incidentally hear something from him which he could turn to account. When he got to Melford he found a Mr. Campbell had been asked to meet him; a young Cambridge rector of a neighbouring parish, of the same religious sentiments on the whole as Bateman, and, though a little positive, a man of clear head and vigorous mind.

They had been going over the church; and the conversation at dinner turned on the revival of Gothic architecture—an event which gave unmixed satisfaction to all parties. The subject would have died out, almost as soon as it was started, for want of a difference upon it, had not Bateman happily gone on boldly to declare that, if he had his will, there should be no architecture in the English churches but Gothic, and no music but Gregorian. This was a good thesis, distinctly put, and gave scope for a very pretty quarrel. Reding said that all these adjuncts of worship, whether music or architecture, were national; they were the mode in which religious feeling showed itself in particular times and places. He did not mean to say that the outward expression of religion in a country might not be guided, but it could not be forced; that it was as preposterous to make people worship in one's own way, as be merry in one's own way. "The Greeks," he said, "cut the hair in grief, the Romans let it grow; the Orientals veiled their heads in worship, the Greeks uncovered them; Christians take off their hats in a church, Mahometans their shoes; a long veil is a sign of modesty in Europe, of immodesty in Asia. You may as well try to change the size of people, as their forms of worship. Bateman, we must cut you down a foot, and then you shall begin your ecclesiastical reforms."

"But surely, my worthy friend," answered Bateman, "you don't mean to say that there is no natural connection between internal feeling and outward expression, so that one form is no better than another?"

"Far from it," answered Charles; "but let those who confine their music to Gregorians put up crucifixes in the highways. Each is the representative of a particular place or time."

"That's what I say of our good friend's short coat and long cassock," said Campbell; "it is a confusion of different times, ancient and modern."

"Or of different ideas," said Charles, "the cassock Catholic, the coat Protestant."

"The reverse," said Bateman; "the cassock is old Hooker's Anglican habit: the coat comes from Catholic France."

"Anyhow, it is what Mr. Reding calls a mixture of ideas," said Campbell; "and that's the difficulty I find in uniting Gothic and Gregorians."

"Oh, pardon me," said Bateman, "they are one idea; they are both eminently Catholic."

"You can't be more Catholic than Rome, I suppose," said Campbell; "yet there's no Gothic there."

"Rome is a peculiar place," said Bateman; "besides, my dear friend, if we do but consider that Rome has corrupted the pure apostolic doctrine, can we wonder that it should have a corrupt architecture?"

"Why, then, go to Rome for Gregorians?" said Campbell; "I suspect they are called after Gregory I. Bishop of Rome, whom

Protestants consider the first specimen of Antichrist."

"It's nothing to us what Protestants think," answered Bateman.

"Don't let us quarrel about terms," said Campbell; "both you and I think that Rome has corrupted the faith, whether she is Antichrist or not. You said so yourself just now."

"It is true, I did," said Bateman; "but I make a little distinction. The Church of Rome has not *corrupted* the faith, but has *admitted* corruptions among her people."

"It won't do," answered Campbell; "depend on it, we can't stand our ground in controversy unless we in our hearts think very severely of the Church of Rome."

"Why, what's Rome to us?" asked Bateman; "we come from the old British Church; we don't meddle with Rome, and we wish Rome not to meddle with us, but she will."

"Well," said Campbell, "you but read a bit of the history of the Reformation, and you will find that the doctrine that the Pope is Antichrist was the life of the movement."

"With Ultra-Protestants, not with us," answered Bateman.

"Such Ultra-Protestants as the writers of the Homilies," said Campbell; "but, I say again, I am not contending for names; I only mean, that as that doctrine was the life of the Reformation, so a belief, which I have and you too, that there is something bad, corrupt, perilous in the Church of Rome—that there is a spirit of Antichrist living in her, energizing in her, and ruling her—is necessary to a man's being a good Anglican. You must believe this, or you ought to go to Rome."

"Impossible! my dear friend," said Bateman; "all our doctrine has been that Rome and we are sister Churches."

"I say," said Campbell, "that without this strong repulsion you will not withstand the great claims, the overcoming attractions, of the Church of Rome. She is our mother—oh, that word 'mother!'—a mighty mother! She opens her arms—oh, the fragrance of that bosom! She is full of gifts—I feel it, I have long felt it. Why don't I rush into her arms? Because I feel that she is ruled by a spirit which is not she. But did that distrust of her go from me, was that certainty which I have of her corruption disproved, I should join her communion tomorrow."

"This is not very edifying doctrine for Reding," thought Bateman. "Oh, my good Campbell," he said, "you are paradoxical today."

"Not a bit of it," answered Campbell; "our Reformers felt that the only way in which they could break the tie of allegiance which bound us to Rome was the doctrine of her serious corruption. And so it is with our divines. If there is one doctrine in which they agree, it is that Rome is Antichrist, or an Antichrist. Depend upon it, that doctrine is necessary for our position."

"I don't quite understand that language," said Reding; "I see it is used in various publications. It implies that controversy is a game, and that disputants are not looking out for truth, but for arguments."

"You must not mistake me, Mr. Reding," answered Campbell; "all I mean is, that you have no leave to trifle with your conviction that Rome is antichristian, if you think so. For if it *is* so, it is necessary to *say* so. A poet says, 'Speak *gently* of our sister's *fall*': no, if it is a fall, we must not speak gently of it. At first one says, 'So great a Church! who am I, to speak against her?' Yes, you must, if your view of her is true: 'Tell truth and shame the Devil.' Recollect you don't use your own words; you are sanctioned, protected by all our divines. You must, else you can give no sufficient reason for not joining the Church of Rome. You must speak out, not what you *don't* think, but what you *do* think, *if* you do think it."

"Here's a doctrine!" thought Charles; "why it's putting the controversy into a nutshell."

Bateman interposed. "My dear Campbell," he said, "you are behind the day. We have given up all that abuse against Rome."

"Then the party is not so clever as I give them credit for being," answered Campbell; "be sure of this—those who have given up their protests against Rome, either are looking towards her, or have no eyes to see."

"All we say," answered Bateman, "is, as I said before, that *we* don't wish to interfere with Rome; *we* don't anathematize Rome—Rome anathematizes *us*."

"It won't do," said Campbell; "those who resolve to remain in our Church, and are using sweet words of Romanism, will be forced back upon their proper ground in spite of themselves, and will get no thanks for their pains. No man can serve two masters; either go to Rome, or condemn Rome. For me, the Romish Church has a great deal in it which I can't get over; and thinking so, much as I admire it in parts, I can't help speaking, I can't help it. It would not be honest, and it would not be consistent."

"Well, he has ended better than he began," thought Bateman; and he chimed in, "Oh yes, true, too true; it's painful to see it, but there's a great deal in the Church of Rome which no man of plain sense, no reader of the Fathers, no Scripture student, no true member of the Anglo-Catholic Church can possibly stomach." This put a corona on the discussion; and the rest of the dinner passed off pleasantly indeed, but not very intellectually.

CHAPTER XVI

After dinner it occurred to them that the subject of Gregorians and Gothic had been left in the lurch. "How in the world did we get off it?" asked Charles.

"Well, at least, we have found it," said Bateman; "and I really should like to hear what you have to say upon it, Campbell."

"Oh, really, Bateman," answered he, "I am quite sick of the subject; every one seems to me to be going into extremes: what's the good of arguing about it? You won't agree with me."

"I don't see that at all," answered Bateman; "people often think they differ, merely because they have not courage to talk to each other."

"A good remark," thought Charles; "what a pity that Bateman, with so much sense, should have so little common sense!"

"Well, then," said Campbell, "my quarrel with Gothic and Gregorians, when coupled together, is, that they are two ideas, not one. Have figured music in Gothic churches, keep your Gregorian for basilicas."

"My good Campbell," said Bateman, "you seem oblivious that Gregorian chants and hymns have always accompanied Gothic aisles, Gothic copes, Gothic mitres, and Gothic chalices."

"Our ancestors did what they could," answered Campbell; "they were great in architecture, small in music. They could not use what was not yet invented. They sang Gregorians because they had not Palestrina."

"A paradox, a paradox!" cried Bateman.

"Surely there is a close connection," answered Campbell, "between the rise and nature of the basilica and of Gregorian unison. Both existed before Christianity; both are of Pagan origin; both were afterwards consecrated to the service of the Church."

"Pardon me," interrupted Bateman, "Gregorians were Jewish, not Pagan."

"Be it so, for argument sake," said Campbell; "still, at least, they were not of Christian origin. Next, both the old music and the old architecture were inartificial and limited, as methods of exhibiting their respective arts. You can't have a large Grecian temple, you can't have a long Gregorian *Gloria*."

"Not a long one!" said Bateman; "why there's poor Willis used to complain how tedious the old Gregorian compositions were abroad."

"I don't explain myself," answered Campbell; "of course you may produce them to any length, but merely by addition, not by carrying on the melody. You can put two together, and then have one twice as long as either. But I speak of a musical piece, which must of course be the natural development of certain ideas, with one part depending on another. In like manner, you might make an Ionic temple twice as long or twice as wide as the Parthenon; but you would lose the beauty of proportion by doing so. This, then, is what I meant to say of the primitive architecture and the primitive music, that they soon come to their limit; they soon are exhausted, and can do nothing more. If you attempt more, it's like taxing a musical instrument beyond its powers."

"You but try, Bateman," said Reding, "to make a bass play quadrilles, and you will see what is meant by taxing an instrument."

"Well, I have heard Lindley play all sorts of quick tunes on his bass," said Bateman, "and most wonderful it is."

"Wonderful is the right word," answered Reding; "it is very wonderful. You say, 'How *can* he manage it?' and 'It's very wonderful for a bass'; but it is not pleasant in itself. In like manner, I have always felt a disgust when Mr. So-and-so comes forward to make his sweet flute bleat and bray like a hautbois; it's forcing the poor thing to do what it was never made for."

"This is literally true as regards Gregorian music," said Campbell; "instruments did not exist in primitive times which could execute any other. But I am speaking under correction; Mr. Reding seems to know more about the subject than I do."

"I have always understood, as you say," answered Charles, "modern music did not come into existence till after the powers of the violin became known. Corelli himself, who wrote not two hundred years ago, hardly ventures on the shift. The piano, again, I have heard, has almost given birth to Beethoven."

"Modern music, then, could not be in ancient times, for want of modern instruments," said Campbell; "and, in like manner, Gothic architecture could not exist until vaulting was brought to perfection. Great mechanical inventions have taken place, both in architecture and in music, since the age of basilicas and Gregorians; and each science has gained by it."

"It is curious enough," said Reding, "one thing I have been accustomed to say, quite falls in with this view of yours. When people who are not musicians have accused Handel and Beethoven of not being *simple*, I have always said, 'Is Gothic architecture *simple*?' A cathedral expresses one idea, but it is indefinitely varied and elaborated in its parts; so is a symphony or quartett of Beethoven."

"Certainly, Bateman, you must tolerate Pagan architecture, or you must in consistency exclude Pagan or Jewish Gregorians," said Campbell; "you must tolerate figured music, or reprobate tracery windows."

"And which are you for," asked Bateman, "Gothic with Handel, or Roman with Gregorians?"

"For both in their place," answered Campbell. "I exceedingly prefer Gothic architecture to classical. I think it the one true child and development of Christianity; but I won't, for that reason, discard the Pagan style which has been sanctified by eighteen centuries, by the exclusive love of many Christian countries, and by the sanction of a host of saints. I am for toleration. Give Gothic an ascendancy; be respectful towards classical."

The conversation slackened. "Much as I like modern music," said Charles, "I can't quite go the length to which your doctrine would lead me. I cannot, indeed, help liking Mozart; but surely his music is not religious."

"I have not been speaking in defence of particular composers," said Campbell; "figured music may be right, yet Mozart or Beethoven inadmissible. In like manner, you don't suppose, because I tolerate Roman architecture, that therefore I like naked cupids to stand for cherubs, and sprawling women for the cardinal virtues." He paused. "Besides," he added, "as you were saying yourself just now, we must consult the genius of our country and the religious associations of our people."

"Well," said Bateman, "I think the perfection of sacred music is Gregorian set to harmonies; there you have the glorious old chants, and just a little modern richness."

"And I think it just the worst of all," answered Campbell; "it is a mixture of two things, each good in itself, and incongruous together. It's a mixture of the first and second courses at table. It's like the architecture of the façade at Milan, half Gothic, half Grecian."

"It's what is always used, I believe," said Charles.

"Oh yes, we must not go against the age," said Campbell; "it would be absurd to do so. I only spoke of what was right and wrong on abstract principles; and, to tell the truth, I can't help liking the mixture myself, though I can't defend it."

Bateman rang for tea; his friends wished to return home soon; it was the month of January, and no season for after-dinner strolls. "Well," he said, "Campbell, you are more lenient to the age than to me; you yield to the age when it sets a figured bass to a Gregorian tone; but you laugh at me for setting a coat upon a cassock."

"It's no honour to be the author of a mongrel type," said Campbell.

"A mongrel type?" said Bateman; "rather it is a transition state."

"What are you passing to?" asked Charles.

"Talking of transitions," said Campbell abruptly, "do you know that your man Willis—I don't know his college, he turned Romanist—is living in my parish, and I have hopes he is making a transition back again."

"Have you seen him?" said Charles.

"No; I have called, but was unfortunate; he was out. He still goes to mass, I find."

"Why, where does he find a chapel?" asked Bateman.

"At Seaton. A good seven miles from you," said Charles.

"Yes," answered Campbell; "and he walks to and fro every Sunday."

"That is not like a transition, except a physical one," observed Reding.

"A person must go somewhere," answered Campbell; "I suppose he went to church up to the week he joined the Romanists."

"Very awful, these defections," said Bateman; "but very satisfactory, a melancholy satisfaction," with a look at Charles, "that the victims of delusions should be at length recovered."

"Yes," said Campbell; "very sad indeed. I am afraid we must expect a number more."

"Well, I don't know how to think it," said Charles; "the hold our Church has on the mind is so powerful; it is such a wrench to leave it, I cannot fancy any party-tie standing against it. Humanly speaking, there is far, far more to keep them fast than to carry them away."

"Yes, if they moved as a party," said Campbell; "but that is not the case. They don't move simply because others move, but, poor fellows, because they can't help it.—Bateman, will you let my chaise be brought round?—How *can* they help it?" continued he, standing up over the fire; "their Catholic principles lead them on, and there's nothing to drive them back."

"Why should not their love for their own Church?" asked Bateman; "it is deplorable, unpardonable."

"They will keep going one after another, as they ripen," said Campbell.

"Did you hear the report—I did not think much of it myself," said Reding—"that Smith was moving?"

"Not impossible," answered Campbell thoughtfully.

"Impossible, quite impossible," cried Bateman; "such a triumph to the enemy; I'll not believe it till I see it."

"*Not* impossible," repeated Campbell, as he buttoned and fitted his great-coat about him; "he has shifted his ground." His carriage was announced. "Mr. Reding, I believe I can take you part of your way, if you will accept of a seat in my pony-chaise." Charles accepted the offer; and Bateman was soon deserted by his two guests.

CHAPTER XVII

CAMPBELL put Charles down about half-way between Melford and his home. It was bright moonlight; and, after thanking his new friend for the lift, he bounded over the stile at the side of the road, and was at once buried in the shade of the copse along which his path lay. Soon he came in sight of a tall wooden Cross, which, in better days, had been a religious emblem, but had served in latter times to mark the boundary between two contiguous parishes. The moon was behind him, and the sacred symbol rose awfully in the pale sky, overhanging a pool, which was still venerated in the neighbourhood for its reported miraculous virtue. Charles, to his surprise, saw distinctly a man kneeling on the little mound out of which the Cross grew; nay, heard him, for his shoulders were bare, and he was using the discipline upon them, while he repeated what appeared to be some form of devotion. Charles stopped, unwilling to interrupt, yet not knowing how to pass; but the stranger had caught the sound of feet, and in a few seconds vanished from his view. He was overcome with a sudden emotion, which he could not control. "O happy times," he cried, "when faith was one! O blessed penitent, whoever you are, who know what to believe, and how to gain pardon, and can begin where others end! Here am I, in my twenty-third year, uncertain about everything, because I have nothing to trust." He drew near to the Cross, took off his hat, knelt down and kissed the wood, and prayed awhile that whatever might be the consequences, whatever the trial, whatever the loss, he might have grace to follow whithersoever God should call him. He then rose and turned to the cold well; he took some water in his palm and drank it. He felt as if he could have prayed to the Saint who owned that pool—St. Thomas the Martyr, he believed—to plead for him, and to aid him in his search after the true faith; but something whispered, "It is wrong"; and he checked the wish. So, regaining his hat, he passed away, and pursued his homeward path at a brisk pace.

The family had retired for the night, and he went up without delay to his bedroom. Passing through his study, he found a letter lying on his table, without post-mark, which had come for him in his absence. He broke the seal; it was an anonymous paper, and began as follows:

"*Questions for one whom it concerns.* (1) What is meant by the One Church of which the Creed speaks?"

"This is too much for tonight," thought Charles, "it is late already"; and he folded it up again and threw it on his dressing-table. "Some well-meaning person, I dare say, who thinks he knows me." He wound up his watch, gave a yawn, and put on his slippers. "Who can there be in this neighbourhood to write it?" He opened it again. "It's certainly a Catholic's writing," he said. His mind glanced to the person whom he had seen under the Cross; perhaps it glanced further. He sat down and began reading *in extenso*:

"*Questions for one whom it concerns.* (1) What is meant by the One Church of which the Creed speaks?

(2) Is it a generalization or a thing?

(3) Does it belong to past history or to the present time?

(4) Does not Scripture speak of it as a kingdom?

(5) And a kingdom which was to last to the end?

(6) What is a kingdom? And what is meant when Scripture calls the Church a kingdom?

(7) Is it a visible kingdom, or an invisible?

(8) Can a kingdom have two governments, and these acting in contrary directions?

(9) Is identity of institutions, opinions, or race, sufficient to make two nations one kingdom?

(10) Is the Episcopal form, the hierarchy, or the Apostles' Creed, sufficient to make the Churches of Rome and of England one?

(11) Where there are parts, does not unity require union, and a visible unity require a visible union?

(12) How can two religions be the same which have utterly distinct worships and ideas of worship?

(13) Can two religions be one, if the most sacred and peculiar act of worship in the one is called 'a blasphemous fable and dangerous deceit' in the other?

(14) Has not the One Church of Christ one faith?

(15) Can a Church be Christ's which has not one faith?

(16) Which is contradictory to itself in its documents?

(17) And in different centuries?

(18) And in its documents contrasted with its divines?

(19) And in its divines and members one with another?

(20) What is *the* faith of the English Church?

(21) How many Councils does the English Church admit?

(22) Does the English Church consider the present Nestorian and Jacobite Churches under an anathema, or part of the visible Church?

(23) Is it necessary, or possible, to believe any one but a professed messenger from God?

(24) Is the English Church, does she claim to be, a messenger from God?

(25) Does she impart the truth, or bid us seek it?

(26) If she leaves us to seek it, do members of the English Church seek it with that earnestness which Scripture enjoins?

(27) Is a person safe who lives without faith, even though he seems to have hope and charity?"

Charles got very sleepy before he reached the "twenty-seventhly." "It won't do," he said; "I am only losing my time. They seem well put; but they must stand over." He put the paper from him, said his prayers, and was soon fast asleep.

Next morning, on waking, the subject of the letter came into his mind, and he lay for some time thinking over it. "Certainly," he said, "I do wish very much to be settled either in the English Church or somewhere else. I wish I knew *what* Christianity was; I am ready to be at pains to seek it, and would accept it eagerly and thankfully, if found. But it's a work of time; all the paper-arguments in the world are unequal to giving one a view in a moment. There must be a process; they may shorten it, as medicine shortens physical processes, but they can't supersede its necessity. I recollect how all my religious doubts and theories went to flight on my dear father's death. They weren't part of me, and could not sustain rough weather. Conviction is the eyesight of the mind, not a conclusion from premises; God works it, and His works are slow. At least so it is with me. I can't believe on a sudden; if I attempt it, I shall be using words for things, and be sure to repent it. Or if not, I shall go right merely by hazard. I must move in what seems God's way; I can but put myself on the road; a higher power must overtake me, and carry me forward. At present I have a direct duty upon me, which my dear father left me, to take a good class. This is the path of duty. I won't put off the inquiry, but I'll let it proceed in that path. God can bless my reading to my spiritual illumination, as well as anything else. Saul sought his father's asses, and found a kingdom. All in good time. When I have taken my degree the subject will properly come on me." He sighed. "My degree! those odious Articles! rather, when I have passed my examination. Well, it's no good lying here"; and he jumped up, and signed himself with the Cross. His eye caught the letter. "It's well written—better than Willis could write; it's not Willis's. There's something about that Willis I don't understand. I wonder how he and his mother get on together. I don't think he has any sisters."

CHAPTER XVIII

CAMPBELL had been much pleased with Reding, and his interest in him was not lessened by a hint from Bateman that his allegiance to the English Church was in danger. He called on him in no long time, asked him to dinner, and, when Charles had returned his invitation, and Campbell had accepted it, the beginning of an acquaintance was formed between the rectory at Sutton and the family at Boughton which grew into an intimacy as time went on. Campbell was a gentleman, a travelled man, of clear head and ardent mind, candid, well-read in English divinity, a devoted Anglican, and the incumbent of a living so well endowed as almost to be a dignity. Mary was pleased at the introduction, as bringing her brother under the influence of an intellect which he could not make light of; and, as Campbell had a carriage, it was natural that he should wish to save Charles the loss of a day's reading and the trouble of a muddy walk to the rectory and back by coming over himself to Boughton. Thus it so happened that he saw Charles twice at his mother's for once that he saw him at Sutton. But whatever came of these visits, nothing occurred which particularly bears upon the line of our narrative; so let them pass.

One day Charles called upon Bateman, and, on entering the room, was surprised to see him and Campbell at luncheon, and in conversation with a third person. There was a moment's surprise and hesitation on seeing him before they rose and welcomed him as usual. When he looked at the stranger he felt a slight awkwardness himself, which he could not control. It was Willis; and apparently submitted to the process of reconversion. Charles was evidently *de trop*, but there was no help for it; so he shook hands with Willis, and accepted the pressing call of Bateman to seat himself at table, and to share their bread and cheese.

Charles sat down opposite Willis, and for a while could not keep his eyes from him. At first he had some difficulty in believing he had before him the impetuous youth he had known two years and a half before. He had always been silent in general company; but in that he was changed, as in everything else. Not that he talked more than was natural, but he talked freely and easily. The great change, however, was in his appearance and manner. He had lost his bloom and youthfulness; his expression was sweeter indeed than before, and very placid, but there was a thin line down his face on each side of his mouth; his cheeks were wanting in fulness, and he had the air of a man of thirty. When he entered into conversation, and became animated, his former self returned.

"I suppose we may all admire this cream at this season," said Charles, as he helped himself, "for we are none of us Devonshire men."

"It's not peculiar to Devonshire," answered Campbell; "that is, they have it abroad. At Rome there is a sort of cream or cheese very like it, and very common."

"Will butter and cream keep in so warm a climate?" asked Charles; "I fancied oil was the substitute."

"Rome is not so warm as you fancy," said Willis, "except during the summer."

"Oil? So it is," said Campbell; "thus we read in Scripture of the multiplication of the oil and meal, which seems to answer to bread and butter. The oil in Rome is excellent, so clear and pale; you can eat it as milk."

"The taste, I suppose, is peculiar," observed Charles.

"Just at first," answered Campbell; "but one soon gets used to it. All such substances, milk, butter, cheese, oil, have a particular taste at first, which use alone gets over. The rich Guernsey butter is too much for strangers, while Russians relish whale-oil. Most of our tastes are in a measure artificial."

"It is certainly so with vegetables," said Willis; "when I was a boy I could not eat beans, spinach, asparagus, parsnips, and I think some others."

"Therefore your hermit's fare is not only the most natural, but the only naturally palatable, I suppose—a crust of bread and a draught from the stream," replied Campbell.

"Or the Clerk of Copmanhurst's dry peas," said Charles.

"The macaroni and grapes of the Neapolitans are as natural and more palatable," said Willis.

"Rather they are a luxury," said Bateman.

"No," answered Campbell, "not a luxury; a luxury is in its very idea a something *recherché*. Thus Horace speaks of the '*peregrina lagois*.' What nature yields *sponte suâ* around you, however delicious, is no luxury. Wild ducks are no luxury in your old neighbourhood, amid your Oxford fens, Bateman; nor grapes at Naples."

"Then the old women here are luxurious over their sixpenn'rth of tea," said Bateman; "for it comes from China."

Campbell was posed for an instant. Somehow neither he nor Bateman were quite at their ease, whether with themselves or with each other; it might be Charles's sudden intrusion, or something which had happened before it. Campbell answered at length that steamers and railroads were making strange changes; that time and place were vanishing, and price would soon be the only measure of luxury.

"This seems the measure also of *grasso* and *magro* food in Italy," said Willis; "for I think there are dispensations for butcher's meat in Lent, in consequence of the dearness of bread and oil."

"This seems to show that the age for abstinences and fastings is past," observed Campbell; "for it's absurd to keep Lent on beef and mutton."

"Oh, Campbell, what are you saying?" cried Bateman; "past! are we bound by their lax ways in Italy?"

"I do certainly think," answered Campbell, "that fasting is unsuitable to this age, in England as well as in Rome."

"Take care, my fine fellows," thought Charles; "keep your ranks, or you won't secure your prisoner."

"What, not fast on Friday!" cried Bateman; "we always did so most rigidly at Oxford."

"It does you credit," answered Campbell; "but I am of Cambridge."

"But what do you say to Rubrics and the Calendar?" insisted Bateman.

"They are not binding," answered Campbell.

"They *are*, binding," said Bateman.

A pause, as between the rounds of a boxing-match. Reding interposed: "Bateman, cut me, please, a bit of your capital bread—home-made, I suppose?"

"A thousand pardons!" said Bateman: "not binding?—Pass it to him, Willis, if you please. Yes, it comes from a farmer, next door. I'm glad you like it.—I repeat, they *are* binding, Campbell."

"An odd sort of binding, when they have never bound," answered Campbell; "they have existed two or three hundred years; when were they ever put in force?"

"But there they are," said Bateman, "in the Prayer Book."

"Yes, and there let them lie and never get out of it," retorted Campbell; "there they will stay till the end of the story."

"Oh, for shame!" cried Bateman; "you should aid your mother in a difficulty, and not be like the priest and the Levite."

"My mother does not wish to be aided," continued Campbell.

"Oh, how you talk! What shall I do? What can be done?" cried poor Bateman.

"Done! nothing," said Campbell; "is there no such thing as the desuetude of a law? Does not a law cease to be binding when it is not enforced? I appeal to Mr. Willis."

Willis, thus addressed, answered that he was no moral theologian, but he had attended some schools, and he believed it was the Catholic rule that when a law had been promulgated, and was not observed by the majority, if the legislator knew the state of the case, and yet kept silence, he was considered *ipso facto* to revoke it.

"What!" said Bateman to Campbell, "do you appeal to the Romish Church?"

"No," answered Campbell; "I appeal to the whole Catholic Church, of which the Church of Rome happens in this particular case to be the exponent. It is plain common sense, that, if a law is not enforced, at length it ceases to be binding. Else it would be quite a tyranny; we should not know where we were. The Church of Rome does but give expression to this common-sense view."

"Well, then," said Bateman, "I will appeal to the Church of Rome too. Rome is part of the Catholic Church as well as we: since, then, the Romish Church has ever kept up fastings the ordinance is not abolished; the 'greater part' of the Catholic Church has always observed it."

"But it has not," said Campbell; "it now dispenses with fasts, as you have heard."

Willis interposed to ask a question. "Do you mean then," he said to Bateman, "that the Church of England and the Church of Rome make one Church?"

"Most certainly," answered Bateman.

"Is it possible?" said Willis; "in what sense of the word *one*?"

"In every sense," answered Bateman, "but that of intercommunion."

"That is, I suppose," said Willis, "they are one, except that they have no intercourse with each other."

Bateman assented. Willis continued: "No intercourse; that is, no social dealings, no consulting or arranging, no ordering and obeying, no mutual support; in short, no visible union."

Bateman still assented. "Well, that is my difficulty," said Willis; "I can't understand how two parts can make up one visible body if they are not visibly united; unity implies *union*."

"I don't see that at all," said Bateman; "I don't see that at all. No, Willis, you must not expect I shall give that up to you; it is one of our points. There is only one visible Church, and therefore the English and Romish Churches are both parts of it."

Campbell saw clearly that Bateman had got into a difficulty, and he came to the rescue in his own way.

"We must distinguish," he said, "the state of the case more exactly. A kingdom may be divided, it may be distracted by parties, by dissensions, yet be still a kingdom. That, I conceive, is the real condition of the Church; in this way the Churches of England, Rome, and Greece are one."

"I suppose you will grant," said Willis, "that in proportion as a rebellion is strong, so is the unity of the kingdom threatened; and if a rebellion is successful, or if the parties in a civil war manage to divide the power and territory between them, then forthwith, instead of one kingdom, we have two. Ten or fifteen years since, Belgium was part of the kingdom of the Netherlands: I suppose you would not call it part of that kingdom now? This seems the case of the Churches of Rome and England."

"Still, a kingdom may be in a state of decay," replied Campbell; "consider the case of the Turkish Empire at this moment. The Union between its separate portions is so languid, that each separate Pasha may almost be termed a separate sovereign; still it is one kingdom."

"The Church, then, at present," said Willis, "is a kingdom tending to dissolution?"

"Certainly it is," answered Campbell.

"And will ultimately fail?" asked Willis.

"Certainly," said Campbell; "when the end comes, according to our Lord's saying, 'When the Son of man cometh, shall He find faith on the earth?' just as in the case of the chosen people, the sceptre failed from Judah when the Shiloh came."

"Surely the Church has failed already *before* the end," said Willis, "according to the view you take of failing. How *can* any separation be more complete than exists at present between Rome, Greece, and England?"

"They might excommunicate each other," said Campbell.

"Then you are willing," said Willis, "to assign beforehand something definite, the occurrence of which will constitute a real separation."

"Don't do so," said Reding to Campbell; "it is dangerous; don't commit yourself in a moral question; for then, if the thing specified did occur, it would be difficult to see our way."

"No," said Willis; "you certainly *would* be in a difficulty; but you would find your way out, I know. In that case you would choose some other *ultimatum* as your test of schism. There would be," he added, speaking with some emotion, "'in the lowest depth a lower still.'"

The concluding words were out of keeping with the tone of the conversation hitherto, and fairly excited Bateman, who, for some time, had been an impatient listener.

"That's a dangerous line, Campbell," he said, "it is indeed; I can't go along with you. It will never do to say that the Church is failing; no, it never fails. It is always strong, and pure, and perfect, as the Prophets describe it. Look at its cathedrals, abbey-churches, and other sanctuaries, these fitly typify it."

"My dear Bateman," answered Campbell, "I am as willing as you to maintain the fulfilment of the prophecies made to the Church, but we must allow the *fact* that the branches of the Church are *divided*, while we maintain the *doctrine*, that the Church should be one."

"I don't see that at all," answered Bateman; "no, we need not allow it. There's no such thing as Churches, there's but one Church everywhere, and it is *not* divided. It is merely the outward forms, appearances, manifestations of the Church that are divided. The Church is one as much as ever it was."

"That will never do," said Campbell; and he stood up before the fire in a state of discomfort. "Nature never intended you for a controversialist, my good Bateman," he added to himself.

"It is as I thought," said Willis; "Bateman, you are describing an invisible Church. You hold the indefectibility of the invisible Church, not of the visible."

"They are in a fix," thought Charles, "but I will do my best to tow old Bateman out"; so he began: "No," he said, "Bateman only means that one Church presents, in some particular point, a different appearance from another; but it does not follow that, in fact, they have not a visible agreement too. All difference implies agreement; the English and Roman Churches agree visibly and differ visibly. Think of the different styles of architecture, and you will see, Willis, what he means. A church is a church all the world over, it is visibly one and the same, and yet how different is church from church! Our churches are Gothic, the southern churches are Palladian. How different is a basilica from York Cathedral! yet they visibly agree together. No one would mistake either for a mosque or a Jewish temple. We may quarrel which is the better style; one likes the basilica, another calls it pagan."

"That *I* do," said Bateman.

"A little extreme," said Campbell, "a little extreme, as usual. The basilica is beautiful in its place. There are two things which Gothic cannot show—the line or forest of round polished columns, and the graceful dome, circling above one's head like the blue heaven itself."

All parties were glad of this diversion from the religious dispute; so they continued the lighter conversation which had succeeded it with considerable earnestness.

"I fear I must confess," said Willis, "that the churches at Rome do not affect me like the Gothic; I reverence them, I feel awe in them, but I love, I feel a sensible pleasure at the sight of the Gothic arch."

"There are other reasons for that in Rome," said Campbell; "the churches are so unfinished, so untidy. Rome is a city of ruins! the Christian temples are built on ruins, and they themselves are generally dilapidated or decayed; thus they are ruins of ruins." Campbell was on an easier subject than that of Anglo-Catholicism, and, no one interrupting him, he proceeded flowingly: "In Rome you have huge high buttresses in the place of columns, and these not cased with marble, but of cold white plaster or paint. They impart an indescribable forlorn look to the churches."

Willis said he often wondered what took so many foreigners,

that is, Protestants, to Rome; it was so dreary, so melancholy a place; a number of old, crumbling, shapeless brick masses, the ground unlevelled, the straight causeways fenced by high monotonous walls, the points of attraction straggling over broad solitudes, faded palaces, trees universally pollarded, streets ankle deep in filth or eyes-and-mouth deep in a cloud of whirling dust and straws, the climate most capricious, the evening air most perilous. Naples was an earthly paradise; but Rome was a city of faith. To seek the shrines that it contained was a veritable penance, as was fitting. He understood Catholics going there; he was perplexed at Protestants.

"There is a spell about the *limina Apostolorum*," said Charles; "St. Peter and St. Paul are not there for nothing."

"There is a more tangible reason," said Campbell; "it is a place where persons of all nations are to be found; no society is so varied as the Roman. You go to a ballroom; your host, whom you bow to in the first apartment, is a Frenchman; as you advance your eye catches Massena's granddaughter in conversation with Mustapha Pasha; you soon find yourself seated between a Yankee *chargé d'affaires* and a Russian colonel; and an Englishman is playing the fool in front of you."

Here Campbell looked at his watch, and then at Willis, whom he had driven over to Melford to return Bateman's call. It was time for them to be going, or they would be overtaken by the evening. Bateman, who had remained in a state of great dissatisfaction since he last spoke, which had not been for a quarter of an hour past, did not find himself in spirits to try much to detain either them or Reding; so he was speedily left to himself. He drew his chair to the fire, and for a while felt nothing more than a heavy load of disgust. After a time, however, his thoughts began to draw themselves out into series, and took the following form: "It's too bad, too bad," he said; "Campbell is a very clever man—far cleverer than I am; a well-read man, too; but he has no tact, no tact. It is deplorable; Reding's coming was one misfortune; however, we might have got over that, we might have even turned it to an advantage; but to use such arguments as he did! how could he hope to convince him? He made us both a mere laughing-stock.... How did he throw off? Oh, he said that the Rubrics were not binding. Who ever heard such a thing—at least from an Anglo-Catholic? Why pretend to be a good Catholic with such views? Better call himself a Protestant or Erastian at once, and one would know where to find him. Such a bad impression it must make on Willis; I saw it did; he could hardly keep from smiling: but Campbell has no tact at all. He goes on, on, his own way, bringing out his own thoughts, which are very clever, original certainly, but never considering his company. And he's so positive, so knock-me-down; it is quite unpleasant, I don't know how to sit it sometimes. Oh, it is a cruel thing this—the effect must be wretched. Poor Willis! I declare I don't think we have moved him one inch, I really don't. I fancied at one time he was even laughing at *me*.... What was it he said afterwards? There was something else, I know. I recollect; that the Catholic Church was in ruins, had broken to pieces. What a paradox! who'll believe that but he? I declare I am so vexed I don't know what to be at." He jumped up and began walking to and fro. "But all this is because the Bishops won't interfere; one can't say it, that's the worst, but they are at the bottom of the evil. They have but to put out their little finger and enforce the Rubrics, and then the whole controversy would be at an end.... I knew there was something else, yes! He said we need not fast! But Cambridge men are always peculiar, they always have some whim or other; he ought to have been at Oxford, and we should have made a man of him. He has many good points, but he runs theories, and rides hobbies, and drives consequences, to death."

Here he was interrupted by his clerk, who told him that John Tims had taken his oath that his wife should not be churched before the congregation, and was half-minded to take his infant to the Methodists for baptism; and his thoughts took a different direction.

CHAPTER XIX

THE winter had been on the whole dry and pleasant, but in February and March the rains were so profuse, and the winds so high, that Bateman saw very little of either Charles or Willis. He did not abandon his designs on the latter, but it was an anxious question how best to conduct them. As to Campbell, he was resolved to exclude him from any participation in them; but he hesitated about Reding. He had found him far less definitely Roman than he expected, and he conjectured that, by making him his confidant and employing him against Willis, he really might succeed in giving him an Anglican direction. Accordingly, he told him of his anxiety to restore Willis to "the Church of his baptism"; and not discouraged by Charles's advice to let well alone, for he might succeed in drawing him from Rome without reclaiming him to Anglicanism, the weather having improved, he asked the two to dinner on one of the later Sundays in Lent. He determined to make a field-day of it; and, with that view, he carefully got up some of the most popular works against the Church of Rome. After much thought he determined to direct his attack on some of the "practical evils," as he considered them, of "Romanism"; as being more easy of proof than points of doctrine and history, in which, too, for what he knew, Willis might by this time be better read than himself. He considered, too, that, if Willis had been at all shaken in his new faith when he was abroad, it was by the practical exemplification which he had before his eyes of the issue of its peculiar doctrines when freely carried out. Moreover, to tell the truth, our good friend had not a very clear apprehension how much doctrine he held in common with the Church of Rome, or where he was to stop in the several details of Pope Pius's Creed; in consequence, it was evidently safer to confine his attack to matters of practice.

"You see, Willis," he said, as they sat down to table, "I have given you abstinence food, not knowing whether you avail yourself of the dispensation. We shall eat meat ourselves; but don't think we don't fast at proper times; I don't agree with Campbell at all; we don't fast, however, on Sunday. That is our rule, and, I take it, a primitive one."

Willis answered that he did not know how the primitive usage lay, but he supposed that both of them allowed that matters of discipline might be altered by the proper authority.

"Certainly," answered Bateman, "so that everything is done consistently with the inspired text of Scripture";—he stopped, itching, if he could, to bring in some great subject, but not seeing how. He saw he must rush *in medias res*; so he added—"with which inspired text, I presume, what one sees in foreign churches is not very consistent."

"What? I suppose you mean antependia, rere-dosses, stone altars, copes, and mitres," said Willis innocently; "which certainly are not in Scripture."

"True," said Bateman; "but these, though not in Scripture, are not inconsistent with Scripture. They are all very right; but the worship of Saints, especially the Blessed Virgin, and of relics, the gabbling over prayers in an unknown tongue, Indulgences, and infrequent communions, I suspect are directly unscriptural."

"My dear Bateman," said Willis, "you seem to live in an atmosphere of controversy; so it was at Oxford; there was always argument going on in your rooms. Religion is a thing to enjoy, not to quarrel about; give me a slice more of that leg of mutton."

"Yes, Bateman," said Reding, "you must let us enjoy our meat. Willis deserves it, for I believe he has had a fair walk today. Have you not walked a good part of the way to Seaton and back? A matter of fourteen miles, and hilly ground; it can't be dry, too, in parts yet."

"True," said Bateman; "take a glass of wine, Willis; it's good Madeira; an aunt of mine sent it me."

"He puts us to shame," said Charles, "who have stepped into

church from our bedroom; he has trudged a pilgrimage to his."

"I'm not saying a word against our dear friend Willis," said Bateman; "it was merely a point on which I thought he would agree with me, that there were many corruptions of worship in foreign churches."

At last, when his silence was observable, Willis said that he supposed that persons who were not Catholics could not tell what were corruptions and what not. Here the subject dropped again; for Willis did not seem in humour—perhaps he was too tired—to continue it. So they ate and drank, with nothing but very commonplace remarks to season their meal withal, till the cloth was removed. The table was then shoved back a bit, and the three young men got over the fire, which Bateman made burn brightly. Two of them at least had deserved some relaxation, and they were the two who were to be opponent and respondent in the approaching argument—one had had a long walk, the other had had two full services, a baptism, and a funeral. The armistice continued a good quarter of an hour, which Charles and Willis spent in easy conversation; till Bateman, who had been priming himself the while with his controversial points, found himself ready for the assault, and opened it in form.

"Come, my dear Willis," he said, "I can't let you off so; I am sure what you saw abroad scandalized you."

This was almost rudely put. Willis said that, had he been a Protestant, he might have been easily shocked; but he had been a Catholic; and he drew an almost imperceptible sigh. Besides, had he had a temptation to be shocked, he should have recollected that he was in a Church which in all greater matters could not err. He had not come to the Church to criticize, he said, but to learn. "I don't know," he said, "what is meant by saying that we ought to have faith, that faith is a grace, that faith is the means of our salvation, if there is nothing to exercise it. Faith goes against sight; well, then, unless there are sights which offend you, there is nothing for it to go against."

Bateman called this a paradox; "If so," he said, "why don't we become Mahometans? We should have enough to believe then."

"Why, just consider," said Willis; "supposing your friend, an honourable man, is accused of theft, and appearances are against him, would you at once admit the charge? It would be a fair trial of your faith in him; and if he were able in the event satisfactorily to rebut it, I don't think he would thank you, should you have waited for his explanation before you took his part, instead of knowing him too well to suspect it. If, then, I come to the Church with faith in her, whatever I see there, even if it surprises me, is but a trial of my faith."

"That is true," said Charles; "but there must be some ground for faith; we do not believe without reason; and the question is, whether what the Church does, as in worship, is not a fair matter to form a judgment upon, for or against."

"A Catholic," said Willis, "as I was when I was abroad, has already found his grounds, for he believes; but for one who has not—I mean a Protestant—I certainly consider it is very uncertain whether he will take *the* view of Catholic worship which he ought to take. It may easily happen that he will not understand it."

"Yet persons have before now been converted by the sight of Catholic worship," said Reding.

"Certainly," answered Willis: "God works in a thousand ways; there is much in Catholic worship to strike a Protestant, but there is much which will perplex him; for instance, what Bateman has alluded to, our devotion to the Blessed Virgin."

"Surely," said Bateman, "this is a plain matter; it is quite impossible that the worship paid by Roman Catholics to the Blessed Mary should not interfere with the supreme adoration due to the Creator alone."

"This is just an instance in point," said Willis; "you see you are judging *à priori*; you know nothing of the state of the case from experience, but you say, 'It must be; it can't be otherwise.' This is the way a Protestant judges, and comes to one conclusion; a Catholic, who acts, and does not speculate, feels the truth of the contrary."

"Some things," said Bateman, "are so like axioms, as to supersede trial. On the other hand, familiarity is very likely to hide from people the real evil of certain practices."

"How strange it is," answered Willis, "that you don't perceive that this is the very argument which various sects urge against you Anglicans! For instance, the Unitarian says that the doctrine of the Atonement *must* lead to our looking at the Father, not as a God of love, but of vengeance only; and he calls the doctrine of eternal punishment immoral. And so, the Wesleyan or Baptist declares that it is an absurdity to suppose any one can hold the doctrine of baptismal regeneration, and really be spiritual; that the doctrine *must* have a numbing effect on the mind, and destroy its simple reliance on the atonement of Christ. I will take another instance: many a good Catholic, who never came across Anglicans, is as utterly unable to realize your position as you are to realize his. He cannot make out how you can be so illogical as not to go forward or backward; nay, he pronounces your professed state of mind impossible; he does not believe in its existence. I may deplore your state; I may think you illogical and worse; but I know it is a state which does exist. As, then, I admit that a person can hold one Catholic Church, yet without believing that the Roman Communion is it, so I put it to you, even as an *argumentum ad hominem*, whether you ought not to believe that we can honour our Blessed Lady as the first of creatures, without interfering with the honour due to God? At most, you ought to call us only illogical, you ought not to deny that we do what we say we do."

"I make a distinction," said Bateman; "it is quite possible, I fully grant, for an educated Romanist to distinguish between the devotion paid by him to the Blessed Virgin, and the worship of God; I only say that the multitude will not distinguish."

"I know you say so," answered Willis; "and still, I repeat, not from experience, but on an *à priori* ground. You say, not 'it is so,' but 'it *must* be so.'"

There was a pause in the conversation, and then Bateman recommenced it.

"You may give us some trouble," said he, laughing, "but we are resolved to have you back, my good Willis. Now consider, you are a lover of truth: is that Church from heaven which tells untruths?"

Willis laughed too; "We must define the words *truth* and *untruth*," he said; "but, subject to that definition, I have no hesitation in enunciating the truism, that a Church is not from heaven which tells untruths."

"Of course, you can't deny the proposition," said Bateman; "well, then, is it not quite certain that in Rome itself there are relics which all learned men now give up, and which yet are venerated as relics? For instance, Campbell tells me that the reputed heads of St. Peter and St. Paul, in some great Roman basilica, are certainly not the heads of the Apostles, because the head of St. Paul was found with his body, after the fire at his church some years since."

"I don't know about the particular instance," answered Willis; "but you are opening a large question which cannot be settled in a few words. If I must speak, I should say this: I should begin with the assumption that the existence of relics is not improbable; do you grant *that*?"

"I grant nothing," said Bateman; "but go on."

"Why you have plenty of heathen relics, which you admit. What is Pompeii, and all that is found there, but one vast heathen relic? Why should there not be Christian relics in Rome and elsewhere as well as pagan?"

"Of course, of course," said Bateman.

"Well, and relics may be identified. You have the tomb of the Scipios, with their names on them. Did you find ashes in one of them, I suppose you would be pretty certain that they were the ashes of a Scipio."

"To the point," cried Bateman, "quicker."

"St. Peter," continued Willis, "speaks of David, 'whose sepulchre is with you unto this day.' Therefore it's nothing wonderful that a religious relic should be preserved eleven hundred years, and identified to be such, when a nation makes a point of preserving it."

"This is beating about the bush," cried Bateman impatiently; "get on quicker."

"Let me go on my own way," said Willis—"then there is nothing improbable, considering Christians have always been very careful about the memorials of sacred things—"

"You've not proved that," said Bateman, fearing that some manoeuvre, he could not tell what, was in progress.

"Well," said Willis, "you don't doubt it, I suppose, at least from the fourth century, when St. Helena brought from the Holy Land the memorials of our Lord's passion, and lodged them at Rome in the Basilica, which was thereupon called Santa Croce. As to the previous times of persecution, Christians, of course, had fewer opportunities of showing a similar devotion, and historical records are less copious; yet, in spite of this, its existence is as certain as any fact of history. They collected the bones of St. Polycarp, the immediate disciple of St. John, after he was burnt; as of St. Ignatius before him, after his exposure to the beasts; and so in like manner the bones or blood of all the martyrs. No one doubts it; I never heard of any one who did. So the disciples took up the Baptist's body—it would have been strange if they had not—and buried it 'in *the* sepulchre,' as the Evangelist says, speaking of it as known. Now, why should they not in like manner, and even with greater reason, have rescued the bodies of St. Peter and St. Paul, if it were only for decent burial? Is it then wonderful, if the bodies were rescued, that they should be afterwards preserved?"

"But they can't be in two places at once," said Bateman.

"But hear me," answered Willis; "I say then if there is a tradition that in a certain place there is a relic of an apostle, there is at first sight a probability that it *is* there; the presumption is in its favour. Can you deny it? Well, if the same relic is reported to be in two places, then one or the other tradition is erroneous, and the *primâ facie* force of both traditions is weakened; but I should not actually discard either at once; each has its force still, though neither so great a force. Now, suppose there are circumstances which confirm the one, the other is weakened still further, and at length the probability of its truth may become evanescent; and when a fair interval has passed, and there is no change of evidence in its favour, then it is at length given up. But all this is a work of time; meanwhile, it is not a bit more of an objection to the doctrine and practice of relic-veneration that a body is said to lie in two places, than to profane history that Charles I was reported by some authorities to be buried at Windsor, by others at Westminster; which question was decided just before our times. It is a question of evidence, and must be treated as such."

"But if St. Paul's head was found under his own church," said Bateman, "it's pretty clear it is not preserved at the other basilica."

"True," answered Willis; "but grave questions of this kind cannot be decided in a moment. I don't know myself the circumstances of the case, and do but take your account of it. It has to be proved, then, I suppose, that it *was* St. Paul's head which was found with his body; for, since he was beheaded, it would not be attached to it. This is one question, and others would arise. It is not easy to settle a question of history. Questions which seem settled revive. It is very well for secular historians to give up a tradition or testimony at once, and for a generation to oh-oh it; but the Church cannot do so; she has a religious responsibility, and must move slowly. Take the *chance* of its turning out that the heads at St. John Lateran were, after all, those of the two Apostles, and that she had cast them aside. Questions, I say, revive. Did not Walpole make it highly probable that the two little princes had a place in the procession at King Richard's coronation, though a century before him two skeletons of boys were found in the Tower at the very place where the children of Edward were said to have been murdered and buried by the Duke of Gloucester? I speak from memory, but the general fact which I am illustrating is undeniable. Ussher, Pearson, and Voss proved that St. Ignatius's shorter Epistles were genuine; and now, after the lapse of two centuries, the question is at least plausibly mooted again."

There was another pause, while Bateman thought over his facts and arguments, but nothing was forthcoming at the moment. Willis continued: "You must consider also that reputed relics, such as you have mentioned, are generally in the custody of religious bodies, who are naturally very jealous of attempts to prove them spurious, and, with a pardonable *esprit de corps*, defend them with all their might, and oppose obstacles in the way of an adverse decision; just as your own society defends, most worthily, the fair fame of your foundress, Queen Boadicea. Were the case given against her by every tribunal in the land, your valiant and loyal Head would not abandon her; it would break his magnanimous heart; he would die in her service as a good knight. Both from religious duty, then, and from human feeling, it is a very arduous thing to get a received relic disowned."

"Well," said Bateman, "to my poor judgment it does seem a dishonesty to keep up inscriptions, for instance, which every one knows not to be true."

"My dear Bateman, that is begging the question," said Willis; "*every* body does *not* know it; it is a point in course of settlement, but not settled; you may say that *individuals* have settled it, or it *may* be settled, but it is not settled yet. Parallel cases happen frequently in civil matters, and no one speaks harshly of existing individuals or bodies in consequence. Till lately the Monument in London bore an inscription to the effect that London had been burned by us poor Papists. A hundred years ago, Pope, the poet, had called the 'column' 'a tall bully' which 'lifts its head and lies.' Yet the inscription was not removed till a few years since—I believe when the Monument was repaired. That was an opportunity for erasing a calumny which, till then, had not been definitely pronounced to be such, and not pronounced in deference to the *primâ facie* authority of a statement contemporaneous with the calamity which it recorded. There is never a *point* of time at which you can say, 'The tradition is now disproved.' When a received belief has been apparently exposed, the question lies dormant for the opportunity of fresh arguments; when none appear, then at length an accident, such as the repair of a building, despatches it."

"We have somehow got off the subject," thought Bateman; and he sat fidgeting about to find the thread of his argument. Reding put in an objection; he said that no one knew or cared about the inscription on the Monument, but religious veneration was paid to the two heads at St. John Lateran.

"Right," said Bateman, "that's just what I meant to say."

"Well," answered Willis, "as to the particular case—mind, I am taking your account of it, for I don't profess to know how the matter lies. But let us consider the extent of the mistake. There is no doubt in the world that at least they are the heads of martyrs; the only question is this, and no more, whether they are the very heads of the two Apostles. From time immemorial they have been preserved upon or under the altar as the heads of saints or martyrs; and it requires to know very little of Christian antiquities to be perfectly certain that they really are saintly relics, even though unknown. Hence the sole mistake is, that Catholics have venerated, what ought to be venerated anyhow, under a wrong name; perhaps have expected miracles (which they had a right to expect), and have experienced them (as they might well experience them), because they *were* the relics of saints, though they were in error as to what saints. This surely is no great matter."

"You have made three assumptions," said Bateman; "first, that none but the relics of saints have been placed under altars; secondly, that these relics were always there; thirdly—thirdly—I know there was a third—let me see—"

"Most true," said Willis, interrupting him, "and I will help you to some others. I have assumed that there are Christians in the world called Catholics; again, that they think it right to venerate relics; but, my dear Bateman, these were the grounds, and not the point of our argument; and if they are to be questioned, it must be in a distinct dispute: but I really think we have had enough of disputation."

"Yes, Bateman," said Charles; "it is getting late. I must think of returning. Give us some tea, and let us begone."

"Go home?" cried Bateman; "why, we have just done dinner, and done nothing else as yet; I had a great deal to say."

However, he rang the bell for tea, and had the table cleared.

CHAPTER XX

The conversation flagged; Bateman was again busy with his memory; and he was getting impatient too; time was slipping away, and no blow struck; moreover, Willis was beginning to gape, and Charles seemed impatient to be released. "These Romanists put things so plausibly," he said to himself, "but very unfairly, most unfairly; one ought to be up to their dodges. I dare say, if the truth were known, Willis has had lessons; he looks so demure; I dare say he is keeping back a great deal, and playing upon my ignorance. Who knows? Perhaps he's a concealed Jesuit." It was an awful thought, and suspended the course of his reflections some seconds. "I wonder what he does really think; it's so difficult to get at the bottom of them; they won't tell tales, and they are under obedience; one never knows when to believe them. I suspect he has been wofully disappointed with Romanism; he looks so thin; but of course he won't say so; it hurts a man's pride, and he likes to be consistent; he doesn't like to be laughed at, and so he makes the best of things. I wish I knew how to treat him; I was wrong in having Reding here; of course Willis would not be confidential before a third person. He's like the fox that lost his tail. It was bad tact in me; I see it now; what a thing it is to have tact! it requires very delicate tact. There are so many things I wished to say, about Indulgences, about their so seldom communicating; I think I must ask him about the Mass." So, after fidgeting a good deal within, while he was ostensibly employed in making tea, he commenced his last assault.

"Well, we shall have you back again among us by next Christmas, Willis," he said; "I can't give you greater law; I am certain of it; it takes time, but slow and sure. What a joyful time it will be! I can't tell what keeps you; you are doing nothing; you are flung into a corner; you are wasting life. *What* keeps you?"

Willis looked odd; then he simply answered, "Grace."

Bateman was startled, but recovered himself; "Heaven forbid," he said, "that I should treat these things lightly, or interfere with you unduly. I know, my dear friend, what a serious fellow you are; but do tell me, just tell me, how can you justify the Mass, as it is performed abroad; how can it be called a 'reasonable service,' when all parties conspire to gabble it over as if it mattered not a jot who attended to it, or even understood it? Speak, man, speak," he added, gently shaking him by the shoulder.

"These are such difficult questions," answered Willis; "must I speak? Such difficult questions," he continued, rising into a more animated manner, and kindling as he went on; "I mean, people view them so differently: it is so difficult to convey to one person the idea of another. The idea of worship is different in the Catholic Church from the idea of it in your Church; for, in truth, the *religions* are different. Don't deceive yourself, my dear Bateman," he said tenderly, "it is not that ours is your religion carried a little farther—a little too far, as you would say. No, they differ in kind, not in degree; ours is one religion, yours another. And when the time comes, and come it will, for you, alien as you are now, to submit yourself to the gracious yoke of Christ, then, my dearest Bateman, it will be *faith* which will enable you to bear the ways and usages of Catholics, which else might perhaps startle you. Else, the habits of years, the associations in your mind of a certain outward behaviour with real inward acts of devotion, might embarrass you, when you had to conform yourself to other habits, and to create for yourself other associations. But this faith, of which I speak, the great gift of God, will enable you in that day to overcome yourself, and to submit, as your judgment, your will, your reason, your affections, so your tastes and likings, to the rule and usage of the Church. Ah, that faith should be necessary in such a matter, and that what is so natural and becoming under the circumstances, should have need of an explanation! I declare, to me," he said, and he clasped his hands on his knees, and looked forward as if soliloquizing, "to me nothing is so consoling, so piercing, so thrilling, so overcoming, as the Mass, said as it is among us. I could attend Masses for ever, and not be tired. It is not a mere form of words—it is a great action, the greatest action that can be on earth. It is, not the invocation merely, but, if I dare use the word, the evocation of the Eternal. He becomes present on the altar in flesh and blood, before whom angels bow and devils tremble. This is that awful event which is the scope, and is the interpretation, of every part of the solemnity. Words are necessary, but as means, not as ends; they are not mere addresses to the throne of grace, they are instruments of what is far higher, of consecration, of sacrifice. They hurry on as if impatient to fulfil their mission. Quickly they go, the whole is quick; for they are all parts of one integral action. Quickly they go; for they are awful words of sacrifice, they are a work too great to delay upon; as when it was said in the beginning, 'What thou doest, do quickly.' Quickly they pass; for the Lord Jesus goes with them, as He passed along the lake in the days of His flesh, quickly calling first one and then another. Quickly they pass; because as the lightning which shineth from one part of the heaven unto the other, so is the coming of the Son of Man. Quickly they pass; for they are as the words of Moses, when the Lord came down in the cloud, calling on the Name of the Lord as He passed by, 'The Lord, the Lord God, merciful and gracious, long-suffering, and abundant in goodness and truth.' And as Moses on the mountain, so we too 'make haste and bow our heads to the earth, and adore.' So we, all around, each in his place, look out for the great Advent, 'waiting for the moving of the water.' Each in his place, with his own heart, with his own wants, with his own thoughts, with his own intention, with his own prayers, separate but concordant, watching what is going on, watching its progress, uniting in its consummation—not painfully and hopelessly following a hard form of prayer from beginning to end, but, like a concert of musical instruments, each different, but concurring in a sweet harmony, we take our part with God's priest, supporting him, yet guided by him. There are little children there, and old men, and simple labourers, and students in seminaries, priests preparing for Mass, priests making their thanksgiving; there are innocent maidens, and there are penitent sinners; but out of these many minds rises one eucharistic hymn, and the great Action is the measure and the scope of it. And oh, my dear Bateman," he added, turning to him, "you ask me whether this is not a formal, unreasonable service—it is wonderful!" he cried, rising up, "quite wonderful. When will these dear, good people be enlightened? *O Sapientia, fortiter suaviterque disponens omnia, O Adonai, O Clavis David et Exspectatio gentium, veni ad salvandum nos, Domine Deus noster.*"

Now, at least, there was no mistaking Willis. Bateman stared, and was almost frightened at a burst of enthusiasm which he had been far from expecting. "Why, Willis," he said, "it is not true, then, after all, what we heard, that you were somewhat dubious, shaky, in your adherence to Romanism? I'm sure I beg your pardon; I would not for the world have annoyed you, had I known the truth."

Willis's face still glowed, and he looked as youthful and radiant as he had been two years before. There was nothing ungentle in his impetuosity; a smile, almost a laugh, was on his face, as if he was half ashamed of his own warmth; but this took nothing from its evident sincerity. He seized Bateman's two hands, before the latter knew where he was, lifted him up out of his seat, and, raising his own mouth close to his ear, said, in a low voice, "I would to God, that not only thou, but also all who hear me this day, were both in little and in much such as I am, except these chains." Then, reminding him it had grown late, and bidding him good-night, he left the room with Charles.

Bateman remained a while with his back to the fire after the door had closed; presently he began to give expression to his thoughts. "Well," he said, "he's a brick, a regular brick; he has almost affected me myself. What a way those fellows have with them! I declare his touch has made my heart beat; how catching enthusiasm is! Any one but I might really have been unsettled. He *is* a real good fellow; what a pity we have not got him! he's just the sort of man we want. He'd make a splendid Anglican; he'd convert half the Dissenters in the country. Well, we shall have them in time; we must not be impatient. But the idea of his talking of converting *me*! 'in little and in much,' as he worded it! By-the-bye, what did he mean by 'except these chains'?" He sat ruminating on the difficulty; at first he was inclined to think that, after all, he might have some misgiving about his position; then he thought that perhaps he had a hair-shirt or a *catenella* on him; and lastly, he came to the conclusion that he had just meant nothing at all, and did but finish the quotation he had begun.

After passing some little time in this state, he looked towards the tea-tray; poured himself out another cup of tea; ate a bit of toast; took the coals off the fire; blew out one of the candles, and, taking up the other, left the parlour and wound like an omnibus up the steep twisting staircase to his bedroom.

Meanwhile Willis and Charles were proceeding to their

respective homes. For a while they had to pursue the same path, which they did in silence. Charles had been moved far more than Bateman, or rather touched, by the enthusiasm of his Catholic friend, though, from a difficulty in finding language to express himself, and a fear of being carried off his legs, he had kept his feelings to himself. When they were about to part, Willis said to him, in a subdued tone, "You are soon going to Oxford, dearest Reding; oh, that you were one with us! You have it in you. I have thought of you at Mass many times. Our priest has said Mass for you. Oh, my dear friend, quench not God's grace; listen to His call; you have had what others have not. What you want is faith. I suspect you have quite proof enough; enough to be converted on. But faith is a gift; pray for that great gift, without which you cannot come to the Church; without which," and he paused, "you cannot walk aright when you are in the Church. And now farewell! alas, our path divides; all is easy to him that believeth. May God give you that gift of faith, as He has given me! Farewell again; who knows when I may see you next, and where? May it be in the courts of the true Jerusalem, the Queen of Saints, the Holy Roman Church, the Mother of us all!" He drew Charles to him and kissed his cheek, and was gone before Charles had time to say a word.

Yet Charles could not have spoken had he had ever so much opportunity. He set off at a brisk pace, cutting down with his stick the twigs and brambles which the pale twilight discovered in his path. It seemed as if the kiss of his friend had conveyed into his own soul the enthusiasm which his words had betokened. He felt himself possessed, he knew not how, by a high superhuman power, which seemed able to push through mountains, and to walk the sea. With winter around him, he felt within like the spring-tide, when all is new and bright. He perceived that he had found, what indeed he had never sought, because he had never known what it was, but what he had ever wanted—a soul sympathetic with his own. He felt he was no longer alone in the world, though he was losing that true congenial mind the very moment he had found him. Was this, he asked himself, the communion of Saints? Alas! how could it be, when he was in one communion and Willis in another? "O mighty Mother!" burst from his lips; he quickened his pace almost to a trot, scaling the steep ascents and diving into the hollows which lay between him and Boughton. "O mighty Mother!" he still said, half unconsciously; "O mighty Mother! I come, O mighty Mother! I come; but I am far from home. Spare me a little; I come with what speed I may, but I am slow of foot, and not as others, O mighty Mother!"

By the time he had walked two miles in this excitement, bodily and mental, he felt himself, as was not wonderful, considerably exhausted. He slackened his pace, and gradually came to himself, but still he went on, as if mechanically, "O mighty Mother!" Suddenly he cried, "Hallo! where did I get these words? Willis did not use them. Well, I must be on my guard against these wild ways. Any one can be an enthusiast; enthusiasm is not truth… O mighty Mother! … Alas, I know where my heart is! but I must go by reason… O mighty Mother!"

CHAPTER XXI

THE time came at length for Charles to return to Oxford; but during the last month scruples had arisen in his mind, whether, with his present feelings, he could consistently even present himself for his examination. No subscription was necessary for his entrance into the schools, but he felt that the honours of the class-list were only intended for those who were *bonâ fide* adherents of the Church of England. He laid his difficulty before Carlton, who in consequence did his best to ascertain thoroughly his present state of mind. It seemed that Charles had no *intention*, either now or at any future day, of joining the Church of Rome; that he felt he could not take such a step at present without distinct sin; that it would simply be against his conscience to do so; that he had no feeling whatever that God called him to do so; that he felt that nothing could justify so serious an act but the conviction that he could not be saved in the Church to which he belonged; that he had no such feeling; that he had no definite case against his own Church sufficient for leaving it, nor any definite view that the Church of Rome was the One Church of Christ: that still he could not help suspecting that one day he should think otherwise; he conceived the day might come, nay would come, when he should have that conviction which at present he had not, and which of course would be a call on him to act upon it, by leaving the Church of England for that of Rome; he could not tell distinctly why he so anticipated, except that there were so many things which he thought right in the Church of Rome, and so many which he thought wrong in the Church of England; and, because, too, the more he had an opportunity of hearing and seeing, the greater cause he had to admire and revere the Roman Catholic system, and to be dissatisfied with his own. Carlton, after carefully considering the case, advised him to go in for his examination. He acted thus, on the one hand, as vividly feeling the changes which take place in the minds of young men, and the difficulty of Reding foretelling his own state of opinions two years to come; and, on the other, from the reasonable anticipation that a contrary advice would have been the very way to ripen his present doubts on the untenableness of Anglicanism into conviction.

Accordingly, his examination came off in due time; the schools were full, he did well, and his class was considered to be secure. Sheffield followed soon after, and did brilliantly. The list came out; Sheffield was in the first class, Charles in the second. There is always of necessity a good deal of accident in these matters; but in the present case reasons enough could be given to account for the unequal success of the two friends. Charles had lost some time by his father's death, and family matters consequent upon it; and his virtual rustication for the last six months had been a considerable disadvantage to him. Moreover, though he had been a careful, persevering reader, he certainly had not run the race for honours with the same devotion as Sheffield; nor had his religious difficulties, particularly his late indecision about presenting himself at all, been without their serious influence upon his attention and his energy. As success had not been the first desire of his soul, so failure was not his greatest misery. He would have much preferred success; but in a day or two he found he could well endure the want of it.

Now came the question about his degree, which could not be taken without subscription to the Articles. Another consultation followed with Carlton. There was no need of his becoming a B.A. at the moment; nothing would be gained by it; better that he should postpone the step. He had but to go down and say nothing about it; no one would be the wiser; and if, at the end of six months, as Carlton sanguinely anticipated, he found himself in a more comfortable frame of mind, then let him come up, and set all right.

What was he to do with himself at the moment? There was little difficulty here either, what to propose. He had better be reading with some clergyman in the country; thus he would at once be preparing for orders, and clearing his mind on the points which at present troubled him; besides, he might thus have some opportunity for parochial duty, which would have a tranquillizing and sobering effect on his mind. As to the books to which he should give his attention, of course the choice would rest with the clergyman who was to guide him; but for himself Carlton would not recommend the usual works in controversy with Rome, for which the Anglican Church was famous; rather those which are of a positive character, which treated subjects philosophically, historically, or doctrinally, and displayed the peculiar principles of that Church; Hooker's great work, for instance; or Bull's *Defensio* and *Harmonia*, or Pearson's *Vindiciae*, or Jackson on the Creed, a noble work; to which Laud on Tradition might be added, though its form was controversial. Such, too, were Bingham's Antiquities, Waterland on the Use of Antiquity, Wall on Infant Baptism, and Palmer on the Liturgy. Nor ought he to neglect practical and devotional authors, as Bishops Taylor, Wilson, and Horne. The most important point remained; whither was he to betake himself? Did he know of any clergyman in the country who would be willing to receive him as a friend and a pupil? Charles thought of Campbell, with whom he was on the best of terms; and Carlton knew enough of him by reputation, to be perfectly sure that he could not be in safer hands.

Charles, in consequence, made the proposal to him, and it was accepted. Nothing then remained for him but to pay a few bills, to pack up some books which he had left in a friend's room, and then to bid adieu, at least for a time, to the cloisters and groves of the University. He quitted in June, when everything was in that youthful and fragrant beauty which he had admired so much in the beginning of his residence three years before.

PART III

CHAPTER I

But now we must look forward, not back. Once before we took leave to pass over nearly two years in the life of the subject of this narrative, and now a second and a dreary and longer interval shall be consigned to oblivion, and the reader shall be set down in the autumn of the year next but one after that in which Charles took his class and did not take his degree.

At this time our interest is confined to Boughton and the Rectory at Sutton. As to Melford, friend Bateman had accepted the incumbency of a church in a manufacturing town with a district of 10,000 souls, where he was full of plans for the introduction of the surplice and gilt candlesticks among his people, and where, it is to be hoped, he will learn wisdom. Willis also was gone, on a different errand: he had bid adieu to his mother and brother soon after Charles had gone into the schools, and now was Father Aloysius de Sanctâ Cruce in the Passionist Convent of Pennington.

One evening, at the end of September, in the year aforesaid, Campbell had called at Boughton, and was walking in the garden with Miss Reding. "Really, Mary," he said to her, "I don't think it does any good to keep him. The best years of his life are going, and, humanly speaking, there is not any chance of his changing his mind, at least till he has made a trial of the Church of Rome. It is quite possible that experience may drive him back."

"It is a dreadful dilemma," she answered; "how can we even indirectly give him permission to take so fatal a step?"

"He is a dear, good fellow," he made reply; "he is a sterling fellow; all this long time that he has been with me he has made no difficulties; he has read thoroughly the books that I recommended and more, and done whatever I told him. You know I have employed him in the parish; he has taught the Catechism to the children, and been almoner. Poor fellow, his health is suffering now: he sees there's no end of it, and hope deferred makes the heart sick."

"It is so dreadful to give any countenance to what is so very wrong," said Mary.

"Why, what is to be done?" answered Campbell; "and we need not countenance it; he can't be kept in leading-strings for ever, and there has been a kind of bargain. He wanted to make a move at the end of the first year—I didn't think it worth while to fidget you about it—but I quieted him. We compounded in this way: he removed his name from the college-boards—there was not the slightest chance of his ever signing the Articles—and he consented to wait another year. Now the time's up, and more, and he is getting impatient. So it's not we who shall be giving him countenance, it will only be his leaving us."

"But it is so fearful," insisted Mary; "and my poor mother—I declare I think it will be her death."

"It will be a crushing blow, there's no doubt of that," said Campbell; "what does she know of it at present?"

"I hardly can tell you," answered she; "she has been informed of it indeed distinctly a year ago; but seeing Charles so often, and he in appearance just the same, I fear she does not realize it. She has never spoken to me on the subject. I fancy she thinks it a scruple; troublesome, certainly, but of course temporary."

"I must break it to her, Mary," said Campbell.

"Well, I think it *must* be done," she replied, heaving a sudden sigh; "and if so, it will be a real kindness in you to save me a task to which I am quite unequal. But have a talk with Charles first. When it comes to the point he may have a greater difficulty than he thinks beforehand."

And so it was settled; and, full of care at the double commission with which he was charged, Campbell rode back to Sutton.

Poor Charles was sitting at an open window, looking out upon the prospect, when Campbell entered the room. It was a beautiful landscape, with bold hills in the distance, and a rushing river beneath him. Campbell came up to him without his perceiving it; and, putting his hand on his shoulder, asked his thoughts.

Charles turned round, and smiled sadly. "I am like Moses seeing the land," he said; "my dear Campbell, when shall the end be?"

"That, my good Charles, of course does not rest with me," answered Campbell.

"Well," said he, "the year is long run out; may I go my way?"

"You can't expect that I, or any of us, should even indirectly countenance you in what, with all our love of you, we think a sin," said Campbell.

"That is as much as to say, 'Act for yourself,'" answered Charles; "well, I am willing."

Campbell did not at once reply; then he said, "I shall have to break it to your poor mother; Mary thinks it will be her death."

Charles dropped his head on the window-sill, upon his hands. "No," he said; "I trust that she, and all of us, will be supported."

"So do I, fervently," answered Campbell; "it will be a most terrible blow to your sisters. My dear fellow, should you not take all this into account? Do seriously consider the actual misery you are causing for possible good."

"Do you think I have not considered it, Campbell? Is it nothing for one like me to be breaking all these dear ties, and to be losing the esteem and sympathy of so many persons I love? Oh, it has been a most piercing thought; but I have exhausted it, I have drunk it out. I have got familiar with the prospect now, and am fully reconciled. Yes, I give up home, I give up all who have ever known me, loved me, valued me, wished me well; I know well I am making myself a by-word and an outcast."

"Oh, my dear Charles," answered Campbell, "beware of a very subtle temptation which may come on you here. I have meant to warn you of it before. The greatness of the sacrifice stimulates you;

you do it because it is so much to do."

Charles smiled. "How little you know me!" he said; "if that were the case, should I have waited patiently two years and more? Why did I not rush forward as others have done? *You* will not deny that I have acted rationally, obediently. I have put the subject from me again and again, and it has returned."

"I'll say nothing harsh or unkind of you, Charles," said Campbell; "but it's a most unfortunate delusion. I wish I could make you take in the idea that there is the chance of its *being* a delusion."

"Ah, Campbell, how can you forget so?" answered Charles; "don't you know this is the very thing which has influenced me so much all along? I said, 'Perhaps I am in a dream. Oh, that I could pinch myself and awake!' You know what stress I laid on my change of feeling upon my dear father's death; what I thought to be convictions before, vanished then like a cloud. I have said to myself, 'Perhaps these will vanish too.' But no; 'the clouds return after the rain'; they come again and again, heavier than ever. It is a conviction rooted in me; it endures against the prospect of loss of mother and sisters. Here I sit wasting my days, when I might be useful in life. Why? Because this hinders me. Lately it has increased on me tenfold. You will be shocked, but let me tell you in confidence—lately I have been quite afraid to ride, or to bathe, or to do anything out of the way, lest something should happen, and I might be taken away with a great duty unaccomplished. No, by this time I have proved that it is a real conviction. My belief in the Church of Rome is part of myself; I cannot act against it without acting against God."

"It is a most deplorable state of things certainly," said Campbell, who had begun to walk up and down the room; "that it is a delusion, I am confident; perhaps you are to find it so, just when you have taken the step. You will solemnly bind yourself to a foreign creed, and, as the words part from your mouth, the mist will roll up from before your eyes, and the truth will show itself. How dreadful!"

"I have thought of that too," said Charles, "and it has influenced me a great deal. It has made me shrink back. But I now believe it to be like those hideous forms which in fairy tales beset good knights, when they would force their way into some enchanted palace. Recollect the words in Thalaba, 'The talisman is *faith*.' If I have good grounds for believing, to believe is a duty; God will take care of His own work. I shall not be deserted in my utmost need. Faith ever begins with a venture, and is rewarded with sight."

"Yes, my good Charles," answered Campbell; "but the question is, whether your grounds *are* good. What I mean is, that, *since* they are *not* good, they will not avail you in the trial. You will then, too late, find they are not good, but delusive."

"Campbell," answered Charles, "I consider that all reason comes from God; our grounds must at best be imperfect; but if they appear to be sufficient after prayer, diligent search, obedience, waiting, and, in short, doing our part, they are His voice calling us on. He it is, in that case, who makes them seem convincing to us. I am in His hands. The only question is, what would He have me to do? I cannot resist the conviction which is upon me. This last week it has possessed me in a different way than ever before. It is now so strong, that to wait longer is to resist God. Whether I join the Catholic Church is now simply a question of days. I wish, dear Campbell, to leave you in peace and love. Therefore, consent; let me go."

"Let you go!" answered Campbell; "certainly, were it the Catholic Church to which you are going, there would be no need to ask; but 'let you go,' how can you expect it from us when we do not think so? Think of our case, Charles, as well as your own; throw yourself into our state of feeling. For myself, I cannot deny, I never have concealed from you my convictions, that the Romish Church is anti-christian. She has ten thousand gifts, she is in many respects superior to our own; but she has a something in her which spoils all. I have no *confidence* in her; and, that being the case, how can I 'let you go' to her? No: it's like a person saying, 'Let me go and hang myself'; 'let me go sleep in a fever-ward'; 'let me jump into that well';—how can I 'let you go'?"

"Ah," said Charles, "that's our dreadful difference; we can't get farther than that. *I* think the Church of Rome the Prophet of God; *you*, the tool of the devil."

"I own," said Campbell, "I do think that, if you take this step, you will find yourself in the hands of a Circe, who will change you, make a brute of you."

Charles slightly coloured.

"I won't go on," added Campbell; "I pain you; it's no good; perhaps I am making matters worse."

Neither spoke for some time. At length Charles got up, came up to Campbell, took his hand, and kissed it. "You have been a kind, disinterested friend to me for two years," he said; "you have given me a lodging under your roof; and now we are soon to be united by closer ties. God reward you; but 'let me go, for the day breaketh.'"

"It is hopeless!" cried Campbell; "let us part friends: I must break it to your mother."

In ten days after this conversation Charles was ready for his journey; his room put to rights; his portmanteau strapped; and a gig at the door, which was to take him the first stage. He was to go round by Boughton; it had been arranged by Campbell and Mary that it would be best for him not to see his mother (to whom Campbell had broken the matter at once) till he took leave of her. It would be needless pain to both of them to attempt an interview sooner.

Charles leapt from the gig with a beating heart, and ran up to his mother's room. She was sitting by the fire at her work when he entered; she held out her hand coldly to him, and he sat down. Nothing was said for a little while; then, without leaving off her occupation, she said, "Well, Charles, and so you are leaving us. Where and how do you propose to employ yourself when you have entered upon your new life?"

Charles answered that he had not yet turned his mind to the

consideration of anything but the great step on which everything else depended.

There was another silence; then she said, "You won't find anywhere such friends as you have had at home, Charles." Presently she continued, "You have had everything in your favour, Charles; you have been blessed with talents, advantages of education, easy circumstances; many a deserving young man has to scramble on as he can."

Charles answered that he was deeply sensible how much he owed in temporal matters to Providence, and that it was only at His bidding that he was giving them up.

"We all looked up to you, Charles; perhaps we made too much of you; well, God be with you; you have taken your line."

Poor Charles said that no one could conceive what it cost him to give up what was so very dear to him, what was part of himself; there was nothing on earth which he prized like his home.

"Then why do you leave us?" she said quickly; "you must have your way; you do it, I suppose, because you like it."

"Oh really, my dear mother," cried he, "if you saw my heart! You know in Scripture how people were obliged in the Apostles' times to give up all for Christ."

"We are heathens, then," she replied; "thank you, Charles, I am obliged to you for this"; and she dashed away a tear from her eye.

Charles was almost beside himself; he did not know what to say; he stood up, and leaned his elbow on the mantelpiece, supporting his head on his hand.

"Well, Charles," she continued, still going on with her work, "perhaps the day will come"...her voice faltered; "your dear father"...she put down her work.

"It is useless misery," said Charles; "why should I stay? Good-bye for the present, my dearest mother. I leave you in good hands, not kinder, but better than mine; you lose me, you gain another. Farewell for the present; we will meet when you will, when you call;

it will be a happy meeting."

He threw himself on his knees, and laid his cheek on her lap; she could no longer resist him; she hung over him, and began to smooth down his hair as she had done when he was a child. At length scalding tears began to fall heavily upon his face and neck; he bore them for a while, then started up, kissed her cheek impetuously, and rushed out of the room. In a few seconds he had seen and had torn himself from his sisters, and was in his gig again by the side of his phlegmatic driver, dancing slowly up and down on his way to Collumpton.

CHAPTER II

THE reader may ask whither Charles is going, and, though it would not be quite true to answer that he did not know better than the said reader himself, yet he had most certainly very indistinct notions what was becoming of him even locally, and, like the Patriarch, "went out, not knowing whither he went." He had never seen a Catholic priest, to know him, in his life; never, except once as a boy, been inside a Catholic church; he only knew one Catholic in the world, and where he was he did not know. But he knew that the Passionists had a Convent in London; and it was not unnatural that, without knowing whether young Father Aloysius was there or not, he should direct his course to San Michaele.

Yet, in kindness to Mary and all of them, he did not profess to be leaving direct for London; but he proposed to betake himself to Carlton, who still resided in Oxford, and to ask his advice what was to be done under his circumstances. It seemed, too, to be interposing what they would consider a last chance of averting what to them was so dismal a calamity.

To Oxford, then, he directed his course; and, having some accidental business at Bath, he stopped there for the night, intending to continue his journey next morning. Among other jobs, he had to get a "Garden of the Soul," and two or three similar books which might help him in the great preparation which awaited his arrival in London. He went into a religious publisher's in Danvers Street with that object, and while engaged in a back part of the shop in looking over a pile of Catholic works, which, to the religious public, had inferior attractions to the glittering volumes, Evangelical and Anglo-Catholic, which had possession of the windows and principal table, he heard the shop-door open, and, on looking round, saw a familiar face. It was that of a young clergyman, with a very pretty girl on his arm, whom her dress pronounced to be a bride. Love was in their eyes, joy in their voice, and affluence in their gait and bearing. Charles had a faintish feeling come over him; somewhat such as might beset a man on hearing a call for pork-chops when he was sea-sick. He retreated behind a pile of ledgers and other stationery, but they could not save him from the low, dulcet tones which from time to time passed from one to the other.

"Have you got some of the last Oxford reprints of standard works?" said the bridegroom to the shopman.

"Yes, sir; but which set did you mean? 'Selections from Old Divines,' or, 'New Catholic Adaptations'?"

"Oh, not the Adaptations," answered he, "they are extremely dangerous; I mean real Church-of-England divinity—Bull, Patrick, Hooker, and the rest of them."

The shopman went to look them out.

"I think it was those Adaptations, dearest," said the lady, "that the Bishop warned us against."

"Not the Bishop, Louisa; it was his daughter."

"Oh, Miss Primrose, so it was," said she; "and there was one book she recommended, what was it?"

"Not a book, it was a speech," said White; "Mr. O'Ballaway's at Exeter Hall; but I think we should not quite like it."

"No, no, Henry, it *was* a book, dear; I can't recall the name."

"You mean Dr. Crow's 'New Refutation of Popery,' perhaps; but the *Bishop* recommended *that*."

The shopman returned. "Oh, what a sweet face!" she said, looking at the frontispiece of a little book she got hold of; "do look, Henry; whom does it put you in mind of?"

"Why, it's meant for St. John the Baptist," said Henry.

"It's so like little Angelina Primrose," said she, "the hair is just hers. I wonder it doesn't strike you."

"It does—it does," said he, smiling at her; "but it's getting late; you must not be out much longer in the sharp air, and you have nothing for your throat. I have chosen my books while you have been gazing on that little St. John."

"I can't think who it is so like," continued she; "oh, I know; it's Angelina's aunt, Lady Constance."

"Come, Louisa, the horses too will suffer; we must return to our friends."

"Oh, there's one book, I can't recollect it; tell me what it is, Henry. I shall be so sorry not to have got it."

"Was it the new work on Gregorian Chants?" asked he.

"Ah, it's true, I want it for the school-children, but it's not that."

"Is it 'The Catholic Parsonage'?" he asked again; "or, 'Lays of the Apostles'? Or, 'The English Church older than the Roman'? Or, 'Anglicanism of the Early Martyrs'? Or, 'Confessions of a Pervert'? Or, 'Eustace Beville'? Or, 'Modified Celibacy'?"

"No, no, no," said Louisa; "dear me, it is so stupid."

"Well, now really, Louisa," he insisted, "you must come another time; it won't do, dearest; it won't do."

"Oh, I recollect," she said, "I recollect—'Abbeys and Abbots'; I want to get some hints for improving the rectory-windows when we get home; and our church wants, you know, a porch for the poor people. The book is full of designs."

The book was found and added to the rest, which had been already taken to the carriage. "Now, Louisa," said White. "Well, dearest, there's one more place we must call at," she made answer; "tell John to drive to Sharp's; we can go round by the nursery—it's only a few steps out of the way—I want to say a word to the man there about our greenhouse; there is no good gardener in our own neighbourhood."

"What is the good, Louisa, now?" said her husband; "we shan't be at home this month to come"; and then, with due resignation, he directed the coachman to the nurseryman's whom Louisa named, as he put her into the carriage, and then followed her.

Charles breathed freely as they went out; a severe text of Scripture rose on his mind, but he repressed the uncharitable feeling, and turned himself to the anxious duties which lay before him.

CHAPTER III

Nothing happened to Charles worth relating before his arrival at Steventon next day; when, the afternoon being fine, he left his portmanteau to follow him by the omnibus, and put himself upon the road. If it required some courage to undertake by himself a long journey on an all-momentous errand, it did not lessen the difficulty that that journey took in its way a place and a person so dear to him as Oxford and Carlton.

He had passed through Bagley Wood, and the spires and towers of the University came on his view, hallowed by how many tender associations, lost to him for two whole years, suddenly recovered—recovered to be lost for ever! There lay old Oxford before him, with its hills as gentle and its meadows as green as ever. At the first view of that beloved place he stood still with folded arms, unable to proceed. Each college, each church—he counted them by their pinnacles and turrets. The silver Isis, the grey willows, the far-stretching plains, the dark groves, the distant range of Shotover, the pleasant village where he had lived with Carlton and Sheffield—wood, water, stone, all so calm, so bright, they might have been his, but his they were not. Whatever he was to gain by becoming a Catholic, this he had lost; whatever he was to gain higher and better, at least this and such as this he never could have again. He could not have another Oxford, he could not have the friends of his boyhood and youth in the choice of his manhood. He mounted the well-known gate on the left, and proceeded down into the plain. There was no one to greet him, to sympathize with him; there was no one to believe he needed sympathy; no one to believe he had given up anything; no one to take interest in him, to feel tender towards him, to defend him. He had suffered much, but there was no one to believe that he had suffered. He would be thought to be inflicting merely, not undergoing, suffering. He might indeed say that he had suffered; but he would be rudely told that every one follows his own will, and that if he had given up Oxford, it was for a whim which he liked better than it. But rather, there was no one to know him; he had been virtually three years away; three years is a generation; Oxford had been his place once, but his place knew him no more. He recollected with what awe and transport he had at first come to the University, as to some sacred shrine; and how from time to time hopes had come over him that some day or other he should have gained a title to residence on one of its ancient foundations. One night in particular came across his memory, how a friend and he had ascended to the top of one of its many towers with the purpose of making observations on the stars; and how, while his friend was busily engaged with the pointers, he, earthly-minded youth, had been looking down into the deep, gas-lit, dark-shadowed quadrangles, and wondering if he should ever be Fellow of this or that College, which he singled out from the mass of academical buildings. All had passed as a dream, and he was a stranger where he had hoped to have had a home.

He was drawing near Oxford; he saw along the road before him brisk youths pass, two and two, with elastic tread, finishing their modest daily walk, and nearing the city. What had been a tandem a mile back, next crossed his field of view, shorn of its leader. Presently a stately cap and gown loomed in the distance; he had gained the road before their owner crossed him; it was a college-tutor whom he had known a little. Charles expected to be recognized; but the resident passed by with that half-conscious, uncertain gaze which seemed to have some memory of a face which yet was strange. He had passed Folly Bridge; troops of horsemen overtook him, talking loud, while with easy jaunty pace they turned into their respective stables. He crossed to Christ Church, and penetrated to Peckwater. The evening was still bright, and the gas was lighting. Groups of young men were stationed here and there, the greater number in hats, a few in caps, one or two with gowns in addition; some were hallooing up to their companions at the windows of the second story; scouts were carrying about *aeger* dinners; pastry-cook boys were bringing in desserts; shabby fellows with Blenheim puppies were loitering under Canterbury Gate. Many stared, but no one knew him. He hurried up Oriel Lane; suddenly a start and a low bow from a passer-by; who could it be? It was a superannuated shoeblack of his college, to whom he had sometimes given a stray shilling. He gained the High Street, and turned down towards the Angel. What was approaching? The vision of a proctor. Charles felt some instinctive quiverings; but it passed by him, and did no harm. Like Kehama, he had a charmed life. And now he had reached his inn, where he found his portmanteau all ready for him. He chose a bedroom, and, after fully inducting himself into it, turned his thoughts towards dinner.

He wished to lose no time, but, if possible, to proceed to London the following morning. It would be a great point if he could get to his journey's end so early in the week, that by Sunday, if he was thought worthy, he might offer up his praises for the mercies vouchsafed to him in the great and holy communion of the Universal Church. Accordingly he determined to make an attempt on

Carlton that evening; and hoped, if he went to his room between seven and eight, to find him returned from Common-Room. With this intention he sallied out at about the half-hour, gained Carlton's College, knocked at the gate, entered, passed on, up the worn wooden steep staircase. The oak was closed; he descended, found a servant; "Mr. Carlton was giving a dinner in Common-Room; it would soon be over." Charles determined to wait for him.

The servant lighted candles in the inner room, and Charles sat down at the fire. For awhile he sat in reflection; then he looked about for something to occupy him. His eye caught an Oxford paper; it was but a few days old. "Let us see how the old place goes on," he said to himself, as he took it up. He glanced from one article to another, looking who were the University-preachers of the week, who had taken degrees, who were public examiners, etc., etc., when his eye was arrested by the following paragraph:

"Defection from the Church.—We understand that another victim has lately been added to the list of those whom the venom of Tractarian principles has precipitated into the bosom of the Sorceress of Rome. Mr. Reding, of St. Saviour's, the son of a respectable clergyman of the Establishment, deceased, after eating the bread of the Church all his life, has at length avowed himself the subject and slave of an Italian Bishop. Disappointment in the schools is said to have been the determining cause of this infatuated act. It is reported that legal measures are in progress for directing the penalties of the Statute of Praemunire against all the seceders; and a proposition is on foot for petitioning her Majesty to assign the sum thereby realized by the Government to the erection of a 'Martyrs' Memorial' in the sister University."

"So," thought Charles, "the world, as usual, is beforehand with me"; and he sat speculating about the origin of the report till he almost forgot that he was waiting for Carlton.

CHAPTER IV

WHILE Charles was learning in Carlton's rooms the interest which the world took in his position and acts, he was actually furnishing a topic of conversation to that portion of it who were Carlton's guests in the neighbouring Common-Room. Tea and coffee had made their appearance, the men had risen from table, and were crowding round the fire.

"Who is that Mr. Reding spoken of in the *Gazette* of last week?" said a prim little man, sipping his tea with his spoon, and rising on his toes as he spoke.

"You need not go far for an answer," said his neighbour, and, turning to their host, added, "Carlton, who is Mr. Reding?"

"A very dear honest fellow," answered Carlton: "I wish we were all of us as good. He read with me one Long Vacation, is a good scholar, and ought to have gained his class. I have not heard of him for some time."

"He has other friends in the room," said another: "I think," turning to a young Fellow of Leicester, "*you*, Sheffield, were at one time intimate with Reding?"

"Yes," answered Sheffield; "and Vincent, of course, knows him too; he's a capital fellow; I know him exceedingly well; what the *Gazette* says about him is shameful. I never met a man who cared less about success in the schools; it was quite his *fault*."

"That's about the truth," said another; "I met Mr. Malcolm yesterday at dinner, and it seems he knows the family. He said that his religious notions carried Reding away, and spoiled his reading."

The conversation was not general; it went on in detached groups, as the guests stood together. Nor was the subject a popular one; rather it was either a painful or a disgusting subject to the whole party, two or three curious and hard minds excepted, to whom opposition to Catholicism was meat and drink. Besides, in such chance collections of men, no one knew exactly his neighbour's opinion about it; and, as in this instance, there were often friends of the accused or calumniated present. And, moreover, there was a generous feeling, and a consciousness how much seceders from the Anglican Church were giving up, which kept down any disrespectful mention of them.

"Are you to do much in the schools this term?" said one to another.

"I don't know: we have two men going up, good scholars."

"Who has come into Stretton's place?"

"Jackson, of King's."

"Jackson? Indeed; he's strong in science, I think."

"Very."

"Our men know their books well, but I should not say that science is their line."

"Leicester sends four."

"It will be a large class-list, from what I hear."

"Ah! indeed! the Michaelmas paper is always a good one."

Meanwhile the conversation was in another quarter dwelling upon poor Charles.

"No, depend upon it, there's more in what the *Gazette* says than you think. Disappointment is generally at the bottom of these changes."

"Poor devils! they can't help it," said another, in a low voice, to his neighbour.

"A good riddance, anyhow," said the party addressed; "we shall have a little peace at last."

"Well," said the first of the two, drawing himself up and speaking in the air, "how any educated man should—" his voice was overpowered by the grave enunciation of a small man behind them, who had hitherto kept silence, and now spoke with positiveness.

He addressed himself, between the two heads which had just been talking in private, to the group beyond them. "It's all the effect of rationalism," he said; "the whole movement is rationalistic. At the end of three years all those persons who have now apostatized will be infidels."

No one responded; at length another of the party came up to Mr. Malcolm's acquaintance, and said, slowly, "I suppose you never heard it hinted that there is something wrong *here* in Mr. Reding," touching his forehead significantly; "I have been told it's in the family."

He was answered by a deep, powerful voice, belonging to a person who sat in the corner; it sounded like "the great bell of Bow," as if it ought to have closed the conversation. It said abruptly, "I respect him uncommonly; I have an extreme respect for him. He's an honest man; I wish others were as honest. If they were, then, as the Puseyites are becoming Catholics, so we should see old Brownside and his clique becoming Unitarians. But they mean to stick in."

Most persons present felt the truth of his remark, and a silence followed it for a while. It was broken by a clear cackling voice: "Did you ever hear," said he, nodding his head, or rather his whole person, as he spoke, "did you ever, Sheffield, happen to hear that this gentleman, your friend Mr. Reding, when he was quite a freshman, had a conversation with some *attaché* of the Popish Chapel in this place, at the very door of it, after the men were gone down?"

"Impossible, Fusby," said Carlton, and laughed.

"It's quite true," returned Fusby; "I had it from the Under-Marshal, who was passing at the moment. My eye has been on Mr. Reding for some years."

"So it seems," said Sheffield, "for that must have been at least, let me see, four or five years ago."

"Oh," continued Fusby, "there are two or three more yet to come; you will see."

"Why, Fusby," said Vincent, overhearing and coming up, "you are like the three old crones in the Bride of Lammermoor, who wished to have the straiking of the Master of Ravenswood."

Fusby nodded his person, but made no answer.

"Not all three at once, I hope," said Sheffield.

"Oh, it's quite a concentration, a quintessence of Protestant feeling," answered Vincent; "I consider *myself* a good Protestant; but the pleasure you have in hunting these men is quite sensual, Fusby."

The Common-Room man here entered, and whispered to Carlton that a stranger was waiting for him in his rooms.

"When do your men come up?" said Sheffield to Vincent.

"Next Saturday," answered Vincent.

"They always come up late," said Sheffield.

"Yes, the House met last week."

"St. Michael's has met too," said Sheffield: "so have we."

"We have a reason for meeting late: many of our men come from the North and from Ireland."

"That's no reason, with railroads."

"I see they have begun our rail," said Vincent; "I thought the University had opposed it."

"The Pope in his own states has given in," said Sheffield, "so we may well do the same."

"Don't talk of the Pope," said Vincent, "I'm sick of the Pope."

"The Pope?" said Fusby, overhearing; "have you heard that his Holiness is coming to England?"

"Oh, oh," cried Vincent, "come, I can't stand this. I must go; good night t'you, Carlton. Where's my gown?"

"I believe the Common-Room man has hung it up in the passage—but you should stop and protect me from Fusby."

Neither did Vincent turn to the rescue, nor did Fusby profit by the hint; so poor Carlton, with the knowledge that he was wanted in his rooms, had to stay a good half-hour *tête-à-tête* with the latter, while he prosed to him *in extenso* about Pope Sixtus XIV, the Jesuits, suspected men in the University, Mede on the Apostasy, the Catholic Relief Bill, Dr. Pusey's Tract on Baptism, Justification, and the appointment of the Taylor Professors.

At length, however, Carlton was released. He ran across the

quadrangle and up his staircase; flung open his door, and made his way to his inner room. A person was just rising to meet him; impossible! but it was though. "What? Reding!" he cried; "who would have thought! what a pleasure! we were just—... What brings you here?" he added, in an altered tone. Then gravely, "Reding, where are you?"

"Not yet a Catholic," said Reding.

There was a silence; the answer conveyed a good deal: it was a relief, but it was an intimation. "Sit down, my dear Reding; will you have anything? Have you dined? What a pleasure to see you, old fellow! Are we really to lose you?" They were soon in conversation on the great subject.

CHAPTER V

"If you have made up your mind, Reding," said Carlton, "it's no good talking. May you be happy wherever you are! You must always be yourself; as a Romanist, you will still be Charles Reding."

"I know I have a kind, sympathizing friend in you, Carlton. You have always listened to me, never snubbed me except when I deserved it. You know more about me than any one else. Campbell is a dear, good fellow, and will soon be dearer to me still. It isn't generally known yet, but he is to marry my sister. He has borne with me now for two years; never been hard upon me; always been at my service when I wanted to talk with him. But no one makes me open my heart as you do, Carlton; you sometimes have differed from me, but you have always understood me."

"Thank you for your kind words," answered Carlton; "but to me it is a perfect mystery why you should leave us. I enter into your reasons: I cannot, for the life of me, see how you come to your conclusion."

"To me, on the other hand, Carlton, it is like two and two make four; and you make two and two five, and are astonished that I won't agree with you."

"We must leave these things to a higher power," said Carlton. "I hope we sha'n't be less friends, Reding, when you are in another communion. We know each other; these outward things cannot change us."

Reding sighed; he saw clearly that his change of religion, when completed, would not fail to have an effect on Carlton's thoughts about him, as on those of others. It could not possibly be otherwise; he was sure himself to feel different about Carlton.

After a while, Carlton said gently, "Is it quite impossible, Reding, that now at the eleventh hour we may retain you? What *are* your grounds?"

"Don't let us argue, dear Carlton," answered Reding; "I have done with argument. Or, if I must say something for manners' sake, I will but tell you that I have fulfilled your request. You bade me read the Anglican divines; I have given a great deal of time to them, and I am embracing that creed which alone is the scope to which they converge in their separate teachings; the creed which upholds the divinity of tradition with Laud, consent of Fathers with Beveridge, a visible Church with Bramhall, dogma with Bull, the authority of the Pope with Thorndike, penance with Taylor, prayers for the dead with Ussher, celibacy, asceticism, ecclesiastical discipline with Bingham. I am going to a Church, which in these, and a multitude of other points, is nearer the Apostolic Church than any existing one; which is the continuation of the Apostolic Church, if it has been continued at all. And *seeing* it to be *like* the Apostolic Church, I *believe* it to be the *same*. Reason has gone first, faith is to follow."

He stopped, and Carlton did not reply; a silence ensued, and Charles at length broke it. "I repeat, it's no use arguing; I have made up my mind, and been very slow about it. I have broken it to my mother, and bade her farewell. All is determined; I cannot go back."

"Is that a nice feeling?" said Carlton, half reproachfully.

"Understand me," answered Reding; "I have come to my resolution with great deliberation. It has remained on my mind as a mere intellectual conclusion for a year or two; surely now at length without blame I may change it into a practical resolve. But none of us can answer that those habitual and ruling convictions, on which it is our duty to act, will remain before our consciousness every moment, when we come into the hurry of the world, and are assailed by inducements and motives of various kinds. Therefore I say that the time of argument is past; I act on a conclusion already drawn."

"But how do you know," asked Carlton, "but what you have been unconsciously biassed in arriving at it? One notion has possessed you, and you have not been able to shake it off. The ability to retain your convictions in the bustle of life is to my mind the very test, the necessary test of their reality."

"I do, I do retain them," answered Reding; "they are always upon me."

"Only at times, as you have yourself confessed," objected Carlton: "surely you ought to have a very strong conviction indeed, to set against the mischief you are doing by a step of this kind. Consider how many persons you are unsettling; what a triumph you are giving to the enemies of all religion; what encouragement to the notion that there is no such thing as truth; how you are weakening our Church. Well, all I say is, that you should have very strong convictions to set against all this."

"Well," said Charles, "I grant, I maintain, that the only motive which is sufficient to justify such an act, is the conviction that one's salvation depends on it. Now, I speak sincerely, my dear Carlton, in saying that I don't think I shall be saved if I remain in the English Church."

"Do you mean that there is no salvation in our Church?" said Carlton, rather coldly.

"I am talking of myself; it's not my place to judge others. I only say, God calls *me*, and I must follow at the risk of my soul."

"God '*calls*' you!" said Carlton; "what does that mean? I don't like it; it's dissenting language."

"You know it is Scripture language," answered Reding.

"Yes, but people don't in Scripture *say* 'I'm called'; the calling was an act from without, the act of others, not an inward feeling."

"But, my dear Carlton, how *is* a person to get at truth, now, when there can be no simple outward call?"

"That seems to me a pretty good intimation," answered Carlton, "that we are to remain where Providence has placed us."

"Now this is just one of the points on which I can't get at the bottom of the Church of England's doctrine," Reding replied. "But it's so on so many other subjects! it's always so. Are members of the Church of England to seek the truth, or have they it given them from the first? Do they seek it for themselves, or is it ready provided for them?"

Carlton thought a moment, and seemed doubtful what to answer; then he said that we must, of course, seek it. It was a part of our moral probation to seek the truth.

"Then don't talk to me about our position," said Charles; "I hardly expected *you* to make this answer; but it is what the majority of Church-of-England people say. They tell us to seek, they give us rules for seeking, they make us exert our private judgment; but directly we come to any conclusion but theirs, they turn round and talk to us of our 'providential position.' But there's another thing. Tell me, supposing we ought all to seek the truth, do you think that members of the English Church do seek it in that way which Scripture enjoins upon all seekers? Think how very seriously Scripture speaks of the arduousness of finding, the labour of seeking, the duty of thirsting after the truth? I don't believe the bulk of the English clergy, the bulk of Oxford residents, Heads of houses, Fellows of Colleges (with all their good points, which I am not the man to deny), have ever sought the truth. They have taken what they found, and have used no private judgment at all. Or if they have judged, it has been in the vaguest, most cursory way possible; or they have looked into Scripture only to find proofs for what they were bound to subscribe, as undergraduates getting up the Articles. Then they sit over their wine, and talk about this or that friend who has 'seceded,' and condemn him, and" (glancing at the newspaper on the table) "assign motives for his conduct. Yet, after all, which is the more likely to be right—he who has given years, perhaps, to the search of truth, who has habitually prayed for guidance, and has taken all the means in his power to secure it, or they, 'the gentlemen of England who sit at home at ease'? No, no, they may talk of seeking the truth, of private judgment, as a duty, but they have never sought, they have never judged; they are where they are, not because it is true, but because they find themselves there, because it is their 'providential position,' and a pleasant one into the bargain."

Reding had got somewhat excited; the paragraph in the newspaper had annoyed him. But, without taking that into account, there was enough in the circumstances in which he found himself to throw him out of his ordinary state of mind. He was in a crisis of peculiar trial, which a person must have felt to understand. Few men go to battle in cold blood, or prepare without agitation for a surgical operation. Carlton, on the other hand, was a quiet, gentle person, who was not heard to use an excited word once a year.

The conversation came to a stand. At length Carlton said, "I hope, dear Reding, you are not joining the Church of Rome merely because there are unreasonable, unfeeling persons in the Church of England."

Charles felt that he was not showing to advantage, and that he was giving rise to the very surmises about the motives of his conversion which he was deprecating.

"It is a sad thing," he said, with something of self-reproach, "to spend our last minutes in wrangling. Forgive me, Carlton, if I have said anything too strongly or earnestly." Carlton thought he had; he thought him in an excited state; but it was no use telling him so; so he merely pressed his offered hand affectionately, and said nothing.

Presently he said, dryly and abruptly, "Reding, do you know any Roman Catholics?"

"No," answered Reding; "Willis indeed, but I hav'n't seen even him these two years. It has been entirely the working of my own mind."

Carlton did not answer at once; then he said, as dryly and abruptly as before, "I suspect, then, you will have much to bear with when you know them."

"What do you mean?" asked Reding.

"You will find them under-educated men, I suspect."

"What do *you* know of them?" said Reding.

"I suspect it," answered Carlton.

"But what's that to the purpose?" asked Charles.

"It's a thing you should think of. An English clergyman is a gentleman; you may have more to bear than you reckon for, when you find yourself with men of rude minds and vulgar manners."

"My dear Carlton, a'n't you talking of what you know nothing at all about?"

"Well, but you should think of it, you should contemplate it," said Carlton; "I judge from their letters and speeches which one reads in the papers."

Charles thought awhile; then he said, "Certainly, I don't like many things which are done and said by Roman Catholics just now; but I don't see how all this can be more than a trial and a cross; I don't see how it affects the great question."

"No, except that you may find yourself a fish out of water," answered Carlton; "you may find yourself in a position where you can act with no one, where you will be quite thrown away."

"Well," said Charles, "as to the fact, I know nothing about it; it may be as you say, but I don't think much of your proof. In all communities the worst is on the outside. What offends me in Catholic public proceedings need be no measure, nay, I believe cannot be a measure, of the inward Catholic mind. I would not judge the Anglican Church by Exeter Hall, nay, not by Episcopal Charges. We see the interior of our own Church, the exterior of the Church of Rome. This is not a fair comparison."

"But look at their books of devotion," insisted Carlton; "they can't write English."

Reding smiled at Carlton, and slowly shook his head to and fro, while he said, "They write English, I suppose, as classically as St. John writes Greek."

Here again the conversation halted, and nothing was heard for a while but the simmering of the kettle.

There was no good in disputing, as might be seen from the first; each had his own view, and that was the beginning and the end of the matter. Charles stood up. "Well, dearest Carlton," he said, "we must part; it must be going on for eleven." He pulled out of his pocket a small "Christian Year." "You have often seen me with this," he continued, "accept it in memory of me. You will not see me, but here is a pledge that I will not forget you, that I will ever remember you." He stopped, much affected. "Oh, it is very hard to leave you all, to go to strangers," he went on; "I do not wish it, but I cannot help it; I am called, I am compelled." He stopped again; the tears flowed down his cheeks. "All is well," he said, recovering himself, "all is well; but it's hard at the time, and scarcely any one to feel for me; black looks, bitter words.... I am pleasing myself, following my own will...well..." and he began looking at his fingers and slowly rubbing his palms one on another. "It must be," he whispered to himself, "through tribulation to the kingdom, sowing in tears, reaping in joy...." Another pause, and a new train of thought came over him; "Oh," he said, "I fear so very much, so very much, that all you who do not come forward will go back. You cannot stand where you are; for a time you will think you do, then you will oppose us, and still think you keep your ground while you use the same words as before; but your belief, your opinions will decline. You will hold less.

And then, in time, it will strike you that, in differing with Protestants, you are contending only about words. They call us Rationalists; take care you don't fall into Liberalism. And now, my dearest Carlton, my one friend in Oxford who was patient and loving towards me, good-bye. May we meet not long hence in peace and joy. I cannot go to you; you must come to me."

They embraced each other affectionately; and the next minute Charles was running down the staircase.

CHAPTER VI

CHARLES went to bed with a bad headache, and woke with a worse. Nothing remained but to order his bill and be off for London. Yet he could not go without taking a last farewell of the place itself. He was up soon after seven; and while the gownsmen were rising and in their respective chapels, he had been round Magdalen Walk and Christ Church Meadow. There were few or none to see him wherever he went. The trees of the Water Walk were variegated, as beseemed the time of year, with a thousand hues, arching over his head, and screening his side. He reached Addison's Walk; there he had been for the first time with his father, when he was coming into residence, just six years before to a day. He pursued it, and onwards still, till he came round in sight of the beautiful tower, which at length rose close over his head. The morning was frosty, and there was a mist; the leaves flitted about; all was in unison with the state of his feelings. He re-entered the monastic buildings, meeting with nothing but scouts with boxes of cinders, and old women carrying off the remains of the kitchen. He crossed to the Meadow, and walked steadily down to the junction of the Cherwell with the Isis; he then turned back. What thoughts came upon him! for the last time! There was no one to see him; he threw his arms round the willows so dear to him, and kissed them; he tore off some of their black leaves and put them in his bosom. "I am like Undine," he said, "killing with a kiss. No one cares for me; scarce a person knows me." He neared the Long Walk again. Suddenly, looking obliquely into it, he saw a cap and gown; he looked anxiously; it was Jennings: there was no mistake; and his direction was towards him. Charles always had felt kindly towards him, in spite of his sternness, but he would not meet him for the world; what was he to do? He stood behind a large elm, and let him pass; then he set off again at a quick pace. When he had got some way, he ventured to turn his head round; and he saw Jennings at the moment, by that sort of fatality or sympathy which is so common, turning round towards him. He hurried on, and soon found himself again at his inn.

Strange as it may seem, though he had on the whole had as good success as Carlton in the "keen encounter of their wits" the night before, it had left an unsatisfactory effect on his mind. The time for action was come; argument was past, as he had himself said; and to recur to argument was only to confuse the clearness of his apprehension of the truth. He began to question whether he really had evidence enough for the step he was taking, and the temptation assailed him that he was giving up this world without gaining the next. Carlton evidently thought him excited; what if it were true? Perhaps his convictions were, after all, a dream; what did they rest upon? He tried to recall his best arguments, and could not. Was there, after all, any such thing as truth? Was not one thing as good as another? At all events, could he not have served God well in his generation, where he had been placed? He recollected some lines in the Ethics of Aristotle, quoted by the philosopher from an old poet, in which the poor outcast Philoctetes laments over his own stupid officiousness, as he calls it, which had been the cause of his misfortunes. Was he not a busybody too? Why could he not let well alone? Better men than he had lived and died in the English Church. And then what if, as Campbell had said, all his so-called convictions were to vanish just as he entered the Roman pale, as they had done on his father's death? He began to envy Sheffield; all had turned out well with him—a good class, a fellowship, merely or principally because he had taken things as they came, and not gone roaming after visions. He felt himself violently assaulted; but he was not deserted, not overpowered. His good sense, rather his good Angel, came to his aid; evidently he was in no way able to argue or judge at that moment; the deliberate conclusions of years ought not to be set aside by the troubled thoughts of an hour. With an effort he put the whole subject from him, and addressed himself to his journey.

How he got to Steventon he hardly recollected; but gradually he came to himself, and found himself in a first-class of the Great Western, proceeding rapidly towards London. He then looked about him to ascertain who his fellow-travellers were. The farther compartment was full of passengers, who seemed to form one party, talking together with great volubility and glee. Of the three seats in his own part of the carriage, one only, that opposite to him, was filled. On taking a survey of the stranger, he saw a grave person passing or past the middle age; his face had that worn, or rather that unplacid appearance, which even slight physical suffering, if habitual, gives to the features, and his eyes were pale from study or other cause. Charles thought he had seen his face before, but he could not recollect where or when. But what most interested him was his dress and appearance, which was such as is rarely found in a travelling-companion. It was of an unusual character, and, taken together with the small office-book he held in his hand, plainly showed Charles that he was opposite a Roman ecclesiastic. His heart beat, and he felt tempted to start from his seat; then a sick feeling and a sinking came over him. He gradually grew calmer, and journeyed on some time in silence, longing yet afraid to speak. At length, on the train stopping at the station, he addressed a few words to him in French. His companion looked surprised, smiled, and in a hesitating, saddish voice said that he was an Englishman.

Charles made an awkward apology, and there was silence again. Their eyes sometimes met, and then moved slowly off each other, as if a mutual reconnoitring was in progress. At length it seemed to strike the stranger that he had abruptly stopped the conversation; and, after apparently beating about for an introductory topic, he said, "Perhaps I can read you, sir, better than you can me. You are an Oxford man by your appearance."

Charles assented.

"A bachelor?" He was of near Master's standing. His companion, who did not seem in a humour for talking, proceeded to various questions about the University, as if out of civility. What colleges sent Proctors that year? Were the Taylor Professors appointed? Were they members of the Church of England? Did the new Bishop of Bury keep his Headship? Etc. Some matter-of-fact conversation followed, which came to nothing. Charles had so much to ask; his thoughts were busy, and his mind full. Here was a Catholic priest ready for his necessities; yet the opportunity was likely to pass away, and nothing to come of it. After one or two fruitless efforts, he gave it up, and leant back in his seat. His fellow-traveller began, as quietly as he could, to say office. Time went forward, the steam was let off and put on; the train stopped and proceeded, and the office was apparently finished; the book vanished in a side-pocket.

After a time Charles suddenly said, "How came you to suppose I was of Oxford?"

"Not *entirely* by your look and manner, for I saw you jump from the omnibus at Steventon; but with that assistance it was impossible to mistake."

"I have heard others say the same," said Charles; "yet I can't myself make out how an Oxford man should be known from another."

"Not only Oxford men, but Cambridge men, are known by their appearance; soldiers, lawyers, beneficed clergymen; indeed every class has its external indications to those who can read them."

"I know persons," said Charles, "who believe that handwriting is an indication of calling and character."

"I do not doubt it," replied the priest; "the gait is another; but it is not all of us who can read so recondite a language. Yet a language it is, as really as hieroglyphics on an obelisk."

"It is a fearful thought," said Charles with a sigh, "that we, as it were, exhale ourselves every breath we draw."

The stranger assented; "A man's moral self," he said, "is concentrated in each moment of his life; it lives in the tips of his fingers, and the spring of his insteps. A very little thing tries what a man is made of."

"I think I must be speaking to a Catholic priest?" said Charles: when his question was answered in the affirmative, he went on hesitatingly to ask if what they had been speaking of did not illustrate the importance of faith? "One did not see at first sight," he said, "how it was rational to maintain that so much depended on holding this or that doctrine, or a little more or a little less, but it might be a test of the heart."

His companion looked pleased; however, he observed, that "there was no 'more or less' in faith; that either we believed the whole revealed message, or really we believed no part of it; that we ought to believe what the Church proposed to us on the *word* of the Church."

"Yet surely the so-called Evangelical believes more than the Unitarian, and the High-Churchman than the Evangelical," objected Charles.

"The question," said his fellow-traveller, "is, whether they submit their reason implicitly to that which they have received as God's word."

Charles assented.

"Would you say, then," he continued, "that the Unitarian really believes as God's word that which he professes to receive, when he passes over and gets rid of so much that is in that word?"

"Certainly not," said Charles.

"And why?"

"Because it is plain," said Charles, "that his ultimate standard of truth is not the Scripture, but, unconsciously to himself, some view of things in his mind which is to him the measure of Scripture."

"Then he believes himself, if we may so speak," said the priest, "and not the external word of God."

"Certainly."

"Well, in like manner," he continued, "do you think a person can have real faith in that which he admits to be the word of God, who passes by, without attempting to understand, such passages as 'the Church the pillar and ground of the truth'; or, 'whosesoever sins ye forgive, they are forgiven'; or, 'if any man is sick, let him call for the priests of the Church, and let them anoint him with oil'?"

"No," said Charles; "but, in fact, *we* do not profess to have faith in the mere text of Scripture. You know, sir," he added hesitatingly, "that the Anglican doctrine is to interpret Scripture by the Church; therefore we have faith, like Catholics, not in Scripture simply, but in the whole word committed to the Church, of which Scripture is a part."

His companion smiled: "How many," he asked, "so profess? But, waiving this question, I understand what a Catholic means by saying that he goes by the voice of the Church; it means, practically, by the voice of the first priest he meets. Every priest is the voice of the Church. This is quite intelligible. In matters of doctrine, he has faith in the word of any priest. But what, where, is that 'word' of the Church which the persons you speak of believe in? And when do they exercise their belief? Is it not an undeniable fact, that, so far from all Anglican clergymen agreeing together in faith, what the first says, the second will unsay? So that an Anglican cannot, if he would, have faith in them, and necessarily, though he would not, chooses between them. How, then, has faith a place in the religion of an Anglican?"

"Well," said Charles, "I am sure I know a good many persons—and if you knew the Church of England as I do, you would not need me to tell you—who, from knowledge of the Gospels, have an absolute conviction and an intimate sense of the reality of the sacred facts contained in them, which, whether you call it faith or not, is powerful enough to colour their whole being with its influence, and rules their heart and conduct as well as their imagination. I can't believe that these persons are out of God's favour; yet, according to your account of the matter, they have not faith."

"Do you think these persons believe and practise all that is brought home to them as being in Scripture?" asked his companion.

"Certainly they do," answered Charles, "as far as man can judge."

"Then perhaps they may be practising the virtue of faith; if there are passages in it to which they are insensible, as about the sacraments, penance, and extreme unction, or about the See of Peter, I should in charity think that these passages had never been brought home or applied to their minds and consciences—just as a Pope's Bull may be for a time unknown in a distant part of the Church. They may be[†] in involuntary ignorance. Yet I fear that, taking the whole nation, there are few who on this score can lay claim to faith."

Charles said this did not fully meet the difficulty; faith, in the case of these persons, at least was not faith in the word of the Church. His companion would not allow this; he said they received the Scripture on the testimony of the Church, that at least they were believing the word of God, and the like.

Presently Charles said, "It is to me a great mystery how the English people, as a whole, is ever to have faith again; is there evidence enough for faith?"

† "Errantes invincibiliter circa aliquos articulos, et credentes alios, non sunt formaliter haeretici, sed habent fidem supernaturalem, quâ credunt veros articulos, atque adeo ex eâ possunt procedere actus perfectae contritionis, quibus justificentur et salventur."—*De Lugo de Fid.*, p. 169.

His new friend looked surprised and not over-pleased; "Surely," he said, "in matter of fact, a man may have more *evidence* for believing the Church to be the messenger of God, than he has for believing the four Gospels to be from God. If, then, he already believes the latter, why should he not believe the former?"

"But the belief in the Gospels is a traditional belief," said Charles; "that makes all the difference. I cannot see how a nation like England, which has lost the faith, ever can recover it. Hence, in the matter of conversion, Providence has generally visited simple and barbarous nations."

"The converts of the Roman Empire were, I suppose, a considerable exception," said the priest.

"Still, it seems to me a great difficulty," answered Charles; "I do not see, when the dogmatic structure is once broken down, how it is ever to be built up again. I fancy there is a passage somewhere in Carlyle's 'French Revolution' on the subject, in which the author laments over the madness of men's destroying what they could not replace, what it would take centuries and a strange combination of fortunate circumstances to reproduce, an external received creed. I am not denying, God forbid! the objectivity of revelation, or saying that faith is a sort of happy and expedient delusion; but, really, the evidence for revealed doctrine is so built up on probabilities that I do not see what is to introduce it into a civilized community, where reason has been cultivated to the utmost, and argument is the test of truth. Many a man will say, 'Oh, that I had been educated a Catholic!' but he has not so been; and he finds himself unable, though wishing, to believe, for he has not evidence enough to subdue his reason. What is to make him believe?"

His fellow-traveller had for some time shown signs of uneasiness; when Charles stopped, he said, shortly, but quietly, "What is to make him believe! the *will*, his *will*."

Charles hesitated; he proceeded; "If there is evidence enough to believe Scripture, and we see that there is, I repeat, there is more than enough to believe the Church. The evidence is not in fault; all it requires is to be brought home or applied to the mind; if belief does not then follow, the fault lies with the will."

"Well," said Charles, "I think there is a general feeling among educated Anglicans, that the claims of the Roman Church do not rest on a sufficiently intellectual basis; that the evidences, or notes, were well enough for a rude age, not for this. This is what makes me despair of the growth of Catholicism."

His companion looked round curiously at him, and then said, quietly, "Depend upon it, there is quite evidence enough for a *moral conviction* that the Catholic or Roman Church, and none other, is the voice of God."

"Do you mean," said Charles, with a beating heart, "that before conversion one can attain to a present abiding actual conviction of this truth?"

"I do not know," answered the other; "but, at least, he may have habitual *moral certainty*; I mean, a conviction, and one only, steady, without rival conviction, or even reasonable doubt, present to him when he is most composed and in his hours of solitude, and flashing on him from time to time, as through clouds, when he is in the world—a conviction to this effect, 'The Roman Catholic Church is the one only voice of God, the one only way of salvation.'"

"Then you mean to say," said Charles, while his heart beat faster, "that such a person is under no duty to wait for clearer light."

"He will not have, he cannot expect, clearer light before conversion. Certainty, in its highest sense, is the reward of those who, by an act of the will, and at the dictate of reason and prudence, embrace the truth, when nature, like a coward, shrinks. You must make a venture; faith is a venture before a man is a Catholic; it is a gift after it. You approach the Church in the way of reason, you enter into it in the light of the Spirit."

Charles said that he feared there was a great temptation operating on many well-informed and excellent men, to find fault with the evidence for Catholicity, and to give over the search, on the excuse that there were arguments on both sides.

"It is not one set of men," answered his companion; "it is the grievous deficiency in Englishmen altogether. Englishmen have many gifts, faith they have not. Other nations, inferior to them in many things, still have faith. Nothing will stand in place of it; not a sense of the beauty of Catholicism, or of its awfulness, or of its antiquity; not an appreciation of the sympathy which it shows towards sinners: not an admiration of the Martyrs and early Fathers, and a delight in their writings. Individuals may display a touching gentleness, or a conscientiousness which demands our reverence; still, till they have faith, they have not the foundation, and their superstructure will fall. They will not be blessed, they will effect nothing in religious matters, till they begin by an act of unreserved faith in the word of God, whatever it be; till they go out of themselves; till they cease to make something within them their standard, till they oblige their will to perfect what reason leaves sufficient, indeed, but incomplete. And when they shall recognize this defect in themselves, and try to remedy it, then they will recognize much more—they will be on the road very shortly to be Catholics."

There was nothing in all this exactly new to Reding; but it was pleasant to hear it from the voice of another, and him a priest. Thus he had sympathy and authority, and felt he was restored to himself. The conversation stopped. After a while he disclosed to his new friend the place for which he was bound, which, after what Charles had already been saying, could be no great surprise to him. The latter knew the Superior of San Michaele, and, taking out a card, wrote upon it a few words of introduction for him. By this time they had reached Paddington; and scarcely had the train stopped, when the priest took his small carpet-bag from under his seat, wrapped his cloak around him, stepped out of the carriage, and was walking out of sight at a brisk pace.

CHAPTER VII

Reding naturally wished to take the important step he was meditating as quietly as he could; and had adopted what he considered satisfactory measures for this purpose. But such arrangements often turn out very differently from their promise; and so it was in his case.

The Passionist House was in the eastern part of London; so far well—and as he knew in the neighbourhood a respectable publisher in the religious line, with whom his father had dealt, he had written to him to bespeak a room in his house for the few days which he trusted would suffice for the process of his reception. What was to happen to him after it, he left for the advice he might get from those in whose hands he found himself. It was now Wednesday; he hoped to have two days to prepare himself for his confession, and then he proposed to present himself before those who were to receive it. His better plan would have been to have gone to the Religious House at once, where doubtless the good fathers would have lodged him, secured him from intrusion, and given him the best advice how to proceed. But we must indulge him, if, doing so great a work, he likes to do it in his own way; nor must we be hard on him, though it be not the best way.

On arriving at his destination, he saw in the deportment of his host grounds for concluding that his coming was not only expected, but understood. Doubtless, then, the paragraph of the *Oxford Gazette* had been copied into the London papers; nor did it relieve his unpleasant surprise to find, as he passed to his room, that the worthy bibliopolist had a reading-room attached to his shop, which was far more perilous to his privacy than a coffee-room would have been. He was not obliged, however, to mix with the various parties who seemed to frequent it; and he determined as far as possible to confine himself to his apartment. The rest of the day he employed in writing letters to friends: his conversation of the morning had tranquillized him; he went to bed peaceful and happy, slept soundly, rose late, and, refreshed in mind and body, turned his thoughts to the serious duties of the day.

Breakfast over, he gave a considerable time to devotional exercises, and then, opening his writing-desk, addressed himself to his work. Hardly had he got into it when his landlord made his appearance; and, with many apologies for his intrusion, and a hope that he was not going to be impertinent, proceeded to inquire if Mr. Reding was a Catholic. "The question had been put to him, and he thought he might venture to solicit an answer from the person who could give the most authentic information." Here was an interruption, vexatious in itself, and perplexing in the form in which it came upon him; it would be absurd to reply that he was on the point of *becoming* a Catholic, so he shortly answered in the negative. Mr. Mumford then informed him that there were two friends of Mr. Reding's below, who wished very much to have a few minutes' conversation with him. Charles could make no intelligible objection to the request; and in the course of a few minutes their knock was heard at the room-door.

On his answering it, two persons presented themselves, apparently both strangers to him. This, however, at the moment was a relief; for vague fears and surmises had begun to flit across his mind as to the faces which were to make their appearance. The younger of the two, who had round full cheeks, with a boyish air, and a shrill voice, advanced confidently, and seemed to expect a recognition. It broke upon Charles that he had seen him before, but he could not tell where. "I ought to know your face," he said.

"Yes, Mr. Reding," answered the person addressed, "you may recollect me at College."

"Ah, I remember perfectly," said Reding; "Jack the kitchen-boy at St. Saviour's."

"Yes," said Jack; "I came when young Tom was promoted into Dennis's place."

Then he added, with a solemn shake of the head, "*I* have got promotion now."

"So it seems, Jack," answered Reding; "but what are you? Speak."

"Ah, sir," said Jack, "we must converse in a tone of befitting seriousness"; and he added, in a deep inarticulate voice, his lips not being suffered to meet together, "Sir, I stand next to an Angel now."

"A what? Angel? Oh, I know," cried Charles, "it's some sect; the Sandemanians."

"Sandemanians!" interrupted Jack; "we hold them in abhorrence; they are levellers; they bring in disorder and every evil work."

"I beg pardon, but I know it is some sect, though I don't recollect what. I've heard about it. Well, tell me, Jack, what are you?"

"I am," answered Jack, as if he were confessing at the tribunal of a Propraetor, "I am a member of the Holy Catholic Church."

"That's right, Jack," said Reding; "but it's not distinctive enough; so are we all; every one will say as much."

"Hear me out, Mr. Reding, sir," answered Jack, waving his hand; "hear me, but strike; I repeat, I am a member of the Holy Catholic Church, assembling in Huggermugger Lane."

"Ah," said Charles, "I see; that's what the 'gods' call you; now, what do men?"

"Men," said Jack, not understanding, however, the allusion—"men call us Christians, professing the opinions of the late Rev. Edward Irving, B.D."

"I understand perfectly now," said Reding; "Irvingites, I recollect."

"No, sir," he said, "not Irvingites; we do not follow man; we follow wherever the Spirit leads us; we have given up Tongue. But I ought to introduce you to my friend, who is more than an Angel," he proceeded modestly, "who has more than the tongue of men and angels, being nothing short of an Apostle, sir. Mr. Reding, here's the Rev. Alexander Highfly. Mr. Highfly, this is Mr. Reding."

Mr. Highfly was a man of gentlemanlike appearance and manner; his language was refined, and his conduct was delicate; so much so that Charles at once changed his tone in speaking to him. He came to Mr. Reding, he said, from a sense of duty; and there was nothing in his conversation to clash with that profession. He explained that he had heard of Mr. Reding's being unsettled in his religious views, and he would not lose the opportunity of attempting so valuable an accession to the cause to which he had dedicated himself.

"I see," said Charles, smiling, "I am in the market."

"It is the bargain of Glaucus with Diomede," answered Mr. Highfly, "for which I am asking your co-operation. I am giving you the fellowship of Apostles."

"It is, I recollect, one of the characteristics of your body," said Charles, "to have an order of Apostles, in addition to Bishops, Priests, and Deacons."

"Rather," said his visitor, "it is the special characteristic; for we acknowledge the orders of the Church of England. We are but completing the Church system by restoring the Apostolic College."

"What I should complain of," said Charles, "were I at all inclined to listen to your claims, would be the very different views which different members of your body put forward."

"You must recollect, sir," answered Mr. Highfly, "that we are under Divine teaching, and that truth is but gradually communicated to the Church. We do not pledge ourselves what we shall believe tomorrow by anything we say today."

"Certainly," answered Reding, "things have been said to me by your teachers which I must suppose were only private opinions, though they seemed to be more."

"But I was saying," said Mr. Highfly, "that at present we are restoring the Gentile Apostolate. The Church of England has Bishops, Priests, and Deacons, but a Scriptural Church has more; it is plain it ought to have Apostles. In Scripture Apostles had the supreme authority, and the three Anglican orders were but subordinate to them."

"I am disposed to agree with you there," said Charles. Mr. Highfly looked surprised and pleased. "We are restoring," he said, "the Church to a more Scriptural state; perhaps, then, we may reckon on your co-operation in doing so? We do not ask you to secede from the Establishment, but to acknowledge the Apostolic authority to which all ought to submit."

"But does it not strike you, Mr. Highfly," answered Reding, "that there *is* a body of Christians, and not an inconsiderable one, which maintains with you, and, what is more, has always preserved, that true and higher Apostolic succession in the Church; a body, I mean, which, in addition to Episcopacy, believes that there is a standing ordinance above Episcopacy, and gives it the name of the Apostolate?"

"On the contrary," answered Mr. Highfly, "I consider that we are restoring what has lain dormant ever since the time of St. Paul; nay, I will say it is an ordinance which never has been carried into effect at all, though it was in the Divine design from the first. You will observe that the Apostles were Jews; but there never has been a Gentile Apostolate. St. Paul indeed was Apostle of the Gentiles, but the design begun in him has hitherto been frustrated. He went up to Jerusalem against the solemn warning of the Spirit; now we are raised up to complete that work of the Spirit, which was stopped by the inadvertence of the first Apostle."

Jack interposed: he should be very glad, he said, to know what religious persuasion it was, besides his own, which Mr. Reding considered to have preserved the succession of Apostles as something distinct from Bishops.

"It is quite plain whom I mean—The Catholics," answered Charles. "The Popedom is the true Apostolate, the Pope is the successor of the Apostles, particularly of St. Peter."

"We are very well inclined to the Roman Catholics," answered Mr. Highfly, with some hesitation; "we have adopted a great part of their ritual; but we are not accustomed to consider that we resemble them in what is our characteristic and cardinal tenet."

"Allow me to say it, Mr. Highfly," said Reding, "it is a reason why every Irvingite—I mean every member of your denomination—should become a Catholic. Your own religious sense has taught you that there ought to be an Apostolate in the Church. You consider that the authority of the Apostles was not temporary, but essential and fundamental. What that authority was, we see in St. Paul's conduct towards St. Timothy. He placed him in the see of Ephesus, he sent him a charge, and, in fact, he was his overseer or Bishop. He had the care of all the Churches. Now, this is precisely the power which the Pope claims, and has ever claimed; and, moreover, he has claimed it, as being the *successor*, and the sole proper successor of the Apostles, though Bishops may be improperly such also.[†] And hence Catholics call him Vicar of Christ, Bishop of Bishops, and the like; and, I believe, consider that he, in a pre-eminent sense, is the one pastor or ruler of the Church, the source of jurisdiction, the judge of controversies, and the centre of unity, as having the powers of the Apostles, and specially of St. Peter."

Mr. Highfly kept silence.

"Don't you think, then, it would be well," continued Charles, "that, before coming to convert me, you should first join the Catholic Church? At least, you would urge your doctrine upon me with more authority if you came as a member of it. And I will tell you frankly, that you would find it easier to convert me to Catholicism than to your present persuasion."

Jack looked at Mr. Highfly, as if hoping for some decisive reply to what was a new view to him; but Mr. Highfly took a different line. "Well, sir," he said, "I do not see that any good will come by our continuing the interview; but your last remark leads me to observe

† "Successores sunt, sed ita ut potius Vicarii dicendi sint Apostolorum, quam successores; contra, Romanus Pontifex, quia verus Petri successor est, nonnisi per quendam abusum ejus vicarius diceretur."—Zaccar. *Antifebr.*, p. 130.

that *proselytism* was not our object in coming here. We did not propose more than to *inform* you that a great work was going on, to direct your attention to it, and to invite your co-operation. We do not controvert; we only wish to deliver our testimony, and there to leave the matter. I believe, then, we need not take up your valuable time longer." With that he got up, and Jack with him, and, with many courteous bows and smiles, which were duly responded to by Reding, the two visitors took their departure.

"Well, I might have been worse off," thought Reding; "really they are gentle, well-mannered creatures, after all. I might have been attacked by some of your furious Exeter-Hall beasts; but now to business.... What's that?" he added. Alas, it was a soft, distinct tap at the door; there was no mistake. "Who's there? Come in!" he cried; upon which the door gently opened, and a young lady, not without attractions of person and dress, presented herself. Charles started up with vexation; but there was no help for it, and he was obliged to hand her a chair, and then to wait, all expectation, or rather all impatience, to be informed of her mission. For a while she did not speak, but sat, with her head on one side, looking at her parasol, the point of which she fixed on the carpet, while she slowly described a circumference with the handle. At length she asked, without raising her eyes, whether it was true—and she spoke slowly and in what is called a spiritual tone—whether it was true, the information had been given her, that Mr. Reding, the gentleman she had the honour of addressing—whether it was true, that he was in search of a religion more congenial to his feelings than that of the Church of England? "Mr. Reding could not give her any satisfaction on the subject of her inquiry";—he answered shortly, and had some difficulty in keeping from rudeness in his tone. The interrogation, she went on to say, perhaps might seem impertinent; but she had a motive. Some dear sisters of hers were engaged in organizing a new religious body, and Mr. Reding's accession, counsel, assistance, would be particularly valuable; the more so, because as yet they had not any gentleman of University education among them.

"May I ask," said Charles, "the name of the intended persuasion?"

"The name," she answered, "is not fixed; indeed, this is one of the points on which we should covet the privilege of the advice of a gentleman so well qualified as Mr. Reding to assist us in our deliberations."

"And your tenets, ma'am?"

"Here, too," she replied, "there is much still to be done; the tenets are not fixed either, that is, they are but sketched; and we shall prize your suggestions much. Nay, you will of course have the opportunity, as you would have the right, to nominate any doctrine to which you may be especially inclined."

Charles did not know how to answer to so liberal an offer.

She continued: "Perhaps it is right, Mr. Reding, that I should tell you something more about myself personally. I was born in the communion of the Church of England; for a while I was a member of the New Connection; and after that," she added, still with drooping head and languid sing-song voice, "after that, I was a Plymouth brother." It got too absurd; and Charles, who had for an instant been amused, now became full of the one thought, how to get her out of the room.

It was obviously left to her to keep up the conversation: so she said presently, "We are all for a pure religion."

"From what you tell me," said Charles, "I gather that every member of your new community is allowed to name one or two doctrines of his own."

"We are all scriptural," she made answer, "and therefore are all one; we may differ, but we agree. Still it is so, as you say, Mr. Reding. I'm for election and assurance; our dearest friend is for perfection; and another sweet sister is for the second advent. But we desire to include among us all souls who are thirsting after the river of life, whatever their personal views. I believe you are partial to sacraments and ceremonies?"

Charles tried to cut short the interview by denying that he had any religion to seek after, or any decision to make; but it was easier to end the conversation than the visit. He threw himself back in his chair in despair, and half closed his eyes. "Oh, those good Irvingites," he thought, "blameless men, who came only to protest, and vanished at the first word of opposition; but now thrice has the church-clock struck the quarters since her entrance, and I don't see why she's not to stop here as long as it goes on striking, since she has stopped so long. She has not in her the elements of progress and decay. She'll never die; what is to become of me?"

Nor was she doomed to find a natural death; for, when the case seemed hopeless, a noise was heard on the staircase, and, with scarcely the apology for a knock, a wild gawky man made his appearance, and at once cried out, "I hope, sir, it's not a bargain yet; I hope it's not too late; discharge this young woman, Mr. Reding, and let me teach you the old truth, which never has been repealed."

There was no need of discharging her; for as kindly as she had unfolded her leaves and flourished in the sun of Reding's forbearance, so did she at once shrink and vanish—one could hardly tell how—before the rough accents of the intruder; and Charles suddenly found himself in the hands of a new tormentor. "This is intolerable," he said to himself; and, jumping up, he cried, "Sir, excuse me, I am particularly engaged this morning, and I must beg to decline the favour of your visit."

"What did you say, sir?" said the stranger; and, taking a notebook and a pencil from his pocket, he began to look up in Charles's face and write down his words, saying half aloud, as he wrote, "Declines the favour of my visit." Then he looked up again, keeping his pencil upon his paper, and said, "Now, sir."

Reding moved towards him, and, spreading his arms as one drives sheep and poultry in one direction, he repeated, looking towards the door, "Really, sir, I feel the honour of your call; but another day, sir, another day. It is too much, too much."

"Too much?" said the intruder; "and I waiting below so long! That dainty lady has been good part of an hour here, and now you can't give me five minutes, sir."

"Why, sir," answered Charles, "I am sure you are come on an errand as fruitless as hers; and I am sick of these religious discussions, and want to be to myself, and to save you trouble."

"Sick of religions discussions," said the stranger to himself, as he wrote down the words in his note-book. Charles did not deign to notice his act or to explain his own expression; he stood prepared to renew his action of motioning him to the door. His tormentor then said, "You may like to know my name; it is Zerubbabel."

Vexed as Reding was, he felt that he had no right to visit the tediousness of his former visitor upon his present; so he forced himself to reply, "Zerubbabel; indeed; and is Zerubbabel your Christian name, sir, or your surname?"

"It is both at once, Mr. Reding," answered Zerubbabel, "or rather, I have no Christian name, and Zerubbabel is my one Jewish designation."

"You are come, then, to inquire whether I am likely to become a Jew."

"Stranger things have happened," answered his visitor; "for instance, I myself was once a deacon in the Church of England."

"Then you are not a Jew?" said Charles.

"I am a Jew by choice," he said; "after much prayer and study of Scripture, I have come to the conclusion that, as Judaism was the first religion, so it's to be the last. Christianity I consider an episode in the history of revelation."

"You are not likely to have many followers in such a belief," said Charles; "we are all for progress now, not for retrograding."

"I differ from you, Mr. Reding," said Zerubbabel; "see what the Establishment is doing; it has sent a Bishop to Jerusalem."

"That is rather with the view of making the Jews Christians than the Christians Jews," said Reding.

Zerubbabel wrote down: "Thinks Bishop of Jerusalem is to convert the Jews"; then, "I differ from you, sir; on the contrary, I fancy the excellent Bishop has in view to revive the distinction between Jew and Gentile, which is one step towards the supremacy of the former; for if the Jews have a place at all in Christianity, as Jews, it must be the first place."

Charles thought he had better let him have his talk out; so Zerubbabel proceeded: "The good Bishop in question knows well that the Jew is the elder brother of the Gentile, and it is his special mission to restore a Jewish episcopate to the See of Jerusalem. The Jewish succession has been suspended since the time of the Apostles. And now you see the reason of my calling on you, Mr. Reding. It is reported that you lean towards the Catholic Church; but I wish to suggest to you that you have mistaken the centre of unity. The See of James at Jerusalem is the true centre, not the See of Peter at Rome. Peter's power is a usurpation on James's. I consider the present Bishop of Jerusalem the true Pope. The Gentiles have been in power too long; it is now the Jews' turn."

"You seem to allow," said Charles, "that there ought to be a centre of unity and a Pope."

"Certainly," said Zerubbabel, "and a ritual too, but it should be the Jewish. I am collecting subscriptions for the rebuilding of the Temple on Mount Moriah; I hope too to negotiate a loan, and we shall have Temple stock, yielding, I calculate, at least four percent."

"It has hitherto been thought a sin," said Reding, "to attempt rebuilding the Temple. According to you, Julian the Apostate went the better way to work."

"His motive was wrong, sir," answered the other; "but his act was good. The way to convert the Jews is, first to accept their rites. This is one of the greatest discoveries of this age. *We* must make the first step towards *them*. For myself, I have adopted all which the present state of their religion renders possible. And I don't despair to see the day when bloody sacrifices will be offered on the Temple

Mount as of old."

Here he came to a pause; and Charles making no reply, he said, in a brisk, off-hand manner, "May I not hope you will give your name to this religious object, and adopt the old ritual? The Catholic is quite of yesterday compared with it." Charles answering in the negative, Zerubbabel wrote down in his book: "Refuses to take part in our scheme"; and disappeared from the room as suddenly as he entered it.

CHAPTER VIII

CHARLES's trials were not at an end; and we suspect the reader will give a shudder at the news, as having a very material share in the infliction. Yet the reader's case has this great alleviation, that he takes up this narrative in an idle hour, and Charles encountered the reality in a very busy and anxious one. So, however, it was: not any great time elapsed after the retreat of Zerubbabel, when his landlord again appeared at the door. He assured Mr. Reding that it was no fault of his that the last two persons had called on him; that the lady had slipped by him, and the gentleman had forced his way; but that he now really did wish to solicit an interview for a personage of great literary pretensions, who sometimes dealt with him, and who had come from the West End for the honour of an interview with Mr. Reding. Charles groaned, but only one reply was possible; the day was already wasted, and with a sort of dull resignation he gave permission for the introduction of the stranger.

It was a pale-faced man of about thirty-five, who, when he spoke, arched his eyebrows, and had a peculiar smile. He began by expressing his apprehension that Mr. Reding must have been wearied by impertinent and unnecessary visitors—visitors without intellect, who knew no better than to obtrude their fanaticism on persons who did but despise it. "I know more about the Universities," he continued, "than to suppose that any congeniality can exist between their members and the mass of religious sectarians. You have had very distinguished men among you, sir, at Oxford, of very various schools, yet all able men, and distinguished in the pursuit of Truth, though they have arrived at contradictory opinions."

Not knowing what he was driving at, Reding remained in an attitude of expectation.

"I belong," he continued, "to a Society which is devoted to the extension among all classes of the pursuit of Truth. Any philosophical mind, Mr. Reding, must have felt deep interest in your own party in the University. Our Society, in fact, considers you to be distinguished Confessors in that all-momentous occupation; and I have thought I could not pay yourself individually, whose name has lately honourably appeared in the papers, a better compliment than to get you elected a member of our Truth Society. And here is your diploma," he added, handing a sheet of paper to him. Charles glanced his eye over it; it was a paper, part engraving, part print, part manuscript. An emblem of truth was in the centre, represented, not by a radiating sun or star, as might be expected, but as the moon under total eclipse, surrounded, as by cherub faces, by the heads of Socrates, Cicero, Julian, Abelard, Luther, Benjamin Franklin, and Lord Brougham. Then followed some sentences to the effect that the London Branch Association of the British and Foreign Truth Society, having evidence of the zeal in the pursuit of Truth of Charles Reding, Esq., member of Oxford University, had unanimously elected him into their number, and had assigned him the dignified and responsible office of associate and corresponding member.

"I thank the Truth Society very much," said Charles, when he got to the end of the paper, "for this mark of their good will; yet I regret to have scruples about accepting it till some of the patrons are changed, whose heads are prefixed to the diploma. For instance, I do not like to be under the shadow of the Emperor Julian."

"You would respect his love of Truth, I presume," said Mr. Batts.

"Not much, I fear," said Charles, "seeing it did not hinder him from deliberately embracing error."

"No, not so," answered Mr. Batts; "*he* thought it Truth; and Julian, I conceive, cannot be said to have deserted the Truth, because, in fact, he always was in pursuit of it."

"I fear," said Reding, "there is a very serious difference between your principles and my own on this point."

"Ah, my dear sir, a little attention to our principles will remove it," said Mr. Batts: "let me beg your acceptance of this little pamphlet, in which you will find some fundamental truths stated, almost in the way of aphorisms. I wish to direct your attention to page eight, where they are drawn out."

Charles turned to the page, and read as follows:

"*On the pursuit of Truth.*

(1) It is uncertain whether Truth exists.

(2) It is certain that it cannot be found.

(3) It is a folly to boast of possessing it.

(4) Man's work and duty, as man, consist, not in possessing, but in seeking it.

(5) His happiness and true dignity consist in the pursuit.

(6) The pursuit of Truth is an end to be engaged in for its own sake.

(7) As philosophy is the love, not the possession of wisdom, so religion is the love, not the possession of Truth.

(8) As Catholicism begins with faith, so Protestantism ends with inquiry.

(9) As there is disinterestedness in seeking, so is there selfishness in claiming to possess.

(10) The martyr of Truth is he who dies professing that it is a shadow.

(11) A life-long martyrdom is this, to be ever changing.

(12) The fear of error is the bane of inquiry."

Charles did not get further than these, but others followed of a similar character. He returned the pamphlet to Mr. Batts. "I see enough," he said, "of the opinions of the Truth Society to admire their ingenuity and originality, but, excuse me, not their good sense. It is impossible I should subscribe to what is so plainly opposed to Christianity."

Mr. Batts looked annoyed. "We have no wish to oppose Christianity," he said; "we only wish Christianity not to oppose us. It is very hard that we may not go our own way, when we are quite willing that others should go theirs. It seems imprudent, I conceive, in this age, to represent Christianity as hostile to the progress of the mind, and to turn into enemies of revelation those who do sincerely wish to 'live and let live.'"

"But contradictions cannot be true," said Charles: "if Christianity says that Truth can be found, it must be an error to state that it cannot be found."

"I conceive it to be intolerant," persisted Mr. Batts: "you will grant, I suppose, that Christianity has nothing to do with astronomy or geology: why, then, should it be allowed to interfere with philosophy?"

It was useless proceeding in the discussion; Charles repressed the answer which rose on his tongue of the essential connection of philosophy with religion; a silence ensued of several minutes, and Mr. Batts at length took the hint, for he rose with a disappointed air, and wished him good morning.

It mattered little now whether he was left to himself or not, except that conversation harassed and fretted him; for, as to turning his mind to the subjects which were to have been his occupation that morning, it was by this time far too much wearied and dissipated to undertake them. On Mr. Batts' departure, then, he did not make the attempt, but sat before the fire, dull and depressed, and in danger of relapsing into the troubled thoughts from which his railroad companion had extricated him. When, then, at the end of half an hour, a new knock was heard at the door, he admitted the postulant with a calm indifference, as if fortune had now done her worst, and he had nothing to fear. A middle-aged man made his appearance, sleek and plump, who seemed to be in good circumstances, and to have profited by them. His glossy black dress, in contrast with the crimson colour of his face and throat, for he wore no collars, and his staid and pompous bearing, added to his rapid delivery when he spoke, gave him much the look of a farm-yard turkey-cock in the eyes of any one who was less disgusted with seeing new faces than Reding was at that moment. The new comer looked sharply at him as he entered. "Your most obedient," he said abruptly; "you seem in low spirits, my dear sir; but sit down, Mr. Reding, and give me the opportunity of offering to you a little good advice. You may guess what I am by my appearance: I speak for myself; I will say no more; I can be of use to you. Mr. Reding," he continued, pulling his chair towards him, and putting out his hand as if he was going to paw him, "have not you made a mistake in thinking it necessary to go to the Romish Church for a relief of your religious difficulties?"

"You have not yet heard from me, sir," answered Charles gravely, "that I have any difficulties at all. Excuse me if I am abrupt; I have had many persons calling on me with your errand. It is very kind of you, but I don't want advice; I was a fool to come here."

"Well, my dear Mr. Reding, but listen to me," answered his persecutor, spreading out the fingers of his right hand, and opening his eyes wide: "I am right, I believe, in apprehending that your reason for leaving the Establishment is, that you cannot carry out the surplice in the pulpit and the candlesticks on the table. Now, don't you do more than you need. Pardon me, but you are like a person who should turn the Thames in upon his house, when he merely wanted his door-steps scrubbed. Why become a convert to Popery, when you can obtain your object in a cheaper and better way? Set up for yourself, my dear sir—set up for yourself; form a new denomination, sixpence will do it; and then you may have your surplice and candlesticks to your heart's content, without denying the gospel, or running into the horrible abominations of the Scarlet Woman." And he sat upright in his chair, with his hands flat on his extended knees, watching with a self-satisfied air the effect of his words upon Reding.

"I have had enough of this," said poor Charles; "you, indeed, are but one of a number, sir, and would say you had nothing to do with the rest; but I cannot help regarding you as the fifth, or sixth, or seventh person—I can't count them—who has been with me this morning, giving me, though with the best intentions, advice which has not been asked for. I don't know you, sir; you have no introduction to me; you have not even told me your name. It is not usual to discourse on such personal matters with strangers. Let me, then, thank you first for your kindness in coming, and next for the additional kindness of going." And Charles rose up.

His visitor did not seem inclined to move, or to notice what he had said. He stopped awhile, opened his handkerchief with much deliberation, and blew his nose; then he continued: "Kitchens is my name, sir; Dr. Kitchens; your state of mind, Mr. Reding, is not unknown to me; you are at present under the influence of the old Adam, and indeed in a melancholy way. I was not unprepared for it; and I have put into my pocket a little tract which I shall press upon you with all the Christian solicitude which brother can show towards brother. Here it is; I have the greatest confidence in it; perhaps you have heard the name; it is known as Kitchens's Spiritual Elixir. The Elixir has enlightened millions; and, I will take on me to say, will convert you in twenty-four hours. Its operation is mild and pleasurable, and its effects are marvellous, prodigious, though it does not consist of more than eight duodecimo pages. Here's a list of testimonies to some of the most remarkable cases. I have known one hundred and two cases myself in which it effected a saving change in six hours; seventy-nine in which its operations took place in as few as three; and twenty-seven where conversion followed instantaneously after the perusal. At once, poor sinners, who five minutes before had been like the demoniac in the gospel, were seen sitting 'clothed, and in their right mind.' Thus I speak within the mark, Mr. Reding, when I say I will warrant a change in you in twenty-four hours. I have never known but one instance in which it seemed to fail, and that was the case of a wretched old man who held it in his hand a whole day in dead silence, without any apparent effect; but here *exceptio probat regulam*, for on further inquiry we found he could not read. So the tract was slowly administered to him by another person; and before it was finished, I protest to you, Mr. Reding, he fell into a deep and healthy slumber, perspired profusely, and woke up at the end of twelve hours a new creature, perfectly new, brand new, and fit for heaven—whither he went in the course of the week. We are now making farther experiments on its operation, and we find that even separate leaves of the tract have a proportionate effect. And, what is more to your own purpose, it is quite a specific in the case of Popery. It directly attacks the peccant matter, and all the trash about sacraments, saints, penance, purgatory, and good works is dislodged from the soul at once."

Charles remained silent and grave, as one who was likely suddenly to break out into some strong act, rather than condescend to any farther parleying.

Dr. Kitchens proceeded: "Have you attended any of the lectures delivered against the Mystic Babylon, or any of the public disputes which have been carried on in so many places? My dear friend, Mr. Macanoise, contested ten points with thirty Jesuits—a good half of the Jesuits in London—and beat them upon all. Or have you heard any of the luminaries of Exeter Hall? There is Mr. Gabb; he is a Boanerges, a perfect Niagara, for his torrent of words; such momentum in his delivery; it is as rapid as it's strong; it's enough to knock a man down. He can speak seven hours running without fatigue; and last year he went through England, delivering through the length and breadth of the land, one, and one only, awful protest against the apocalyptic witch of Endor. He began at Devonport and ended at Berwick, and surpassed himself on every delivery. At Berwick, his last exhibition, the effect was perfectly tremendous; a friend of mine heard it; he assures me, incredible as it may appear, that it shattered some glass in a neighbouring house; and two priests of Baal, who were with their day-school within a quarter of a mile of Mr. Gabb, were so damaged by the mere echo, that one forthwith took to his bed and the other has walked on crutches ever since." He stopped awhile; then he continued: "And what was it, do you think, Mr. Reding, which had this effect on them? Why, it was Mr. Gabb's notion about the sign of the beast in the Revelation: he proved, Mr. Reding—it was the most original hit in his speech—he proved that it was the sign of the cross, the material cross."

The time at length was come; Reding could not bear more; and, as it happened, his visitor's offence gave him the means, as well as a cause, for punishing him. "Oh," he said suddenly, "then I suppose, Dr. Kitchens, you can't tolerate the cross?"

"Oh no; tolerate it!" answered Dr. Kitchens; "it is Antichrist."

"You can't bear the sight of it, I suspect, Dr. Kitchens?"

"I can't endure it, sir; what true Protestant can?"

"Then look here," said Charles, taking a small crucifix out of his writing-desk; and he held it before Dr. Kitchens' face.

Dr. Kitchens at once started on his feet, and retreated. "What's that?" he said, and his face flushed up and then turned pale; "what's that? It's the thing itself!" and he made a snatch at it. "Take it away, Mr. Reding; it's an idol; I cannot endure it; take away the thing!"

"I declare," said Reding to himself, "it really has power over him"; and he still confronted Dr. Kitchens with it, while he kept it out of Dr. Kitchens' reach.

"Take it away, Mr. Reding, I beseech you," cried Kitchens, still retreating, while Charles still pressed on him; "take it away, it's too much. Oh, oh! Spare me, spare me, Mr. Reding!—nehushtan—an idol!—oh, you young antichrist, you devil!—'tis He, 'tis

He—torment!—spare me, Mr. Reding." And the miserable man began to dance about, still eyeing the sacred sign, and motioning it from him.

Charles now had victory in his hands: there was, indeed, some difficulty in steering Kitchens to the door from the place where he had been sitting, but, that once effected, he opened it with violence, and, throwing himself on the staircase, he began to jump down two or three steps at a time, with such forgetfulness of everything but his own terror, that he came plump upon two persons who, in rivalry of each other, were in the act of rushing up: and, while he drove one against the rail, he fairly rolled the other to the bottom.

CHAPTER IX

CHARLES threw himself on his chair, burying the Crucifix in his bosom, quite worn out with his long trial and the sudden exertion in which it had just now been issuing. When a noise was heard at his door, and knocks succeeded, he took no farther notice than to plant his feet on the fender and bury his face in his hands. The summons at first was apparently from one person only, but his delay in answering it gave time for the arrival of another; and there was a brisk succession of alternate knocks from the two, which Charles let take its course. At length one of the rival candidates for admission, bolder than the other, slowly opened the door; when the other, who had impetuously scrambled upstairs after his fall, rushed in before him, crying out, "One word for the New Jerusalem!" "In charity," said Reding, without changing his attitude, "in charity, leave me alone. You mean it well, but I don't want you, sir; I don't indeed. I've had Old Jerusalem here already, and Jewish Apostles, and Gentile Apostles, and free inquiry, and fancy religion, and Exeter Hall. What *have* I done? Why can't I die out in peace? My dear sir, do go! I can't see you; I'm worn out." And he rose up and advanced towards him. "Call again, dear sir, if you are bent on talking with me; but, excuse me, I really have had enough of it for one day. No fault of yours, my dear sir, that you have come the sixth or seventh." And he opened the door for him.

"A madman nearly threw me down as I was coming up," said the person addressed, in some agitation.

"Ten thousand pardons for his rudeness, my dear sir—ten thousand pardons, but allow me"; and he bowed him out of the room. He then turned round to the other stranger, who had stood by in silence: "And you too, sir…is it possible!" His countenance changed to extreme surprise; it was Mr. Malcolm. Charles's thoughts flowed in a new current, and his tormentors were suddenly forgotten.

The history of Mr. Malcolm's calling was simple. He had always been a collector of old books, and had often taken advantage of the stores of Charles's landlord in adding to his library. Passing through London to the Eastern Counties Rail, he happened to call in; and, as his friend the bookseller was not behind his own reading-room in the diffusion of gossip, he learned that Mr. Reding, who was on the point of seceding from the Establishment, was at that moment above stairs. He waited with impatience through Dr. Kitchens' visit, and even then found himself, to his no small annoyance, in danger of being outstripped by the good Swedenborgian.

"How d'ye do, Charles?" he said, at length, with not a little stiffness in his manner, while Charles had no less awkwardness in receiving him; "you have been holding a levee this morning; I thought I should never get to see you. Sit you down; let us both sit down, and let me at last have a word or two with you."

In spite of the diversified trial Charles had sustained from strangers that morning, there was no one perhaps whom he would have less desired to see than Mr. Malcolm. He could not help associating him with his father, yet he felt no opening of heart towards him, nor respect for his judgment. His feeling was a mixture of prescriptive fear and friendliness, attachment from old associations, and desire of standing well with him, but neither confidence nor real love. He coloured up and felt guilty, yet without a clear understanding why.

"Well, Charles Reding," he said, "I think we know each other well enough for you to have given me a hint of what was going on as regards you."

Charles said he had written to him only the evening before.

"Ah, when there was not time to answer your letter," said Mr. Malcolm.

Charles said he wished to spare so kind a friend…he bungled, and could not finish his sentence.

"A friend, who, of course, could give no advice," said Mr. Malcolm drily. Presently he said, "Were those people some of your new friends who were calling on you? They have kept me in the shop this three-quarters of an hour; and the fellow who has just come down nearly threw me over the baluster."

"Oh no, sir, I know nothing of them; they were the most unwelcome of intruders."

"As some one else seems to be," said Mr. Malcolm.

Charles was very much hurt; the more so, because he had nothing to say; he kept silence.

"Well, Charles," said Mr. Malcolm, not looking at him, "I have known you from this high; more, from a child in arms. A frank, open boy you were; I don't know what has spoiled you. These Jesuits, perhaps.… It was not so in your father's lifetime."

"My dear sir," said Charles, "it pierces me to the heart to hear you talk so. You have indeed always been most kind to me. If I have erred, it has been an error of judgment; and I am very sorry for it, and hope you will forgive it. I acted for the best; but I have been, as you must feel, in a most trying situation. My mother has known what I was contemplating this year past."

"Trying situation! fudge! What have you to do with situations? I could have told you a great deal about these Catholics; I know all about them. Error of judgment! don't tell me. I know how these things happen quite well. I have seen such things before; only I thought you a more sensible fellow. There was young Dalton of St. Cross; he goes abroad, and falls in with a smooth priest, who persuades the silly fellow that the Catholic Church is the ancient and true Church of England, the only religion for a gentleman; he is introduced to a Count this, and a Marchioness that, and returns a Catholic. There was another; what was his name? I forget it, of a Berkshire family. He is smitten with a pretty face; nothing will serve but he must marry her; but she's a Catholic, and can't marry a heretic; so he, forsooth, gives up the favour of his uncle and his prospects in the county, for his fair Juliet. There was another—but it's useless going on. And, now I wonder what has taken you."

All this was the best justification for Charles's not having spoken to Mr. Malcolm on the subject. That gentleman had had his own experience of thirty or forty years, and, like some great philosophers, he made that personal experience of his the decisive test of the possible and the true. "I know them," he continued—"I know them; a set of hypocrites and sharpers. I could tell you such stories of what I fell in with abroad. Those priests are not to be trusted. Did you ever know a priest?"

"No," answered Charles.

"Did you ever see a Popish chapel?"

"No."

"Do you know anything of Catholic books, Catholic doctrine, Catholic morality? I warrant it, not much."

Charles looked very uncomfortable.

"Then what makes you go to them?"

Charles did not know what to say.

"Silly boy," he went on, "you have not a word to say for yourself; it's all idle fancy. You are going as a bird to the fowler."

Reding began to rouse himself; he felt he ought to say something; he felt that silence would tell against him. "Dear sir," he answered, "there's nothing but may be turned against one if a person is so minded. Now, do think; had I known this or that priest, you would have said at once, 'Ah, he came over you.' If I had been familiar with Catholic chapels, 'I was allured by the singing or the incense.' What can I have done better than keep myself to myself, go by my best reason, consult the friends whom I happened to find around me, as I have done, and wait in patience till I was sure of my convictions?"

"Ah, that's the way with you youngsters," said Mr. Malcolm; "you all think you are so right; you do think so admirably that older heads are worth nothing to the like of you. Well," he went on, putting on his gloves, "I see I am not in the way to persuade you. Poor dear Charlie, I grieve for you; what would your poor father have said, had he lived to see it? Poor Reding, he has been spared this. But perhaps it would not have happened. I know what the upshot will be; you will come back—come back you will, to a dead certainty. We shall see you back, foolish boy, after you have had your gallop over your ploughed field. Well, well; better than running wild. You must have your hobby; it might have been a worse; you might have run through your money. But perhaps you'll be giving it away, as it is, to some artful priest. It's grievous, grievous; your education thrown away, your prospects ruined, your poor mother and sisters left to take care of themselves. And you don't say a word to me." And he began musing. "A troublesome world: good-bye, Charles; you are high and mighty now, and are in full sail: you may come to your father's friend some day in a different temper. Good-bye."

There was no help for it; Charles's heart was full, but his head was wearied and confused, and his spirit sank; for all these reasons he had not a word to say, and seemed to Mr. Malcolm either stupid or close. He could but wring warmly Mr. Malcolm's reluctant hand, and accompany him down to the street-door.

CHAPTER X

"THIS will never do," said Charles, as he closed the door, and ran upstairs; "here is a day wasted, worse than wasted, wasted partly on strangers, partly on friends; and it's hard to say in which case a more thorough waste. I ought to have gone to the Convent at once." The thought flashed into his mind, and he stood over the fire dwelling on it. "Yes," he said, "I will delay no longer. How does time go? I declare it's past four o'clock." He then thought again: "I'll get over my dinner, and then at once betake myself to my good Passionists."

To the coffee-house then he went, and, as it was some way off, it is not wonderful that it was near six before he arrived at the Convent. It was a plain brick building; money had not been so abundant as to overflow upon the exterior, after the expense of the interior had been provided for. And it was incomplete; a large church had been enclosed, but it was scarcely more than a shell—altars, indeed, had been set up, but, for the rest, it had little more than good proportions, a broad sanctuary, a serviceable organ, and an effective choir. There was a range of buildings adjacent, capable of holding about half-a-dozen fathers; but the size of the church required a larger establishment. By this time, doubtless, things are different, but we are looking back at the first efforts of the English Congregation, when it had scarcely ceased to struggle for life, and when friends and members were but beginning to flow in.

It was indeed but ten years, at that time, since the severest of modern rules had been introduced into England. Two centuries after the memorable era when St. Philip and St. Ignatius, making light of those bodily austerities of which they were personally so great masters, preached mortification of will and reason as more necessary for a civilized age—in the lukewarm and self-indulgent eighteenth century, Father Paul of the Cross was divinely moved to found a Congregation in some respects more ascetic than the primitive hermits and the orders of the middle age. It was not fast, or silence, or poverty which distinguished it, though here too it is not wanting in strictness; but in the cell of its venerable founder, on the Celian Hill, hangs an iron discipline or scourge, studded with nails, which is a memorial, not only of his own self-inflicted sufferings, but of those of his Italian family. The object of those sufferings was as remarkable as their intensity; penance, indeed, is in one respect the end of all self-chastisement, but in the instance of the Passionists the use of the scourge was specially directed to the benefit of their neighbour. They applied the pain to the benefit of the holy souls in Purgatory, or they underwent it to rouse a careless audience. On their missions, when their words seemed uttered in vain, they have been known suddenly to undo their habit, and to scourge themselves with sharp knives or razors, crying out to the horrified people, that they would not show mercy to their flesh till they whom they were addressing took pity on their own perishing souls. Nor was it to their own countrymen alone that this self-consuming charity extended; how it so happened does not appear; perhaps a certain memento close to their house was the earthly cause; but so it was, that for many years the heart of Father Paul was expanded towards a northern nation, with which, humanly speaking, he had nothing to do. Over against St. John and St. Paul, the home of the Passionists on the Celian, rises the old church and monastery of San Gregorio, the womb, as it may be called, of English Christianity. There had lived that great Saint, who is named our Apostle, who was afterwards called to the chair of St. Peter; and thence went forth, in and after his pontificate, Augustine, Paulinus, Justus, and the other Saints by whom our barbarous ancestors were converted. Their names, which are now written up upon the pillars of the portico, would almost seem to have issued forth, and crossed over, and confronted the venerable Paul; for, strange to say, the thought of England came into his ordinary prayers; and in his last years, after a vision during Mass, as if he had been Augustine or Mellitus, he talked of his "sons" in England.

It was strange enough that even one Italian in the heart of Rome should at that time have ambitious thoughts of making novices or converts in this country; but, after the venerable Founder's death, his special interest in our distant isle showed itself in another member of his institute. On the Apennines, near Viterbo, there dwelt a shepherd-boy, in the first years of this century, whose mind had early been drawn heavenward; and, one day, as he prayed before an image of the Madonna, he felt a vivid intimation that he was destined to preach the Gospel under the northern sky. There appeared no means by which a Roman peasant should be turned into a missionary; nor did the prospect open, when this youth found himself, first a lay-brother, then a Father, in the Congregation of the Passion. Yet, though no external means appeared, the inward impression did not fade; on the contrary, it became more definite, and, in process of time, instead of the dim north, England was engraven on his heart. And, strange to say, as years went on, without his seeking, for he was simply under obedience, our peasant found himself at length upon the very shore of the stormy northern sea, whence Caesar of old looked out for a new world to conquer; yet that he should cross the strait was still as little likely as before. However, it was as likely as that he should ever have got so near it; and he used to eye the restless, godless waves, and wonder with himself whether the day would ever come when he should be carried over them. And come it did, not however by any determination of his own, but by the same Providence which thirty years before had given him the anticipation of it.

At the time of our narrative, Father Domenico de Matre Dei had become familiar with England; he had had many anxieties here, first from want of funds, then still more from want of men. Year passed after year, and, whether fear of the severity of the rule—though that was groundless, for it had been mitigated for England—or the claim of other religious bodies was the cause, his community did not increase, and he was tempted to despond. But every work has its season; and now for some time past that difficulty had been gradually lessening; various zealous men, some of noble birth, others of extensive acquirements, had entered the Congregation; and our friend Willis, who at this time had received the priesthood, was not the last of these accessions, though domiciled at a distance from London. And now the reader knows much more about the Passionists than did Reding at the time that he made his way to their monastery.

The church door came first, and, as it was open, he entered it. It apparently was filling for service. When he got inside, the person who immediately preceded him dipped his finger into a vessel of water which stood at the entrance, and offered it to Charles. Charles, ignorant what it meant, and awkward from his consciousness of it, did nothing but slink aside, and look for some place of refuge; but the whole space was open, and there seemed no corner to retreat into. Every one, however, seemed about his own business; no one minded him, and so far he felt at his ease. He stood near the door, and began to look about him. A profusion of candles was lighting at the High Altar, which stood in the centre of a semicircular apse. There were side-altars—perhaps half-a-dozen; most of them without lights, but, even here, solitary worshippers might be seen. Over one was a large old Crucifix with a lamp, and this had a succession of visitors. They came each for five minutes, said some prayers which were attached in a glazed frame to the rail, and passed away. At another, which was in a chapel at the farther end of one of the aisles, six long candles were burning, and over it was an image. On looking attentively, Charles made out at last that it was an image of Our Lady, and the Child held out a rosary. Here a congregation had already assembled, or rather was in the middle of some service, to him unknown. It was rapid, alternate, and monotonous; and, as it seemed interminable, Reding turned his eyes elsewhere. They fell first on one, then on another confessional, round each of which was a little crowd, kneeling, waiting every one his own turn for presenting himself for the sacrament—the men on the one side, the women on the other. At the lower end of the church were about three ranges of moveable benches with backs and kneelers; the rest of the large space was open, and filled with chairs. The growing object of attention at present was the High Altar; and each person, as he entered, took a chair, and, kneeling down behind it, began his prayers. At length the church got very full; rich and poor were mixed together—artisans, well-dressed youths, Irish labourers, mothers with two or three children—the only division being that of men from women. A set of boys and children, mixed with some old crones, had got possession of the altar-rail, and were hugging it with restless motions, as if in expectation.

Though Reding had continued standing, no one would have noticed him; but he saw the time was come for him to kneel, and accordingly he moved into a corner seat on the bench nearest him. He had hardly done so, when a procession with lights passed from the sacristy to the altar; something went on which he did not understand, and then suddenly began what, by the *Miserere* and *Ora pro nobis*, he perceived to be a litany; a hymn followed. Reding thought he never had been present at worship before, so absorbed was the attention, so intense was the devotion of the congregation. What particularly struck him was, that whereas in the Church of England the clergyman or the organ was everything and the people nothing, except so far as the clerk is their representative, here it was just reversed. The priest hardly spoke, or at least audibly; but the whole congregation was as though one vast instrument or Panharmonicon, moving all together, and, what was most remarkable, as if self-moved. They did not seem to require any one to prompt or direct them, though in the Litany the choir took the alternate parts. The words were Latin, but every one seemed to understand them thoroughly, and to be offering up his prayers to the Blessed Trinity, and the Incarnate Saviour, and the great Mother of God, and the glorified Saints, with hearts full in proportion to the energy of the sounds they uttered. There was a little boy near him, and a poor woman, singing at the pitch of their voices. There was no mistaking it; Reding said to himself, "This *is* a popular religion." He looked round at the building; it was, as we have said, very plain, and bore the marks of being unfinished; but the Living Temple which was manifested in it needed no curious carving or rich marble to complete it, "for the glory of God had enlightened it, and the Lamb was the lamp thereof." "How wonderful," said Charles to himself, "that people call this worship formal and external; it seems to possess all classes, young and old, polished and vulgar, men and women indiscriminately; it is the working of one Spirit in all, making many one."

While he was thus thinking, a change came over the worship. A priest, or at least an assistant, had mounted for a moment above the altar, and removed a chalice or vessel which stood there; he could not see distinctly. A cloud of incense was rising on high; the people suddenly all bowed low; what could it mean? The truth flashed on him, fearfully yet sweetly; it was the Blessed Sacrament—it was the Lord Incarnate who was on the altar, who had come to visit and to bless His people. It was the Great Presence, which makes a Catholic Church different from every other place in the world; which makes it, as no other place can be, holy. The Breviary offices were by this time not unknown to Reding; and as he threw himself on the pavement, in sudden self-abasement and joy, some words of those great Antiphons came into his mouth, from which Willis had formerly quoted: "O Adonai, et Dux domûs Israel, qui Moysi in rubo apparuisti; O Emmanuel, Exspectatio Gentium et Salvator earum, veni ad salvandum nos, Domine Deus noster."

The function did not last very long after this; Reding, on looking up, found the congregation rapidly diminishing, and the lights in course of extinction. He saw he must be quick in his motions. He made his way to a lay-brother who was waiting till the doors could be closed, and begged to be conducted to the Superior. The lay-brother feared he might be busy at the moment, but conducted him through the sacristy to a small neat room, where, being left to himself, he had time to collect his thoughts. At length the Superior appeared; he was a man past the middle age, and had a grave yet familiar manner. Charles's feelings were indescribable, but all pleasurable. His heart beat, not with fear or anxiety, but with the thrill of delight with which he realized that he was beneath the shadow of a Catholic community, and face to face with one of its priests. His trouble went in a moment, and he could have laughed for joy. He could hardly keep his countenance, and almost feared to be taken for a fool. He presented the card of his railroad companion. The good Father smiled when he saw the name, nor did the few words which were written with pencil on the card diminish his satisfaction. Charles and he soon came to an understanding; he found himself already known in the community by means of Willis; and it was arranged that he should take up his lodging with his new friends forthwith, and remain there as long as it suited him. He was to prepare for confession at once; and it was hoped that on the following Sunday he might be received into Catholic communion. After that, he was, at a convenient interval, to present himself to the Bishop, from whom he would seek the sacrament of confirmation. Not much time was necessary for removing his luggage from his lodgings; and in the course of an hour from the time of his interview with the Father Superior, he was sitting by himself, with pen and paper and his books, and with a cheerful fire, in a small cell of his new home.

CHAPTER XI

A VERY few words will conduct us to the end of our history. It was Sunday morning about seven o'clock, and Charles had been admitted into the communion of the Catholic Church about an hour since. He was still kneeling in the church of the Passionists before the Tabernacle, in the possession of a deep peace and serenity of mind, which he had not thought possible on earth. It was more like the stillness which almost sensibly affects the ears when a bell that has long been tolling stops, or when a vessel, after much tossing at sea, finds itself in harbour. It was such as to throw him back in memory on his earliest years, as if he were really beginning life again. But there was more than the happiness of childhood in his heart; he seemed to feel a rock under his feet; it was the *soliditas Cathedrae Petri*. He went on kneeling, as if he were already in heaven, with the throne of God before him, and angels around; and as if to move were to lose his privilege.

At length he felt a light hand on his shoulder, and a voice said, "Reding, I am going; let me just say farewell to you before I go." He looked around; it was Willis, or rather Father Aloysius, in his dark Passionist habit, with the white heart sewed in at his left breast. Willis carried him from the church into the sacristy. "What a joy, Reding!" he whispered, when the door closed upon them; "what a day of joy! St. Edward's day, a doubly blessed day henceforth. My Superior let me be present; but now I must go. You did not see me, but I was present through the whole."

"Oh," said Charles, "what shall I say?—the face of God! As I knelt I seemed to wish to say this, and this only, with the Patriarch, 'Now let me die, since I have seen Thy Face.'"

"You, dear Reding," said Father Aloysius, "have keen fresh feelings; mine are blunted by familiarity."

"No, Willis," he made answer, "you have taken the better part betimes, while I have loitered. Too late have I known Thee, O Thou ancient Truth; too late have I found Thee, First and only Fair."

"All is well, except as sin makes it ill," said Father Aloysius; "if you have to lament loss of time before conversion, I have to lament it after. If you speak of delay, must not I of rashness? A good God overrules all things. But I must away. Do you recollect my last words when we parted in Devonshire? I have thought of them often since;

they were too true then. I said, 'Our ways divide.' They are different still, yet they are the same. Whether we shall meet again here below, who knows? But there will be a meeting ere long before the Throne of God, and under the shadow of His Blessed Mother and all Saints. 'Deus manifeste veniet, Deus noster, et non silebit.'"

Reding took Father Aloysius's hand and kissed it; as he sank on his knees the young priest made the sign of blessing over him. Then he vanished through the door of the sacristy; and the new convert sought his temporary cell, so happy in the Present, that he had no thoughts either for the Past or the Future.

THE END

Designed by Fiona Cecile Clarke, the Cluny Media *logo depicts a monk at work in the scriptorium, with a cat sitting at his feet.*

The monk represents our mission to emulate the invaluable contributions of the monks of Cluny in preserving the libraries of the West, our strivings to know and love the truth.

The cat at the monk's feet is Pangur Bán, from the eponymous Irish poem of the 9th century. The anonymous poet compares his scholarly pursuit of truth with the cat's happy hunting of mice. The depiction of Pangur Bán is an homage to the work of the monks of Irish monasteries and a sign of the joy we at Cluny take in our trade.

"Messe ocus Pangur Bán,
cechtar nathar fria saindan:
bíth a menmasam fri seilgg,
mu memna céin im saincheirdd."

Made in the USA
Middletown, DE
06 February 2025

70350028R00181